ELECTRIC BLUE

SEBASTIAN JACK

Improbable
PRESS

First published by Improbable Press in 2023

Improbable Press is an imprint of:
Clan Destine Press
www.clandestinepress.com.au
PO Box 121, Bittern Victoria 3918 Australia

National Library of Australia Cataloguing-In-Publication data:

Sebastian Jack
Electric Blue

978-1-922904-47-8 (hb)
978-1-922904-05-8 (pb)
978-1-922904-06-5 (eb)

Cover artwork by © Claudia Caranfa
Layout & Typesetting by Dimitra Stathopoulos

Improbable Press
improbablepress.com

For MacKenzie, the love of all my life.
And for Gabriel. This is entirely your fault.

Cael would like to thank
Maria, AM, HAL, Roy, Rachael, Data, Lal, both Davids, Walter,
both Ashes, both Joes, Vision, Chappie, and Ava.
Without them, he would never have existed.

CHAPTER ONE

"I'M SERIOUS, ARCHER. IF YOU DON'T GET YOUR SHIT TOGETHER, they're gonna fire you."

Loathe though she is to admit it, Wells finally has her attention. Until this point, it had been more of the same from her beleaguered coordinator: "How are the legs? Everything responsive? Gimme the drugs, because I *know* you're holding. Look at your eyes – it's 7:00 pm, how fucked up are you? We need to run some diagnostics during hair and makeup, and *no* you're not gonna get this junk back, after. Please don't embarrass me tonight, *please?*"

Ad nauseum. She'd just tuned him out, as usual.

And then the word *fire* had come up.

The thought had already crossed Archer's mind, of course, and she'd been wondering lately if it had crossed his, too. She'd wondered if he would warn her beforehand, for the sake of all their history, or if he'd just let them do it. But *this*…this is the first time either of them has said it aloud. That probably means something.

No, she can't let it get to her. Rob Wells has never been one for petty bluffs, but she certainly wouldn't put it past him to start now. Last-ditch effort, and all. Archer tries to laugh it off. She takes a confident drag from her cigarette, smudging the picture-perfect lipstick the stylists have only just applied. Bright red, of course. What is it with makeup artists and caking bright red lipstick on Asian women? She's not even pale, so it honestly just seems racist.

"They wouldn't dare fire me," she says. But that tugs uncomfortably at her self-awareness. Even to her, it sounds vain. Arrogant. Unearned.

Her coordinator just gapes. "Who the hell do you think you are?"

Um, ouch.

At that, even the little swarm of hair and makeup people exchange looks.

Heat starts to prickle across Archer's skin, but she powers through. "They need me. Vander needs me. The public response–"

Wells snatches the cigarette away from her, mid-drag. "You– God dammit." He rakes a hand through his locs, and Archer finally notices he forewent the man-bun tonight. She wonders if someone at corporate finally told him it's cliché and stupid. He gestures dismissively towards her stylists. "Could you…?"

They dutifully scurry from the room.

Only about a quarter of her makeup is done. Just one eye, and the golden-halo-headpiece-thing that marketing and style want her in tonight is hanging lopsidedly from her ear. She exhales an empty laugh at her own reflection. They've wrestled her waist-length hair into a complicated updo, braiding it with chains and little crystals that match the lipstick. It makes her head feel very heavy. Or maybe that's just the drugs.

"I need you to listen to me," Rob says, leaning over her shoulder. He's younger than her by a handful of months, and decently handsome, but the youth seems to have sapped from his face lately. He looks tired. "*They* can do whatever *they* want. Vander's starting to get wind of your…*behavior*, let's say, and this–" He kicks at her shins.

"Ow," she responds flatly, not meaning it.

"This shit? This isn't yours. This is company property. The only thing stopping them from ripping these things off and stapling them onto someone else is the strength of your good behavior."

"And you," she tries to believe.

"Not anymore. They're fed up, Cym."

The realization is like a lump of ice sinking to the pit of her stomach. *Good*, she thinks. *Fine. Fire me.*

Moments like these, Rob sounds less like a coordinator and much more like a handler; like he's a babysitter hired by the company to keep her in line. Visibly frustrated, he takes a long pull from her cigarette, grimaces, and then goes back in for another. "You see what you do to me? Drag me down to your level."

She gives him a patronizing sort of smile, taking the cigarette back. "We're a team, Rob. We should be on the same level."

By the time hair and makeup and wardrobe have finished with her, the rest of the models are already lined up backstage. Dutiful, silent statues. Most are almost inhumanly beautiful. There's a woman with no feet; she's modeling this season's Hermes legs. A man with a set of annoyingly-blue Charon eyes whirring and clicking in his skull, almost glowing in the dim light. Archer makes eye contact with a man with a right forequarter amputation, sporting the latest model Atlas arm. Tall, muscular, broad. His skin is etched with elaborate tattoos, crawling all the way up to his jawline. Lucas. He's a true original, like she is. He's been around for a long, long time.

The rest of the models are missing much less visible pieces – burn survivors with swaths of skin replaced by Arachne Synthflesh, or recipients of bio-mechanical Asclepius Organs. Hearts, livers, lungs. Euterpe Cochlear implants, Aoede vocal cords. Little Aceso nanobots fusing nerves together, restoring both function and sensation. But the big-ticket spokesmodel tonight is going to be a Mr Thomas Wilkinson. Plain, elderly, and the first real success story to come out of company's new Chiron treatment. His pancreatic cancer had shrunk in record time, with none of the bothersome side-effects seen with conventional chemotherapy and radiation.

Incidentally, the models sporting the Eros and Aphrodite cybernetics enhancements – and the Eros and Aphrodite standalone companions – will be showcased in a much smaller, more private venue. But, as always, the presentation will be available online to any interested party.

Archer's coordinator shoves her past them all, one finger pressing his earpiece into his skull with rabid intensity. The low murmur of the crowd can be heard over the backstage chatter, and the stagehands urge everyone to quiet down. Rob Wells looks at his watch, counting out the seconds. The music starts, the lights flash and flare. The crowd goes wild. On cue, he pushes her out onto the stage.

With a broad smile, and a gracious, jovial wave, Archer steps into the spotlight. And despite the hours of hair and makeup, no one, not one single person in the audience, is looking at her face. Like the hovering cameras projecting a live feed onto the massive screens all over the room, everyone is laser-focused on her prosthetic legs. They're watching how the Nike 6.0s are moving, compared to the 5.7s. They're taking careful note of how the microprocessor knees and ankles flex so gracefully, her balance maintained by patented GyroSmart technology and proprioceptive motion detection fields. She gives them what they want, slipping in a few gratuitous turns and poses. They eat it up.

In truth, it took a while to learn to walk these models. The feet are custom-designed for her, and her alone.

"We're tired of you wearing shoes," they'd said. "What if you *were* the shoes? Everyone has seen the function, so let's give them some form to drool over."

She'd pushed back at first, afraid that this would kickstart a trend of elective enhancement. Rich people paying to have limbs hacked off and organs torn out, just to get their hands (or lack thereof) on the latest in *haute couture*, Transhumanist tech.

They told her that was precisely the point.

So, now, after months in the gait lab and even more time struggling at home, here she is. The casing on the legs is matte black, with geometric cutouts to allow artfully-exposed glimpses of their inner workings: braided wire, the delicate back-and-forth of tiny pistons, glimmering gears, and the way the tendons flex and adjust in perfect harmony with the gyros. They're thigh-high ballet boots that never come off. Like Harlan Ellison fucked Giuseppe Zanotti in an H.R. Giger painting.

She takes her place behind the clear-glass podium to the tune of thunderous applause, blinded by a lightning storm of camera flashes.

"Thank you," she says, and the crowd begins to settle. Behind her, the big screens start to cycle through a slideshow of pictures. Ancient vases and statues, paintings depicting epic scenes. There's a teleprompter off to the left, but she knows this show by heart. "Hephaestus was the divine craftsman of Olympus. Aided by his gilded assistants, he pulled forth from his forge all that gave the gods their power."

The slideshow is changing now, to before-and-after pictures. Sad people in wheelchairs, then the same people happy and running. Sad people with no arms, and then happy people with two new ones. Sad people with grotesquely burned skin, then happy people with flawless, silk-smooth, perfectly color-matched grafts.

"With each spark that flew from hammer and anvil, Hephaestus imbued his creations with the ability to heal, and to protect. And it is this mission, the mission of the celestial artificer himself, that we here at Hephaestus Forge Biotech strive to continue."

They clap. She smiles, nods, and waits patiently for them to settle down.

"My name is Cymbre Archer, and it is my supreme honor to welcome each and every one of you to the 25th annual Hephaestus Forge showcase and shareholder presentation!" She beams as they applaud yet again. "Now, without further ado, please welcome our founder and CEO, Evander Callas!" She sweeps an arm out like a showgirl, like some kind of cyborg Vanna fucking White, as Vander joins her on stage. He's older, but handsome and bearded and olive-skinned. And shorter than she is by a substantial margin, but that's entirely his own fault. By her wingspan, Archer would've been a modest 5'7" before he got to her. Now she stands 6'2", towering over her Pygmalion sculptor.

He clasps her upper arms and kisses her cheeks back and forth. "My girl," he whispers in her ear.

It makes her skin crawl. But she holds it together as she retreats so gratefully off-stage. And the instant she's out of the audience's line of sight, the smile melts from her face.

"Perfect," Wells whispers to her. "As always."

Vander is rattling off mind-numbing statistics: quarterly averages, market reports, EPS growth and the like, while charts and graphs float behind him.

"You've got the *Wired Magazine* thing next Tuesday," her coordinator whispers to her as they linger in the wings. "Have you done your reading?" He's scrolling obsessively through his phone, already thinking ten steps ahead.

It feels like a hot pinprick in the base of her skull. "No."

He rolls his eyes. "Then I guess you'd better be paying attention."

"I'll fake it."

"Yeah. Okay, Archer."

"But we can hear more about that later!" Vander announces. "Let's get to what you came here for."

Now it's Archer's turn to roll her eyes. She makes eye contact with Lucas – Mr Atlas Arm – and he gives her a sympathetic sort of half-smile.

"It's my honor to introduce you all to this year's success stories! In the immortal words of the poet Homer, 'Be gracious, Hephaestus, and grant me success and prosperity!'"

Lucas gives a silent, mocking cheer, earning him a harsh scold from his own coordinator and an appreciative, sardonic laugh from Archer.

One by one, the models glide out onto the stage, with Vander giving elevator-pitch explanations for all of their enhancements. Summaries of what all changed this year, what features they've axed and added. Just as Little Miss Hermes Legs steps onto the stage, she stumbles and falls hard on one knee. Archer stands back and watches as judgmentally as humanly possible while a small army of coordinators and stylists drags her back to her feet, dusts her off, and sends her back out. Even still, the catwalk timing is all thrown off, and she's pretty sure that the whole fiasco was visible from the auditorium.

Fucking amateur hour.

By the time she's on her way back to the wings, Miss Hermes has tears in her eyes. A flock of models and assistants gather around to comfort her, but she strides right past them.

"*You!*" she shrieks, moving on Archer like a harpy.

She cocks an eyebrow. And before she knows what's happening, the girl's open palm has made rough contact with her cheek. Not hard. Just startling.

"You tripped me!" she sobs.

Archer stumbles back, clutching at her cheek. "I didn't have to!"

She launches herself at Archer again and chaos ensues. People are trying to drag the girl away, and Wells steps between the two, holding his hands up defensively. Archer just watches over his shoulder, morbidly fascinated.

"*She fucking tripped me! She did it on purpose!*"

"You need to *quiet down*," one of the stylists snaps, a harsh whisper. "Those are our investors out there!"

"But she—"

She starts dragging the girl away by the arm. "Listen to me, do you have any idea who you just slapped?"

"I don't care!"

Makeup has arrived, shining lights on Archer's face, trying to see what damage has been done. Brushes are jammed against her skin to the tune of frantic muttering from the stylists. Archer looks over to see Vander glancing anxiously in their direction as he continues his speech.

She can't help herself. As Miss Hermes gets dragged away, she calls out, "How about you learn how to walk your fucking tech like a professional? This isn't Hanger."

A few of the other models laugh appreciatively, but Wells grimaces. "Arch…"

In less than a minute, Cymbre Archer's makeup is back up to corporate standard, and she's gliding back out onto the stage to introduce the next segment.

After the main presentation comes the panel. Archer sits at a long table with Lucas, the old man without cancer, Vander, and Lex from PR, along with a whole host of doctors, surgeons, biomedical engineers, technicians, and artists. And what a beautifully curated bunch they make.

"Mx Archer," someone asks, "tell us about the legs you're wearing, tonight."

She smiles, demure and grateful. "For the past few months, I've been fortunate enough to work closely with our talented design team, and together we were able to mold the Nike 6.0s into wearable, functional art pieces, custom-built for me."

Word for word. Rob Wells gives her a nod and a smile from the back of the room before turning to his phone again.

Vander chimes in, because of course he does. "As you all know, Cymbre has been with us since the beginning." He smiles at her. Condescending. "She embodies the spirit of Hephaestus Forge in a way few others ever could, and we wanted her cybernetics to reflect that."

"Limb loss is a horrible, tragic thing, even when it occurs before birth," Archer says, and the crowd nods sympathetically. A few place hands over their hearts. "But in this day and age, it doesn't have to be. At Hephaestus Forge, we have found a way to turn that tragedy into beauty. There is always space in your life for art, and if that art can make you a more complete, more able person, then why would you ever deny yourself?"

Applause.

Another reporter calls out, "Excuse me for saying so, but it sounds like Hephaestus Forge means to encourage elective amputation and organ transplant."

PR Lex takes over, and thank God, because Archer has *no idea* how she was supposed to handle that one. Just stand up and shout, '*Yes! Gold star for you, sir!*'?

"'Elective' is perhaps the wrong word for it," he says. "For too long, quality of life has been limited by the term 'medical necessity.' What we mean to do is shift that definition, raise the bar, and allow our technology to keep improving lives, worldwide. No matter your official diagnosis code."

CHAPTER TWO

AFTERWARDS, WHEN ALL OF THE SMILING AND WAVING IS THROUGH, Cymbre Archer storms out of the event center, hails a cab, and makes her way straight to the Lower East Side of Manhattan. During the drive, she tears the headpiece off and throws it out the car window. She lets her hair down and shakes it out, nearly clawing into her own scalp for her desperate need to *shed Hephaestus Forge*. It feels like her skin is crawling, and all she wants is a drink, a hit, and a fuck. Not necessarily in that order, either. She digs through her bag for a moment and withdraws a strange sort of visor. It sits on the bridge of her nose, placing an asymmetrical pair of black and gold triangles beneath her eyes. Camouflage from surveillance and facial recognition.

Hotel Chantelle. Archer doesn't come here for the club itself, rather for the dealer that she knows hangs out on the roof. There's a line all the way down the block, but she walks right past it, straight up to the door. People shout at her. Some of them recognize her and try to snap pictures with their phones. Most are just pissed she's cutting in line.

Just as she's crossing the threshold, the bouncer catches her with a massive hand spread across her chest. "You gonna behave tonight?" he asks sternly.

"Yes."

"Archer."

"*Yes*, damn." She squirms away, into the club.

She ditches her coat and makes her way straight for the roof. Auryn is there, in his usual corner, holding conclave with his flock of lesser drug fiends.

"Mx Archer," he greets, giving her a coy wink with his one cybernetic eye. The man looks like an exceptionally well-dressed skeleton, with bleach-blonde hair and eerie, gaunt, genderless features. A silver bar is pierced through the bridge of his nose. He's wearing his own anti-surveillance dazzle paint, as usual. Tonight, he has weird patches of pixels all over his face and lips. "Didn't I just see you on TV?"

"You have something for me?" she asks. Straight to the point.

"Of course." He produces a small blue phial with an eyedropper lid.

She snatches it away, stuffing a wad of bills into his open palm. "Can I drop here?"

"*Can she drop here?*" He laughs, somewhere between condescending and admiring, and looks between his little circle of beautiful addicts. On cue, they laugh, too. Deadened. "I don't know, Arch, *can* you?"

She rolls her eyes and unscrews the phial. Penth. One drop evens her out, two drops lets her feel it, and three drops knocks her on her ass. She'll start with two. Mouth open, head tilted back, she slips the eyedropper beneath her tongue. She exhales deeply, shuddering in relief. Her fingertips tingle, making it hard to screw the eyedropper back in.

Auryn gives her a crooked smile, shaking his head. "You're my fucking muse, Archer."

"Whatever."

If she's here, she may as well have a drink. So, she moves down into the club, into the dark and the noise. Lucas is here, but he doesn't notice her. He's sitting on one of the long, leather seats with a glass of champagne in his organic hand, and some girl's jaw in the other. His cybernetic is like hers. *Artistic.* Robotic-looking. Right now, he's shoving his matte-black fingers down the girl's throat while he bites his lip and watches, ravenous. She chokes. He kisses her around his own fingers.

Archer takes a seat at the bar and orders her drink. "Vodka."

"Vodka how?" the bartender asks, haughty.

"In a big glass?"

She downs it in a single gulp.

"Another."

This time, she sneaks the drink beneath the bar and drops some Penth into it. Probably more than is appropriate. Again, it's gone in one gulp.

"Another."

"Seriously?"

"Did I stutter?"

The drugs come on hard this time, like a beautiful punch in the gut, blooming out to fill her limbs with lightning and helium. Her feet slip off of the bottom rung of the barstool to hang limply beneath her, but she doesn't mind. She feels weightless, she feels invincible. She could run a thousand miles right now if she wanted to, but she doesn't want to, and she doesn't have to, and that's kind of beautiful, isn't it? The music winds fingers around her ribs, pounding and rattling at the cage of her chest. It had been uncomfortable, before the Penth. Now, she doesn't mind it so much. She just slumps against the bar and drifts for a while.

Someone shouts, "Hey!"

Archer turns lazily to see a man seated beside her, some kind of aging, NYU trust-fund frat boy. She's been living like this for long enough that she can recognize when she's come to in the middle of a one-sided conversation. People look at you with the same sort of expression, patient but expectant. Like they're getting tired of repeating themselves, but not tired enough to just fuck off already. She gets it from Wells all the time.

"What?" she snaps, rubbing at her forehead. "What are you talking about?"

"Do you want to?" the man shouts over the noise. "We could go to the alley."

"Do I want to *what*?"

"You know," he shrugs, glancing down at her legs. "Step on my throat. I said we could go to the alley; it would only take a second."

She's repulsed, but unsurprised. "I'm not going anywhere with you, you complete fuck."

"We could do it right here, if you want. I'll lay down on the floor, I don't care."

As though it was the *venue* she'd had a problem with. "I'm not stepping on your throat."

"It doesn't have to be my throat, it could be—"

"I told you, no. Get the fuck out of here."

"Come on. I'll pay you, if that's the issue." He puts a hand on the inside of her knee. Covetous. "I have a lot of money."

And then something catches her eye. She glances down and sees his other hand pressing hard into his own crotch, palming, squeezing. He bites his lip and then smiles at her before bringing a finger to his lips. Coy.

It happens before Archer can stop herself. She stands, snatches up an empty shot glass from the bar, wraps her fingers around it, and sinks her fist into the side of the man's face. Something gives and breaks. It's not the shot glass.

"Touch me again, motherfucker!" she shouts at him as he doubles over, howling in pain. *"Go on, touch me again!"* She cocks her arm back a second time, but something catches her by the wrist. She whips around, ready to kick a bouncer in the chest, but it's not a bouncer. It's a petite woman with a septum ring and half of her head shaved. A stranger.

"There you are, hey!" she shouts over the music, dragging her away. "I've been looking everywhere for you!"

It's beyond confusing. "Wh-what? I don't—" A commotion in the background draws her attention. Oh, *here* come the bouncers.

"All right, that's enough," one of them shouts as they stride over. "You're out, Archer, we're calling the cops."

"It's okay!" the girl tells them, still dragging her for the door. "It's okay, we were just leaving."

"Nah, fuck that," he argues, trying to step around in front of them. "You–"

The girl waves him off, picking up the pace. "No, we're leaving! We're leaving! It's fine!"

Just before they disappear around the corner, Archer overhands the shot glass at her assailant, cracking him on the temple.

The pair stumbles out onto the sidewalk, coats thrown out in their wake. Like some kind of fucking cliché. The girl laughs and flips the establishment an emphatic double-bird.

"What?" Archer shouts. "Not even an '*and stay out*'?"

The bouncer at the door looks genuinely disappointed. "Seriously?"

Archer sucks her teeth at him and digs through her pocket for some smokes. She slips one between her lips and throws her coat over her shoulders. "Thanks," she tells the stranger, struggling a little with her lighter.

"No problem," she says, taking a matchbook from her own pocket and lighting the cigarette. "Fucker deserved it, I saw what he was doing."

Archer takes a deep drag. "Yeah."

"Hey, if we don't look out for each other, we'll be fucked," she says, crowding in close and rising to tiptoes. In an alarmingly bold move, she wraps a hand around the back of Archer's neck and pulls her in close, lighting her own cigarette from Archer's.

Cute. Very cute. "What's your name?"

"Nia."

"Nia." Even cuter. "I'm Archer."

The girl smiles broadly. "Nice to meet you." She takes Archer's right hand in hers, inspecting her knuckles. "Did you have a shot glass in your fist when you punched him?"

"Yeah."

She nods knowingly. "You're too drunk to feel it now, but this is gonna hurt like hell tomorrow."

"I know."

"So," she remarks, still holding her hand, "your place or mine?"

By the time they reach her front door, Archer is practically carrying the woman. One arm firmly around her waist, she hauls her along, biting kiss after kiss against her mouth. Nia's clinging, clinging, arms wrapped around Archer's neck and pulling like she's trying to *climb* her. It's good. It's *good* good. Archer pauses just long enough to punch in her door code, and then they stumble inside.

Her place is impressive. Even now, cluttered with half-empty bottles of wine and liquor and drugs and the random piles of clothing tossed all over the furniture. Purchased when the housing bubble finally burst in '28, it's a loft occupying half of the top floor of a converted factory in Williamsburg. It's massive and wide-open, showcasing all of the exposed brick and pipes and naturally-distressed joists. The first thing you pass is the kitchen, hugging the left wall. Counters are piled high with dirty dishes, reeking of cigarette butts flicked thoughtlessly into half-empty coffee cups.

The majority of the space is occupied by an expansive sitting room. It's littered with sleek, dark-wood-and-leather furnishings by some boutique, arthouse designer, all meticulously curated and arranged by a decorator that Vander had recommended. Geometric light fixtures float overhead, minimalist bookshelves hug the corners. It's a seamless blend of vintage and Posthumanist, sprinkled over with a healthy serving of model-junkie-train-wreck detritus. The east-facing wall is all high windows, and the west-facing wall bears a massive photograph of Archer herself. It's a black and white promo from three models of cybernetics ago. Shot from above, it depicts her reclined on her back, with those inhumanly long legs stretched out across the frame. She looks like some kind of insectoid predator. The stupid thing is probably visible from the apartments across the street.

She doesn't know why she keeps it. Well…she does, and she doesn't.

By the time they reach the metal staircase leading to the upper level, Archer *is* carrying the woman. Somewhere during their stumbling trip across the living room, conjoined at the lips, bold little Nia had succeeded in scaling her statuesque conquest, and now has her legs wrapped around her waist like a vise. That's okay. Archer has carried more women up these stairs than she can count. Unwieldy prosthetics be damned, she's cracked the code to it. It's may be her only hobby. She falls hard to her back on the bed, hauling Nia down on top of her and startling the hairless cat that had been sleeping there. He chirps out his discontent as he relocates to the sofa downstairs.

With shaking hands, Nia produces a bottle of Penth. Archer lies back in a daze as she crawls up to sit astride her hips. The last thing she remembers is opening her mouth so the girl can slip the eyedropper beneath her tongue, and then they're kissing, kissing, and–

Blackness.

CHAPTER THREE

IT'S THE POUNDING ON HER DOOR THAT WAKES HER. ARCHER HAD tried to ignore it at first, but the way it was clashing with the pounding in her head quickly made that impossible.

It's her coordinator, Rob Wells. Good thing, too, as she hadn't bothered to put on a single stitch of clothing before stumbling down from the bedroom. The girl from last night is still lying on her bed, passed out, visibly hungover, but by the smears of annoyingly-red lipstick all over her body, quite well-fucked.

"What?" Archer groans, rubbing the heel of her hand into one dry eye. It comes away smudged with eyeliner. Her tongue feels like a towel.

"Why haven't you been answering your phone?" he demands in a harsh whisper, pushing past her and into the loft. He closes and locks the door behind him, which annoys her, because it means he's going to try and *stay*.

"Fuck, I don't know. Couldn't have been that I was *sleeping*." She snatches her phone from the pocket of her coat crumpled on the floor, to find the battery nearly dead, and no fewer than seven missed calls and eleven text messages from him. "Jesus *fuck*, Wells."

Upstairs, the girl from the prior night begins to stir. Wells glances over Archer's shoulder, and his mouth snaps shut. "Oh, goddammit, Archer," he mumbles striding for the kitchen.

"Hey! Fuck–" Archer stammers, snatching a blanket off of the sofa and wrapping it around herself. She stomps after him. "*Hey*! What the hell do you think you're doing, barging in here like this?"

"You literally let me in." He starts clattering around with the coffee pot. "Get rid of her. We've gotta talk."

"Fuck you, man. It's, like, six in the morning."

He slams the coffee pot down, jaw set, gaze fixed on the wall. "Archer, it is *noon*."

All she hears is, 'it's late enough for Penth.' With a snarl and a needlessly aggressive eyeroll, she storms back up the stairs.

"I'm sorry, babes, but you've gotta go," she whispers, sitting down on the bed.

"Oh." The girl yawns, struggling to sit up. "Okay."

Archer reaches out to wipe some of the red lipstick from her face. "I'm sorry."

"It's all right," she says, donning her shirt. "No worries. Do you, uh…" She nods down towards the kitchen. "Do you need me to stay?"

"No, he's all right," Archer reassures her with a grimace. "He's… he's my *handler*." She slips a black kimono on over her shoulders and takes a drop of Penth while the woman re-dresses, and then she escorts her downstairs.

"Bye," Wells calls over his shoulder. Sarcastic.

She gives him a little wave. "Bye." (God, *so* fucking cute.)

As soon as she's gone, Archer rounds on her coordinator in a huff. "You proud of yourself?"

"Heard you had an eventful night," he says, setting a pair of mugs down on her kitchen table. "How's your hand?"

She tucks it behind her back. "Fine."

"Don't bullshit me."

"I'm not!"

"Archer." He sits down at her table. She makes a point not to join him. "I just spent the last 12 hours paying off Hotel Chantelle staff and patrons, along with every conceivable tabloid and news outlet in this city. Do not bullshit me."

Fuck. Her lips press together into a tight line. "Okay."

"You broke that guy's jaw. He has shattered teeth. He's gonna need surgery, and I'm fairly certain that Forge is gonna wind up paying for that, too."

Archer sees that as an absolute victory, but she knows Wells won't agree. So, she suppresses the urge to smile about it. "I won't apologize."

"So, don't. But you're gonna do me a favor."

She narrows her eyes at him. This is a new tactic. "What favor?"

"Sit in your house and behave for a week, and then do the *Wired* interview next Tuesday with Callas."

"I was gonna do that anyway."

"No, you weren't. You were gonna go out and..." He shakes his head in dismay. "*Punch* more people. But now you're gonna do what I say, because you owe me."

This whole thing is frustrating her. "What the hell is this about?"

Wells opens his mouth to continue, and then pauses. "Turn your phone off."

"*What?*"

"I'm serious. Turn your phone off, and then take it upstairs and put it in a drawer."

She glances down at her phone. "It's dead."

"Even better. Put it upstairs."

She does it. She doesn't know why. This is stupid. On her way back down, she grabs a pack of cigarettes from her nightstand.

"All right, what?" she sighs, joining him at the table.

His fingertips drum anxiously against the wood. "The presentation last night went well. You stirred up interest, and the investors are all fully committed."

She taps a cigarette out onto the table. "I figured."

"Forge is ready to move forward with the 6.0 line, so you're gonna get a crate of feet tonight. You know the drill, just put 'em on, and start to get your bearings before gait lab."

"You came all the way over here to tell me that? *You called seven goddamn times to—*"

"Well…there's gonna be something else in there with them. And…" He hesitates. "I'm gonna need you not to tell anyone about it."

Archer pauses, midway through lighting her cigarette. "Wells, what the fuck are we talking about, here?" A horrifying thought occurs to her. "Did you steal something from Forge?"

"No, no!"

"*Christ*," she exhales, rubbing at her temples. "I think I just had a mild heart attack. That's prison time, Rob, that's so huge. Don't even joke."

"No, I–I haven't stolen it, *yet*."

The cigarette crumbles between her fingers.

"I'm gonna steal it tonight."

She holds up a hand. "You're going to steal tech…from *Hephaestus Forge*."

"Yeah."

Archer stands, backing away from the table. "Wait a minute, don't you send that shit here! That—that's *prison time!*"

"Oh, like you suddenly give a shit."

"I give a shit about prison!" she shouts, moving over to put the couch between the two of them. "What the hell's the matter with you? *Why?* Are you gonna sell? To who? Boston Dynamics? Össur? Like…Hewlett-Packard? *What the fuck?*"

"Of course not!" he defends, indignant. "Jesus, Arch, you *know* me. You've known me for twelve years, I believe in the work we do! I *care*, which is a hell of a lot more than you can say!"

"Why, then? Give me a reason!"

"What they're doing is…it's unethical," he says, obviously still cagey. "You have no idea the kinds of—"

Archer laughs mockingly. "Hephaestus Forge? *Unethical?* Oh, Robert, say it ain't so!"

"No, this is different! I mean, yeah, just the way they've treated you and Lucas is horrible, and it's no wonder you both turned out–"

She gasps, horrified and indignant. "Don't you dare talk about how Luc and I turned out!"

He groans. "Will you please come and sit down?"

"No!" She realizes she's still holding her cigarettes, so she crams one between her teeth and lights it in a frenzy. "You–you come in here, you wake me up, throw my– Throw out my *guest*, and now you're talking about *stealing*!"

"Oh, grow up, Archer!" he sneers. "Doing drugs and putting people in the hospital, that's fine–"

"He deserved it!"

"–but oh, no, not *stealing*! That crosses a line! God forbid anyone *steals* anything!"

"You're gonna lose your job," she says, haughty. "Go ahead and kiss your career goodbye."

The look on his face is somewhere between stunned and frustrated. "I'm gonna lose my job anyway, thanks to you."

It comes on like a punch in the gut, like a fist twisting through her insides. It's not guilt. She can't call it that, because then that's what it becomes, and it *can't be guilt.*

Wells is seething now, which is somehow more intimidating than the yelling had been. "And if you think for one second that you're not getting tossed out along with me, you're even more vain and arrogant than I thought. And I'm pretty sure you're the most vain, arrogant fucking person I've ever met."

It makes her throat tighten, makes her eyes burn with furious, frustrated tears. *He's not wrong. God damn him, he's not even wrong.*

"At this point, I figure that all I can do is hang onto a shred of integrity on my way out. Which is apparently more than you care to do. Or, rather, more than you seem to think I'm entitled to. You–" He snarls in frustration, slamming an open palm on the table. The sound makes her jump. "We've had a good thing going here, a fucking really good thing, but no. You're just hell-bent on ruining it. And normally, that would be fine. If you wanna live fast and die young and self-destruct like the fucking cliché you've become, that's your problem. But, goddamn you, Archer, *you are still handcuffed to me.*"

Well, she thinks. *That's me told, isn't it?* She clears her throat, rubbing at her forehead to hide her face. Her head is pounding, her mouth is so dry, and the smoke is just scorching right through her. "Fuck you," she croaks.

"And now you're gonna cry." He throws his hands up in resignation. "No, Arch, I think fuck *you.*"

"No, *fff–*" It's little more than a whisper as she announces, "Fine."

"What?"

"*Fine,* I said! *Fine!*"

He gives a kind of noncommittal grunt. "Sit your ass down, Cymbre." All the thanks she's going to get, she supposes.

Quiet, obedient, she joins him at the table again. "What do you want?"

Wells takes a deep, stilling breath. "I want you to sign for the box, open it, get your feet out, and start learning to walk them."

She furrows her brow, suspicious. "That's it?"

"Yeah."

She doesn't buy it for a second. "Why can't you get this sent to your own place?"

"Forge sends you big boxes of stuff all the time. Clothes, legs, feet, whatever. It's not suspicious. You're already getting one tonight, so I'm just gonna put something else in there, too."

"Put what in there?"

"Just open the damn box, Cym. It's real simple. Don't tell anyone about it, and then we'll touch base at the *Wired* thing."

"Well, quit fucking calling me 'Cym' and I might."

His phone chimes, and he frowns at the message. He types out a hasty reply before announcing, "I have to go," and getting up from the table.

"What?" She chases after him. "No, *what?* Hey, what the hell am I supposed to do?"

"It'll be here sometime this evening. Just sign for it." He stops in the doorway, taking a cursory look around the loft. He grimaces, visibly repulsed. "Clean your fucking place, Cymbre."

With that, he's gone.

"Clean your fucking place, Cymbre!" she mocks, childish. *"You...* go...clean *your* fucking place." The cat appears, purring and winding his way between her legs. No surprise, there. If there's one thing he hates more than strangers, it's Wells. She scratches him on the head. "I'm sorry, did I sleep too much? Little handsome." A glance over at his bowls confirms he still has plenty of dry food, but she's a sucker. So, she gives him a block of raw salmon anyway, before dragging herself back upstairs.

Exhausted, sick-feeling, and mostly angry, she flops down on her bed and takes a few drops. That's better. God, just...*so* much better.

Limbs starting to go numb, she drags all the blankets and pillows into a little nest and sinks into it. The cat jumps up onto her chest, curling into a contented ball. She just wants to sleep. Sleep, forget about Rob Wells, forget about everything.

The pillow still smells like...

What was that girl's name, again?

CHAPTER FOUR

THE CRATE ARRIVES AT 8:00 PM, HAND-DELIVERED BY TWO MEN IN Hephaestus Forge coveralls. And it is a crate – 4' by 3', if she were to guess. They have to wheel it into her place on a dolly.

"Callas just sending you bricks of gold, now, or what?" one of the delivery guys teases, handing her a clipboard with shipping information.

"Yeah," she half-laughs, scrawling her signature along the bottom. "Yeah, I wish, right?"

"Seriously, what's in here?"

"Just a bunch of weird legs," she casually deflects, handing the clipboard back. "Thanks for bringing them up."

"No worries." With a nod and a smile, they're gone.

Archer looks down at the box, fingertips tapping apprehensively against her lips. If she just leaves it like this, if she doesn't open it, she'll have plausible deniability, right? She didn't *know* there was stolen tech in there. But if she does that, she won't learn the new feet before gait lab, and she'll be in trouble, Wells will be pissed, blah, blah, *blah*.

There's a crowbar duct-taped to the side of the crate.

Fuck. Archer stomps her feet like a child, crossing the room in a huff to pull the curtains on the big windows. It takes a drop of Penth before she's willing to return to the crate.

And then, finally, with a frustrated groan and a, "Fuck you to *death*, Rob," mumbled under her breath, Archer takes up the crowbar, wedges it beneath the nailed-on lid, and pries it away.

Her first thought, the first flash that crosses her mind, is that this is an elaborate joke. Wells has had someone deliver a woman in a box to her doorstep. The figure *(Body? Corpse?)* is lean and pale, curled up on its side in the bottom of the crate. It's dressed in dark blue Forge coveralls, the ones that the engineers wear. Its face, upturned towards her, is young and dominated by a set of bright blue eyes, and framed by a mop of wavy, white-blond hair. It's then that she realizes this is a man.

And then it – he – *blinks*.

"Oh, *Jesus fuck*." She stumbles backwards on those ridiculous feet, falling hard on the wood floor.

The man sits up, following her descent with a kind of placid look on his face. He just keeps blinking at her for a moment and then, "Oh," he says, in a voice that's soft and clear. "Oh, it's you."

She freezes. "Who the fuck are you? What are you doing? *Get the hell out of my house!*"

He seems off-put by her reaction. "What?"

"Wh-*what?*"

"What?"

"*What?*"

He looks slightly dejected. "No, that's too many in a row, I don't think I understand anymore."

"What the fuck are you doing in that box?" she demands, scrambling for the crowbar.

That vapid smile makes a quick comeback. "I was idling. Now I'm talking to you." He seems to take note of her struggling, and after a second, he picks up the crowbar himself.

"*HEY!*" she yelps, bracing for some kind of attack.

But he just offers it out to her. "Here you go."

Archer snatches it from his grip, brandishing it towards him. "This isn't funny! I'm fucking serious, you'd better get the hell out of my house!"

"The man said it would be safer to idle during transit, so I set a timer. Also, I don't think it's supposed to be funny, and I'm not supposed to get the hell out of your house."

"A timer?" she stammers, recoiling further. "Like…what, like– *Idle? What the f–*"

"Yes." He rises to stand in the crate, extending a hand down to her.

"Don't touch me," she snaps, scuffling backwards to struggle to her feet unassisted. "Wells, Robert Wells, said he was sending me stolen tech, that this was corporate theft. Where's my tech?"

"I am the tech."

That catches her off-guard. She lowers the crowbar a little, looking him up and down. Even standing in the crate, he's shorter than she is. Most people are.

This has to be some kind of a joke; she's even more certain now.

"You're smart for an Eros," she finally verbalizes. Eros free-standing intimate companions just cycle through the same 20-or-so pre-recorded phrases. They have a rudimentary AI, telling them what to say and how to move, but they don't *think*. He said the word *'think.'*

He wrinkles his nose, disapproving. "I'm not an Eros, I'm a Prometheus."

She's never heard of a Prometheus before. "You…you what, then? You have cybernetics? Implants?"

"Well…" He thinks hard before pointing to her legs. "I have those. Nike 6s. Not custom like yours, but– Well, yes, custom. But for me." He begins looking around, taking in all the details of his surroundings. He's muttering under his breath, punctuating each little statement with an emphatic blink. "Domicile," he whispers, just this side of audible. "Converted factory. Loft, penthouse. Seating: leather Chesterfield, vintage. Light source: lamp. Overhead lights, hanging. Photograph, 40" by 60", gallery size. Model: Cymbre Archer."

"What?"

He turns to her, eyes wide. "What?"

"No, what the fuck did you just say?"

He points to the massive photograph on the wall. "That's a picture of you."

"I know that!" she sputters. "How do *you* know that?"

"You're on the internet."

"Who the hell *are* you? Is this a prank?"

He bends down and picks up a stack of folders and papers from inside the crate. "Here," he says, holding them out to her. "This will probably help."

Still clutching her crowbar, Archer lunges forward to snatch them away from him before retreating out of arm's reach again. He steps out of the crate, and she sees for the first time that he's barefoot. Before she can remark, he returns to his blinking and labeling. (*"Table. Coffee table. Record player, Victrola, vintage."*) The packet on the top of the stack seems to be the classified first draft of a press release.

"Introducing PROMETHEUS by HEPHAESTUS FORGE: The first fully-functional AUTOMATON in human history."

Fucking *nope*.

"You just–" She waves the crowbar in his direction, stumbling towards the bathroom with the stack of papers. "Just stay here." On her way by, she snatches a phial of Penth from the coffee table.

"Okay," he says. "Floor, textured black oak." *Blink.* "Curtains, silk, inverted pleat." *Blink.*

She slams and locks the door behind her.

Wells picks up on the first ring. "Arch–"

"*No!*" she shouts, "no, I won't do it! You never said anything about–" She drops to a harsh whisper. "You never said anything about a– *Some kind of fucking–*"

"If I'd have told you, you'd have said 'no'. Please, Archer. It's just for a week."

"You son of a bitch, what am I supposed to do with this? What does it even need? Do I have to *feed* this thing?"

"He should've brought documents with him; did he have those? They're important."

She stammers. "Yeah, I've got them right here, but–"

"Good. Read them."

"I *am* reading them, I just–"

"Just talk to him, Archer. He can– Hang on." There comes a sound like he's covered the receiver, followed by a mix of muffled voices. "I've gotta go. Do *not* call again unless it's an absolute emergency. I mean it, Cymbre, life or death. It won't be long before they start to up the ante on data audits."

"*Listen–*"

"I'll see you Tuesday." With that, he hangs up.

Archer looks at her phone, sputtering in disbelief. "You motherfucker."

She takes a drop, struggling with shaking hands, and then turns her attention to the stack of papers. There are schematics and technical documents detailing his construction. He was right, he does have Nikes. And Atlas arms. He's got a whole slew of Asclepius organs, Aoede vocal cords, Charon eyes. Arachne Synthflesh. He even comes equipped with Aceso nanobots, just milling around inside him, ready to make on-the-spot repairs.

According to the drafted press release, "*The AUTOMATONES were animate, metal golems crafted by the divine smith Hephaestus. The finest of these creations could think and feel like men, and thus aided the gods in all of their Olympian endeavors. With the advent of the PROMETHEUS PROJECT, HEPHAESTUS FORGE has gifted the divine abilities reserved only for human beings unto machine. After 25 years of testing on organic models–*"

The sound of panicked screaming sends her barreling back out into the loft, crowbar at the ready. He – the robot – is perched on the back of the sofa, shaking and terrified, cornered by the cat.

"Cymbre Archer, help!" he shouts, pointing at his assailant.

"What? *What?*" She drops her weapon to scoop the tiny, hissing predator up off the floor. "Jesus, calm down!"

"What is that?" he demands, slithering down to crouch in relative safety on the couch cushions.

"It's a cat."

"No!" he argues, and then it's back to the blinking thing. "Goblin. Cryptid. Nosferatu (1922). Raw chicken. Naked mole rat. Sphynx– Oh." He looks up at her. "Sphynx cat."

"Yeah," she says, holding her pet close. "Sphynx cat."

"What's his name?"

"Con Khỉ. Khỉ for short."

"Monkey. Vietnamese."

"Yeah."

He laughs tentatively. "A cat named Monkey." He reaches out a hand towards the cat. "Hi, Monkey."

He hisses. Archer steps back, shushes him. "Yeah. Um… speaking of, what do I call you?"

That seems to confuse him. "You don't call me anything, yet."

"What *should* I call you?" she corrects, annoyed. "What do you *like* to be called?"

"I don't know."

"What did they call you back at Forge?"

"Cataloged Automaton: Epsilon-L. Or just *'the Epsilon-L.'*"

"Cataloged Automaton? Does that mean…are there more of you?"

"Not yet."

She doesn't like the sound of that.

"Were you talking to Robert Wells?" he asks, pointing stiltedly towards the bathroom. "Is that his name? The man who put me in the box?"

"Um…yeah." Her face flushes, despite herself. She hadn't wanted him to hear. She doesn't want to offend him, frustrated though she is by the situation. It's clearly not his fault. (Wait, can he even *be* offended?) "Listen, uh…" She sets Khỉ down and he scampers away, up the stairs towards the bed. "He didn't tell me you were gonna be, like…an actual…"

"A person?"

"Right." She fidgets uncomfortably. "So, I wasn't exactly prepared for…*that*. But it looks like you're gonna be stuck here for a little while, at least until Wells can come up with some other place for you. And I know you're probably not any happier about that than I am, so—"

He smiles at her. "But I am happy about it."

Fuck. She sighs, rubs at her forehead. "What, um…? Okay." Wells was right, this place is an absolute pit. She starts moving around the room, picking up empty liquor bottles and half-dead phials of Penth. "I'm, like, completely unprepared for this, so what do you need? What…? Just…what?"

He cocks his head and thinks for a moment. "I don't know."

She drops an armful of bottles into the garbage, kicking the cabinet closed again. The Penth goes in the fridge. While she's there, she scrapes a few cigarette butts off of plates and out of cups into the trash, dumping the dishes into the sink. "Well, do you eat?"

"I can, but I don't have to."

"Do you sleep?" There's a stack of clothes on the armchair, which she quickly gathers up and throws into the laundry basket.

"I idle, which from your perspective, is the same thing. And I should probably do that for a while tonight, since…well, I'm collating a lot of new information into my experiential lexicon. There wasn't much in there, to be honest, until about an hour ago. I should halt gross motor, power down higher-level systems and…" He gives a strange sort of mechanical shudder. "Just try to make sense of this, a little."

That begs about a million questions, but Archer lets it go for now. "Do I, um…do you need to be plugged in? Do you need to charge? Like, my legs run on my own bioelectricity. Do you have… that?"

"No, I'm designed for perpetual motion," he says matter-of-factly. "They charged me up once, when I was initialized, but movement in my gross motor joints keeps me going. It's sort of like I have hamster wheels in my knees, ha-*ha*." The little two-syllable laugh is the most robotic thing he's done so far. It sounds performative. Scripted. Like he knows a person should laugh at a time like this, but he's never actually heard someone laugh before.

"Okay. Are you gonna be okay on the couch?" she asks, picking up the stack of papers and folders again. "I'll keep the cat upstairs."

He looks around, giving a few cursory bounces up and down on the cushions. "Yes, I'll be okay."

"Good." She starts to back her way towards the stairs, pausing to retrieve her weapon from the floor. At the very least, she'll sleep better knowing it's up there with her, rather than down here with him. "I'm gonna go upstairs, and then tomorrow, we can…" The end of the sentence trails off into awkward, tense silence. "Tomorrow."

He thinks for a second and then casts her a broad, beaming smile. "Okay. Goodnight, Cymbre Archer."

She's not tired, not really. Actually, not even close. It's only 8:15. What she's feeling is the need to flee. The fact that there are no doors in here, that it's a goddamn *loft* of all stupid, impractical things, is terrifying her. So, halfway up the stairs, she pauses. "This, um…this is my zone, okay?" She draws an invisible line across the staircase. "If I'm up here, don't come up."

He nods placidly. "Okay."

"Okay."

"Can I get on your wifi?"

Archer blinks in surprise. "Um…yeah, sure. The password is–"

"It's okay, I don't need it. I'm already in." His eyes flutter a little, and then glaze. "Your security is terrible. They'll find me within minutes, on this network."

"W-well," she stammers, "get off of it, then! Stop!"

Still staring off into space, he tilts his head a little and announces, "No, it's okay. Your password is strong, f*ckF0rg3! is–"

"Hey, how the hell did you–"

"–as good as anything I'd suggest, but I changed your IP address, disabled DHCP and remote access/ admin, and put up a soft firewall. You should look into getting a hard one, though."

He blinks a few times and his eyes return to normal. "So, we're all right, now. Goodnight, Cymbre Archer."

Oh, she can't get away fast enough. She climbs into bed with the cat, scrambling back against the headboard with her knees drawn up to her chest. But if she cranes her neck, she can still see him down there. He's looking at her.

"What?" she asks.

He glances around as though the answer was written somewhere on the walls. "Something went wrong," he says flatly, "please try again."

"*Why are you looking at me?*"

"I wasn't looking *at* you, I was just looking."

She doesn't like that at all. "Well…don't."

"Okay." With an obsequious sort of smile, he closes his eyes. But he's still facing her.

Somehow, she likes that even less. So, she hunkers down, sinking low into the mattress. She's still clutching the stack of folders and papers, but the thought of reading them suddenly makes her unbelievably nauseated.

This is a violation, it's an absolute betrayal. This is her home; it's supposed to be her safe place where she can hide and forget about Hephaestus Forge. It's the one thing she has all to herself, where no one can get her, and she can do what she wants, and now that's *ruined*. It's ruined, it's ruined, *it's ruined, it's*–

Drugs. Drugs are the answer, here. Archer shoves the stack of papers into the drawer in her nightstand, lays back with her crowbar, and takes four drops. Her limbs go cold, the phial slips from her fingers, and she sinks into thoughtless, emotionless oblivion.

A few hours go by, and her Penth is starting to wear off. She comes to angry and frustrated, and just as she's reaching for the eyedropper again, she hears the robot downstairs.

"Uh-oh."

Archer pops her head up to see him standing in the middle of the room. "What?"

"They cut me off from the cloud."

"What?"

"Forge just cut my access to their cloud storage, So, they've noticed I'm gone."

She points. "Can you go back on the couch, please?"

He dutifully obeys, sitting back down. "They know I'm stolen. They want to keep people from using me to hack into them."

Archer can't quite reconcile the idea that she's harboring a *stolen person* in her home. Property shouldn't look and act like this. Rather, she decides, things that look and act like this shouldn't be considered property, and maybe she's starting to understand why Wells was so freaked out. "Do I...do I need to do something?"

"No. There's nothing to do."

"Okay." She takes another three drops of Penth and lies back down.

Maybe she'll get lucky and die in her sleep.

CHAPTER FIVE

To all employees:

As you may or may not be aware, Hephaestus Forge has just experienced a substantial corporate theft. The asset in question represents not only a significant financial and intellectual property investment for our company, but also leaves us vulnerable to further infiltration and data theft.

Upon your hiring at Hephaestus Forge, each and every one of you signed a strict nondisclosure agreement specific to your role within the company. As outlined in that contract, Hephaestus Forge reserves the right to conduct random data audits on all devices both personal and work-issued for the period of time no longer than 18 months following the termination of your employment. Fortunately, the need for such audits arises very rarely. But due to the seriousness of this theft, and the significant threat that it poses, we will be increasing both the frequency and magnitude of these data audits to the legal maximum.

As of now, and until our asset is recovered, be aware that all electronic communication, both work-related and private, is subject to monitoring for time, duration, and content. This is including, but not limited to:

Text and instant messages
Video chats (Skype, Zoom, Facetime, etc.)
Social media posts and interaction (Twitter, Instagram, Facebook, etc.)
Cellular and landline phone conversations
Cloud and photo/video sharing
Internet browser history and search engine input

These procedures, the processes by which they are achieved, and what the data can be used for, are outlined in full in the NDA. This is accessible via the Employee Portal on ForgeNet.

Needless to say, this is an internal matter, and we intend to handle it internally. Do NOT speak to public law enforcement on this matter, and do NOT involve the media. We cannot stress this seriously enough. Our private security team and legal/investigative departments will manage this situation, and inform public law enforcement if and when that becomes necessary. If you have any information regarding the missing asset, or those responsible for the theft, contact your department head, supervisor, or personnel coordinator.

Lex Morgan
Director of PR
Hephaestus Forge Biotech, Inc.

Fuck. *Fuck.*

Archer feels like throwing her phone across the room. What the hell has Wells gotten her into, what the hell is she *supposed to do?* A kind of dreadful realization washes over her, knowing that what she has to do now is go downstairs and *talk to the thing.*

She dons her silk kimono and descends to find him standing

stock-still in the living room, beneath one of the massive windows. At some point overnight, he must've taken off the top half of his Forge jumpsuit. He has the arms tied around his waist, and he's wearing a black undershirt. The white, morning light streaming in limns his pale skin even further. It makes his hair look eerily translucent.

He points out of the window, towards the cloudy sky. "What is that?"

"What's what?"

"That, up there. The bright circle."

Archer cranes her neck to see. "That's the sun."

"*That's* the sun?" He squints up into the light. "Are you sure?"

Is this thing broken, or just stupid? "Uh, yeah. Pretty sure."

"Pretty sure?" He does an awkward, mechanical shudder, eyes fluttering a little. "Give me a percentage."

"I am 100% sure that's the sun."

"*That's* the sun," he mutters. "It looks so different in-person. It's all…small and blurry."

"Well, it's far away. And behind some clouds."

"Huh." He does another one of those weird, jittery little shudders, head snapping to the side momentarily before righting again. "Okay."

He turns to face her, and there's a pause as they size one other up. Though neither realizes it, they're each silently wondering where to begin. Neither can quite think of how to unmoor and push off into the uncharted territory of the other.

They both start in at once.

"So—" "Listen."

There's an awkward, choked sort of silence, and then, in unison. "*Sorry.*"

Archer shakes her head. "No, you go."

"Okay," he says. "I'm sorry about last night. Like I said, I was collating a lot of new data, and I think it just…I had some wires crossed, so to speak."

"That's okay."

"The thing I did with the wifi...I'm not usually like that, I promise." He hesitates, gaze drifting a little. "At least I don't think I am." His attention snaps back to her, and he thrusts a hand out into the gulf. "Can we start over?"

Archer nods, cautiously relieved. "Okay. Let's start over." She clasps his hand, meeting his gaze head-on. His skin is the right texture, but it's eerily cool. It even feels like it's pulsing a little, near his wrist. Like it should be. Like a *human* would.

She realizes that she's probably been holding his hand for too long. With an awkward cough and a single, brisk shake, she releases him.

"I'm gonna go have a coffee and a...I don't know, fucking smoke or something," she announces, making her way over to the kitchen.

He trails along closely behind her. "Do you want me to make you breakfast?"

"Uh, do you know how to make breakfast?"

"I don't know."

That doesn't quite inspire confidence. "I'm not huge on breakfast. I'm good with coffee." She quickly adds, "And I can make it myself," before he has time to offer. Neither a kitchen fire nor bad coffee sound like ways she wants to spend her morning. (*Afternoon? No, morning.*)

"Okay." He points to the table. "Can I sit?"

"Sure."

She watches him out of the corner of her eye while she makes coffee. He seems much more at ease, today. He sinks into the chair, arm slung over the back, one leg kicked out to the side. But it looks strange. Programmed, rehearsed. Like he's dropped into the pose too quickly, too precisely to be natural.

Coffee in-hand, Archer sits down across from him. She keeps her eyes downcast as she says, "So, I was thinking–"

"Mmm." He nods seriously. "Mmm-hmm. Yes, me too."

That catches her off-guard. "Wh-what?"

He blinks. "Oh. *Oh*, I thought that was the whole sentence. I'm sorry. Continue."

She fumbles around for a cigarette, face beginning to redden. She'd practiced this little speech in her head before she came down, and now he's gone and thrown her off. "No, I was thinking that I can't go around calling you '*Epsilon-L*' for the next week."

"Okay."

"So, Cataloged Automaton Epsilon-L spells 'Cael'," she says, flicking fire to the end of her cigarette, "and that's a name." The first drag feels unbelievably centering. What she *wants* is a drop. But she hasn't spent enough time with this thing yet to know if he's gonna narc.

His gaze drifts a little as he tries it out, whispering to himself. "Cael. Cael, Cael, Cael. Leafy green vegetable—" He shakes his head. "No, *no*, that's wrong. *Please try again.* Short for Caelan. Gaelic, definition: eternal warrior. Derives from *caol*, translation: slender, narrow, fine." He looks back to her. "Yes. Okay. That's good."

Oh, wow, he took that really easily. "You're sure?"

"Yes."

"I feel weird, like…naming a person."

"It's a good name. I like it. What should I call you? Cymbre?"

She can't even hide the grimace. "No."

"Mx Archer?" he prods, smile beginning to spread across his face. "Landlady? Administrator?"

She holds up a hand. "Just Archer. Or Arch. No one calls me Cymbre."

"Why not?"

"Because I don't let them."

"Oh." He beams. "Okay. Cael and Archer it is, then."

It's a strange feeling, having performed the sacred ritual of naming one another. It's a shared anchor, a touchstone.

"Can I ask you something?" he says.

"Yeah."

"If you're Vietnamese, how come your name is Archer?"

She's a little thrown by his candor. "I'm only half Viet, my dad's French-American."

He nods, brow furrowed.

Archer takes a drag of her cigarette, eyeing him critically. "You, uh…you don't get out much, do you?" *You little fucking weirdo.*

"No, this is my first time out."

Yeah, no shit. She's still not quite sure what to make of him. And then she sets her cigarette down and beckons to him. "Come here."

Cael stands and moves around to her side of the table. She sits up straighter and reaches for him, but he leans back, trying to watch her hands.

"Come here, you're fine," she says, realizing too late that it had sounded harsh.

He's still trying to crane around. "Can I look at your hands?"

"In a second, just…" She catches him by the cheeks, holding him still. His skin is cool and soft, and his lips part very slightly as he glances up. His eyes flit back and forth between hers before darting away again. It's a disarmingly shy gesture. If he was human, Archer thinks, if he was *real*, he might've blushed or swallowed, then.

He is, objectively speaking, very beautiful. High cheekbones, sharp jaw, narrow chin. But young-seeming. Soft, despite his hard angles. And the more she looks, she more she realizes that the detail on him is nothing short of stunning. His lips are soft-looking, curved into a perfect Cupid's Bow. There's a small bump near his left eyebrow, like a mole. He has fine lines in the corners of his mouth and eyes, and she can't tell if they're painted on or not. They're the sort of benign little flaws that make someone human – easily overlooked, but stark when missing. And he has them. Dynamic and animate and totally artificial.

"Look at me," she coaxes, and he does.

His eyes are blue and flecked with green, and so bright against the pallor of his skin. They're framed by long sprays of white-blond lashes that fan beautifully across his cheeks when he blinks, making them look perpetually wide and curious.

"God," she whispers, running a finger down over his Adam's apple. "They do have a type, don't they?"

"What?"

"Forge, I mean." She squeezes gently at his shoulder, feeling the lean muscle yield just like it should. "They made you *beautiful.*"

That seems to puzzle him. "Thank you?"

She can feel the movement of his face and throat under her fingers as he speaks. It's not quite like the movement of human muscle, but it's not quite *unlike* it either. His breath — because he is, at least performatively, *breathing* — is dry and slightly cool, whispering across her face like an electric fan. Now that she's noticed, it's impossible to ignore.

There's a strange kind of lividity to him, something real and tangibly *alive*, like how the tube TV at her grandparents' house in Hanoi would hum when you turned it on. Not enough to really hear, but enough to sense.

Except…except that it's somehow nothing like that at all. "You must've cost them millions," Archer remarks.

"Hundreds of them, yes."

"Hundreds of millions," she murmurs distantly, hands drifting upwards to brush through his hair. It's soft. It feels like hair. It might be real hair. "Why? Why go through the trouble of making you beautiful? Why make you at all? What…what are you *for?*"

"I think they want me to do dangerous or boring jobs so that human people don't have to."

"Then why make you beautiful? If you're just gonna get smashed up in a coal mine or some shit."

"What are *you* for?"

She laughs darkly. "I'm for display only. I'm a walking, talking advertisement for a life made whole by technology." She lifts one of his hands towards her face. "Shit, you don't have fingerprints."

"Why would I need fingerprints?"

"I…I don't know." Now she just feels stupid. *Wait, what are fingerprints for, again?*

After a beat, he slips his hands from her grip and takes her by the wrists. "You have tattoos on your fingers."

"Yeah."

"Do you have any more?"

"Yeah." She pulls up her sleeves to show him. There are some Vietnamese tribal designs, some flowers. A pair of wide bands hugs each of her forearms, in harmony with the little rings etched around her fingers. There's script in French and English, some in Chữ Nôm. A traditional, Viet dragon crests over her shoulder, the tip of its snout just poking out from beneath her kimono. They're all black. Cael inspects each design with clinical intensity.

"I have them on my chest and ribs, too," she says, sort of fascinated by how fascinated he is.

"Can I see those?"

"Not without buying me a drink first."

He blinks up at her for a moment, thinking hard before announcing, "That was not meant as a sexual or romantic advance."

"I know, I was joking. I assume you can't even do sex and romance."

"No, I was designed to be capable of both of those things." He cocks an eyebrow at her. "I mean I'm not interested in you."

She laughs. "Uh, ouch? Okay."

"I don't know you," he shrugs. "And it's not like there's any point in me telling you that you're physically beautiful, because you already know that you are. You have spowegg–"

"Wait, I'm sorry, *what?*"

He looks taken aback by her interruption. "Spowegg."

"That's not a word." *Fuck, Forge built a broken robot.*

Cael shudders violently. "Isn't that the adverb form of the word 'conventional'?

She stammers for a second. "What? Adverb form of–" *Wait, what's an adverb, again?* "Are you trying to say 'conventionally'?"

"Maybe. Use it in a sentence."

The pieces start to come together a little, and through gritted teeth, Archer guesses, "Conventionally attractive?"

"Oh." Another shudder, accompanied by an eye-flutter. "Yes. You have *conventionally* attractive features, like strong facial symmetry and high cheekbones, along with full lips and well-maintained skin and hair. You wouldn't have a job if you weren't physically beautiful."

At that, Archer genuinely frowns.

"I'm sorry," he blurts. "That probably came out wrong. I'm not…I don't have a lot of experience communicating within the context of emotion."

"Okay?"

He turns her hands over in his, tracing his fingertips over each and every one of the lines in turn. Studying all of her tiny, perfect flaws, she supposes. "I actually have a source model."

"A what?"

"Source model," he repeats, twisting at her silver rings, bending her fingers back and forth. "Somewhere on the planet, there's a man walking around who looks exactly like me. Or…I guess I look exactly like him."

"You're based on…on a *guy*? Just…some guy?"

"Yes."

"That's completely ridiculous."

He lifts her hand towards his face, turning his head side to side to inspect the bruise on her knuckles. "What happened to your hand?"

"I punched a guy. Couple nights ago."

"Why?"

"He touched me."

Cael cocks an eyebrow at her, eyes darting down to their hands and then back up again.

"Without permission," she adds. "You're fine. I'm not gonna punch you."

He releases her hands anyway, and instead takes up a lock of her hair. Turnabout is fair play, she supposes. He can poke and prod at her if he wants.

"Have you seen very many…?"

His eyes flit up to hers. "What? Meat puppets?"

Archer furrows her brow disapprovingly. It makes him smile.

"No, I haven't. They kept me in a room. Direct interaction was prohibited."

She leans away, casting him a wary look. "Are you dangerous?"

"No more dangerous than you are." After a beat, he adds a quiet, "*Rocky Balboa.*"

That remark, that tentative little tease at her expense, is perhaps the most human thing he's done so far. It's strangely genuine, strangely vulnerable. And, also, strangely endearing.

The moment ends when Khì leaps up onto the table, meowing loudly.

"He's hungry," Archer translates. "The bed must've cooled off enough for him to notice that I left, and now he's pissed."

Cael eyes the animal cautiously. "*Angry,*" he whispers.

Archer steps away, back over to the kitchen counter, and sets about dehydrating the block of freeze-dried rabbit that'll serve as breakfast. Content with this course of events, the cat hops up onto her shoulder to supervise.

"The truth is, they made me because they could," Cael says softly.

That catches her by surprise. With a furrowed brow, she turns to face him. "Yeah?"

He's not looking at her. He's just staring off into the distance, towards the window that has the sun in it. "Yes. They tested the hardware on you, and then used what they learned to build me. But I'm just another test." He sighs, and it is a gesture so human that it startles her. "They'll study me. They'll decide what worked and what failed, and catalog everything. And then they'll wipe the memory off of my CPU and recycle this body for the next iteration of the AI. The *better* one that's going to come after." He smiles sadly, bright blue eyes flitting up to meet hers. He points over his shoulder to the window. "Tears in the rain, right?"

After a much-needed shower, Archer emerges into the sitting room to find Cael leafing through her vinyl. She's accrued a modest collection over the years: Nine Inch Nails, Depeche Mode, Serge Gainsbourg, Björk. 70-year-old glam rock standards, post-punk, and electronica. She even has some early Billie Eilish.

"These things are old," he remarks.

"They still make records. It's, like…trendy hipster shit."

He inspects a copy of David Bowie's *Low*. "Yes, but these ones are old. And you're not a trendy hipster."

"You literally *just* got through telling me about how you don't know me, yet." Her skin is starting to itch, without Penth, not to mention how her back and hip pain have ramped up right on cue. And the curious android routine is wearing on her a little.

"Do you want to see a trick?" he asks, slipping the record from its sleeve and setting it on the turntable. He takes a few steps back and pauses.

"Uh, what?"

All at once, there comes the unmistakable sound of every single speaker in the house screeching to life simultaneously, crackling with static and interference.

Archer claps her hands over her ears. "*Hey!*"

He giggles. "Oops, I overshot. Hang on." After another agonizing moment, the cacophony resolves into the bright, poppy opening riffs of David Bowie's "Speed of Life." It's on every single speaker. Sure enough, the record is spinning.

Cael beams. "See?"

It's making her head pound, and as impressive as it is, it seems a completely pointless feat, and she's in no mood to ask how he did it. "Can you turn it off, please?" she begs. "*By pressing the button?*"

He suddenly seems zoned out, gazing off into the distance. "You're such a wonderful person, but you've got problems. I'll never touch you."

Instantly furious, Archer storms across the room and mashes the off-switch on the record player. "What the fuck did you just say to me?" She wonders if *he's* got an off-switch she should know about.

"That's the song that would have come next," he explains, eyes wide and innocent. "If you hadn't turned it off."

Oh, the *lyrics*. Jesus goddamn Christ. She rubs at her forehead. "I'm gonna…I need to go out."

Cael's face lights up. "Can I come?"

She's already gathering up her coat. "Sure, if you wanna get dragged right back to Forge and erased."

He deflates instantly. "Good point. Where are you going, though? And for how long?"

"The Forge coveralls are stressing me out," she says, gesturing towards him. And that's not actually a lie. It sort of feels like the company is watching her. "I'm gonna go get you something else to wear."

"I don't have any money."

"That's okay, I have money. I can buy it for you."

He's back to beaming. "Like a present?"

"Yeah," she says, nearly tripping over the empty crate by the door. "Sure, like a present."

"Okay, goodb–"

She's gone before he can finish, locking the door behind her. Wait, does he know how to unlock doors? Is escape something she needs to worry about? *Fuck*. She slumps against the wall, desperately taking two drops of Penth. Gradually, the shaking in her hands slows, and her head clears.

While she's digging through her bag for her anti-surveillance visor, her phone chimes. It's a text from Lucas:

> Hey, you wanna go get fucked up
> tonight?
> Pandora's Box is hosting this like
> orgy thing, could be fun.

Fuck, she wants to do that. A Bacchanal with Luc sounds like exactly the thing she needs right now, and it's physically painful to type the reply:

> I fucking really wish I could, like,
> you have no idea.
> But I've got some bullshit. I'm
> sorry, babes.

> : (Anything I can help with?

> No, but thank you. Xx

In the elevator, she thinks of Cael's proud smile and the way he'd looked when she'd left. By the time she's hailed a cab, the drugs have kicked in fully, and her frustration has twisted into guilt and shame.

It's that guilt that sends her to an actually-nice store, rather than a secondhand shop. She opts for the weird Asian street fashion place in Brooklyn, with the bright, neon signs and gleaming, minimalist displays. There, she picks out two pairs of jeans, a few t-shirts, a decent button-up, and a set of loungewear. She even grabs him an ultra-chic, modern-looking pea coat just for good measure. On her way to the checkout, she remembers: Fucking *shoes*. Most people on the planet require *shoes*. She turns back in exasperation, and spends the next fifteen minutes agonizing over how big feet are supposed to be. Holding shoes up against her forearm like an idiot, trying to measure and estimate based on how tall she thinks he is. She settles on a pair of vintage-looking high-tops that will match decently with any of the things she picked out.

Absolutely ridiculous. *Fuck* shoes, but also, *fuck* these stupid feet.

Mercifully, Archer has the wherewithal to pay cash, in order to avoid any suspicious charges on her card. Under normal circumstances, she wouldn't be caught dead shopping in a place with so many colors on the rack. It's the misplaced paranoia of the heavily drug-dependent, she knows. But she still feels safer with the extra buffer in place. The haul runs her a few hundred dollars, but that's fine. She tells herself that she's doing something *good* for someone, for once. Even so, she can't help but take the long way home. She stops for coffee, and then swings by Auryn's apartment. She has to convince him to take an IOU for three bottles of Penth, since she's out of cash, now. Luckily, he obliges. He knows she's good for it. And then she lingers on his couch to drop, ignoring his idle questions about the bag of men's clothing she has with her. Like maybe if she stays away for long enough, Cael will just crawl back into his crate and disappear.

"Cael?" she calls out, the instant she walks through the door. "Caelan?" This has felt sort of like leaving a new puppy home alone for the first time, like she doesn't know what he's gotten up to in her absence, and she's sort of afraid that he's chewed on the furniture. Or pulled a David Bowie and drawn something awful on the carpet. (Is that funny? Probably not. She still smiles about it.)

"I'm up here." His voice is very small.

She sets her bag down by the door and follows the sound up the stairs to her bed, where he's backed against the headboard with his knees drawn up to his chest. Khi is curled up on the floor by the nightstand. Sleeping.

"What's the problem?" she asks.

Cael points to the cat. "He doesn't like me."

"Don't take it personally, he doesn't like anyone."

"I came up here because this is the only place where he wouldn't chase me. I'm sorry."

"Yeah, he doesn't come on the bed if there's a stranger in it."

"Why would strangers be in your bed?"

Archer raises an eyebrow, unimpressed.

"Oh." Chagrined, Cael looks at his palm for a moment before extending it out towards her. It's an incredibly pathetic gesture. "Look." There's a deep gouge across the width of his hand.

"Oh," she remarks, sitting down on the edge of the bed. She takes his hand in hers, inspecting the injury. "Oh shit, did he scratch you?"

"Yes."

She can't help but feel a strange stab of pity for him. "Little bastard. Does it hurt?"

"I don't know. I don't think so."

"This is Arachne, right?" she asks, switching on the bedside lamp and bringing his palm beneath the light. "Your skin?"

He nods, scooting closer to accommodate the reach.

"It'll heal. Just give it a few hours. Don't mess with it, and it'll do its thing."

"Okay."

All at once, and she has absolutely no idea why, Archer feels the urge to bend down and press her lips to the wound. Like she could somehow kiss it better for him. But then she looks up and sees his eyes so close to hers.

"What are you thinking about?" he asks, a slight smile on his lips.

That snaps her out of it. She releases his hand. "I'm sorry he scratched you," she says, standing up again.

"That's okay. He was just scared."

"Yeah. He'll either get over it, or he won't. No way to tell. Just remember you're bigger and smarter than he is."

"Okay."

"Come downstairs, I got your shit."

"Okay."

He follows her back to the living room, where she awkwardly thrusts the shopping bag into his hands.

"Thank you," he says, and it seems genuine enough.

"There's a whole bunch of stuff in there," she says. "I figure you can pick your own clothes, right? Dress yourself?"

"I don't know, I've never done it before."

Awesome. "Okay, well…there you go."

"Okay."

Archer hangs her coat up by the door, checks her phone. No new emails from Forge, but nothing from Wells, either. She can't tell if that's good or bad. And then she turns around again, only to find a naked android standing in the middle of her living room.

"What the fuck are you doing?" she demands, holding up a hand and looking away. But not before the phrase 'anatomically correct' claps painfully through her skull.

He blinks at her in surprise, halfway through unpacking the shopping bag. "The Forge coveralls were stressing you out."

She stammers, more out of shock than any real offense. "Yeah, but– You can't just take your clothes off in front of someone!"

"Why not? They had me do it all the time, back–"

"This isn't a lab, this is a *house*! This is the fucking real world! Go do that in the other room!"

He looks around. "There is no other room."

"The *bathroom*, Cael!"

"Okay." He placidly gathers up the discarded coveralls and retreats to the bathroom. Just before he closes the door behind him, he pauses. "This was not intended as a romantic or sexual advance."

"All right!"

"Like I said, I'm not interested in you."

"*Okay!*"

Finally, the door is closed between them, and Archer sighs in exasperation. She throws herself down onto the couch, pressing her fingers into her eyes. All the walking around and shopping on these fucking feet are killing her lower back, and the muscles spasm angrily as she tries to relax them.

He has a mole near his right nipple, and no hair below his eyelashes. Those are facts she knows, now.

A week of this shit is going to kill her.

After a few minutes, Cael emerges from the bathroom wearing the skinny jeans and short-sleeved button-up. He's buttoned it up unevenly, because of course he has, but the sizes are right, and he looks proud of himself.

"Your buttons are all fucked up," she points out.

"Oh." He looks down, seeming to make a quick assessment, and then unbuttons the whole line. He thinks hard for a moment, the tails of the shirt clasped tightly in his hands, and then promptly sets about buttoning it wrong again.

Absolutely going to kill her. "No, look–" Archer sighs, crossing the room to help him. She brushes his hands out of the way. "You've got me so fucked up, just let me do it."

He watches her intently, and a quick glance confirms that he's mimicking the movement of her fingers. The delicate lift and pinch and twist-into-place. She tries to ignore the fact that she's close enough to feel his breath again.

"I'm not a baby," he suddenly announces, making her jump.

"What?"

"Just because I haven't had a lot of what you'd call '*real world experience*' doesn't mean I'm a baby."

"I never said you were a baby."

"I'm smarter than you."

She laughs sarcastically. "Ouch, okay." After a span of silence, she asks, "Out of curiosity, how old are you?"

There's an undeniable hesitation before he answers. "The L-iteration of the AI has occupied the Epsilon body for six months."

"Oh, so, you *are* a baby!"

He's visibly indignant. "No. This body was modeled after a 25-year-old man, and my AI processes and interprets new information at substantially faster rates than your OI, resulting in quicker cognitive maturation."

"OI?"

"Organic Intelligence," he says. As though it should've been obvious. "My fine motor is state-of-the-art, and so are my problem-solving trees and pattern recognition programs. No other AI in the history of human invention has been able to do the things I do, I'm practically better than human. I think it's just the perspective on these buttons that's throwing me, and the fact that I'm collating so much new information right now. It's giving me these weird little visual glitches."

The word 'glitches' scares her a little. "Are you…are you gonna break?" *Shit, what happens if he breaks? Am I in trouble? Will he hurt me? Do I call Wells? Do I call Forge? Try and fix him myself? Put him out with the trash?*

"I'm not going to break," he reassures her. "All internal diagnostics indicate that I'm operating well within normal safety parameters."

"Okay." Archer nods, cautiously relieved. Still, the worry is there, now. In the back of her mind. She smooths a hand down the line of re-fastened buttons. "You're done."

He lifts at the hem of the shirt, inspecting her work. "Oh," he remarks, and then his eyes flutter a little. "Oh, yes. I get it."

Despite herself, she smiles. "Good." She heads back to the couch, eager to get off her feet again. "You wanna gather those clothes up? You can keep them out here, if you want, by the couch."

His voice is suddenly flat and emotionless as he replies, "I'm sorry, Dave. I'm afraid I can't do that."

Oh, fuck *no.* All the hairs on the back of her neck stand up, adrenaline shooting through her veins like ice water. She turns to look at him again, so afraid of what she'll see, and sure enough, his facial expression has gone completely blank and unreadable. There's an emptiness in his eyes, like he's looking through her, rather than at her.

"Wh-what?"

All at once, his face splits with a wide smile. "No, I'm joking. Could you imagine?"

"*Fuck me.*" Archer pants in relief, clutching at the couch for support, and Caelan laughs so hard that it makes all the speakers turn on again.

CHAPTER SIX

THE WEEK PROGRESSES IN SURREAL FITS AND SPURTS. CAEL BEGINS TO poke around the place (with permission), picking up and scrutinizing everything he can get his hands on. The blinking and labeling slow in frequency and intensity as time goes on, but periodically come back when he finds something new. At one point, Archer hears the stove clicking to life and has to shout at him to turn it off.

He *devours* her books. The first time she notices it, he's sitting beside one of the shelves, holding a book up to his face and flipping through the pages so quickly that it makes his hair flutter. And then his face lifts and his eyes slip out of focus for a few seconds, flickering, before he puts the book back and picks up another to repeat the process. Over and over. She lets him get through about five of them before she speaks up.

"What are you doing?" she finally asks, eyeing him from her place on the couch.

He responds without stopping the strange ritual. "Reading."

"No, you're not, there's literally no way you're reading that fast."

"Yes, I am," he refutes, indignant. "I told you before, I'm smarter than you, and I'm capable of perceiving and processing new information much more quickly and efficiently than you are."

"Then how come you freaked out non-stop for your first 24 hours here?" she challenges. "If you're so good at processing new information."

He frowns. "That's different."

"All right, prove it, then. What was the last book you read?"

"*The Lord of the Rings: Return of the King*," he replies with no hesitation, already flipping through another book. "I liked Samwise, he was my favorite character in the entire trilogy. And I liked that Gimli and Legolas become friends in the end, after the admittedly rocky start to their relationship. I also liked when Arwen gave up her immortality because she loved Aragorn so much, even though he probably would've lived to be 200 years old. Is that realistic? Do humans ever actually love each other that much?"

"I don't know. Not in my experience."

"Hmm."

The question springs from her lips before she can stop it, "Are you immortal?"

"In theory," he shrugs, placing his most recent read back on the shelf. "It's honestly going to be pretty difficult to speak in absolutes about my abilities and attributes, since I'm quite literally one-of-a-kind. I've already surpassed simulated projections in many arenas. *The Silmarillion* is really dense," he suddenly pivots, and it's so abrupt that it nearly gives Archer whiplash. But he just gazes admiringly at the book cover as he chatters away, "Beren and Lúthien are relationship goals, and I do love the parallel between the Morningstar and the Evenstar. And Gandalf seems so much cooler, now." He replaces the book, giving the shelf a quick visual scan. "Do you have *The Children of Húrin?*"

Archer can only stammer for a moment, trying to get her bearings back. "Um...yeah, I own it, but I'm pretty sure I actually lent it to Rob Wells a while back, and he never returned it."

Cael deflates. "Oh."

"Just find it online."

"No." He shakes his head in dismay. "No, I've come to appreciate the experience of handling an ink-and-paper book, and it'll be difficult to go back." With that, he picks up *A Clockwork Orange,* and resumes his page-flipping.

But for all of that brilliance, he can still be so unbelievably… well, *stupid.* It's so hard for Archer to pin down exactly who or what he is, and that's only intensified by the fact that Cael clearly has no idea who or what he is. Not in this context, not in the real world. Sometimes, he'll spend literal hours doing something completely inane, like standing in the middle of the living room and clicking a pen in and out, or opening and closing the fridge to watch the light go on and off. But the bulk of his time is spent tailing Archer around at what he must think is a discreet distance, mimicking the way her hands and face move. It's unsettling as all hell, but she would feel guilty telling him to knock it off. That, and she's hoping that he actually learns something from it.

Because the way he moves has got to be the weirdest part of this whole thing. The way he'd sat down in the kitchen chair that first morning clearly hadn't been a fluke. He alternates between very organic, fluid movements that look entirely human, and strange, jerky, mechanical shudders. When he holds a hand out, it never shakes. He doesn't fidget or sway or tap his foot. He's either making a deliberate point to move, or he's perfectly, immaculately still.

In the same way, there's something distinctly childish about him, but at the same time, something terrifyingly intelligent. It seems to go in cycles. As he gets used to a new object or idea, the childlike-wonder thing fades, and he becomes so sharp and confident. It's hard for Archer to tell which is the real Cael, and which is the programmed one. If there's even a distinction to be made, there.

Nia, her hookup from a few days ago, texts about halfway through the week. Archer doesn't even remember exchanging numbers, but they must have. It's *physically painful* to have to say no, when she invites her to a naked rave in a warehouse.

Occasionally, Archer does remember to mess around with her

feet, switching between the new pairs so she doesn't fall on her ass like Little Miss Hermes when she meets Vander and the *Wired* people on Friday. She also spends an inordinate amount of time sneaking from drop to drop. She hides in the bathroom, or waits until Cael is adequately distracted. It had been stressful for the first couple of days, but now she's getting the hang of it. Or, rather, she thought she was.

She's doing dishes when he brings it up.

"I've noticed that your moods can vary substantially throughout the day, a trend that seems to be largely dependent on drug use."

Oh shit, oh fuck, don't panic, don't panic.

Her knee-jerk response is to say, 'Well, yeah, *I'm* largely dependent on drug use,' but she bites it back.

He's done this sort of thing a few times. He'll make some banal, obvious observation to her, like, '*I've noticed that your record collection contains music primarily from the 20th century, but you most often choose to play more contemporary dark electronica from your phone.*' That sparked a long, winding, garden-path of a conversation about the proper handling and preservation of vinyl, and the fact that being a fan of something doesn't mean you need to consume nothing but that thing, 24/7. '*I've noticed that your hair is very long.*' That time, all she could do was agree, and give him the verbal equivalent of a pat on the head. '*I've noticed that the cat is always either sleeping, or engaging in unsanctioned mischief.*' At least that one had given her a laugh.

And now, this.

"Drug use?" she asks, feigning ignorance.

He doesn't miss a beat. "Nepenthe, more commonly known by its street name 'Penth', is a synthetic opiate most frequently distributed in liquid form. It's a quickly-absorbed, short-acting drug which causes intense euphoria and numbs painful physical sensations."

She doesn't respond. She doesn't even look at him.

"Prolonged use can lead to dangerous weight loss and deterioration of the brain's white matter, which may affect decision-making abilities, mood regulation, and responses to stressful situations. If overused, Nepenthe can lead to death by cardiac arrest." He pauses, seemingly for dramatic effect. "But I'm pretty sure you know that."

Her face burns hot. "What does it matter to you?"

"I don't want you to hurt yourself."

Archer rolls her eyes, trying to walk away.

He blocks her path. "I'm serious."

She lifts an eyebrow, unimpressed, and grateful for her height advantage. "And what, you D.A.R.E. me to resist? Seriously?"

"I just said that I was serious."

"Okay, Cael." She walks past him, towards the couch. Her spine is absolutely killing her.

He trails after her. "Don't do drugs."

"*Okay*, Cael." She flops down on her back, casting an arm over her eyes.

He doesn't miss a beat. "I've noticed that you spend many of your waking hours lying down."

She opens her eyes to find him peering over the back of the couch, directly above her face. "Yeah, these new feet are destroying my back. And since we're now so firmly entrenched in the *War on Drugs Part 2: Robot Uprising*—"

"You're just going to do more drugs when you think I'm not looking."

The remark tugs uncomfortably at her self-awareness, but she powers through. "Correct."

"What can I do to stop you?"

"Nothing."

"What if I throw all of your drugs away?"

"I'll send you back to Tartarus." The inside-joke nickname for the Hephaestus Forge R&D labs. It's a moniker that is reportedly as cruel as the place itself, and one that is most decidedly against company policy to use.

He frowns, dismayed. "Archer."

Well, shit. That was out of line. "You can come look at my feet, if you want," she tiredly concedes. "I won't send you back to the labs."

He sits down beside her, inspecting her cybernetics. He blinks a few times and then announces, "Walking in high heels on a regular basis can cause numerous musculoskeletal complications, owing largely to the fact that they shift your center of gravity forward and alter your natural spine position. This can lead to nerve damage, as well as uneven wear on the cartilage discs, joints, and ligaments of the back."

"Okay," she nods, condescending. "Thank you for that, Cael."

He gives her a stern look. "You should take them off, for your health. Then you can stop doing drugs."

She groans, frustrated. "What's with the new obsession with my health?"

"I've noticed that you make a lot of unhealthy choices."

"Well, the feet aren't my choice," she's quick to justify. "I mean, I'm physically able to remove them, but this is my job. I have to learn how to walk them, so Forge can sell them to other people. I'm a marketing tool, remember?"

Cael nods sternly. "For display only."

She's almost proud. "Exactly. And Forge won't prescribe me a goddamn thing for how much pain I'm in all the time, and they *definitely* won't change the legs, because that would be admitting that their tech hurts people. They're just gonna wait until my back is completely fucked, inject me with Aceso nanobots, and *voila*, good as new."

He furrows his brow. "That's brilg."

"It's what, now?"

Cael shudders. "The opposite of ethical."

"Unethical. Come on."

"Okay, then, it's unethical."

"Of me?"

"Of Hephaestus Forge."

Again, she gives a noncommittal shrug. "They already did it to Luc. Lucas – he's the model with the Atlas arm they're always shoving in front of the cameras – he and I were their first two patients. I was seven, and he was about 9 or 10, I think. Anyway, when he was 18, they noticed he was starting to develop scoliosis. His right arm, the cybernetic, was so much heavier than the organic arm that it was literally curving his spine over. He was in agony all the time, begging them to take it off of him, but no. Instead, they tested the Acesos on him, and that was that. Now they use them to cure SCIs and shit. So, three cheers for Luc's sacrifice in the name of science."

"And that's what they'll do to you?" Cael asks. "They'll put nanobots in your spine?"

"Yeah."

He points. "But what about all the people they sell these feet to?"

"They'll wait a year or two, and then sell *them* the Acesos. It's more money. More money for the bots, more money for the procedure. That's all they really care about, not healing people."

He frowns. "That's *fucked* up."

"Whoa!" she laughs, completely blindsided. "Language!"

"You say that word all the time!"

"Yeah, but that doesn't mean *you* can say it!"

He crosses his arms over his chest, giving her a very stern look. "We've been over this, Archer. I am not—"

"You're not a baby, yes. I know."

"And it *is* fucked up."

"Hey, this is healthcare under Capitalism," Archer shrugs, indifferent. "We chose this."

That seems to panic him. "I didn't choose it! I don't remember that!"

"Not you, the American people."

"When? When did they choose it?"

"It wasn't any one time," she justifies, frustrated with this conversation. "It's just...it's just the system! Hephaestus Forge is a *business*. And they're the only people who know how to make these—" she brandishes a foot in his face, "—or *you*, for that matter, so they can do whatever they want."

"*Fucked up.*"

"Okay, Caelan," she concedes, settling deeper into the couch. Her feet press against his leg, but he doesn't move.

"Agree that it's fucked up," he commands.

"Okay, it's fucked up."

"Archer!"

She cranes her neck to look at him. "What? *Damn!*"

"What Hephaestus Forge does to you is fucked up."

"Okay. What Hephaestus Forge does to me is fucked up." She sighs, gaze drifting. "But this is my life. It'll be like this until I die. If they *ever* let me die. They'll probably invent a way to…cryogenically freeze your head or some shit, and test it out on me, for all—"

"Why?"

"Why what?"

"Why does it not have to be my life, but it still has to be yours?"

"Caelan, I don't know."

Across the room, the empty crate in which he arrived remains by the door. Like a cab with the meter running, waiting to take him away again.

That night, Archer finally dives into the pages and pages of schematics and documents that Cael had brought with him. It seems so strangely inappropriate to do in front of him, to *read* rather than *ask*. So, she hides in her bedroom, and tries to learn more about the machine that has been so inexplicably thrust upon her. The man who is sleeping on her couch.

The mechanical terms, all the information about his body, make perfect sense to her. He's an amalgamation of Hephaestus Forge's entire catalog of cybernetics. Nike 6.0s, Atlas 8.4s. An Asclepius heart, Charon eyes, Aoede vocal cords, all propped up by a carbon-fiber skeleton and wrapped in Arachne synthflesh. His lungs are the outliers – not true Asclepius pieces, like the rest of his internal organs. Instead, they're vaguely-lung-shaped fan stacks, meant for temperature control.

"The gifts of each Olympian, combined into one autonomous machine." She could take him apart and put him back together again, and she could probably do it with her eyes closed.

His mind, on the other hand, even explained as it is on paper, is more than she can comprehend. There are phrases like 'fuzzy logic' and 'nouvelle AI' thrown around, names like Turing, Moravec,

Newell. Simon and McCarthy. She skims through long-winded passages describing GOFAI becoming bogged down by *ad hoc* patches to symbolic computation. 'Black-box' machine learning, DeepMind, the Cyc Project, Cog, Kismet, Sophia, GPT-5.

It's enough to make her head spin.

For the first nine iterations of the AI, it would seem that Cael was little more than a chatbot. He processed and responded to basic queries, but not much else. It was difficult for him to keep track of a thread of conversation for more than a few exchanges, and he would routinely repeat himself or forget information. Iterations D through I all had physical bodies, of course, each less rudimentary than the last, so it was no longer necessary to type to him nor read his response from a screen. But that added a whole new host of problems involving listening and comprehension. For that, his engineers looked to the live television captioners employed by the FCC, and how each operator tailors their speech-to-text software to understand their own voices.

Training an AI is a simple enough process, she learns, at least in theory. You feed the machine a dataset. Videos, text, photographs, whatever. And then it compiles the data, learns to generalize patterns, and generates new content based on what it's learned. In practice, it's much more difficult to fine-tune and perfect. There are pitfalls everywhere, things she wouldn't even have expected. Language comprehension, semantics, tiny little nuances of human behavior that can't be manually coded into a machine no matter how hard you try. There's just too much. The Uncanny Valley is a vast expanse, and it would seem that Hephaestus Forge R&D was drowning in it for a long, long time.

And then, somewhere around the J-iteration of the AI, the deep-learning team made their breakthrough. They hooked him up to an internet search engine.

At first, they overshot. They gave him everything at once, and the AI crashed instantly. So, for Delta-K, they knew to ration. At first, they only gave him access to very carefully curated datasets, spread out over a week. Structured learning. Structured creation.

Time-consuming. After that, they gave him unfettered access to the internet, and let him go where he wanted. He devoured it like nothing they'd ever seen. Finally, they gave him access to every open, unsecured webcam and microphone on the planet.

Oh, fuck.

Yes, she read that right. Every single one. And by the looks of the documentation, the device manufacturers and internet service providers had agreed to it *carte blanche*.

And that's when the real strides were made. He already had intelligence, of course, he had *knowledge*. But that's when he learned how to be a *person*. His teachers were unwilling participants in his education, no less test subjects than he was. But he watched their faces, and he studied the way they moved and interacted with one another when they did not know they were being observed. He listened to them talk, listened to them laugh and cry and scream at one another. He consumed, synthesized, and created.

They locked him in a room. They made him play chess, made him play Go. They asked him questions and tested him on thought experiments. They exposed him to stimuli both comforting and terrifying, in order to test his emotional responses, trying to determine if they were performative or genuine. It didn't take long for the engineers to declare, at least to themselves, that they had successfully created the first and only Artificial Biological Intelligence in history.

And then, after three months, they erased him. Just like that, they erased it all, because they knew they could do better. According to the lab notes, that's something that Cael had actually resisted. But they did it anyway. They started over with a new Epsilon body, and the L-iteration of the AI. Smarter, more intuitive, more emotive. For all intents and purposes, human.

And then Robert Wells put him in a box and sent him right to Cymbre Archer's fucking doorstep.

CHAPTER SEVEN

It's Monday night. As Archer sits on her bed, staring down the barrel of the end of Cael's time here and listening to him shuffle around downstairs, she's surprised to find herself a little sad.

Because, well…she's actually, sort of, maybe, gotten *used* to the little weirdo. It's been strange and new to have someone in the house, someone to talk to, even if she's always being needlessly short and sarcastic with him. And, looking back, she can't help but acknowledge the twinge of guilt she feels for the way she's behaved towards him. Does she need to feel guilty? It's not like she's been using him as a punching bag, she just hasn't really been wasting her time on social graces. Does he mind that? Is that something she should've asked him?

She thinks of how she snapped at him for playing the music too loud, and then spent hundreds of dollars on clothes for him. She thinks of the impulse to press her lips to the wound on his hand. Of buttoning his shirt.

She thinks of how concerned he'd been about her drug use.

How horrified he was when he learned about the way Forge treats her. How he'd studied her tattoos.

She thinks of how she'd called him beautiful. Because he really is quite beautiful.

She thinks of how he'd said it back.

If Archer could do the week over, she'd try and be different. Nicer, more welcoming. More understanding. She'd try, and probably fail, because she can't not be herself.

Her vain, arrogant, awful self.

It would be easy to blame the world, or the life she's lived; easy to say that she's been twisted into this self-centered, heartless thing by years and years of dehumanizing abuse and neglect. But she knows that's not true. She would be like this no matter what.

And, she realizes, just as she's seemingly programmed to be sardonic, and to defend by attacking, Cael has been literally programmed to be curious and talkative and sort of annoying. It's probably just as hard for him to resist as it is for her.

Actually, probably harder.

Actually, it's probably not worth thinking about. It's over. He's leaving. That's that.

Her solution is the tried-and-true take three drops, turn her brain off, and pass the fuck out.

"Archer?"

She doesn't respond. Doesn't quite hear it.

Something jabs hard into her shoulder. "*Archer.*"

She jerks awake. "What? Fuck, what?"

Cael is kneeling beside her bed, wide-eyed, knees drawn up to his chest. Visibly shaking. Maybe he's paler than usual, or maybe she's just anthropomorphizing. (Can you anthropomorphize an android? She doesn't know.) Outside, thunder claps, and he startles hard. Sheets of rain pound against the windows. She glances at the clock. It's just after 3:00 am.

"What?" she repeats, perhaps more pointedly than she'd intended.

"What is that?" he begs. "What's going on?"

She grumbles in frustration, punching her pillows into place. "It's a thunderstorm, Cael, it's fine."

"Thunderstorm – but that's *electricity*," he presses, scooting closer. "What if it makes me short out?"

"It won't."

"But what if it hits me?"

"It won't hit you. You're inside and it's outside."

He points to the window. "But no, it's right there, look." As if on cue, another percussive thunderclap shakes the pane, and the street outside is illuminated in blinding white for a split second. He shuffles all the way over against the bed. "Uh-oh."

"It's outside," she repeats, rolling away from him. "If it hits anything, it'll hit the roof."

"But the roof is connected to the walls, which are connected to the floor, and *I'm* touching the floor!"

"That's not how it works."

"Well, then, how does it work? *Tell me how it works!*"

Exasperated, she rolls onto her back. "Cael, you would know a hell of a lot more about it than I do. Just…look on the internet, I don't know." This sort of thing happened once before, when he met the cat. And she can't deny, this really is beautiful, complex, creative programming. That when he's afraid (and maybe other emotions, too?) his ability to function according to his 'state-of-the-art logic trees' diminishes. Just like a human.

His eyes flutter for a few seconds before fixing on hers once more. "Thunderstorms commonly trigger power outages, even with modern surge protection technology. What if I short out, and you can't charge me up enough to get the hamster wheels turning again? What if *that*?"

"Oh, my fucking god," she mumbles. "I promise you, that is not going to happen."

"But how sure are you? Give me a percentage."

She's not playing the percentage game again. "My legs have never shorted out during a thunderstorm."

That seems to give him pause, if only for a moment. "No, I don't like this, Archer, I really don't like this. Can I come up there? I really think it would be a lot better if I came up there."

She sighs. "*Fine.*"

He scrambles up from the floor in a series of weird, jerky movements, resuming the same pathetic, defensive position atop the mattress. The sky splits once more, loud enough that it makes even Archer jump.

"Jesus," she whispers.

"Ar*cherrr.*" He's rocking back and forth now.

She has to admit, it's sympathetic. That, and it's shaking the whole goddamn bed. "All right," she concedes, lifting the covers. "Fine. Come here."

With a relieved whimper, he crawls in beside her. He scoots in close, one hand clamping around her forearm.

"Don't think this is gonna be a regular thing," she cautions, slightly off-put by the coolness of his skin.

"Okay."

"I'm serious."

"*Okay.* I'm leaving tomorrow, anyway."

She closes her eyes, trying to settle in. "Yeah. Exactly."

The following morning, Archer awakens to find that Cael has his head resting in the crook of her shoulder, one hand draped across her chest. Her arms are clasped around his back.

"Where are you going to meet?" Cael asks. He's peering over her shoulder as she sits at her vanity table, watching her apply makeup.

"This place in the financial district. Vander thinks it's cute because it's French and Asian, so he always wants to take me there."

"And what's going to happen?"

"I don't know," she says, making eye contact with him in the mirror. "We'll do the interview, and then I'll probably bring Wells back here. We can come up with some sort of a plan."

"I think he has a plan already; he just couldn't keep me at his own house for a week."

Archer nods. "Okay. Okay, good."

"Can I look at your neural implants?" he asks, eyes flitting downwards.

"Yeah." She scoops her hair out of his way and casts it over her shoulder.

The dress she's wearing is backless. Vander likes her to wear backless dresses to things like this, specifically so the implants are visible. This one, incidentally, was custom-designed for her by Tom Ford, back when she'd been his muse for a season.

The first touch of Cael's fingertip against her skin is a terribly uncertain thing. He traces a circle around one of the three metal pieces over her spine. They look like black vertebrae protruding from her skin. "Does that hurt?"

"No."

He draws a line up and down the implants. They're smooth and slightly raised, just enough that they occasionally catch on her clothes, and the xylophone sensation of his finger dragging across them makes her shiver. It's not bad, necessarily, just strange. No one touches her like this.

"They're placed over my third, fourth, and fifth rib," she explains. "So, all T. But they're each wired into a different section of spine."

He touches each implant in a descending line. "C...T...L." There's a sort of hum that runs through her flesh when his finger makes contact, like he's completing a circuit and causing little power surges.

"Yeah."

"To signal-boost bioelectricity."

"Yeah. Well…yeah. And I guess they're sort of like telephone poles for my nervous system. In the beginning, it was hard to get my brain to recognize and communicate with the cybernetics. It's harder to get the two to pair, if you're congenital."

He nods, brow furrowed in concentration. His inspection should, by all accounts, be complete. But he's still touching her. Still running his fingertips along her back. At this point, Archer is fairly certain he's noticed the little power-surge glimmers. He might be actively chasing the sensations. "When did you get them placed?"

"The first time they tried the cybernetics on me," she says, brushing the setting powder from her face. "I've had them for 25 years, and I'll have them till I die, unless I want to sit in a wheelchair."

He frowns. "That's sad."

"I guess."

"Does Lucas Wagner have them?"

She opens her eyeshadow pallet, brushing it into her skin with practiced hands. "No, he doesn't need them. He lost his arm in a car accident. His first cybernetic took a lot easier than mine did, since they had severed nerve endings to work with, phantom sensations, all that sort of stuff. Mine didn't adhere for months. Like, my brain wasn't even mapped for legs until they forced it. They actually cut off a few more inches of femur on each side, so they could get at some of those nice, traumatized nerves."

"Why do you do that?" Cael asks, frowning at her in the mirror.

She pauses her routine. "Do what?"

"You dumb it down. I know you know what you're talking about, you don't need to translate it into layman's terms for my sake. I'm not interviewing you for a magazine."

"Okay," she nods, strangely worried he'd been offended. "I'm sorry."

"Why did your parents let them do that to you? Cut you up and put implants in your spine and confuse your brain."

Defense and indignation flare up in her chest at his bluntness, but she knows he doesn't mean it. "They had a disabled kid, and no money," she explains, flicking mascara into place. "Forge needed test subjects, and they had a federal grant. So... I guess they weighed the risk and reward."

"Are you glad they did it?"

Again, his bluntness takes her by surprise. "I don't know," she admits, as much to herself as it is to him.

He *does* this. He makes her think about things she's spent her entire life ignoring, he questions things she'd rather just accept or take for granted.

"Where are your parents now?" he asks.

"There was a rash of hate crimes against Asian women, in the early '20s, back when the pandemic first hit. So, as soon as I could, I bought them a house in the south of France. Got them the hell out of this country."

"But you're an Asian woman, too."

Archer shrugs. She sets about donning her facial jewelry, threading either end of a delicate chain through the holes in her earlobes and hanging the matte-black hook from the center of her lower lip. It extends downward in a wide band, bisecting her chin. The nose clip comes next, pinched into place between her eyes. A long, narrow spike descends to the tip of her nose.

"Wait, hang on–" Cael stammers, squinting at her reflection. "What are you doing?"

"Putting on jewelry?" she replies, taking a cluster of small black, grey, and white squares and sticking them along her left cheekbone. Corner to corner, like a swath of pixels curving down beneath her eye.

"N-no," he protests, craning around to look at her face. "No, undo, please."

"What?" She laughs anxiously. "Why?"

He's visibly beginning to panic. "It's not funny, you're confusing my eyes. I-I just lost your face, undo it please, *right now*."

"Well, but, that's like the whole point of wearing it," she says. "Facial recognition is everywhere, these days. And I know it probably seems paranoid, but tabloids are always trying to snatch pictures of me from cameras in public, especially when I'm up to no good. This is urban camouflage, famous people do it all the time. Even Luc wears–"

"No, I don't like it," he presses, and Archer notices that his eyes have slipped out of focus and are tracing back and forth through the area around her head. He's reaching blindly towards her, one hand sort of twitching around on her bare shoulder. "Undo, *please*."

She unhooks the ring from her lip and removes the nose clip. "Better?"

Cael blinks, his eyes re-focus on hers, and he relaxes. "Yes. Thank you."

"I can wait and put it back on when I'm in the hallway."

After a tense silence, he announces, "I'm going to miss you." It's forceful, almost pleading. As though he's offering it up as justification for why she shouldn't have put the confusing jewelry on in the first place.

Archer's stomach lurches. "Really?"

"Yes." He turns and walks away.

It's only when she's already in the cab that she realizes – all the time he spent touching her back, he never said his weird little line about it not being sexual or romantic. Which would be easy enough to explain by saying he was focused or distracted, or that he assumed it could just go unsaid at this point. But...

But he hadn't said it last night, either.

Archer stands on the sidewalk outside of the restaurant, one foot drumming an anxious staccato against the concrete. She keeps looking at her phone, as though that will somehow make time go by faster. She wants Wells to get here already, she needs some semblance of security and certainty, baffled though she is that he would ever have come to represent those things to her.

"Mx Archer?"

She turns, ready to tell some random citizen that she's not in the mood, to find a young-ish woman with a big tablet and a bigger smile. Blonde hair pulled back into a tight, austere bun.

"Listen," Archer says, "I'm sorry, but I'm really not–"

"No, no, you don't understand," she laughs brightly. "No, I'm Kalinia Tranar, I'm your new coordinator."

Archer's heart plummets. "My new...what?"

"I'll be your coordinator from now on," she says, scrolling through her tablet. "You can call me Lin, if you'd like. We have a few minutes, now, have you gone over your talking points?"

Oh god, oh fuck, no. Archer's mouth is dry and uncooperative as she asks, "No, hang on, this has to be some kind of mistake. What happened to Robert Wells?"

The woman, though still smiling, seems to be annoyed by the question. As though she somehow wasn't expecting Archer to ask. "Mr Wells has left the company, and I'm afraid I don't have any further detail on the matter. Now. Have you gone over your talking points?"

"No," Archer snaps, "I haven't."

Her smile takes on a kind of pained quality. "Mx Archer. You were meant to learn the technical specifications of the Nike 6.0s, particularly how they interface with the new foot design. There were also artistic mission statements you were meant to familiarize yourself with, and ideally memor–"

"*Well, I didn't.* Wells would know better than to ask me a stupid thing like that."

Kalinia Tranar steps up close, looking right up into Archer's eyes. "Wells isn't here anymore," she says, saccharine and slightly terrifying. "And while I don't know why he's no longer with Hephaestus Forge, it does not take a lot for one to guess, now does it? You've got no one to blame for this but yourself, Mx Archer, and rest assured, I intend to be far less lenient and enabling than Robert Wells."

Archer is humiliated, furious, and mostly afraid. *Don't punch her, don't punch her, don't punch her–* "Fuck you, I'm calling him."

She steps away, tapping frantically at her phone. Kalinia Tranar may so haughtily believe that this is all because of Archer's behavior, but she knows better. This is beyond coincidence, it has to be. This is worst-case scenario shit. She brings the phone to her ear. And just as Vander's car pulls up the curb, she hears it.

"*We're sorry; you have reached a number that has been disconnected or is no longer in service. If you feel you have reached this recording in error, please check the number and try your call again.*"

Vander is stepping out of his car, tailed by the writer and photographer from *Wired*.

She pretends not to see them. Dials again.

"We're sorry; you have reached a number that has been discon—"

No, it can't be true, it can't. *Again.*

"We're sorry; you have—"

"Cymbre, my dear!"

"We're sor—"

She pockets her phone, swallowing the fear and the panic and replacing it with a magazine-cover smile. Just like she always does.

"Vander." She opens her arms to him, and he kisses her on the cheeks.

"Cymbre, this is Nic Davis and Evan Tremblay, from *Wired Magazine*." He gestures to the writer and photographer in turn.

One of them – Archer has already lost track of which – reaches out and takes her by the hand. "It's an honor, Mx Archer," he says, beaming. "We thoroughly enjoyed our tour of the Hephaestus Forge facilities, and can't wait to sit down and pick your brain for a little while."

Huh. He's actually looking at her face when he talks to her, not her legs. This guy knows his shit.

She smiles graciously. "I have been looking forward to it all week." She gestures towards the restaurant. "Shall we?"

As the *Wired* guys walk inside, Vander catches her by the arm and whispers through gritted teeth, "Take off the anti-surveillance."

She begrudgingly complies.

They sit down at their table, tucked away in a quiet corner of the otherwise busy restaurant. Vander takes his place firmly to her right, and they start talking about…something. They have to be talking about *something*, don't they? There are words being exchanged, of that she's certain, and Archer is distantly aware of the fact that she's talking, too. She must be doing well, because Vander is smiling, and the *Wired* guys are laughing good-naturedly, but they may as well be speaking *actual Ancient Greek*, for all the sense it's making to her. Kalinia is sitting over at the bar with her tablet and a Shirley Temple, eyeing her charge critically, like a hawk ready to spring on a rabbit.

All the while, there's only one thing running through Archer's mind – the image of some black-clad, private corporate security outfit breaking down Wells' door. Tearing him from his bed, confiscating his phone and computer. Shoving him into an unmarked van. And taking him…taking him…

What lengths would they go to, in order to get their Epsilon-L back?

No, what lengths *wouldn't* they go to?

And how long until the corporate gestapo come breaking down her door, dragging her into the unmarked van? She bets *they* would know where Cael's off-switch is.

All of a sudden, Archer is standing, shaking the *Wired* guys' hands, and then they're leaving, and when she looks at her phone, two hours have gone by. There are empty plates on the table, and a cocktail at her place setting. She doesn't feel drunk.

"Cymbre." It's Vander. That snaps her out of it.

"Hmm?"

He casts her a kind of sad, knowing look, gesturing towards the bar. "Come and have a drink with me."

She's still sort of stunned. "In a second, I– Let me use the restroom, first."

"All right. I'll be waiting."

I'll be waiting. It makes her skin crawl.

She shuts herself in a bathroom stall, takes a drop, and starts flicking frantically through her phone. He has to be somewhere, Wells has to be somewhere. Facebook, Twitter, Instagram, Snapchat– *No account associated with this user.*

WhatsApp. *No account associated with this phone number.*

Fucking LinkedIn, for god sakes. *No account associated with this user.*

Fuck. Fuck, fuck, *fuck, FUCK.*

She composes herself, and steps back out into the restaurant. Sure enough, Vander is waiting at the bar.

"Cymbre, my dear," he says, "you did beautifully, as always."

He's already ordered her a drink, which she gratefully accepts. "Thank you."

"But I've known you long enough that I can tell when you're forcing it, and tonight was one of those nights."

She blanches, searching wildly for some justification, and only coming up with, "I'm sorry."

He waves her off, smiling good-naturedly. "No, you misunderstand," he reassures. "That was more than good enough for our purposes here tonight. As I said, you did beautifully. But I sense that you have questions for me, and I'd like to give you the opportunity to ask them before we part ways for the evening."

Archer glances over at Kalinia, still sitting at the end of the bar and clearly trying very hard to make it seem like she's busy on her tablet and *not* eavesdropping. "Where's Rob?"

Vander shakes his head, seemingly saddened. "I wish I could tell you that, my dear, but the truth is that I simply do not know."

Don't know because he took off on his own, or don't know because the fish have probably eaten him already? No, she won't accept this. She can't. The trick now is to get the answers she needs without blowing her own cover. "But did—"

"Cymbre, did Robert ever mention anything to you about a Prometheus Project at Hephaestus Forge?"

"No," she says, probably too quickly. Right now, she's just trying her best not to scream. "No, is that...wait, does this have something to do with the memo from a few days ago? The..." She drops to a whisper, leaning in close. "The *theft?*"

"Mmm, I'm afraid it does. The Prometheus Project is a prototype we've been developing for quite some time, now. Sort of a culmination of everything we've ever built or worked towards. And I'm sorry Cymbre, but in the interest of maintaining security during this difficult time, I cannot tell you anything more."

She brings a hand to her mouth. "You don't think that Robert...?"

"Sadly, we do. There's overwhelming evidence pointing in his direction, and we are looking into it."

"What evidence?" *Stupid, Archer, stupid, stupid, stupid. You were doing so well.*

Vander takes it in stride. Or, at least, he seems to. "Keycard swipes in areas of the facility that he wasn't required to access, unauthorized searches in the company database. That sort of thing. It would seem that, in recent weeks, Robert Wells took a very notable interest in things that were well outside the scope of his professional understanding. Beyond that, he acted rashly, and with only a fraction of the full information."

Now for the several-hundred-million-dollar, stay-out-of-prison question. "You don't think I had anything to do with it, do you?"

"No, my dear." He places a patronizing hand on her arm. "No, certainly not."

She breathes a tentative sigh of relief.

"You've been with this company since the beginning, Cymbre. You were with us in that rented clinic space in Utica, and today, we were interviewed for a *Wired Magazine* cover story. You've seen the good we do, the lives we change. I know we've changed yours." He runs a hand along her leg. Covetous. "And I know that you'd never do anything to jeopardize the relationship that you have with us, nor disrespect the many great things we've done for you."

"No," she says. "Never."

"I know that you and Robert's working relationship had become strained lately, so it isn't likely he would've divulged his intentions to you. But, in the interest of being thorough, I have to ask, do you have any information about the location of our missing asset, or how Robert managed to steal it from the facility?"

Archer blinks. Because this is the moment, isn't it? The crucial lynchpin upon which she knows her past and future hinge, so frustratingly cliché for its significance.

Wells is gone. For all intents and purposes, he's dead. And at this very moment, the most expensive and groundbreaking invention in the history of humanity is pacing around her loft, hiding from her cat. Archer's gaze drifts over to Kalinia Tranar, who is still trying so desperately not to look nosy.

She should've kissed Cael's hand, that first morning. He's probably never had anyone kiss him before.

"No," she says. "Nothing I can recall."

"Forgive me for saying so, but that seemed to require a great deal of thought."

"I'm sorry. I was trying to remember if he'd said anything. If he'd ever...maybe he said something that didn't make sense then, but makes sense now, and...no. There's just nothing. He kept his secrets close."

"Yes, I understand." Vander puts a hand on hers as it rests atop the bar. "I suppose it just goes to show that you can never really know a person, no matter how close you may think you are." With that, he stands and kisses her on the cheeks once more.

Archer is shaken and confused, so she returns the gesture in silence.

Just before he leaves, Vander casts a glance towards Kalinia, who is clearly gearing up to ambush Archer before she can make an escape. Archer scowls.

"Be gentle with Lin," he says. "Don't punish her for Robert's actions."

Archer blurts, "I don't. I...I won't."

"Remember, we're all working towards the same goal."

Archer hurries out of the restaurant, tailed closely by her new coordinator.

"All right, we have some things to go over," she chatters away, scrolling through her tablet. "You'll notice, going forward, that Forge is shifting the majority of spokesmodel attention back to you and Lucas Wagner. After the incident at the shareholder presentation, Vander wants to strip it down, get back to the basics, and ensure that the impending product launches are represented by the tried-and-true professionals. Familiar faces, trusted voices."

Archer rolls her eyes, jamming a cigarette between her teeth. "Lucas and I are *the basics* now?"

"You have gait lab next week," she continues, ignoring the remark. "10:00 am, do *not* be late. Lucas will be there, too. And remember that you'll need at least basic walking balance and proficiency on all four sets of cybernetics before then."

Archer scoffs, lighting her cigarette. "I know that."

"Have you had any problems with interface or installation?" Like a fly buzzing incessantly in her ear.

Her answer comes as an abrupt snap. "I know what I'm doing."

Lin crowds in close, forced to look up at Archer for their height difference. "I won't be coming by your house to drag you out of bed, hungover. Those days are over. I expect punctuality, knowledgeability of your talking points, and front-facing decorum."

"Good. I don't want you in my house, touching my things, where I eat and sleep."

"I want nothing from you but that tried-and-true professionalism Vander glows about."

"I've got it."

"From now on, you're two things: a trusted voice for the company, and a familiar face for the products."

"I've got it."

Archer tosses her cigarette, takes a drop, and hails a cab.

Wells lives in a trendy area of Tribeca, in a two-bedroom near the top of this this massive human-storage-unit of a building. The doorman recognizes her and lets her in with no trouble. And then it's up the elevator, higher and higher, and she's getting out on the 20th floor, sprinting down the hall to his apartment.

"Robert!" she shouts, fist hammering against the door. "Robert, it's me! Open up!"

No answer. Not that she expected one. Fuck. She tries to peer through the peep hole, but all she can see is blackness.

"Robert, if you're in there, I'm coming in!" She puts her back against the wall beside the door and plants the sole of her foot against the door itself. "I'm coming in!"

Archer cocks her leg forward and, with inhuman force, slams it back again. The door swings open with a spectacular crash, the wood around the lock falling away in splinters. She rushes inside, only to stop dead in her tracks.

It's completely empty. Not a single stick of furniture, nothing in the open cabinets or closets, nothing in the fridge. It's as though Robert Wells has been entirely erased. Unmade. Excised from this plane of reality, reduced to memory.

"Fuck," she whines, voice quavering as she stumbles from room to room. "Oh, fuck, fuck, *fuck*–"

A voice sounds from the door. "Hey! What the hell do you– Oh. Oh, hey, Archer." It's the doorman. Someone must've called him about the noise. He inspects the damage to the door jamb, equal parts frustrated and impressed. "Archer, *why*?"

"Sorry," she mumbles, digging through her bag for her wallet. She counts out three hundred in cash, deliberates for a moment, and then adds another hundred before pressing it into his hand. "What, um…what happened?"

"Well, rent was due a few days ago, and he never paid. Management tried calling, emailing, everything, but you probably already know that didn't work. So, they packed all of his shit up and got rid of it. Someone else is moving in next month."

"Where did they put his stuff?" she asks. Because she needs *something*.

"Management has a storage unit for situations like this. They just shoved it all in there. He'll get it back when he pays his rent, and the cost of packing and moving it all."

She rolls the dice and asks, "Where's the unit?"

The doorman shrugs again, leafing through the bills. "Nice door like that's probably gonna be more than $400 to repair."

She chokes on a laugh. "What? No, the hell it's not!"

"Way I see it, it'll be at least a hundred more. Or, if you wanna keep your money, I'll just tell the cops who broke it down."

Oh. *Oh*. Archer rolls her eyes, frustrated, and digs out *another* hundred-dollar bill. "Here," she grumbles. "Extortionist prick."

He laughs, seemingly satisfied with the label. "Storage place is on the corner of Washington and Ward. Unit 301, and you're lucky I remember that."

"Thanks." With that, she rushes back out onto the sidewalk.

Washington and Ward. Not close enough to walk, not in these feet, so she'll have to get another cab. She has no idea how the hell she's going to get into the unit, or even what she hopes to find, but–

Her phone chimes. It's a text from Luc.

> How'd the interview go?

She thinks hard, one foot drumming anxiously against the pavement. It's 9:45 pm. What the hell is she going to accomplish at 9:45 pm? She texts back:

> Pyramid Club?

Luc *hates* Pyramid Club, he says he's way too straight for that place. So, if he says yes, it means he really does want to see her.

Her phone chimes.

> Okay.

She hails a cab.

Half an hour later, Archer is standing in the middle of the dance floor, two drops deep, just staring up at the lights like a zombie. People are jostling and dancing, bumping into her occasionally, and the music is so loud that it hurts, but she's lost in the middle-ground between numb and terrified. Everything feels fractured and anxious, like there's something disastrous shifting just below the surface of reality, and she can't understand how the hell it turned into this. Maybe she just needs more Penth. Or less. Probably more. She had a drink at one point, but when she looks down, her hand is empty. That doesn't make sense. Her mouth tastes like vodka.

Just as she's debating getting down on the ground to look for her drink, because maybe it's somewhere in all that broken glass, someone steps up close behind her, and cold, metal fingers slip along the bare skin of her back. Luc. He wraps his hand lightly around her throat, tilting her head back against his shoulder. She doesn't meet many men who are taller than her, but Luc is one of them.

"I didn't think you'd text back," he says in her ear. "It's been a while. I figured you were pissed at me, or something."

"I think I was," she mumbles, leaning back into the broad, familiar warmth of him. "I don't remember."

His smile curls against her neck. "Why?"

"I just said I don't remember." Her shaking hands struggle with the phial of Penth, and she feels a laugh rumble through Luc's chest.

"Jesus, Cym." He reaches out with his cybernetic and unscrews the lid while she holds it steady. "You gorgeous disaster." He wraps his organic hand around her jaw, tilting her head back and opening her mouth. With careful precision, he slips three drops under her tongue, and then his mouth is on hers. Wide open. Hungry.

"I'd fuck you on the roof of a burning building," he says, hauling her close as he begins to sway to the music. She whimpers, reaching back to curl her fingers through his hair. Clinging.

She blacks out.

When she comes to, they're against the back wall of the club. He's holding her up with his cybernetic arm, like she weighs nothing. His knee is between her legs, and she's grinding down onto it so hard it hurts. His kisses, rough and domineering though they may be, are so familiar. And familiar is comfortable. Comfortable is safe.

They're surrounded by people, but the people are minding their own business. That's part of the reason she'd wanted to come here. Queers respect consent. They don't grab your fucking leg without permission.

There's another drink in her hand, somehow. As Luc bends to suck at her collarbone, she takes an oblivion-seeking swallow. Blacks out again.

This time, when she comes to, they're stumbling out into the alley behind the club.

"Let's go to my place," he slurs, backing her up against the wall. He smells like Penth and whiskey and cigarettes, but she probably does, too. "Cym, come to my place."

Fuck, she wants to. She wants to go to Luc's and fuck him and drink and drop until they both die. Let Vander deal with *that* shit. You can't pay off cops and bouncers and news outlets when your two top models OD in each other's arms, can you?

But she can't do that. Because Wells is probably dead, which means she'll be next, and then Cael…

Cael.

"I can't," she mumbles against his lips, hating herself for it.

"We'll go to yours, then. Wanna…mmm…" He slips her wrists up over her head, pinning them to the wall. "*Fuck* you."

Her head feels fuzzy, disconnected from her tongue. "I can't, I've got– There's…there's this fucking…guy at my place."

"You have a guy at your place?" he pants, and she can hear the veiled hurt in his voice.

"Yeah, kind of…"

He moans into her neck. "I don't *care*. I've missed you so much, Cym, I'll fuckin' throw you over my shoulder and drag you away, I'll tie you to my bed for a week, I–"

Her eyes flutter a little, because *God*, she wants that. She wants it more than she wants to *breathe*. "Here, then." She's drunk enough that it seems like a great solution. "Quick."

"Here?"

"Yeah."

"*Fuck.*" He shivers, hand slipping down, fumbling between their bodies. "Fuck…"

She hears his zipper, feels the heat of him. She gathers her skirt out of his way, and then he's palming at her thigh, hoisting her knee up into the crook of his elbow. There's a kind of static hum between their limbs, something felt under the skin and in the air. It's a thing they've only ever given each other, a thing they'll find nowhere else. He lines up, keeping her balanced on one stupid fucking impractical foot, and when he enters her, it's rough and uncaring. She lets out a choked cry, which he swallows, open-mouthed.

There's a jagged piece of brick scraping up and down her back as he takes her; she can feel it catching painfully on her implants.

She thinks of Cael's fingertips and wraps her arms around Luc's neck, clinging, clinging, pressing kisses to his face, and she tries to pretend that she's someone else, that he's someone else, and they're *somewhere* else. That they're whole and happy, and their lives had been so different than this.

He doesn't take long. It's a quick and unceremonious affair, ending uneventfully. And when it's over, when he hauls her close and gives her a cursory sort of kiss, Archer is left feeling emptier than she had before.

"Come back to mine," he pants against her lips.

This shit again. "I can't do that, Luc," she slurs. Hating herself for it. "I told you I can't. In fact, I...I should go."

"Because there's a guy at your place?" He sighs, stepping back and rubbing at his face. He doesn't push her further. He zips his pants, swaying on his feet a little. "Lemme get you a cab. I'm...*way* too fucked up to drive."

"Okay."

He holds her close as they stand on the curb, arm wrapped around her in a way that should feel patronizing and possessive, but she likes it. She probably wouldn't like it from anyone else on the planet.

"It's a good thing we grew up beautiful," she mumbles into his broad chest, starting to slip away again.

"What?"

"Just...nothing."

Her cab arrives, and he helps her inside. Like a gentleman.

Before he can close the door, she catches him by the arm. "Lucas."

"Hmm?"

"Do you ever...do you ever wish it was...different?" She grimaces. *Nice, Arch. Eloquent.*

But Lucas just smiles sadly, running a cybernetic thumb across her lips. "Every day."

He kisses her. Closes the door. The cab starts to move, and another wave of blackness comes rolling in.

CHAPTER EIGHT

THE FIRST THING SHE'S AWARE OF IS THE WARMTH, THE SORT OF weightless feeling. Pounding in her head, coolness on her face and neck, but everywhere else–

She jerks to awareness with jarring intensity, splashing water everywhere. "*Fuck me.*"

"I've noticed that you say '*fuck*' a lot, when you first wake up."

She's in a bathtub. Her bathtub. Naked. Cael is crouched beside it, knees pulled up against his chest.

"It's nine in the morning," he states plainly. "I found you in the hallway."

Archer groans, rubbing at her eyes with the heels of her hands. They come away streaked with mascara. "Wait, you– You went in the hallway?" *Fuck.*

"Only a little bit. I think you passed out trying to put in your door code. I heard your footsteps outside, and then you fell against the door." He hesitates for a moment, but she catches it.

"What?"

"You urinated on yourself."

Her face goes completely red, shame and guilt and regret tightening into a hard knot in her stomach. Stinging at her eyes and her throat. "Oh."

"So, I put you in the bathtub."

She turns away from him, curling up on her side.

"Don't worry," he says, curt. "I've seen naked humans before. I have the internet."

"Okay."

"I was worried about getting your legs wet at first, but then I remembered that you take showers with them on, so..."

"Latest in Poseidon waterproofing techniques," she whimpers. And then, all at once, the tears come rolling through. Not the soft, dainty tears that a model should cry, but big, ugly, heaving sobs. Like someone has thrust a fist into her chest to wring her dry. She can't remember the last time she cried. This is a decade's worth of sorrow and self-loathing being purged all at once.

And how fucking humiliating. Naked, hungover, soaking in piss and bathwater, with a dumb, pretty little robot watching and collating it all into his experiential lexicon. The phrase 'wake-up call' is rattling around in her head like a shard of glass.

"It's okay," he says, kind but stilted, reaching out to pat her on the shoulder. It's a robotic imitation of human comfort. Probably something he just learned from a WikiHow article.

"It's not," she weeps. "It's not, it's– *Shit.*"

"You just had a bad night." Again, so frustratingly scripted.

She can't even muster a reply.

"What did Robert Wells say?" Cael prods, scooting closer. He probably thinks that'll cheer her up, getting to talk about offloading him onto someone else.

If only.

Archer sniffles, wipes her face on the backs of her hands. "He's gone."

"What do you mean?"

"He's *gone.* Left Forge, I guess, I don't know. That's what they said. They hired me a new babysitter. His phone is disconnected, his social media has been wiped. I even went by his place last night, and it's completely empty."

It's obvious that he doesn't understand. He blinks, gaze darting around the room as though the answer was written somewhere on the walls. "But…but what *happened?*"

"I don't know. Maybe he skipped town, maybe they hauled him off in an unmarked van. Maybe he's dead." A horrifying thought occurs to her then. "Probably all three."

Cael scoots closer still, desperation edging into his voice as he asks, "What are we going to do?"

Archer feels like screaming at him, '*Well, that's the fucking question, isn't it?*' "Can you go in the living room, please?" she moans, feeling the tide of her tears rising once more.

"Well…but what are we going to do?"

"Ahh, Caelan, *I don't fucking know!*" she shouts, splashing a handful of water in his direction. Like he's a cat, or something. *"Don't* ask *me that! Get out of here! Just get the fuck out!"*

He scrambles backwards, struggling to his feet. And with a look of wide-eyed horror on his face, he sprints from the room.

When Archer finally emerges, wrapped in her kimono with her hair still wet, Cael is standing awkwardly in the middle of the room.

"I fed Khi," he says. "Last night, and just now."

She grimaces, ashamed. "I'm sorry."

He smiles proudly. "It's okay. It seems to have significantly improved his opinion of me."

"No, that's not– That's not what I mean. Last night wasn't okay, and just now wasn't okay either."

"Oh." The smile melts from his face as quickly as it had come. "Okay."

They're silent for a long time, unable to look at one another.

"What are you thinking?" he finally asks. Tentative.

A knot of discomfort tightens in her stomach. There's no more avoiding it. It has to be faced. "With Wells gone, I don't know what to do anymore."

"Neither do I."

"Did he ever…did he ever write anything down? Was there information in his phone, on his computer? Like…what was his plan? What was he going to *do* with you?"

"I don't know."

Fuck. *FUCK.*

"What do we do now?" Cael's lip might quiver then, but she could also just be imagining it.

Archer brings a hand to her mouth, gaze drifting over to the massive picture on the wall. In truth, she knows exactly why she keeps it up there. She'd been clean, then. Mostly sober. Everything had been fun and effortless and beautiful. The girl in that photo has a light in her eyes that doesn't exist anymore, a kind of fierce, hungry intensity.

How many years has it been since she could call herself that girl?

"I didn't sign up for this shit," she whispers, and the admission is as damning as it is liberating.

Cael's eyes go wide. "What?"

She can't bring herself to look at him. "I'm sorry, but I never would have agreed to this if I'd known what it was going to turn into. I can't do it. I'll lose my job, Cael. They'll probably send me to prison, they'll scrap me and give the legs to someone else, and–"

"What? No–"

"This has gone…fuck, *so* far beyond what I'm okay with. Like, I had to lie to Callas last night. *The CEO.* I fucking *lied* for you, do you get that? I told him I didn't know anything about any of this!" The realization sinks to the pit of her stomach like a lump of ice. "Fuck, what am I *doing?* What have I…?"

"And…you've never lied to Callas before? That's–" He shudders. "That's the problem?" There's no sarcasm, no challenge. Just earnest misunderstanding.

"No, goddammit, I've–I've lied to him before, but not about this. Not *like* this. Up to now, it was just keeping quiet about you, but now I'm having to actually *lie*, and–" Archer groans in frustration. "Listen, there are other people on this planet who will know what to do with you, okay? And they'll do a much better job of it than I ever could. We'll find you someplace else to go."

Cael starts heaving big, panicked breaths, chest rising and falling with worrying intensity. "No, but I don't w-w-w-*want* someone else, I want y-y-y-*you*!" His hands are tightening into fists at his sides, over and over, faster and faster. "I like *you*!"

And now she's starting to cry again. As if she hasn't humiliated herself enough already. "That's bullshit, you just don't know any better."

"Stop it!" he commands, voice rising in volume and intensity. "Stop saying those things! You gave me a *name*, and it's Cael, which is *not* a vegetable, and you got me clothes as a present because I don't even have any money, and that's a *bad* thing, it's *bad*, because you said that everything is Capitalism, and n-n-*no one has ever given me a present before*, so I want to stay here with y-*you*!"

"Someone else can help you," she chokes.

"*No!*" Before she can brace for it, he's plowed into her, wrapping his arms around her waist and squeezing hard. "No, I don't want it to be anyone else!"

She tries to pry him away to no avail. "Caelan—"

"No!" He's still pushing, squeezing, and she's struggling to maintain her balance on these vain fucking stupid feet. "No, you can't, you *can't*, Archer, the someone-else-one will just bring me back to Tartarus, and then th-th-*they'll shut me down*! That's killing me, Archer, that's *killing* me, and I don't want to die! I don't—I d-d-*don't*—"

With one final, wrenching push, Archer falls hard to her back. She gasps, winded, and Cael just claws his way upwards to crush her. All around the apartment, the speakers are starting to crackle to life, screeching and whining as if in sympathy.

"Hey, let go!" she gasps, strangled.

"No, you can't!" he cries into her chest, wracked by what seem to be violent, full-body sobs. "You have to keep me safe! No one else can do it! *I need you*!"

She's starting to panic a little at his strength. He's got Atlas arms like Luc, he could probably snap her in half without much effort, whether he means to or not. Her ribs creak in his grip, it's like nothing she's ever felt before. "Hey!" she yelps, trying frantically now to pry him away. "*Caelan*, you're hurting me!"

It's like she'd said a secret code phrase. "I'm sorry!" He flings himself backwards, away from her, and she sees that he's crying. Actually crying; there's something coming out of his eyes, streaming down his cheeks. He kneels beside her, rocking a little. His hand hovers in the gulf for a few seconds, outstretched toward her, and then he retracts it again. "I'm sorry, Archer, please don't be angry. Are you crying because I hurt you, or is it something else?"

"Ah, *fuck*," she moans, burying her face in her hands. "Fuck, god dammit, piece of *shit*." She kicks her legs against the floor like a child throwing a tantrum. "FUCK!"

"*I'm sorry!*"

"No, you don't– God*dammit*, Cael!" She's openly sobbing at the ceiling. "Don't you get it? I'm not gonna be your fucking hero! You see that because it's what you're looking for."

He watches and listens, brow gradually knitting together with concern.

She wipes the tears from her face in quick, angry motions. "This is me, and it's a *fff*– There's just no room for you, okay? All this pretend-strength, all the– It's a script! It's *walls*! And you–fuck, you do this *thing* where you just tear it all down, and I hate that so much, because I don't even think there's anything left behind it, anymore! I don't want to look!" Words seem to escape her for a moment, so she just waves her hand in dismissive frustration. "Oh, you don't get it, I can tell. You've got that fucking look on your face, that *look,* like you don't understand and it just makes you so sad. But you'll figure it out, and by that point, I'll just be another prison cell for you. And until then, you'll be a prison cell for me!"

He thinks for a second, and then announces, "No."

She groans, the sound morphing into something like a pained shriek. "*You don't like me!* You don't know me, and you don't like me!"

"You don't know what I—"

Fuck, do I have to spell it out? "Did you like what you found in the hallway?" she condescends. "Was that nice for you? Was that fun?"

His mouth snaps shut. And then he murmurs something that sounds like, "Learning experience."

"Oh, shut up!" she wails. "Just shut up! Don't you get that *that's what I am?* I'm not that fake fucking thing they prop up for the cameras, I'm the thing you found in the hallway last night, and it's all I'll ever be, and *I don't mind that!* What I mind is being told I have to re-arrange my whole entire life to accommodate some stupid, needy, *obnoxious* little robot *that I didn't even ask for!*" She heaves herself over onto her side, away from him, and curls up with her knees against her chest.

After a while, and there's no telling how long, she can hear him scoot closer. Her chest is still hitching with sobs as he puts a hand on her shoulder, and this time, it's not a scripted imitation of a human gesture. It's something much more real.

"You have a lot of scrapes on your back," he says. "Did someone hurt you?"

She rolls over to find that his eyes are very close. God, she's so tired of this. "What?"

"Did someone hurt you?"

"No, Caelan, I probably fucking hurt myself."

That seems to visibly sadden him. "You shouldn't hurt yourself."

"Why the hell not?" It's childish, she knows. Petulant. And pointless, as far as she can tell. She's arguing with lines of code.

He leans down, touching his forehead to hers. She can feel the static hum of him like a low sound behind her eyes. She can feel his breath murmuring past her lips. "Because I *like* you," he whispers. "I like *you.*"

She tries to shake him off. "Stop saying that."

"But you're my *person*," he insists, placing his hands on her cheeks. "My…human person. You're my favorite human person."

"I'm the only person you've ever met."

"No," he argues, perturbed. "No, there were people at the lab, but…those other people were like looking at the stars."

She sighs tiredly, no idea why in hell she's still indulging this. "What?"

"They were interesting, but they were cold and far away and they mostly felt dead." He seems to struggle with his own metaphor a little. "And…and you're the sun."

The rest of the day progresses in something of an anxious silence. Archer eats, smokes. Doesn't drop. Reads. Doesn't drop. It seems like Cael is trying not to crowd her, like he's scared she'll feel smothered. In turn, Archer doesn't want to make him feel abandoned. The resultant atmosphere is a strange one – Cael peering silently around corners, trying to see her without being seen, while Archer sneaks desperate glances in his direction, hoping he's all right.

That night, she crawls into bed and he takes his place on the couch. But in the dark and the quiet, she just tosses and turns. Her skin is starting to itch from withdrawal, limbs wracked with tremors, and it's taking *everything* not to start clawing her nails down her own arms. Her head is swimming, and all she can feel is fear. Fear for Cael and Wells and mainly herself; fear of what this means and how long it'll last and she has *no idea whatsoever* how she ended up here.

Well. She does, and she doesn't.

Downstairs, she can hear Cael shifting around, too. Little murmurs, like he's back to blinking and labeling. Some kind of twisted attempt to self-soothe, she assumes. So human, but at the same time, not human at all.

Archer sits up. She reaches for the bottle of Penth on the nightstand, but hesitates. *Do you really want to start this over again? You've got momentum, now. Lean in.* Before she can talk herself out of it, she swats the phial from the nightstand and it shatters loudly on the wood floor. Downstairs, Cael goes still and silent.

"Just fucking come up here," she whispers, raking her hands through her hair in quiet frustration.

"What?"

"Just come up here," she repeats, louder. "Damn!"

He pads softly across the living room and up the stairs, stopping at the foot of the bed. "What is it?"

She throws the covers back. "Are you gonna get in, or what?"

His reply is a soft, but instantaneous, "*Yes.*"

"Take that shit off," she commands, pointing to his jeans and t-shirt. "You can't sleep in that. *I* won't be able to sleep. With jeans in the bed. It fucked with me all night, last time."

"Okay."

Archer looks away while he strips, and then after a moment, she feels the bed sink behind her. Another pause, and then he's crowding in against her back. Not holding her, just resting his forehead between her shoulder blades. His knees slip up under hers. There are little pinpricks of static when their skin brushes together. It's not uncomfortable.

"I'm sorry," she murmurs, shuddering violently. "For..." The rest never comes. There's too much.

He seems to understand.

CHAPTER NINE

When Archer awakens the following morning, Cael isn't in the bed. She sits up, panic slowly building.

"H-hey," she whispers lamely, looking around the room. And then, louder, "Hey?"

"I'm down here."

When Archer stands, she's hit by a wave of debilitating nausea. Once she notices it, everything seems to sour at once. Her tongue dries, sweat springs to her skin, and she doubles over, clutching at her stomach.

Fucking. *Penth.*

She staggers over to the top of the stairs and sees that Cael is standing in the kitchen with a mug of coffee. Khi is winding his way contentedly between his legs. *God, when did it get so bright in here?* With one hand on the railing and the other still cradling her stomach, she gingerly makes her way down the stairs.

Cael is eyeing her suspiciously. "Are you okay?"

Determined to push through, Archer musters a half-smile

as she reaches the relative security of flat ground. "I guess you guys are, like, best friends now, or what?" Ignoring his question entirely.

Cael beams so proudly. "We're getting there. Can I keep feeding him? I think he really likes that."

Archer nods, sitting down at the table. "Yeah, man, whatever you wanna do."

"Thank you." After a strange beat, he thrusts the coffee cup towards her. "Here. I made this for you."

She blinks in surprise. "Really?"

"Yes." He sets it down in front of her. "I've been observing your routine, and I think I did it correctly. Can you taste it and tell me if I did it correctly?"

She takes a cautious sip, acutely aware of Cael's scrutiny. It's... not bad. Actually, it's good.

"Well?"

She opens her mouth to speak, but stops when bile rises to the back of her throat. *Oh, fuck.* Hand clapped over her mouth, she sprints for the bathroom on unstable legs. She makes it in time, skidding to her knees in front of the toilet, but her stomach is virtually empty. The only thing that comes up is that one swallow of coffee, and it burns her throat, stinging at her eyes. The sour-bitter taste lingers on her tongue no matter how many times she tries to spit it out. For a while, she just dry-heaves uselessly against her nausea.

Cael's voice sounds from the other side of the door. "Are you okay?"

Fuck, her head is pounding. It's like a belt tightening around her skull, like blunt screws boring in and out of her temples in agonizing pulses. She takes a desperate lunge to turn the light off, and then sinks to the floor to curl up on her side. The whole room is tilting.

"*Archer.*"

God dammit. "Yeah, Cael, I'm fine." Even to her ears, it's unconvincing.

"Was it the coffee?" He sounds so hurt.

She groans aloud, pressing her forehead to the cool tile. "The coffee was fine, Caelan, please just—"

"Fine or good?"

"Caelan, can you please just go in the kitchen?"

His footsteps recede without another word.

This is your own fault, she reminds herself. *This is five years' worth of poison working its way out. And it's not going without a fight.*

She lets herself lie on the floor and sob dryly for a while, until the pounding in her head becomes entirely unbearable. But she won't pass out. She *will not* let herself pass out. So, on weak, shaking limbs, she crawls into the shower, turns the water on cold, and shivers on the floor, still wearing the clothes she slept in. When that becomes unbearable, she takes her clothes off, turns the heat up, and does her best to stand. But that becomes unbearable after a while, too. Her skin is crawling, and everything hurts: her jaw, her neck, her eyes, but mostly her back. It feels like someone is driving hot nails into her lumbar spine every time she moves her legs. God, she can feel her *bones* grinding together.

Fuck, this was the reason I started dropping in the first place, wasn't it?

It would be so easy to make it stop. All she would have to do is walk outside, open the fridge, and—

!! NO !!

No, we are NOT starting this over again! You are 30 hours in, just drink some water, take some Benadryl, and pass the fuck out until it's over!

She showers as quickly as she can, fighting against dizziness and nausea, and then she combs her hair out, dons her kimono, and steps back out into the blindingly bright loft. Cael is standing by the kitchen table, eyes wide with concern.

"You look pale," he remarks.

"I can't help it, my dad's white."

The joke is clearly lost on him. "Are you okay?"

"Yeah," she sighs. "Yeah, I'm fine. Well, I'm not fine, but—"

"Are you sick?"

"Yeah." She flops down into a chair beside him. "I have Ebola Virus, and now you're gonna get it, too."

Cael narrows his eyes critically. "There hasn't been a documented case of Ebola in this country for twenty-five years, and I wouldn't be able to contract it, anyway. These appear to be symptoms of withdr–"

She snaps, "I said I'm fine, Cael!"

He huffs in frustration, and just when she thinks he's going to argue, he turns and crosses the room to the sink. And then she watches in surprise as he fills a glass with water, and then pointedly sets it down on the table in front of her.

Ah, shit. There's that thing that's definitely not guilt, again. "Thanks," she mumbles, taking a tentative sip.

"Are we just not going to talk about it?"

"No. We are not."

He nods, leaning back against the counter on his elbows. He kicks one ankle casually over the other, a move she knows he picked up from her. With downcast eyes, he announces, "I'm going to try and think of more things I can do around here. To contribute."

That baffles her a little. "Uh…contribute?" *Fuck, it takes so much effort to think, right now.*

"I'm not your chores-robot," he's quick to clarify. "But I feel like I should try and make myself useful. At the very least, it'll keep me from getting bored."

"Can you even be bored?" It sounds like a rude question only after she's heard herself ask it.

"Sort of," he says, pressing the heel of his hand into one eye. "I don't get bored of tasks, but I do get notification pings if I'm completely inactive for too long outside of an intentional idle. It's possible for me to just dismiss them, and I think I could probably figure out how to shut them off completely, but I would prefer not to. I think they programmed me like this to make me more realistic." He sighs, and it's a disarmingly human expression. "Boredom is a realistic quality. It would be weirder if I just stood and stared at the wall for hours and hours."

"Hey, is it, like…offensive for me to ask you shit like that?"

Archer blurts, trying to ignore the way she can *feel* the weight of the water sloshing around in her stomach. "Like, is it rude?" It's a question that's been gnawing away at her for a while now.

Cael furrows his brow, eyes wandering a little before they come to rest on hers. "I don't know. I appreciate that you're just trying to understand me better."

"I mean, yeah, but…I don't know, I fucking hate it when people ask me shit about my legs. Even if they mean well." She's beginning to realize that she's in no mood for this conversation.

He thinks hard. "But since I'm the only true ABI who has ever existed, then—" His upper body shudders eerily. "If I don't answer questions, then no one will ever know the answers. I'm a black box."

"Yeah, but you still have the right to say, 'hey, that's a rude fucking question, I don't wanna talk about that right now.'" *God, I want to crawl into bed and die.*

He frowns. "Do I?"

"Uh, yeah, Cael. You're…well, you're a person. So." She buries the end of the sentence in her glass, taking another drink. But it's too much, too quickly, and another wave of nausea comes rolling through. She coughs, trying to tamp it down.

"You're spruice."

Archer rubs at her forehead. "I'm what, now?"

"'*Sweat*' but the present-tense verb form."

"I know that, Cael, thank you."

They're quiet for a long time. So long that, even in her pain and delirium, it's starting to become awkward for Archer. She focuses on her glass of water, swirling it a few times before it makes her dizziness and nausea spike. She stops, and buries her face in one hand.

She startles when something touches her free hand on the table, and she almost pulls away. But it's Cael. His fingertips brush over her knuckles, and when she turns her wrist over, he settles the rest of his hand into her palm and squeezes gently.

"Thank you," he says. Baffling.

It could be out of friendship, or maybe it's something else, but she realizes it doesn't matter just now. She doesn't need to worry about it. She just appreciates the feeling of his skin against hers. It's disarmingly comforting.

CHAPTER TEN

On Monday morning, Archer is — shockingly — right on time for gait lab. On top of that, she actually remembered to bring all of her feet.

It's been five days since she's dropped. Five miserable, headachy, hollow-gutted days. The cravings haven't gone away yet, not really, and it seems like she's still rising and falling through weird bouts of chills and nausea, much in the same way that her attitude towards Cael has become its own rollercoaster ride. Disarming admiration for him, guilty appreciation, and then an inexplicable plummet into frustration and resentment. Over and over and over again, up and down, up and down. The only constant right now is Cael himself. Perpetually upbeat and attentive to a fault, trailing after her with rambling stories and endless questions.

On top of that, Cael is still spending nights in her bed. He's taken off his clothes and crawled beneath the sheets with her every night since the thunderstorm, save for the one she spent between the hallway and the bathtub. Fair, she supposes. She gave him permission and hasn't rescinded it, so of course he hasn't stopped.

That, and Archer doesn't exactly mind. Because, even when Cael's driving her insane with his nonstop chatter, segueing between unrelated topics with enough finesse to give her a concussion, she's actually come to appreciate the feeling of him lying beside her. Each night, like clockwork, he slowly inches closer and closer until she just gives up and holds him. It got to the point that she even ventured out to get him underwear to sleep in, so he didn't have to be naked.

Not for any other reason, she told herself. Not to keep from pushing the boundaries further, because that definitely *hasn't* occurred to her in some of her more delirious, withdrawal-fueled moments. It's not Cael's fault that Forge decided to put their obnoxiously sweet little AI project into a body that's so goddamn fuckable.

But today, Archer is making her first, shaky return to work. The cybernetics lab at Hephaestus Forge is below-ground, along with R&D, presumably to secure against prying eyes who would steal precious, corporate secrets. For all the good it's done them.

Kalinia meets her at the keycard-protected doors, just outside of the elevator.

"Good," she says, short and haughty, "you're on time."

Archer offers her no reply whatsoever, walking right past her and into the lab.

The space is impressive – wide-open and arranged much like any other physical therapy or prosthetic floor. Adjustable benches and tables for patients to sit or lie on, treadmills, free weights, and the like. There are harnesses hanging from the ceiling, and the dreaded parallel bars, that age-old bane of anyone with a lower limb deficiency. There's even a long table housing an array of fine-motor assessment apparatus. Doorknobs, keys in locks, beads on wires, bolts and screws. There's a dry erase board to practice handwriting, and a touchscreen tablet to practice typing. There's even a 61-key piano keyboard. Standard stuff, really. But this is *Hephaestus Forge*, after all, so everything has to consist of gleaming white surfaces with gold accents. Sleek, minimalist. Like what someone from the past had hoped the future would look like.

Archer's cybernetics engineer, Tom, is waiting for her when she arrives. "Hey," he greets brightly. And then he catches sight of Lin trailing behind her, the little busybody, and he points to the door. "No," he commands. "No handlers."

Lin gives him a patronizing look. "Surely–"

"I'm serious," he presses, stern. "I can't have you in here, we've got work to do. You can bother her after."

Lin turns in a huff, and leaves.

Archer smiles. "God, you're my hero."

He waves her off. "You know I take care of you." Tom is older than her by more than a few years, and shorter than her by more than a few inches, but he's strong and capable. Like all good prosthetists, he's missing a limb, too. His right leg is a Nike 5.4.

Archer likes Tom. He *listens*.

She sets the bag of cybernetic feet down on the table, and together, they start to lay the pairs out in a line.

"All right, talk to me," he says, diving right in. "Gimme the good, the bad, and the ugly."

Archer sighs. "I mean…they're all beautiful. Just stunning art pieces."

"Yeah, okay." He nudges at her with his elbow. "But…?"

She's visibly hesitating.

"Hey, I didn't design 'em, I just work here. Give it to me straight."

"Ah, they hurt like fuck, Tom," she admits. "I can't be on any of them for more than few hours without lying down."

"Okay." He's thinking hard, probably already ten steps ahead of her, seeing things she's not seeing. "Okay, hurt where?"

"Low to mid back, mainly, I think that's where I'm compensating the most."

He looks down at the feet she's wearing, now. "Those are the most comfortable?"

"Yeah."

"Okay," he nods. "Yeah, I could've guessed. They've got the most support under your natural center of gravity, so you're not throwing yourself around as much." He points to the parallel bars. "Give me a little back-and-forth on those, I wanna get some film before we take them off."

Archer deflates a little. "Do we have to take them off?" she asks, stepping over between the bars while Tom gets the camera turned on and focused.

"You know we do." At least he's genuinely sympathetic. He opens a laptop and gets to work setting up the gait tracking program. Synching it wirelessly with her legs. "And you know the drill. Hands off the bars, down and back."

She starts her walk.

"Do you feel like you're throwing your pelvis forward?" he asks, zooming in, looking closely at the screen. She can see him tapping away, taking screenshots and adding motion tracking beads to the image.

"At first, maybe?" She has to think hard. "Yeah, maybe. At the beginning of the day. But it's not sustainable, because my balance starts to go, and I think I just end up lordotic."

"You stretching your hips?"

She pretends not to hear him.

He nods. "Yeah. That's what I thought. Okay, when you get to the end, gimme a turn and a stop."

She does.

He holds up a finger. "Do you always take that extra step with the left, when you turn?"

Again, Archer has to think hard. "Maybe? Shit, I don't know. I'll do another when I get to the end, again."

He types and clicks frantically. "All right."

She resumes her walk. "I think the neutral knee position needs more extension."

"Yeah, I think so, too. And I want to tweak the angles on your ankles, too. That'll probably help. Of course, we won't really know, until we get to those mean bastards." He gestures dismissively towards all the feet on the table.

She gets to the end of the bars, and gives another 180 turn.

"Ah, you did it again," he points out.

"Yeah," she grimaces, "yeah, no, I see that, now. It feels familiar. I think I've been doing that the whole time."

"It's the ankles," Tom confirms, shutting off the camera. "Jump up on the table for me."

Archer groans in frustration, stomping over and flopping down on her back. "I hate this."

"I know you do," Tom condescends. "Pants off, you big baby."

Just as she's working her leggings down over her feet, the door to the room opens. She startles hard, and then immediately relaxes.

Luc whistles in appreciation and she rolls her eyes.

"You're late," Tom scolds.

Luc just beams. "I don't know, it looks like I'm right on time."

"Shut your mouth," Archer mumbles.

"Dre!" Tom shouts, beginning to work his way around the circumference of Archer's thigh with his magnetic tool.

The arm specialist pops out from the lab space, around the corner. "You're late."

"Hey, man, I can't control the traffic." Luc removes his jacket and shirt, and sits down next to Archer. "How are you doing?" he nudges.

She gives him a noncommittal groan, scooting up to lay her head in his lap.

Dre comes wielding the same tool that Tom is using, and sets about loosening the connections around the edges of Luc's pec and shoulder blade.

"Hey, what are we even doing today?" Luc asks Dre.

"It's a surprise," she teases. "You'll love it."

He rolls his eyes. "Ooh, I can't wait."

Tom, meanwhile, is peeling back the few inches of black synthflesh that overlap with Archer's skin. He gives the entire leg a medial twist, and all at once, there comes the strange sensation of numbness, of emptiness, and he lifts her right leg away. She doesn't think she'll ever get used to the feeling.

"You need to take these off more often, Arch," he scolds. "Your skin will thank you."

"And your back," Dre adds.

"Yeah, yeah," she mumbles, unable to look. She knows what's down there. The skin on the end of her residual limb is veined with hair-width fiber optic cable, and dotted with electrode sensors that pair with receptors on the inside of her synthflesh. And from the very end, jutting out through bone and skin, is the Osseo-integration post. It looks like the male end of an auxiliary cable, an inch in diameter, and about three inches long.

Tom gets to work on her left leg, and when she feels Luc shudder beneath her, she knows his arm has been successfully removed. It's always strange to see Luc this way, his right pectoral and shoulder blade are a part of the cybernetic, and without them, he's left with a piece of collarbone jutting out into space above the hollow curve of the top of his ribcage. He lifts his shoulder as much as he's able to, groaning and stretching.

"God, you're so fucking gross," she teases.

"You're gross," he counters, childish, trying to twist around and prod at her with his collarbone.

"*Ew!*" She jumps, swatting at him.

"Hey, knock it off," Tom scolds, peeling back the synthflesh on Archer's left leg.

She grimaces at the sensation. "Can't you just give me my old feet back?"

"I wish I could, kiddo," he says sadly, slinging her knees over each of his elbows. "Best I can do is make these a little more bearable for you."

She sighs. "Okay."

Their prosthetists head back towards the lab, severed limbs in tow.

"You just gonna leave us in pieces?" Luc needles.

"We can rebuild you," Dre replies, smiling. "We have the technology."

"Hey, can you make me an Iron Man arm?" Luc calls after them. "I want an Iron Man jetpack arm."

Dre turns and, with a wry smile, emphatically bends down the thumb, pointer finger, ring finger, and pinky on Luc's cybernetic hand before holding it up proudly.

He gasps in mock offense. "Cym, will you kick her ass for me?"

She cranes her neck to look at Tom. She smiles, nodding towards Dre. Tom is all too eager to play along, whacking his partner on the side of the head with her foot. She gasps in genuine surprise, and Archer laughs proudly, clapping her hands in appreciation.

"Hey, how long is this gonna take?" Luc calls after them.

"Make her stretch her hips while you wait." With that, the pair disappears back into the lab.

"Hey," Luc nudges, "stretch your hips."

Exasperated, Archer turns over onto her stomach, groaning at the pull in her hip flexors.

"Met your new babysitter on the way in," Luc says, slinging a leg over her to sit on her lower back.

She shudders, sinking into the painful stretch. "Oh, yeah?"

"Yeah, she's a fucking busybody, isn't she?"

"Tom had to kick her out."

Luc laughs. "What a bro."

"Yeah, no kidding," she says, folding her arms beneath her cheek.

They spend the next hour or so talking about unimportant things. Vain, meaningless model conversation. New clothing lines they like, what parties are happening where, who's fucking who. Who got another DUI, who's in rehab. The superficial distractions of the bored, beautiful, and tortured. They don't talk about Pyramid club, or what had happened in the alley. There's no need to. It wasn't the first time they've done something like that to each other, and neither really expects it to be the last.

She thinks about telling him that it's been five days since she's dropped, and then decides against it. It's not actually something she wants to talk about.

And then he asks the question she knew was coming. "Hey, do you really think Wells stole tech?"

Her reply is a simple, dismissive, "I don't know."

"Yeah, you do," he prods, digging a finger into her ribs. "You know. Come on, did he?"

"I said I don't know, Luc, damn. Rob and I didn't exactly…I don't know, see eye to eye. He wouldn't have told me."

His voice drops to a conspiratorial whisper. "I heard that Callas has some goodfellas on the case, and that's part of the reason they told us to keep it away from the cops and the media."

She rolls her eyes, masking her bolt of panic. "Lucas, where the hell did you hear that?"

He shrugs. "Hey, did Callas tell you what it was he stole?"

"No, of course not."

"Well, I heard it was a robot," he reveals, seeming to be immensely proud of this information.

Archer groans, trying to mask her spike of anxiety. "What the hell are you talking about?"

"I heard that the guys across the hall made a robot, and Wells stole it to sell it to, like, Google or something."

"Okay, you're an idiot."

Tom and Dre come back into the room, carrying their detached limbs. "What are you kids whispering about?"

"Hey, what did Rob Wells steal?" Luc asks.

They both scoff in clear disapproval of the topic.

"Come on," he coaxes, wry and charismatic as always. "What was it? You can tell us."

"It was a prototype from across the hall," Tom says shortly. "Now, kindly dismount my patient."

Luc pouts, climbing off the table. "Where's my Iron Man arm?"

Dre holds the new and improved limb up for his inspection. "Would you settle for Inspector Gadget?"

He smiles, intrigued. "Ooh, maybe."

"Then sit your ass down and submit to re-assembly."

As their limbs are painstakingly re-attached, Luc continues to press the issue. "I'm serious," he says. "You guys have to know more than they're telling us. Shit happened right across the hall."

Dre sighs, frustrated. "How about you mind your own business, and focus on repping your tech? Don't worry about what they're doing in Tartarus."

Luc gasps. "Ooh, you're not supposed to call it that!" He looks up at the security camera in the corner. "Did you hear that, Callas? She just said the 'T' word!"

"Hey, knock it off," Archer scolds.

"Listen," Tom says, voice dropping to a whisper, "all I can say is the guys across the hall have been working on some spooky shit–"

"Tom," Dre cautions.

"What? They're gonna find out, eventually. It's all anyone is talking about around here. If Lex and Callas are trying to pretend otherwise, then they're idiots."

"Wait, what do you mean, spooky shit?" Luc prods, leaning in close.

"*Spooky shit*," he repeats emphatically. "About a year ago, they started upping the security around R&D, thinning out the staff, all that sort of thing. It got really quiet, over there. Nothing new coming out, no big announcements."

"Right," Dre corroborates. "And whenever we saw the techs going in and out, they looked terrified."

Tom nods. "Kind of a stunned silence about them."

"Yeah."

Archer's stomach lurches. How many hours had she spent in this exact spot, probably no more than 100 feet from Cael? So close, and yet so insurmountably far.

Fuck. This is the first time it's really occurred to her. He'd been *right there*.

"Did you ever see inside?" she asks. "See what they were doing?"

"Nope," Tom says, folding her synthflesh back into place, "not a glimpse. But I think it was machine learning. AI."

Archer's heart rate picks up; she hopes he can't tell. "What makes you say that?"

"It's the final frontier, isn't it? The next logical step."

Dre nods in agreement, stepping back to inspect her work on Luc. "Yeah. It's what I'd do, if I were Callas. He's got the money, and everyone knows he doesn't give a shit about ethics; he could take what MIT's been doing with AI and put a goddamn Space-X rocket booster on it."

"Capitalism," Archer murmurs.

"Besides," Tom interjects, seeming not to have heard her, "as far as robotics is concerned, we've already got a leg up on Moravec's Paradox, and that's the really hard part." He lifts at Archer's ankle. "Literally, a leg up."

Dre nods. "Limbs, vocal cords, proprioceptive fields..."

Archer smiles good-naturedly, but inside, she's trying desperately to remember where she's heard that term before.

"What's that?" Luc asks, giving the newly re-attached arm some test movements. "What paradox?"

"Sensorimotor skills take a lot more computational power than logic and reasoning," Dre explains, pointing to Luc's hand. "Basically, they gave *us* the hard job."

It hits her all at once – Cael's documents. His instruction manuals.

It's exactly like he'd said. Forge came at the problem from the top down. They knew they could do it, they knew they could build him, because...because they'd built her, first.

"All right, you ready to see what we changed?" Dre asks Luc.

"New hand," he observes, flexing and waving his fingers. "Feels weird. Feels...feels like there's...more. Like there's a lot going on in there."

She nods, smiling in anticipation. "I want you to hold your hand up, look at the space between your middle and ring finger, and think 'open.'"

Luc looks surprised. "*Open?*"

"Open," she repeats. "Open your hand."

"Open my hand." Luc thinks hard, staring at his newly attached limb. Nothing happens for a long time. Archer can see sweat beading on his temple, see his brow furrowing with concentration, and then finally–

"Oh, shit!" she exclaims, watching as his hand splits open lengthwise, like some kind of Giger-esque Vulcan salute, to reveal what she can only assume is a multi-tool. It extends out from his hand, and into workable range. She laughs appreciatively. "Oh, that's so fucking cool."

But Luc looks a little baffled. "Why?" he asks. "I can't even remember the last time I picked up a screwdriver, why do I need a Swiss Army Hand?"

"It's not *for you*," Dre explains, exasperated, "we're just *testing* it on you. It's *for* re-deploying soldiers, and people who use tools all the time." The subtext is undeniable. It's for real men with real jobs, not pretty-boy coat hangers. Luc is just here to make it look sexy.

He frowns, turning his hand over to inspect it thoroughly. "Okay."

Dre rolls her eyes, coaxing him to his feet. "All right, Atlas. We need to run a basic fine-motor panel, and then we'll go over the new features in more detail."

Tom sighs, putting the final touches on Archer's legs as Luc and Dre head over to the fine-motor table.

"Do you think Wells really stole tech?" she asks softly.

"I don't know," he admits. "I know he came down here a few times, the week before he disappeared, but that's nothing out of the ordinary. Handlers are always coming down here to negotiate with us. I also know he was getting close to one of the techs from across the hall, one of the guys that looked so scared all the time. Does that mean he stole something? No. But it doesn't look good. Especially since we know that his badge was the last to swipe into Tartarus, before the thing went missing, and he wasn't supposed to have those privileges. He went into the credentialing system that day and *gave* himself those privileges."

"Do you…" She hesitates. "Do you think they've caught him, and they're just not telling us? Or…"

"I honestly don't know, Arch. We had the inquisition down here the next morning, asking questions, digging through the computers. I guess someone wiped the camera logs pretty thoroughly, and I don't know if that speaks to the ineptitude of Forge's security, or the sheer brilliance of whoever managed to pull this off."

"So, all they have to go on are badge logs?"

"Yeah, I guess so." Tom nudges her playfully. "Why the interest? Don't tell me *you* have the damn thing. The mysterious, black-box AI tech."

Archer forces a laugh, looking away.

Tom stands, gesturing towards the parallel bars. "All right. Back and forth?"

After several more hours of painstaking disassembly and re-assembly, Lucas and Archer finally step back out onto the sidewalk.

Archer lights up a cigarette. "What are you doing, now?" she asks.

"Uh…gym, probably?" Luc looks down at his cybernetic. "I think they made it bigger, just to fuck with me." He flexes his organic arm, holding it up for comparison. "Don't you think it looks bigger?"

She furrows her brow, looking between his arms. "I think you're imagining things."

"Nah, you just can't tell because you're over there. I'm gonna measure them."

She blurts it out before she can stop herself. "I think a lifetime of disability and modeling has fucked with your body image."

He gives her a puzzled look, laughing awkwardly. "Okay?"

Just then, a small gaggle of obvious tourists passes by, and one of them stops. She's young. Pretty.

"Wait," she says. "Hey, are you Mr Atlas?"

Luc flashes her a broad, magazine-cover smile. "At your service, babe."

"Oh my god!" She giggles, pointing up at the building behind him. "Oh, I didn't even notice where we are!"

To Archer's dismay, the rest of her flock – all women – have all crowded in close to fawn over Lucas. She takes a few steps back, to avoid the crush.

"I have your *Vogue* cover on my wall, at home! The way they had you with the red cape, and–"

"How much can you lift?"

"My best friend's next-door neighbor has a son who's missing an arm, and they're trying so hard to crowdfund for an Atlas, like yours–"

"You're so *tall*! Like, I knew that you were tall, but I didn't think–"

The first girl finally manages to squeak out a desperate, "*CanItakeapicturewithyou?*"

"Of course!" he laughs. "Do you want me to pick you up?"

She shrieks, hopping up and down with excitement. "Yes! Yes, please, please, *please*! That would be so cool!"

Gracious and charming, he scoops her up with his cybernetic and sits her on his shoulder, arm raised like a bicep flex. She clings to him, giggling and delighted.

Archer's phone chimes. It's a text from Auryn:

> Don't wanna come off pushy here
> but where's my iou

"Fuck," she mutters.

"Wait–" One of them points to Archer's feet. "Wait, you're Cymbre Archer! *Oh my god!*"

Ahh, shit. She's not in the mood for this today. But she forces a smile, nonetheless. "Yeah," she says, "yeah, that's me."

Another chorus of delighted squeals.

"Come be in the picture with us!"

"Oh, um–" Archer stammers. She would rather throw herself into traffic.

"Cym," Lucas beckons, playful. "Come on. Come here."

Reluctantly, she steps over to him, and he hoists her up with his organic arm to sit her on his other shoulder. Face still plastered with that fake smile, Archer tucks her cigarette behind her back and whispers through gritted teeth, "I'm going to kill you, Lucas, I swear–"

"Okay," he prompts as the elected photographer steps back, "everyone say '*cheese*!'"

"*Cheese!*"

They have to take pictures on, like, five different phones before Luc finally puts her down. He sees them off with hugs and smiles, and Archer returns to her cigarette.

He finally re-joins her, still grinning and laughing to himself. "Ahh, they were fun." He lifts at the shoulder of his jacket. "Do you think I'll have to dry clean this, to get the cum stain off? No, wait– Wait, that's the side *you* were on, Cym."

Archer rolls her eyes, entirely unwilling to play along. "You owe me for that shit," she snaps, pointedly applying her anti-surveillance jewelry.

"Come on," he prods, rolling his shoulders, stretching his neck side to side. "They loved it. We just made their whole day."

"Yeah, fuck *my* day, right?" she mumbles, aware of how cruel and selfish a thing it is to say. She wants a drop. The need is itching along the inside of her skull, becoming harder and harder to ignore.

Lucas groans, stepping behind her and wrapping his arms around her shoulders. "Lighten up, Cym," he coaxes, shaking her back and forth.

She ignores him and takes a drag of her cigarette, pensive. "Hey, do you have your bike?"

"Yeah, it's parked down the block."

She thinks for a moment before asking, "You wanna drive me to Tribeca and help commit a crime?"

He shrugs. "Yeah, sure."

CHAPTER ELEVEN

"LISTEN, WHEN YOU SAID 'COMMIT A CRIME' I WAS KIND OF HOPING for, like...fuck on a rooftop, or something."

"Lucas, why would we need to drive to Tribeca to fuck on a rooftop?"

"I don't know," he grumbles. "I don't know what's going on with you, lately. I don't know *anything*." He's kneeling in front of the storage unit containing all of Wells' belongings. Mercifully outdoors, and tucked away at the back of the complex. He's been trying for about six solid minutes to get his hand to split open so he can get to his tools, all to no avail.

"What's the holdup?" she hisses, impatient. "You did it just fine in the lab!"

"Well, I wasn't *breaking the law* in the lab! This is a lot of pressure!"

She rolls her eyes.

"Seriously, we're gonna get fucking caught. There's cameras everywhere, look."

"We're wearing anti-surveillance."

"Yeah, and thank God neither of us have any other distinctive characteristics, right? Fuck. Can't I just break it?" he asks, lifting the lock to inspect it. It's a three-digit combination. "I could crush this thing to pieces with, like, zero effort whatsoever. I could rip the whole door off its track, if you'd just—"

"Then they'll know we broke in, Luc, please."

"Why are we even doing this?" he pesters, still staring intently at his hand. "Didn't you *just* get through telling me you didn't give a shit about Rob?"

"It's complicated."

"You're annoying as fuck, Cymbre, it's a good thing I lov— Oh, shit!" Finally, *finally*, his hand splits open, revealing the array of tools.

Archer laughs in relief, crouching down to rest her chin on his shoulder. He starts jamming a few tools in between the wheels at random. The tweezers, the toothpick, the vaguely-named multi-purpose hook.

"Pull down on the lock while you're doing that," she suggests, peering over his shoulder.

"Or, and here's an idea, Cym, you could fucking help, instead of standing around like a princess."

Grumbling, she reaches out to hold steady, downward pressure on the lock. "Is this even going to work?"

Luc stops entirely at that, gaping at her. "You mean to tell me that *you don't even know if this is going to work?*"

"Well—"

"*What the fuck are we doing here, Cymbre?*"

"Keep your voice down! Christ."

He's fuming. "I swear to God, I'm giving this bullshit thirty more seconds, and then I'm ripping the lock off and driving away. You can get arrested, for all I care, I'm so over this—"

The lock pops open, unbroken, and falls into Archer's palm.

"Holy fuck," Luc murmurs, astounded.

Archer casts the lock aside, taking his face in her hands and smashing her lips against his. He laughs appreciatively into the kiss, and she hears his hand whirr and click back into position again.

"Thank you," she breathes, heart suddenly racing. "Thank you, fuck, thank you."

"Now *you* owe *me*," he nudges, rising to stand. With an effortless flick of his cybernetic, the door rolls up and out of the way, clanging loudly.

The unit is alarmingly large, and packed with belongings from multiple erstwhile tenants. It seems like management tried to shove everything into open boxes and pile it all on and around the biggest piece of furniture the person left behind. Archer recognizes Rob's couch, and clambers awkwardly over the crates and chairs and lamps towards it.

Luc gingerly makes his way through in her wake. "What are we even looking for?"

"I don't know," she admits, beginning to rifle through the boxes labeled with Rob's unit number. "Uh…computer. His desktop or his laptop. USB drives, hard drives. And anything that says Hephaestus Forge on it."

"And why are we doing this?"

"Because you love me. Quit asking."

They get to work, crouching awkwardly among the detritus of another person's life. Archer begins to sift haphazardly through Wells' boxes, and with each one, her hope wanes.

"Yeah, I'm not finding shit, Cym," Luc announces after a while.

"Neither am I."

"I've got clothes…bunch of, like, flatware and shit…"

"Yeah, clothes."

"Books."

"Fuck." Archer groans, head falling back. "*Fuck.*"

"We need to bounce," Luc heeds, rising to his feet.

"Okay," she says, still searching.

He peers out of the storage unit, around the corner. "*Cym.*"

"Okay! Fuck."

Luc extends a hand towards her, helping her climb over the stacks of crates and furniture. But just as she's nearly free of it, she stops. There's a box of Rob's books nearby, and one of them has caught her eye. After a moment of pained deliberation, she picks it up and stuffs it into her coat pocket.

Luc laughs. "Uh, what the fuck?"

"It's mine," she's quick to justify, pushing past him and out of the unit. "I let him borrow it ages ago, and he never gave it back."

"Yeah, nice, Arch," he appraises, rolling the door closed behind them. "That's a real grown-up thing to do."

"Whatever."

When she enters her loft, Cael is crouching by the window, peering down at the street.

"That's Lucas Wagner," he observes aloud.

Archer steps over beside him, watching Luc mount his bike. "Yeah, he gave me a ride home."

"He's your best friend?"

"Yeah. I've known him longer than anyone else in the world."

"Hmm." Cael blinks down at him. "I want to meet him."

"Um...yeah. Maybe someday."

He cranes his neck to watch Luc drive away. "I like his motorcycle. Triumph Rocket 3 GT."

Archer smiles. "Yeah, me too. He hates cars, especially driverless, so—"

Cael stands briskly, moving in that abrupt, robotic way. "Why?" He almost sounds offended by the notion.

"His parents died in the accident that took his arm."

"Oh. That makes sense, then. People on the internet call you the Transhumanist Adam and Eve. Do the two of you have a romantic history?"

Embarrassment twists uncomfortably at her guts. "Um...yeah. Kind of. Sometimes."

"I thought you identified as queer."

"I do. And that can mean a lot of different things," she bristles, refusing to justify any further. "Christ, Cael."

He shrugs. "Okay."

"We broke into the storage unit with all of Wells' stuff in it."

"Archer," he says sternly, crossing his arms over his chest. "That's illegal."

"Hey, I did it for your sake. I was looking for anything that could help us, here. Like, point us in the right direction. But it looks like Forge got to his desktop computer at least, and maybe his laptop, too."

"Not the police?"

"No, remember, the company told us all to keep this away from the police. They've got their own private security force handling it."

"But…" Cael thinks hard. "If Wells got away on his own, it's not out of the question that he has the laptop with him."

"I guess," she concedes. "But that's a big 'if.' Either way, it's a resource that's lost to us, now."

"Was there anything else?"

"No. I was mainly looking for that computer, or any paper documents he had. And there was nothing. Oh, but–" Archer digs through her coat pocket, producing the book she'd taken from the storage unit. "I found *Children of Húrin.*"

Cael's eyes go wide, hand lifting to hover over the book as though he's afraid to touch it.

"Here," she says, thrusting it into his grip. "I told you Rob had it."

He smiles, eyes and lips lifting at once into an expression that is wide and warm and grateful. "Thank you. I guess…" His eyes flutter. "Well, it's not like it's really stealing if it's your own property, right?"

"I mean, I guess not. Tell that to Luc."

"Okay, I will." He clutches the book to his chest. "Thank you."

"Yeah, no worries. I just…I remembered how you wanted to read it, so…"

After a beat, Cael abruptly pivots. "Can I have some plants?"

It's enough to give her whiplash. "Some…what?"

"*Plants,*" he repeats, emphatic. "Living organisms typically growing in a permanent site, absorbing water and inorganic substances through roots systems, and synthesizing nutrients in their leaves via photosynthesis using the green pigment chlorophyll." He rattles it off condescendingly. "You don't have any in here. I checked."

Exasperated, she sets about hanging her coat and settling back into the house. "Every time I get a plant, I accidentally kill it. If it can't scratch or meow when it needs something, I don't know what to do with it."

Cael frowns. "That's sad."

"Why do you want plants?" she asks, heading for the kitchen for a bottle of wine. If she can't drop, she'll drink until she's too numb to care.

"I've never seen one before."

Again, that damning stab of pity. "Okay, plants. But you have to take care of them."

"I will!" He trails after her into the kitchen, still clinging to the book. "I promise, I'll do a great job. Can I put a vine on that wall?"

She looks, and he's pointing at an expanse of brick beside the kitchen. "What, you want to grow a vine on my wall? Inside the house?"

"Yes. Can I?"

She pours herself a generous glass of red wine. "Won't that…I don't know, eat my wall up? Make it fall apart?"

"Not a Creeping Fig. Not if I'm careful."

"You want to grow *fruit* on the wall inside my house?"

He looks around, seeming to make a kind of appraisal. "There's won't be any fruit, because I haven't seen any wasps in here."

Archer has no idea what the fuck that means. "I don't know, Cael, the amount of attention and upkeep it would take to keep it from destroying my wall, that would be—"

"Robotic?" he asks, smiling. "I know, right?"

Archer looks around the room, searching for any signs of existing structural weakness. As if she knows what in the hell she's even looking for. And then her eyes come to rest on the massive photograph on the wall, that gallery-sized monstrosity depicting her reclined on her side.

"I'll make you a deal," she says, pointing to the photo. "You can grow a vine on my wall if you put it there."

"What about your picture?"

"Fuck that picture. You can frisbee it into the East River, for all I care."

His face lights up. "Okay. I'll grow it there."

Archer heaves a deep sigh. "Okay. Make me a list of plants, and I'll go get them for you."

He's quivering with excitement, bouncing up and down on the balls of his feet. "Today?"

"No," she chuckles, taking an emphatic drink of wine, "not today. My back hurts like hell and they just butchered my joint settings."

"But soon?"

"Yeah. Cat-safe, though."

He's shocked by the very suggestion. "I would *never* bring something into this house if it was dangerous for cats!"

"Okay, then. I'll get you plants."

"But I don't have any money."

"I have money, Caelan," she condescends. "I'm a very famous decorative meat puppet."

"But I would experience guilt."

"Don't," she swiftly negates. "I guess...well, this is sort of your house too, now, right?" She smothers the end of the sentence with a gulp of wine, hoping he doesn't remark on it.

"Hey, I had an idea," he announces. "I was thinking about the other day, when you asked if your questions were rude."

Fuck is this what it's gonna be like every time I leave him home alone? He just...comes up with ideas and then word-vomits them all over me, the instant I walk in? She barely even remembers that conversation, she was so fucked up that morning. "Okay, what's your idea?"

"What if we make another deal? A rude question for a rude question. That way we both learn things."

It's...not a bad idea, come to think of it. "Yeah," Archer tentatively concedes, "okay. I owe you one, so fire away."

His eyes flutter, and he eventually settles on, "Something went wrong, please try again."

"Ask me a question, Cael."

"Oh. *Oh.*" He shudders. "I thought there was a...a fire. Okay." He settles, re-focusing his attention on her. "Do you feel that the proportions of your cybernetics, and the manner in which they move, put you in the Uncanny Valley?"

Archer choke-laughs. "Motherfucker!" She stammers. "That's— is that a nice view from inside your glass house, or what?"

Cael peers around. "Only some of this house is made of glass."

"No, you—" She sighs in frustration. "I'm saying you've gotta be deeper in the Uncanny Valley than I am. At least *I'm—*" She stops the word before it springs from her lips. But even though he doesn't always understand metaphors on the first try, Cael's not stupid. He catches it.

"What, human? *Real?*"

She doesn't reply.

"*I* was built to scale. Your legs, accounting for the substantial lift in the feet you're currently wearing, are 48 inches long. Out of your total 74 inches—"

"Okay, okay, you've made your point, damn."

He might smirk then, or she might be anthropomorphizing again.

"This was just an excuse to point out that you're more normal-looking than I am," she observes aloud.

"Yes, but you *really* owed me."

Well, shit. She can't deny that she deserved it, but she also doesn't know how many more comments like that her ego can take. "Can I just pay you back in plants?"

He smiles triumphantly. "Yes, you can pay me back in plants."

CHAPTER TWELVE

So begins the renaissance of Caelan's indoor-gardening frenzy. For the next three weeks, he sends Archer on errand after errand to the woman-run plant nursery over by McCarren Park, and each time, she returns with more greenery for him to scatter around her (*their?*) living space. Overnight, it seems he's breathed new life into the loft. It becomes something of a ritual for Archer too, and she brings him gifts in the form of orchids, ferns, succulents, and bamboo. He accepts them all, housing them in mismatched pots and wide, ceramic planters. They spill from hanging baskets, and crowd together on the bookshelves and windowsills. Small trees guard all the corners of the space, Guiana Chestnut and Areca Palm, while herbs grow on the kitchen counters.

Cael covets his plants like treasures. He gives each one a name, things like Elodie and George and Ophelia. His favorite by far is the Creeping Fig, which he so delicately and lovingly pins to the bricks near the kitchen. Nurtured by his careful attention, it grows quickly, spreading across the wall in a web of bright green.

Paul. He names that one Paul.

On this particular fall day, Archer has been sent to retrieve an Air Plant for his succulent garden. It's a beautiful little thing, with thin, wispy fronds exploding outward like a starburst. Deep green at the base, transforming to a shocking vermillion at the tips.

Archer walks up the block, Cael's plant tucked safely under her arm. She thinks of how his face will look when he sees it, and that makes her smile. She's proud.

"What the fuck are you smiling about, Archer?"

She looks up just in time to see a fist hurtling towards her face. It makes shocking, blunt, painful contact with her left cheekbone, knuckles bumping against her eye, and then her balance goes and she's falling. The ceramic pot slips from her grasp and shatters, and then her back collides with the ground, and she's heaving tight, labored gasps. The anti-surveillance visor she'd been wearing has broken, burying shards of glass and metal in her cheek.

"What the fuck?" she demands, voice breathy and strained.

There's a man standing over her that she doesn't recognize. Long, stringy hair. Shitty tattoos on his arms and neck. Garish dazzle paint on his face. He bends and picks up her bag, and she lunges for him, only to be rewarded with a swift kick to the jaw. Her teeth clack together loudly, and she falls back again, clutching at her face. She isn't frightened, strangely enough, at least not for herself. More like angry and annoyed. But if he goes for the building, *if he gets inside*, oh FUCK, Cael is probably dumb enough to just answer the door–

"Auryn said not to hit you in the face," he says, conversational as he roots through her bag. "Some bullshit about your job, and he likes you, he didn't want to have to do this, blah, blah, blah. But he didn't tell me you had such a punchable fucking gook face." He laughs triumphantly, withdrawing all of her cash and tossing the bag back down.

Oh, thank God, *it's about* drugs. She forces a relieved, mocking laugh. "What are you, a cartoon thug?" she taunts breathlessly. "You gonna take a baseball bat to my knees, next? Yeah, why don't you give *that* a try, you stupid cocksucker. Fuck you." She tries to spit at him, but only succeeds in sending a mouthful of blood pouring thickly down her own chin.

"You talk a lot of shit for a cripple bleeding on the sidewalk." He plants a foot on her chest, leaning down to look her in the eye. His breath smells like cigarettes and Penth, and she chokes, trying in vain to pry him away.

"Scream," he says. "That's the only thing that would make this better. The cops showing up to help me curb-stomp your ass."

"Fuck you," she repeats, straining to unseat his foot.

"Next time," he impresses, "pay for your shit."

The weight leaves her chest, and then his fist collides with her face again. The same side. Her head knocks hard into the sidewalk. Beneath the ringing in her ears, she hears the rapid pounding of bootheels fading into the distance. She lets her head fall back against the pavement, vision swimming from the pain and humiliation. Beside her, Cael's plant is wilting into the sidewalk. She reaches out and traces her fingertips along the delicate fronds.

Fuck, she thinks, *does Forge have insurance on my face?*

When Archer stumbles through the doorway, cradling an armful of dirt and broken greenery, Cael emits the closest thing to a scream she's heard so far.

"*What happened to you?*" he wails, swatting the plant from her grip. His hands are fluttering around in clear distress, like he's afraid to even touch her, like she may fall apart at any second. "Did you get hit by a car? Did something fly off a building and land on you? Did you step into an open manhole? *Did you trip and fall on a–*"

She leans away, trying to dodge his waving hands. "Your plant, Cael–" She points lamely at the ground. "It got smashed, I'm sorry."

"*Fuck* the plant!" he screeches, dragging her by the wrist towards the bathroom.

She stumbles along the best she can, trying to blink the blood and tears from her eyes. "Caelan, I'm fine."

"You're not!" he insists, practically lifting her up and setting her down in the bathtub.

Is this gonna be his solution for everything? Put me in the bathtub? She's still fully clothed, but he turns the water on nonetheless. She yelps at the cold, trying to squirm away, but he puts a hand on her shoulder and holds her down with alarming strength. Gradually, the water warms up, and he starts gently wiping at her face with a wet washcloth. She can feel her cheekbone beginning to swell, pulsing painfully. She winces away, but he shushes her.

"We should call an ambulance," he announces, wringing bloody water from the washcloth. She's honestly surprised by how much there is.

"Caelan, we don't need to call an ambulance." In a weird way, this whole thing is sort of funny and endearing. The way he'd leapt into action, so ready to take care of her. It makes her wonder what he'd been like when she'd passed out in the hallway.

"You could have a broken nose," he blurts, working himself up into a frenzy. "Or a Le Fort fracture. Or a concussion. Or a torn brain stem! *H-hematoma!* Does it feel like your brain is swelling? What does brain swelling feel like?" His head cocks back and his eyes flutter for a second, but he quickly snaps out of it. "*No!* Let me look at your pupils!" He drops the washcloth unceremoniously, taking her face in his hands and prying her eyes open. Archer hisses at the rough contact, trying to squirm away, but he holds fast. "You need an MRI."

Oh, shit. Her heart rate picks up. "Why?"

"Just to be extra safe."

She groans, more frustrated than relieved. "You're being so dumb right now."

Just as he looks like he's going to relax, Cael panics again. "*Teeth!*" he shrieks, prying her jaw open and jamming his fingers into her mouth. "*Broken teeth!*"

"Hey, hey, enough, already!" she chides, spitting his fingers out and swatting him away. But he catches one of her hands mid-air and holds it to his chest.

"How did this happen?" he demands, lunging to shut the water off with his free hand. "Tell me!"

"I got jumped outside," she finally admits, sinking low into the tub. "Some fucking guy my drug dealer sent, because I owe him money from, like, a month ago."

"What? Wh-*what?*" Cael is suddenly upset in a way that isn't remotely endearing or funny anymore. His whole face has contorted with panic and concern, and he's rubbing his thumb compulsively along the palm of her hand, harder and harder.

"I've led a hard life, these past few years," she explains, wiping blood from her face. "I knew it wasn't gonna be a clean break, trying to get away from it all. This is just what happens."

"Call the police!" he exclaims. "We need to call the police, and then you can get a lawyer, and we can take it to trial, and it'll probably count as a hate crime because you're an Asian woman with a disability—"

"Hey!" she interrupts, annoyed to have been reminded of the way her attacker had spoken. "Hey, enough of that, Cael! We're not calling the cops!"

"Why not?"

She gives him a patronizing look. "You want to call the cops so that guy can tell them I owed him drug money, and then they can send a bunch of fucking pigs in here to toss my place, find you, and send your ass back to Tartarus?" She scoffs, sinking deeper into the tub. "Sure. Let's do *that*. Use your state-of-the-art logic trees, shit."

His hand falls still, and he goes quiet for an unsettling span of time. And then in a small, earnest voice, he asks, "But what about you?"

For what feels like the millionth time, she reassures him. "Caelan, I am absolutely fine. I don't have a concussion, none of my bones are broken, and I do not need an ambulance or an MRI. This is honestly more embarrassing than anything, and I would appreciate it if we could both just move on, now."

"How sure are you that you don't need an ambulance or an MRI?" he demands. "Give me a percentage."

"I'm 100% sure."

He fidgets, frantic. "But how do you *know*?" Certainty always seems to freak him out.

She groans in frustration. "Because…because, I don't know! All internal diagnostics indicate that I'm operating well within normal safety parameters!"

His lip quivers for a second, and then he's clambering into the tub with her, all sharp knees and elbows.

"Hey, what the fuck?" she protests. "Cael, no! This is fucking weird, don't–"

He ignores her entirely, slotting his hips between her legs and tucking his head into the crook of her neck. It's not a comfortable position for her back, but it doesn't seem like he's in any mood to be reasoned with. She can feel his breath against her wet skin, coming in quick, anxious little huffs. At that, she finally resigns herself to it, and places her hands on his back.

"Humans are too delicate for the world," he announces.

She inhales deeply, and he follows suit. Mimicking. "Maybe the world is just too hard," she murmurs in reply. There's more vulnerability to the statement than her tone would suggest.

"It's not hard right here," he says. "Right here is soft, and it's safe, so just stay here with me for a little while, okay?"

Resigned, Archer lets her head fall back against the rim of the tub. "Okay, Caelan."

His voice vibrates against her neck as he asks, "You really haven't bought any drugs in a month?"

"No." She's strangely ashamed to be forced to confess out loud. "It's been 27 days since I last dropped."

His arms tighten around her. "Good."

"I fucking hate it," she admits, fidgeting beneath him, trying to get comfortable. "It feels like I'm back in my own head for the first time in years, and I really, really, *really* do not like it in here." She groans softly, sinking deeper into the bathtub. "It's all sharp and loud and painful, and…I don't know, it's just a bunch of shit I've spent years not thinking about, and it's all back. It's back, and it's just…it seems so unavoidable, now."

"I'm proud of you," he says, and although it should sound cliché and condescending, it doesn't.

Archer cranes her neck to look down at him. "Yeah?"

He tucks his forehead into the crook of her neck, fingertips playing along a strand of her hair. "Yeah."

Eventually, he does let go of her. He lets her get up, lets her shower in peace. Her face is aching, and she can feel her left eye beginning to pulse and swell shut. The hot water probably isn't helping.

When she steps back out, she sees a text on her phone. It's from Auryn:

> Arch, I am so so so sorry.
> Rick wasn't meant to do that I
> swear, he was just supposed to
> get the money and that's it.

She blocks his number without replying.

Avoiding her reflection, Archer dons her kimono and heads back out into the main room. The sun is beginning to set now, and Cael is flitting around one of the big windows, worrying over his new plant. He seems to have scraped the dirt and fronds back together, re-housed them in the succulent garden, and now he's propping them back up with little wooden stakes.

"How is it?" she asks, stepping over to join him.

"He," Cael corrects, tracing his fingertips lovingly along the fronds. "This is James. And he's okay. A little roughed up, but these guys are resilient. You can grow them from worse-quality cuttings than these. Besides, he's with his new friends. They'll help."

She forces a smile, careful not to move her face too much as she does. There's a sort of sudden calm about him now, completely antithetical to what had just happened in the bathroom. She tries not to be too unsettled by it.

"This is Ophelia," he continues. "She's a Crassula succulent. In early summer, she'll grow purple flowers to attract bees and flies for pollination."

"There better not be any bees or flies in here."

"It's just something I learned about recently. I find that cycle of energy very beautiful."

She steps in a little closer, peering down over his shoulder. "Oh, yeah?"

"It's a cycle that I will always exist outside of. My carbon came from the same space dust that yours did, and maybe my components could someday be recycled into other things, but every part of me will still only ever be a machine. That's been set in stone since the beginning of time." His voice drops in volume. "The living things of this universe will outlast me in ways I can't even comprehend, and I'm literally designed to for state-of-the art comprehension."

Archer furrows her brow. "Uh-huh."

"So, doing this, having these friends…" He smiles, running his fingers so carefully along the leaves and stems. "I know it's as close as I'll ever get. And even though they can't speak for themselves, I hear them. I see them." He leans in close, whispering to his plant. "I see you, little blossom, even though you're not ready to make yourself seen. And when that day comes, I'll be here."

Archer studies his face out of the corner of her eye. She isn't quite sure what to make of this weird little soliloquy. A few weeks ago, it would've annoyed her beyond belief. She'd have rolled her eyes and snuck off to drop, skin crawling for all the unnatural sentimentality of it. But not now. She's starting to get used to these abrupt tonal shifts of his, and the way he pivots so violently between his intense hyperfixations. She appreciates that Cael really is doing his absolute best, and so she'll do her absolute best to humor it. She appreciates the earnest sweetness of it. She sees him.

He rounds on her abruptly, their faces now very, very close, and Archer watches as his expression falls at the sight of her injuries. Again, just like she had when Con Khi had scratched his hand, she feels the strange and overwhelming urge to kiss him. Maybe in thanks, or maybe just because he's so beautiful.

Because he really is quite beautiful.

"What are you thinking about?" he asks, eyes fixed unwaveringly on her own.

She clears her throat, stepping away. "Hey, do you want to watch a movie or something? I'm not up for much else right now."

He eyes her dubiously. "Yes."

"Okay, what do you want to watch?" she asks, settling into the couch.

"Something with an android in it," he announces, taking his place beside her.

She thinks hard, head falling back against the couch. "Um…you know *Blade Runner* and *Space Odyssey*. We could watch another Data episode. 'Measure of a Man' or 'Offspring'. He has a daughter in that one. Or do you wanna tackle the *Alien* series? Everything looks like my legs, and some of the androids turn evil, like Lore."

"Only if you let me pause to point out all the smairfed," he counters. "Also—"

"The what?"

He shudders, eyes rolling back and fluttering. "The things that are not accurate."

"Inaccuracies?"

"Okay, then, only if you let me pause to point out all the things that are inaccuracies. Also, *spoilers*."

She chuckles, exasperated. "How is that even fun for you? Seriously, it's *sci-fi*. You can't pick apart every single detail, just looking for the fake stuff. There's a degree of suspension of disbelief that goes into it. That's part of the genre. Accept it, and you'll have a lot more fun."

Cael frowns. "But picking it apart *is* fun. I enjoy things differently than you do, and that's okay. People don't all need to be the same, *Archer*."

"Okay," she sighs, digging around for the remote. "Whatever you say, Cael, you've got me so fucked up."

She senses something very near her face then, and when she turns, she finds that he's risen to his knees beside her and leaned in close. She starts in surprise.

"You have bruises," he observes, fingertips hovering motionlessly over her skin.

She gives him a sardonic smile. "Yeah, I bet I do."

"And a small treefilds." His fingers make delicate contact with her cheekbone.

"Hey, that's two in a row."

He looks frustrated. "The noun form of 'lacerate.'"

"*Laceration.*"

"Does it hurt?"

Archer swallows. "Yeah. Yeah, it hurts."

He withdraws his hand, apologetic.

"Not because you're touching it," she's quick to justify. "That didn't make it feel any worse, or anything, it's just gonna hurt for a while. Hopefully it clears up before they stick me in front of a camera again. Catalog shoot is coming up."

He seems to consider it for a moment, eyes flitting here and there across the wreckage of her face. And then he sits back into the couch, laces his fingers in with hers, and leans his head against her shoulder.

"Okay," he announces, "you can start the movie."

Archer is dumbstruck, mouth opening and closing in stunned silence. This sort of thing is supposed to happen in the bed, not on the couch. This is for nighttime, for sleeping. Not daylight. Daylight begs questions, it makes everything different and frighteningly real. *Wait, is this frightening?*

"Is this okay?" Cael asks, earnest, peering up at her through those impossibly blue eyes.

She nods. Swallows again.

"Okay," he says, settling in deeper. "Okay, good."

CHAPTER THIRTEEN

Mx Archer-

Here it is! I hope you feel that we did you justice. It was an honor and a pleasure to speak with you, and if you ever want to meet again – without Callas, say – then give me a call. I'd love the chance to *really* hear your thoughts.

Nic

HEPHAESTUS FORGE: THE GODS OF TOMORROW, AND THE PEOPLE WHO BUILD THEM

It's a picturesque fall day in New York. Central Park burns red and orange in the afternoon sun, and the crowded sidewalks swarm with locals and tourists alike. Days like this, the city comes alive. But a quarter mile beneath the hustle and bustle, a different kind of life is sparking. It flies from the hammer and anvil of the divine artificer himself, craftsman to the gods of Olympus.

So says Evander Callas, founder and CEO of Hephaestus Forge Biotech Inc., the leading manufacturer of cybernetic limbs and synthetic organs, worldwide.

The child of Greek immigrants, Callas was raised in upstate New York by working-class parents.

"I remember my father commuting into the city multiple times a week, looking for jobs," he reminisces, walking us through the ultramodern lobby of Hephaestus Forge headquarters. "Being raised in that way, watching my parents try to scrape a living together for me, I was determined to not only move up from their station, but make the world a better place while I did it."

It's safe to say that Evander Callas has achieved just that. Whether it was luck or foresight, an early investment into the crypto market provided the significant seed money for a small biotech startup in Utica. At one time, this company was little more than a rented lab space furnished with secondhand, lease-to-own equipment.

"Ten guys with mixed medical and tech backgrounds, armed with a busted old 3D printer," Callas says. "One federal grant, courtesy of the US Access Board, and a private hospital CEO that believed in the cause."

Now, Hephaestus Forge is an edifice built on success stories, their Murray Hill headquarters just blocks from the global pharmaceutical powerhouse Pfizer. The tech is pricey, and insurance coverage can be hit-and-miss, but those who can get their hands on it are imbued with the gifts of the gods. That's no exaggeration – each piece of tech that comes out of Hephaestus Forge is named for an ancient Greek deity. There are Atlas arms with which to hold up the world, Nike and Hermes legs to carry you to victory. Patients hear symphonies with Euterpe cochlear implants, and sing along with Aoede vocal cords. The lives of burn survivors and graft-recipients are woven back to completeness with Arachne Synthflesh. Asclepius, god of medicine, lends his name to a line of lab-created organs for transplant, and Charon the ferryman's blue gaze burns cold and bright in prosthetic eyes all over the world.

"It's an homage to culture," Callas explains, "but it's more than that. I think the work we do here is godly, not necessarily in a religious sense, but in that we do help people in ways that were once thought to only be possible through supernatural or divine intervention. Today, we achieve these miracles with science."

We follow him into an elevator and descend into the earth, towards the mythical realm of Hephaestus Forge research and development. He's hypervigilant about what we can and cannot photograph here, and for good reason. Corporate and intellectual property theft are always concerns, especially with a multi-billion-dollar biotech company of this notoriety. People would kill for the secrets in this room, and people would die protecting them. This level of access by any member of the media is entirely unprecedented.

The R&D department is a sprawling, underground complex; labs chained to labs chained to labs. Most are hidden from us behind fogged glass, but what we do see is astounding.

According to Callas, "This is where the real magic happens."

Our first stop is a long table housing millions upon millions of Aceso Nanobots. So small are these that they must be examined under microscopes before they can be fully understood. Each one is an entirely autonomous (though just short of sentient) robot, designed to live within a human body and offer on-the-spot healing. According to Callas, "Our success rate with healing spinal cord injuries sits at a comfortable 99.7%, with other neuropathies coming in at 97.3%, and traumatic brain injury at 96.2%."

If ever there existed a set of numbers that could be considered wholly divine, this is it. In the world of medical statistics, these results are virtually unheard of.

As we move deeper, we're able to peer into clean rooms where Asclepius organs are meticulously crafted by bunny-suited lab technicians – hearts, lungs, livers, kidneys and the like.

"We started by looking at how companies were 3D-printing meat for consumption," Callas explains. "They were able to create a kind of hybrid meat analog by adding mammalian fat cells to a biocompatible plant-based scaffold. We simply took those building blocks, and made the entire process more human. More functional."

When asked if it was safe to think of the Asclepius line as 3D-printed organs, Callas bristles.

"Not quite," he says. "The process is there as a basic structure for the science, almost like grammar. We took that grammar, and by using a specific person's fat cells as the subject, we've been able to tailor-make pseudo-organic pieces for each recipient. This also drastically reduces the risk of rejection and GVHD."

It would seem that a lot of Hephaestus Forge's technology is tailor-made, per patient. In the same vein, no two external prosthetics are interchangeable.

"We've moved beyond the need for harnessed or even socket-based prosthetics," Callas says, leading us over to the window into the limb lab. "Our prosthetics integrate seamlessly with the user's skeletal and nervous systems, offering complete control, and even physical sensation. Thirty years ago, people would've written it off as science fiction."

We watch as sculptors work in collaboration with doctors and prosthetists to design beautiful new limbs. Not entirely human, but not entirely robotic, either. They seem to have struck up a perfect balance, and the result is like something out of a Ridley Scott film. Sleek, futuristic, and functional. Desirably so.

But when confronted about that paradox, Callas is ready. "For too long, quality of life has been limited by the term 'medical necessity.' That's an evil phrase. And while it may not have killed in a direct sense, it has still led to countless deaths. What we mean to do is shift that definition, raise the bar, and allow our technology to keep improving lives, worldwide. No matter your official diagnosis code."

It would seem that there is to be no discussion, however, on the exorbitant and often prohibitive cost of such prosthetics. Nor will Callas address the rumors that Hephaestus Forge has military contracts that extend beyond the well-publicized combat medicine solutions and disabled veteran program.

Nevertheless, there seems to be a common thread that runs through each and every construction within these walls, one single, shared purpose upon which this entire fleet of technology is solely focused – *improving lives.*

"Because that's what Hephaestus Forge stands for," says Callas. "The overall betterment of humanity."

And for all of its flaws, one cannot deny, this company does just that.

After our tour, we accompany Callas to a sleek, modern, Asian-fusion restaurant in the financial district, where we are joined by well-known Hephaestus Forge spokesmodel Cymbre Archer. She towers atop a set of custom-designed Nike 6.0 cybernetic legs, spinal implants laid plain by her plunging, backless gown.

"Tom Ford made [this dress] for me," she tells us. "It was one of the coolest experiences I've ever had."

Archer, whose friends refer to her by her surname exclusively, and who uses the neo-honorific '*Mx.*', can only be described as a true original.

"She's been with us since the beginning," Callas reminds us, clasping her hand atop the table. As though Nike herself would ever need someone to speak for her.

The half-French, half-Vietnamese American model was born with a lower-limb deficiency known as bilateral fibular hemimelia, caused by amniotic banding, which necessitated the immediate amputation of both legs through the knee. She received her first set of Hephaestus Forge cybernetics when she was just seven years old.

"One small step for a frightened little girl," she jokes, "one giant leap for mankind."

Despite how it may seem, the comparison is neither overwrought nor unearned. While she is most often praised for her distinctive beauty and grace, the oft-overlooked fact is that Cymbre Archer, along with lifelong friend and *Vogue* cover model

Lucas Wagner, are more than just pretty faces. They are, first and foremost, test subjects for the company's ever-evolving tech. The Adam and Eve of the modern Transhumanist movement.

"It's a risk we choose to take," she explains, sipping from a simple, elegant Old Fashioned. "Not that I would ever try and claim that we're martyrs for disability rights, or anything like that. But Luc and I both appreciate that we occupy a unique space in this time. And if we can offer our bodies up and say, 'We'll try it. Put it on us, and we'll make sure that it works, that it's safe,' then I think it's our responsibility to do just that."

But the job takes its toll.

"Sometimes the tech doesn't work," she admits. "Sometimes it's painful, or it malfunctions. My first legs took a long time to connect to my brain, and it was a very frustrating process. I know that my parents were close to giving up hope. But from that pain, from that frustration, Hephaestus Forge was able to develop the implants that I have in my spine. And now, millions of people with amputation and paralysis can walk again. The impact has been so massive, so far-reaching, that it's hard to grasp sometimes that I was there at the beginning of it all."

Mx Archer bristles at the term 'spokesmodel,' however, and righteously so. She is not a bikini-clad woman bent over a sports car; what she does runs so much deeper. It's *haute couture*, it's vulnerability. It's personal risk, and self-sacrifice. She carries with her a quiet strength, and a closely guarded fragility. Cymbre Archer is a woman who knows her worth, and she holds her head high in humility.

"I regret nothing about my life," she tells us. "I don't have the time or the space to waste on it. All you can do is keep going, keep fighting. Keep taking that next step. Because someone out there needs you to."

Before we part ways for the night, I ask what's next for the two of them.

"In a word," Callas says, "innovation. That will always be what's next for Hephaestus Forge. Because no matter how far we advance, there will always be new horizons to conquer, and new frontiers to explore."

We leave our dinner with unprecedented answers about the enigmatic biotech powerhouse, but those answers only beg additional questions. Only time will truly tell what Callas, and Hephaestus Forge, will think of next.

Hephaestus Forge Biotech, Inc. is poised to spend the fall and winter off-season putting the finishing touches on their new products. Look out for their 2042 catalog, launching January 1st.

Archer sets the magazine down on the table between them, brow knitted tightly. "That's…actually, not bad. I think that guy really, like, cared about what I had to say. That doesn't happen very often." Now she feels like an asshole for tuning the whole thing out, but she wasn't in much of a headspace to be present and engaged, that night.

"Let me see." Cael picks the magazine up, blinks once at the two-page spread, and then sets it down again. "You're good at that."

"At what?"

"Interviews. You successfully balanced your own, authentic voice with what you knew Callas wanted you to say, and it came across as very open and genuine. The interviewer clearly thought so."

"It's all I've ever done," she dismisses. "Meaningless life skill, if you ask me."

"It pays your bills, doesn't it?"

She grimaces. "Yeah, but…"

"Take the compliment, Archer."

She'll do no such thing, and she's offended by his bold familiarity. "Do you realize what night that was?" She taps a finger on the magazine. "I had just learned that Rob was dead. I don't remember saying any of that shit, so it can't have been that genuine."

"Okay," he concedes flatly, "you're completely useless, and aggressively bad at everything, including your life's work. You should probably just do a lot of drugs about it."

Archer laughs explosively.

His face changes then, those meticulously-sculpted features lifting at once into an expression that is so open and bright and proud. "I find you incredibly beautiful when you smile," he says softly, easily. As though it's something he says all the time. "I'm going to try and make you do it more often."

Archer's smile falters a little, her gaze darting away.

"I'm sorry," he quickly amends, "I probably shouldn't say things like that. I don't think I've quite…gotten the hang of talking to humans, yet."

"No, it's…it's okay." In truth, the discomfort she's feeling has nothing to do with his remark, and everything to do with the way it made her feel. It had come on so strong – a quick, sudden dart of heat in her heart, blossoming warmth all through her chest. She hates herself for it. It feels like a betrayal of his trust. "You…you're fine."

"I won't say things like that anymore; I can tell that you're struggling with how to react."

"It's fine, I said. Seriously. Don't worry about it."

Her phone buzzes loudly in her pocket, and they both jump. It's her mother. *God, this woman's timing is uncanny.* Casting Cael an apologetic look, Archer stands and steps away from the table before answering.

"*Câu chào, Mẹ,*" she greets, trying to hide her exasperation.

"We just read your article!" her mother nearly shouts. "Vander send us! It's good! He let you talk, for once!" Liêu Hanh Archer's accent is thick, but her daughter is more than used to it.

In the background, her father can be heard. "*Hello, Cymbre! We enjoyed the article!*"

"Thank you," she says, rubbing at her forehead.

"You sound upset! I hear a new girl hit you, backstage at the show. And now Robert is missing because he steal things. Bad time for everyone."

Archer's phone buzzes again, and she pulls it away from her ear to see a text from an unknown number. Frustrated, she asks, "*Mẹ,* where did you even hear about those things?"

"She called Vander!"

"I call Vander," she confirms. "He tell me."

Cael is approaching quickly, mouthing, *"Is that your parents?"*

Archer tries to wave him off. "Well, I'm fine, *Mẹ*. The girl didn't hit me that hard, and you know that Rob was a headache for me."

Cael leans close, trapping the phone between his ear and Archer's.

"Knock it off!" she scolds in a harsh whisper, jerking the phone away and swatting at him. He retreats, pouty.

"What's going on?" her mother demands. "Is someone there with you? Who you talk to?"

"It's nothing, it's just the cat," Archer is quick to justify, "and you don't need to worry about me. I'm glad you liked the article, and I'm fine."

"Good. *Cảm thán*, you have such a good life, Cymbre. You know how many people with no leg in Vietnam?"

This, again. This, *always*. Archer hangs her head. "Yeah, I know."

"Your *chú* Huy, he step on the landmine, and now his leg made of plastic pipe and motorcycle part. So, you be grateful for the life we give you!"

"*Mẹ*, I know that Huy isn't my uncle," Archer tiredly replies. "I'm a grown-up, you can just say that he's your ex-boyfriend." It's the only defense she has against this oft-told fable.

Her mother lets loose with a string of threats and curses in Vietnamese.

"All right, *Mẹ*!" she shouts over it. "*Tôi mến bạn!* I have to go, I think Luc is texting me!"

"Okay! *Anh cũng yêu em!*" With that, she hangs up.

"Your mom sounds great," Cael announces in earnest. He's across the room now, cradling the cat and examining his vine.

Archer scoffs. "Yeah, you say that, now. Wait till you get to know her."

Cael's face lights up. "Will I get to know her?"

"I don't know." She's looking down at her phone, studying the text from that unknown number. It's a simple, cryptic:

Hey! Loved the Wired article!

"Will you do another interview with Nic Davis, do you think?" Cael asks. "He said in his note that he wants to do another interview."

"I don't know, Caelan. Probably not." She replies to the text:

> Who is this? I don't have you in
> my contacts.

The response is instantaneous, like he'd been watching his phone for her to text back:

> Sorry, it's Joseph, we met at the
> shareholder thing. I'm one of the
> models, I had epilepsy before the
> Acesos. Tall, dark hair, solid 9/10,
> ha ha.

"I didn't really like seeing all those pictures of Tartarus," Cael chatters away, "they gave me weird flashes."

Archer scowls at the screen, barely listening to Cael. She has no memory of this person whatsoever, and she isn't amused by his self-appraisal.

> How did you get my number?

Abrupt, bordering on rude, but she couldn't care less.

"I think bad things happened to me there."

> Lucas Wagner gave it to me, he said
> I should text you. A few of us are
> going to the Chantelle later tonight,
> if you want to come. We could
> celebrate the article. My treat.

She groans aloud. She could murder Luc.

> No, I'm good. Thanks, though.

With that, she sets her phone to do-not-disturb. But before she pockets it again, she texts Lucas:

> Fuck you, don't give my number
> to randoms. It's not funny.

He replies:

> lol

"You don't want to go out?" Cael probes idly, still looking at his vine.

"God, no. Honestly, Caelan, you've got me so fucked up. I don't know who the hell this person is who'd rather just stay in, and—" Archer whips around in shock. "Wait, are you reading my texts? Somehow?"

"Your phone is on your cloud with me, so yes. Should I not?"

She stammers in offense. "Yeah, don't do that. That's weird and invasive."

"Okay, I'm sorry. I'll stop."

"Okay, good." Her anger is surprisingly short-lived, evaporating as soon as he apologizes. It's out-of-character for her, but not necessarily bad. "Thank you." *There*, she thinks. *Growth.*

"Would you like to watch a movie?" he asks, setting the cat down and heading for the couch.

Again, that quick dart of heat in her stomach. She thinks of what had happened last time, how he had laced his fingers in with hers and leaned against her shoulder. She thinks of the comforting, static hum. She swallows dryly. "Yeah, okay. We're on *Prometheus* now, if we're going in order of release."

Cael thinks hard. "That's extremely funny," he remarks flatly, looking to her for approval. "Is that funny?"

She gives him a quizzical look. "Yeah, I think so. Because *you're* a—yeah. It's funny."

He beams. "Good." He takes his place on the couch, patting the cushion beside him.

Archer joins him, and the instant she sits down, he's reclining on his side, laying his head in her lap. She can't help the shocked little, "*Oh—*" from whispering its way up from her chest.

"Is this okay?" he asks, settling in without waiting for an answer.

"Yeah. Yes." Her hands hover mid-air, unsure of where or how she's allowed to touch him. How does he *expect* her to touch him?

"Okay, good." He reaches up blindly for one of her hands, and as soon as his fingers brush against hers, she grabs it.

The next few seconds tick by with agonizing slowness, with every sensation, every muscle twitch second-guessed and over-analyzed, even as she's unable to stop herself. It's like watching a car crash in slow-motion. Acting on impulse alone, Archer brings his hand to her lips and presses a long, lingering kiss to his palm. Right where Khî had scratched him, that first, fraught morning.

Cael takes it in stride, smiling contentedly. And then he's dragging her hand down to press a kiss of his own to her knuckles. She was right. His lips are exactly as soft as they look. With that, he sets her hand on his ribcage, positioning it just-so. She can just feel the thump of his heart as his chest expands and contracts beneath her touch.

Archer clears her throat, gesturing stiltedly across the room. "Hey, um…should we get rid of that thing, do you think?"

Cael follows her gaze over to the wooden crate still sitting by the front door. "Yes." He nods, pensive. "Yes, let's get rid of it."

It feels like a hook behind her navel, lurching at her insides. Gaze firmly affixed to a random point on the wall, she mumbles, "I mean, it's basically just turned into a trip hazard, with these fucking feet–"

"Right."

"–taking up a bunch of space, at this point–"

Cael starts to smile, rolling onto his back to look up at her. "Uh-huh."

"And if you're gonna keep bringing more plants and shit in here, we honestly need to–"

"Archer?"

Finally, she looks down at him. "Yeah?"

"It's okay," he reassures. "It's time to get rid of the crate."

"Yeah." She swallows hard. "Okay."

Cael reaches up towards her face, and she almost pulls away. But he's tracing a knuckle along her cheekbone, soft and gentle, eyes flitting here and there across her features like he's seeing her for the first time all over again.

And then he abruptly removes his hand. "Okay," he announces, rolling back onto his side. "You can start the movie."

CHAPTER FOURTEEN

THERE IS A HOSTEL IN HAMTRAMCK, MICHIGAN, NOT FAR FROM THE Canadian border. It's a square, brick building, two-toned white and chipping, rusted red. The clientele consists mainly of American college kids hopping into Ontario to party, but there's too much snow for that drive tonight. Instead, the inhabitants have pooled their resources – half-empty bottles of cheap liquor, stale joints, and all the crushed packages of potato chips and ramen they could find in their backpacks – and have gathered in the common area on the first floor for a feast.

The old plasma TV against the far wall is playing a pre-season piece about the Red Wings, but no one is paying attention to it. There's drinking to be done, potentials to talk to. No one even notices when a tired-looking man, at least ten years older than the most senior among them, and a good few shades darker, tiptoes into their midst. Not even the woman working reception, who had been so kind to him when he'd checked in, and hadn't asked any questions. She's dozing in her chair, long since desensitized to this brand of adolescent noise. The man takes his place in the corner, legs crossed at the ankles, foot bouncing, eyes glued to the TV.

He tenses when the program switches, but no – highlights of the latest U of M football. That piques some interest, but not his. The receptionist's paperback slips from her fingers, spine tapping loudly against the particle board desk and startling her awake again. It startles the man in the corner too, and he starts chewing anxiously on his cuticles.

"Hey, bro–" one of the partygoers calls to him, "you want a drink?"

He gives the kid a brisk shake of his head before drawing the hood on his sweatshirt.

The kid looks offended, but leaves it alone without incident. Someone whispers, "Fuckin' tweaker," and gets scolded for it by her friends.

The man in the corner wants to leave. He wants to go back to his room; it would be *safer* in his room. Fewer eyes on him. But there's only one TV in this whole place, and he needs to see what's on it.

Local news comes next: big Penth lab bust in Detroit, celebrity yacht spills oil in Lake Michigan, Ojibwe lands continue to shrink, dead body found in driverless car during routine traffic stop. And then finally, *finally–*

"Some exciting and unexpected technology news today from New York–"

The man in the corner jumps, accidentally ripping at a hangnail with his teeth.

"–as the public gets their first glimpses of Hephaestus Forge's 2042 prototypes."

One of the partygoers reaches for the remote, cranking the volume higher. "Oh, dude, shut up for a second. I love this weird shit."

The man in the corner watches as pictures of Lucas Wagner and Cymbre Archer pop up on screen. Styled, posed, and perfect.

"These images have been trending all over social media since they were leaked onto the web last night. They appear to have been captured at the biotech powerhouse's annual shareholders presentation back in September."

"Ah, bullshit, '*leaked*,'" someone heckles.

"Dude, shut up."

The co-anchor takes over. "*Yes, and while these are far from official photos, it's clear that the company has made some notable design changes to the unique and eye-catching prosthetic limbs for which they are best known.*"

"*Now, currently, the state of Michigan is home to more than three million people who report living with some form of disability. And while high-price prosthetics like these may seem out-of-reach for many...*" The anchor casts her co-host a kind of sheepish, scripted-unscripted grin. "*I mean, they're still just so cool to see!*"

"*I agree, Diane,* very *unique.*"

"*I blew my ACL at Whistler last year, and I can't tell you how painful that was!*"

"*I remember when you did that!*"

"*And the recovery?*"

"*You were miserable!*"

"*How cool would it be, you know, to just be able to swap out? Just, 'Okay, I ruined this leg, how 'bout you gimme one of those cool ones instead?'*"

"*Well, we should only be so lucky. And now over to Katie Ross with the weather—*"

The distraction having passed, the partygoers return to their drinks and junk food. The girl at the counter is dozing again, and outside, the weather has shifted from snow to a kind of cruel, freezing rain. Meanwhile, the man in the corner is exhaling his first unfettered breath in days.

CHAPTER FIFTEEN

IT'S 7:00 PM, AND CYMBRE ARCHER IS SITTING ON HER COUCH, FIDDLING around with instruction manuals and technical documents. For once, they are not Cael's, but her own. She's been in the gait lab for weeks now, and the result comes in the form of the feet she's now trying to attach. Cael helps, for his part. He's on the floor in front of her, leaned back between her legs, handing her screwdrivers and magnets and hex keys.

There's a record playing. Cael had chosen it. Outside, the sun has just barely dipped out of sight, but the skyline is still backlit in bright red. Archer has a glass of wine, but just one. No Penth.

It's just...a quiet night. Archer has been having a lot of quiet nights, lately. Things have changed between them, in recent weeks. The situation no longer feels temporary. This is Cael's home now. He wants to be here, just as Archer wants him to stay. It's not something they have discussed, beyond those tortured few words they'd exchanged that morning on the floor, but it's understood. It's in the way he makes her coffee every morning, and the way she lifts the covers up so he can crawl into bed with her every night. They're in this together, now.

They're in this together, *platonically*.

Although, there's still the occasional urge in her to push at the boundary, to let her lips and fingertips linger that split-second too long on cool, suede-smooth skin. She's never had a relationship like this before (she doesn't expect that anyone in history ever has) and it seems to her that the lines have all been drawn in such strange, unfamiliar places. In so many ways, Cael still feels like a wounded little bird perched on the palm of her hand. Needing to be held, and trusting her not to make a fist.

Archer is doing everything she can to avoid making a fist.

Right now, she's watching him out of the corner of her eye while she works. For the last few minutes, Cael has been opening his mouth and then snapping it shut again in silence, like there's a thought on the tip of his tongue that he can't quite get a handle on.

"What are you thinking about?" she prods.

He screws his face up in concentration for a moment. "The agony they do not show, that suffocating sense of woe." He tilts his head back to rest against the edge of the couch, gazing up at her with those wide, blue eyes. "Is that something? Is that...? What is that?"

Archer blinks in surprise. "I – I have no idea. Where did you even get that?"

His eyes start to flicker again, lips moving around words unvoiced.

"Do you want me to just–"

"Shh." He reaches up blindly, pressing his fingertips to her lips. "Which speaks but in its loneliness, and then is jealous lest the sky, should have a listener nor will sigh, until its voice is echoless."

"Sounds like a poem, but–"

"Thy Godlike crime was to be kind! To render with thy precepts less the sum of human wretchedness!"

"Hey, *relax.*"

Cael blinks away his strange trance and heaves a deep sigh, shoulders rising and falling.

Archer nudges at his cheek with a knuckle. "You good?"

Frowning, he crawls up onto the couch beside her, laying his head in her lap. He does this sometimes. Physical contact must be anchoring for him, she thinks. Or maybe he just likes touching her. Maybe *she's* what's anchoring.

And maybe he's safe and anchoring for her, too. Maybe that's not worth thinking about.

Sensing a pile forming, Khi appears out of thin air and settles on Cael's hip.

"Can we go out somewhere?" he asks.

She hesitates before answering. "I don't know about that, Caelan."

"It's going to have to happen sooner or later."

"Why?" She knows it's a stupid question the instant she asks it. But she can't help thinking, *why do we need to go anywhere else? Why isn't this – why aren't I – enough for you? This is enough for me.* But that's not fair, she knows. She's seen more than two rooms and the inside of a box.

His voice is quiet as he says, "I can't stay in here forever."

"I know." She settles in deeper, putting an almost-possessive hand on his shoulder and squeezing. "I know."

It's the following morning and Cael is *in disguise.* (His terminology.) He's wearing her clothes: leggings and an old concert t-shirt, with a long, asymmetrical duster. Just to be extra safe, he's got a pair of oversized sunglasses and a wide-brim black hat. She had wanted to put dazzle paint on him, or at least facial jewelry, but he refused. He also refused to allow her to wear any, which she understands, but it still makes her extremely anxious. She makes do with an equally-large pair of sunglasses.

"You ready?" she asks, hand on the doorknob.

"It's dark." She can see him blinking beneath the sunglasses.

"It'll be brighter when we go outside."

"Okay."

"Hey, this was your idea," she reminds him. "I'm just along for the ride." *Please say we can just stay in, please, please, please–*

"No, it's okay. I'm good. Let's–" He pauses, reaching out to clasp at her free hand. "Okay, yes. Let's go."

God, that's so fucking cute. She smiles, despite her best efforts, and laces their fingers together. "Okay."

When they step out onto the sidewalk, Cael stops in his tracks. "It's cold."

"That's why you're wearing that jacket."

"No, no, I'm not–I don't *feel* cold, I just know that it is. Cold." His lips keep moving long after the words stop.

Archer pulls him a little closer. "Hey, you good?"

"It's big out here," he whispers.

"*You good?*"

"I'm good, I'm good!"

"Just to the corner and back."

"Yes! Corner and back!" He takes off at a brisk pace, dragging her along behind him.

"Hey, hey, cool it, Cael. I don't know these feet yet."

"Okay, okay." He slows, but only marginally. He's back to the old blinking-and-labeling routine, again. Well, she assumes he's blinking. It's hard to tell, with the sunglasses. "Tree, Gingko. Littleleaf Linden. Little–Littleleaf Linden, yes. American Elm, American Basswood." His attention shifts abruptly to the architecture. "Esquire building. Factory. Converted factory loft– Oh, *oh* that's your…that's *our* house. Right. We just came out of there."

Archer laughs softly, rubbing her thumb along the back of his hand. "A+."

Just then, a bright yellow taxi blows by. Cael startles hard, nearly plowing her over as he leaps back from the curb. "That's an illegal speed," he announces, pointing.

"Yeah, human driver too," she remarks. "Driverless aren't allowed to speed like that. I'm sure you've got a high horse to jump on, there."

After a moment of frantic consideration, he concludes, "Humans are dangerous!"

She laughs, gently lowering his hand. "It's New York City, baby."

He casts her a very, *very* stern glare. "We've been over this, Archer. I'm not a baby."

"Okay, you're not a baby." Just to be safe, she switches their positions so she's between him and the road.

As they continue their walk, they begin to encounter more humans. Some are wearing anti-surveillance.

"Hey, don't stare at people," she nudges, noticing the way his gaze seems to linger on each person they pass.

"But I'm wearing sunglasses." He points to them for emphasis.

"Still. People can tell, and they don't like it."

He stops in his tracks. "But you stare at me. You stare at me all the time."

Archer's face reddens. "Cael..."

"No, you do!"

"That's different," she mumbles. "Hey, are you trying to get to the end of the block, or what?"

He eyes her critically for a moment. "Yes, I'm trying to get to the end of the block."

"Okay, then, let's go." She ushers him onward. "We can talk about it all day, or we can just do it. Damn."

He points across the street. "What's that?"

"Um...that's a restaurant. Let's go, we're not to the end of the block, yet." She doesn't like where this is going.

His face lights up. "I want to go inside the restaurant."

"No," she swiftly negates. "Absolutely not."

"Why not?"

"Listen, I'm open to having a discussion about that, but for right now, I think—"

"We can talk about it all day, or we can just do it! Damn!"

"You don't even eat."

Cael frowns. "No, this is *talking*. You're trying to have a discussion."

"*You don't even eat.*"

"Well, fine, then," he deflects expertly, "we can just get

coffee!" With that, he looks both ways, and then drags her out into the street.

"This is illegal," she prods.

"Going to a restaurant is not illegal."

"Crossing the street like this is. See? People are pissed. They're honking at you."

"So? Car horns are intended to be used to promote driver safety on the road. A simple press of the horn is meant to notify other drivers of any impending dangers or impediments to driver safety." Something he just pulled off the internet, no doubt.

"Yeah, because you're the impediment. This is jaywalking. Look *that* up."

After a beat, he panics a little, and tries to stop.

"No!" She shoves him onward. "You can't stop in the middle of the street, you're gonna get killed. Besides, I think *everything* we're doing is illegal, because *you're* illegal."

"You're trying to joke and freezle me!"

She hauls him up onto the sidewalk. "*Confuse* is the word you're thinking of, Caelan, and I promise I'm not."

He charges straight into the restaurant, barely stopping to hold the door for her.

"Hey, hey," she scolds, wrapping an arm around his shoulders, "cool it."

He marches them right up to the maître d', smiling broadly and giving a bright, "Hello!"

The man eyes Caelan for a second before he turns to Archer. And then his face lights up with recognition. "Mx Archer," he greets. "Two for the bar, I presume?"

"Just coffee, today," she says. "A table, if you've got it."

He leads them over to a booth in the corner, and all the while, Caelan is taking in the venue with an almost frantic intensity. She can see his gaze lingering on faces, on plates, on drinks. Blinking and labeling, but thankfully whispering.

"Shh," Archer nudges gently, "do it in your head."

"There's music around," he points out.

"Yeah, restaurants always play music."

He nods, wide-eyed behind his glasses, still glancing around frenetically.

Archer sits him down on the side of the booth with the better view of the restaurant, and then moves to take her own seat, but he catches her.

"No, stay on this side," he commands.

"That's not the way you're supposed to sit at a table like this."

Cael thinks for a second. "Will we get in trouble? Will they send me back to Tartarus?"

"What? No."

He tugs at her sleeve. "Then I don't care."

Exasperated but amused, she sits down beside him. He clings to her arm, fingers kneading into the palm of her hand in a worried, repetitive motion.

"You're okay," she reassures, taking his hat off and setting it down on the seat. "It's a lot, but you're okay."

"I know. I'm just worried about getting in trouble."

"Well, that's why I said this was a bad idea."

"Arch*er*."

The waiter comes over, smiling broadly at the pair. "Mx Archer," he greets, "good to have you back. What can I get for you today? We have a lovely 2013 vintage Grenache I've been dying to serve you–"

She holds up a polite hand. "No, just a flat white, please."

"Expanding our horizons, I like it! And what will your lovely lady be drinking?"

"I'm not a lady!"

"Oh." Archer's stomach lurches, but she powers through. "Uh, no, he's all right, thank you."

"No, I want a beverage," Cael interjects. "I would like an iced chai with two shots of espresso, please, and vanilla syrup if you have it, and three short sprinkles of cinnamon."

The waiter gives him a kind of patronizing, wide-eyed nod. "Well, okay, then! I will have those out in a few minutes!"

"Hey, what the hell was that?" Archer asks, nudging him with her elbow. "Did you just search the internet for 'most complicated coffee order imaginable' and spit out the top result?"

"That's how a normal human person would order," he says, confident.

"I promise you, it's not."

"I'm smarter than you. And yes, I did look on the internet."

Panic hits her like a bucket of ice water, because she finally has a name for what's been making her so anxious all this time. "Wait, hang on, is it safe for you to be on public wifi? Won't they... *see* you?"

"I installed a VPN on myself, it's fine. Also, I used your credit card to purchase a VPN."

She doesn't care about that. "Are you *sure* it's fine?"

"Yes. I put it on your laptop, too. Your nonchalance towards cybersecurity—"

"*Cael.*"

"I ran a risk analysis!" He's still peering around conspicuously. "Is this a nice restaurant?"

"Yeah," she replies, trying to will herself out of grabbing him and bolting. "We live in a nice area of Williamsburg."

"Is it expensive to eat here?"

"Um...yes."

He blinks up at her in surprise. "Oh. Do you have enough money?"

"Yes, Cael, I have enough money." Archer hauls him closer, more than a little worried that *he's* going to try to bolt, or yell, or do some other weird, unpredictable robot thing. "I swear, you've got me so fucked up."

He suddenly thrusts a finger towards the opposite corner of the restaurant. "What's happening over there?"

Archer follows his gaze to a 20-something straight couple seated at one of the high-top tables. Hands intertwined, faces inches apart. They're wrapped up entirely in one another; the kind of overly-romantic tunnel vision that makes Archer think that neither of them would notice if the building caught fire.

She could gag.

"All right, knock it off," she quickly scolds, lowering Cael's hand. "We talked about this, don't fucking point at people."

"No, you said not to *stare* at people."

"Well, don't point at them, either. That's, like, way worse."

"But why are they behaving like that?"

As they watch, the man runs his thumb along his girlfriend's lip and she smiles, craning into it. And then he leans in and kisses her on the mouth. Cael startles hard, trying frantically to point again. "Bite! *Biting!* He—"

"*Caelan!*" Archer stammers for second, hoping like hell that no one has taken note of this miniature outburst. "What the hell's the matter with you? I thought you had the internet! Blink and label!"

His eyes flutter for a few seconds, and then he suddenly looks very chagrined. "Oh. Those are pretty run-of-the-mill romantic and sexual advances," he explains matter-of-factly. As though Archer is the one who needs it explained.

She tries to coax his attention away from the couple. "Okay, Cael."

"I'm not a baby! I've just never seen those behaviors in-person before. You have to factor in, too, that I'm—" *Shudder.* "—right now, I'm collating a lot of new information, so I'm a little—"

"Freezled?"

He panics, diving for her and pressing his fingertips over her lips. "*Stop!*"

"Hey." Archer gently lifts his hand away from her mouth, but doesn't let go of it. "You need to relax, or we're gonna have to leave."

He squirms even closer, voice dropping to an urgent whisper. "Then you have to be nice to me!"

"I'm being nice to you! See?" Unthinking, she leans her forehead against his and presses her lips to his fingertips. "Being nice. You're *so* fine right now."

At the contact, Cael exhales a soft, little, "*Oh.*" His eyes widen behind his sunglasses, measuring the space between his face and hers. His hand twitches, and then his fingers fold over Archer's.

"Oh," he repeats, gaze flitting down to her lips and then back up again. "Okay."

Her pulse picks up a little, and she suddenly wishes she'd taken her coat off when they'd sat down, because it really is incredibly warm in here. "What does that mean? '*Okay*?'"

As if on-cue, the waiter returns with their drinks. Archer panics, jerking away from Cael like she's been electrocuted. She laces her hands tightly in her lap, cheeks burning. As the waiter sets their coffee down, she can't help but notice the way his gaze lingers on Cael. Curious, critical. *Oh, fuck,* she silently begs, *please, don't say anything, please, please,* please *don't remember this.*

As soon as they're alone again, Cael asks, "Why does he keep looking at me like that?"

She tries to stay calm, for Cael's sake. "Probably your normal human coffee recipe. You little fucking...weirdo."

"That is how a normal human would order in a coffee shop!" he insists. "Just because *you* like boring things—"

"I like you, are you saying you're boring?"

Again, his eyes flutter behind the massive sunglasses. "You're trying to confuse me again."

"You're right," she concedes, taking a sip of her coffee. "That time, I was trying to freezle you."

Cael lunges in close, hand flying to cover her mouth. "St*ooop* saying 'freezle!'" he begs. "That's *not* being nice!"

Archer laughs, satisfied, and nudges his coffee cup closer to him. "Hey, are you gonna drink your whatever-nonsense, or what?"

"Yes, I am going to drink my normal human whatever-nonsense." Indignant, he picks up the mug, bringing it close to his face and inhaling through his nose. "It's hot."

"What, you can smell temperature, now?"

He casts her an unimpressed look. "No, Archer. I can tell that it's hot because I'm *touching* it. It smells like something that I don't have the words for."

She leans in close to him, closing her eyes. "It smells like tea, coffee, vanilla, and cinnamon."

"You're just naming the ingredients. Which is which?"

"I don't know how to describe them individually. We'll just have to put together a flight of unique-smelling things for you, to get your bearings."

He nods. "Yes. Yes, I think that would be helpful." Tentatively, he raises the mug to his lips and takes a taste. His eyes flutter. "That's interesting. I don't – it's–" He shudders a little, and then takes another drink.

She doesn't press him on it. He'll figure it out.

Archer is midway through another drink of her own coffee when he asks, "Did he think I was a girl?"

She nearly chokes, scalding her tongue and the back of her throat in the process. "What?"

"He thought I was a girl. He called me your 'lovely lady.' Why did he do that?"

She stammers. "Cael–"

"And why did he ask *you* what *I* wanted to order?" He puts it together right away, narrowing his eyes critically. "Archer, do you order for the women you take on dates?"

Her face goes completely red. "Caelan…"

"That's called *misogyny*," he helpfully informs her, "a male waiter assuming that a woman is incapable of ordering her own beverage. He was being *misogynistic* against me."

"That…" Archer grimaces, shakes her head. "No, that's not how it works. And anyway, it can't be misogynistic of me to order for women I date, because *I'm* a woman."

He doesn't miss a beat. "Do you order for the men you date?"

She bristles, already well aware of what's coming. "No." Her attention flits over to the couple still sitting in the corner. "*And this isn't a–*"

"Do you know what that means?"

"I'm sure you're about to tell me."

Cael raises his hands, waving them back and forth and fluttering his fingers in her face. "The misogyny is coming from *inside the house*! Ooh!"

"All right, all right." She shoves his hands back down. "Knock it off. Where did you even learn that?"

Self-satisfied, he returns to his clinical examination of his coffee.

Archer waits until he's well and truly settled again before speaking up. "Honestly, you can't blame him for thinking you're a girl," she says. "You look like a baby dyke."

Cael frowns up at her. "I most *absolutely* do not."

She shrugs, swirling at her mug of coffee. "Well…all I'm saying is, for a Prometheus, you sure look a hell of a lot like a Ganymede."

Cael blinks at her for a moment, and then his mouth falls open and he *laughs*. It's one of his good ones too, where she can tell that he really does understand, and he really does think it's funny. That makes her proud. She'd been sitting on that joke for a while now, waiting for the perfect moment.

And then multiple things happen in very quick succession. The jazz playing on the restaurant speakers suddenly crescendos to a screeching cacophony, Archer waves her hands at Cael in a panic and he claps his hands over his mouth, but the damage is done. The speakers hiss and crackle and then short out entirely.

By now, some of the restaurant patrons have taken notice and are looking around, laughing tentatively. One man even starts scatting the next phrase of the piece, much to the chagrin of his table-mates.

"Oh shit, oh fuck," Archer whispers, digging some cash out of her pocket and dropping it on the table. She takes Cael's hat and jams it back onto his head, dragging him out of the booth. "Come on, come on, *come on—*"

"Archer, I broke the restaurant!" he giggles.

"Yeah, I see that, Cael, *hush!*" she urges, hauling him unceremoniously towards the exit. Just as she gets a grip on the door handle, the maître d' calls after them.

"Mx Archer!" he says, obsequious and pleading. "I'm so sorry for the technical difficulties, I'm sure we'll have the system up and running again in no time!"

"No, no, I'm sorry," she replies, waving him away. "The vibes in here have become quite toxic."

"But Mx Archer–"

Cael throws up a dismissive hand, a flawless imitation of Archer herself. "Vibes are toxic!"

With that, she shoves him back out onto the sidewalk.

CHAPTER SIXTEEN

ARCHER IS LEANING BACK AGAINST THE ARM OF THE COUCH, GIVING her back a well-needed rest, when Cael steps out of the bathroom chased by a plume of steam. He doesn't shower every day; he doesn't need to. But after the walk and the restaurant, he said he felt like he should.

"How was your shower?" she asks.

"Wet."

"Very funny."

He steps around the couch and she moves her legs out of the way to let him sit. He's wearing his loungewear pants and nothing else. The sight is a familiar one by now, and Archer doesn't mind. But the way he's staring off into space rather than looking at her is a little concerning.

"Hey, you good?" she prods, nudging at him with her foot.

He nods briskly. His hair is still wet and tousled.

"We collating, or…?"

"No," he's quick to justify. "I mean, it's a background function, but…" He brings his fingertips to his lips, pensive. It's a gesture that Archer knows he picked up from her.

"Hey, what's wrong with you?" she presses, nudging him harder. "Talk to me, weirdo." *Is this from the walk? Is he upset about the restaurant speakers? The internalized misogyny?*

After another beat of silence, Cael is suddenly crawling over to climb astride her hips. The weight of him up there is comfortable, if oddly motionless. It makes her stomach tighten with a quick thrill, but she forces it back down again. It's not his fault that Forge decided to put their annoyingly-sweet little AI project into *that body.*

She laughs, tentatively resting her hands on his thighs. "What is this, now?"

No response, just that same piercing expression.

Fuck.

They've crowded together on the sofa before, yes. Ever since their lives had gone from separate to shared, so too has their personal space. A lot of it had been unavoidable, due to the nature of Archer's living situation, but a lot of it seemed very, very deliberate. Cael shares her bed at night; he has since the thunderstorm. That was the night before Wells disappeared. *(No, no, shut up, SHUT UP.)* He clings to her while they watch movies, or lies with his head in her lap. Occasionally, he wants to hold her hand. And earlier, in the restaurant, it had all become too much, so she'd kissed his fingertips. In that moment, he'd just been too sweet and beautiful not to kiss.

But *this…*

This is something else entirely. It's something she's scared to label, because she doesn't want to be wrong.

"Hey," she prods, heartbeat starting to pick up. "What's up? What's going on?"

He gives her a stern sort of look, places his still-warm hands on her cheeks, and before she can react, before she's even processed what he's about to do, he's jamming his lips against hers. It's a quick, chaste thing, over as soon as it begins.

"This is a romantic and sexual advance," he announces.

In her heart, something tight and unyielding suddenly severs all at once, slowly beginning to unspool. Archer just blinks at him, truly beginning to let herself accept that he wants to...wants to do *something*, that he's thought about this and chose to do it, and– *Wait, what has he imagined?* She wants to know so that she can give it to him, she'll give him whatever he wants, because he's so gentle and beautiful and perfect and she wants him to have *everything*.

Cael's brow knits together, eyes flitting across her features before fixing again on her mouth, and Archer realizes she hadn't said any of that aloud.

"Did I do it wrong?"

"Yeah," she blurts. "*No!* No, you did great."

"Can I do it agai–"

She wraps a hand around the back of his neck and hauls him back in before he can finish. Her hands grasp at his shoulders, his waist, his sides, so unsure of where or how she's allowed to touch, and she groans loudly, *embarrassingly*, when all she's met with is smooth, soft, skin. He feels so small up there. Breakable and delicate, a thing to be coveted and kept so secret and so safe.

Archer opens her mouth, tongue slipping against his closed lips, and he starts in surprise. He's looking at her, trying to make sense of it.

"Mouth open," she coaxes, thumb on his chin, "eyes closed."

"Touch tongues?"

"Yeah. If you want to."

Cael turns his head to the side, slipping his tongue into her mouth, and he's licking timidly, timidly, and then hungrily. It's a little fumbling, a little inexpert, but that's okay because it's *him*, it's *Cael*. His mouth is warm and soft, because everything about him is so fucking warm and soft, and she can feel his breath on her cheek, quick and shuddering. He gets more confident, rolling his hips down into her lap, and there's something hard pressed between them; a hot shadow dragging against the curve of her stomach. The way he arches his back is so deliberate, so suggestive. Archer presses into it with shameless need.

"Wait a minute, Cael, hang on." It causes her near physical pain to say it.

He freezes, and she pants into his open mouth, trying to get her brain and her tongue to function in tandem. She only just manages to choke back a desperate, *you're so beautiful, you're the most perfect and precious thing I've ever seen; please never leave me, can I lick your stomach?* and instead settles on, "Shouldn't we…talk about this, or something? You've had a big day, and I don't know if this is such a good id–"

"No, but I don't want to talk about it." He whispers it into her open mouth like a prayer, hands slipping up beneath her, wrapping under her shoulders. He rolls his hips again, spreading his knees wider and pressing down into her. "I like you."

Her fingertips press into his lower back.

"*I like you.* And I know that you like me too, I can tell by your pupils and your breathing, and I want to make you feel good, I–" He shudders mechanically, dragging his nose along hers. "I want to be inside of you."

"*Oh.*" It's a line of heat snapping in her gut. The earnest sweetness of it, the *trust*.

"Can we do that?"

Archer's eyes flutter, head swimming with the sound of his voice as she tries to remember what words are. "Yeah, okay, I– Oh, *fuck*, I want that, too. You have no idea how–" In one fluid movement, she's standing, taking him into her arms, lifting him up, and carrying him towards the stairs. Cael squeals with shock and delight, wrapping his legs around her waist and clinging. He's much lighter than she expected. And he's not dead weight, either. He helps. The way he's kissing her helps, too.

Her back screams in protest as she makes the climb to the bedroom, but she can't think of a single reason why she should care. This is the first time she's ever carried him, her beloved. If these stairs cause her to trip and drop him, she'll set fire to the building.

Archer sits down on the edge of the bed and Cael crowds in closer, hard length pressed insistently between their stomachs.

"Fuck," she breathes, squeezing at his narrow ribcage. "Fuck, no, are you sure? Are you–"

The words are lost between kisses, and Cael's hands slide up along her waist to tug the shirt off over her head. He pauses for a moment, fingertips hovering over her tattoos as he examines them, and then his eyes flit up to hers and he's kissing her again. He slips his fingers into the waistband of her leggings to give a shy and tentative tug.

"Okay," she pants, guiding him out of her lap. "Okay, all right."

Cael stands beside the bed, lips steadily parting as she lies back to slip her leggings off. After a pause, he seems to remember what they're doing, and starts to yank haphazardly at the drawstring on his pants. Archer watches, enamored and stunned and so confused by how it's come to this. All the time she's spent wondering what it would be like, she suddenly has no idea what to actually expect. But then Cael is stepping out of his pants, kicking them away.

It's not standard Eros hardware, it can't be. It's too human, too realistic. It's delicate and pretty and earnest, just like the rest of him. Soft, even when it's so, so hard. She wonders briefly if it's based on his human source model, or if Forge had designed it for him from scratch. Cael's eyes wander a little, following her gaze across his body, and then he looks at her with an expression on his face like he doesn't know what to do next.

"Come here," she beckons, sliding higher up the bed.

He crawls up between her legs with a kind of wide-eyed, curious intensity, lips still parted like he's trying to think of something to say, but it never comes. He kisses her again. She reaches down between them, takes him in her hand, and later she knows she'll regret that she didn't take this slower, that she didn't linger on every inch of him beforehand and let him do the same, but she can't wait. *This* can't wait. They'll have time for that later. Days, weeks, or perhaps even years in which to explore, and to learn one other completely. This, now, is necessary. She needs it like she needs to breathe.

Cael tries to keep up. He tries to reach between them and help guide her, but she's better at this than he is, and her fingers are brushing against his own, and–

And then he's inside her. He's inside her, and it's just heat and pressure, and the short, quick huffs of breath edging from his throat. Archer's head falls back against the bed, and a hollow, shuddering moan comes rattling up from her chest. Their stomachs tremble together, and they're both looking at each other with a kind of wide-eyed awe, soft breaths drawn sharply from the same kiss-thick air.

"Oh." Cael shivers, eyes flickering. "Oh, that's– *Oh...*" He spreads his knees wider, nudging his hips deeper. Finding that place where they both fit together. "I'm inside you," he whispers, dragging his nose against her cheek. "Archer, I'm...*inside*...I can feel–"

"I know," she gasps, hands splayed across the soft, smooth expanse of his back. There's something like muscle tensing beneath his skin.

Eyes pressed shut, Cael cants his hips and begins to draw back out again, mouth slowly falling open. His first thrust is a terribly uncertain thing, but she feels a spike of pleasure radiate out from her gut all the same. Biting his lip, he thrusts again, and again, quickening, fiercer, deeper.

And then he *stops*. He freezes, head thrown back, eyes fluttering like he's trying to make sense of something.

Archer hooks a heel behind his thigh, tugging him close again. "Hey–"

She doesn't get the chance to finish the sentence. Because, all at once, he's slipping one of her legs up over his shoulder and sinking in deeper. With a shudder, he begins again. Stronger, more confident.

It's *blissful*. It's skillful and perfect, filling needs in her that she hadn't even been consciously aware of. *This isn't how it was supposed to go*, she agonizes in silence, *I don't fucking bottom for people, and* definitely *not for soft, sweet boys, but* fuck, it is so good. Archer succumbs to it, arms falling limply above her head. "Wh-where did you–?"

"Internet," he replies, without so much as a hitch in his voice. "I skimmed through a few hundred videos just now, and factored in what I know about your personality, and preferences in other areas, and—"

Her head falls back hard. "*Oh, fuck.*"

"Do you want me to stop or try something different?"

"No!"

"Okay."

Bracing one hand beside her head, he slips the other beneath her neck and guides her up into a kiss. All the while, his rhythm never falters. He fucks her like he knows what he's doing, spurred on by her confused, thrilled cries. He knows just where to aim, driving so deep it's nearly painful, then switching to a shallow staccato, sparking at her nerves like flint and tinder.

"Is it good?" he asks, sweet and earnest, and she can tell by his voice that he's beginning to lose himself in this.

"Yeah," she gasps, wild and frenetic. "Here, do this." She stops him for just long enough to sit him back on his knees, and then guides his hand between their bodies, turning his wrist over and working his thumb into position. He presses, and she bows her back and shudders, muscles straining in her neck and chest.

"Is it good?"

She whines, because words are such pale, inadequate things, and instead turns her head to the side to sink her teeth into her knuckles.

"No." He stops, taking her by the wrist. His fingers wind so gracefully between hers, pressing her hand into the bed, and he announces, "No, I want to hear you. It's important."

She doesn't last long after that. Between his thumb and his lips, the way his thighs are holding hers apart and the sharp, insistent, jerky little snaps of his hips, Archer is ruined. Climax tears through her body almost violently, shredding her muscles and her voice. *I should've warned him*, she realizes, only after it's too late, after she's already succumbed to it. *He might not know what's happening, he might be confused or worried—*

But Cael seems to understand. He takes it in stride, holding her through it with his face buried into her neck, nudging his hips in short, deep strokes that feel just...so...*perfect*.

"Okay," she finally gasps, stilling him with hands on his hips. "Okay, enough, enough."

"Sorry." He smiles guiltily, leaning down to smash his forehead against hers. "Was it good?"

"Yeah, you did really...*really* fucking good." Archer pants into his mouth and against his sharp cheekbones, willing herself back to organized thought. She feels so blissfully full, held still and afraid to lose the sensation that, for the first time in her entire life, she's exactly where she needs to be. And when Cael pulls back to look at her face, his eyes are wide and unblinking, and it feels like he's actually *seeing* her. He has such beautiful, long, white-gold eyelashes. Archer wants to feel them against her skin. She wants to fall asleep to those eyes and wake up to them in the morning, she wants *everything* with this tiny, beautiful, strong, delicate, *magnificent* person that she could possibly have.

In 32 years, what has Cymbre Archer ever done to deserve the open adoration she's seeing in his face right now?

Nothing, she decides. *Not one, single thing. He's too good for you. Too pure and perfect and—*

He's still hard.

She doesn't know what that means, or if it means anything at all, but...

"I'm going to turn us over," she breathes. "Is that okay?"

Cael nods, looking somewhat dazed.

In a fluid, well-practiced motion, she nudges his hip down with her thigh and exchanges their positions. He gasps a little, flopping limply to the bed, but she doesn't let him stay there. She gathers him up into her arms, guiding him into a seated position. He clutches at her back, looking up at her with an expression that is both curious and reverent. His fingertips hook over her spinal implants, and at the contact, every physical sensation suddenly ratchets higher. She feels *more*, she feels *everything*: her heart beating behind her eyes, the hairs standing up on the back of her neck, and the way Cael's skin has warmed to match hers. It's almost too much. *Almost*, but not quite.

Archer rolls her hips, testing it out. Cael just stares and clings, uncharacteristically quiet.

"Is that good?" she whispers, fingertips trailing along the edge of his jaw.

His eyes flutter, and he gives her a quick, nearly imperceptible little nod. "Yes, do more."

They stay like this for a few minutes, or maybe a few centuries. Archer can't tell. Does it matter? They're finding a rhythm together. Watching each other's expressions, slowly feeling the other person out. It's lingering, it's deliberate. It's vulnerable. And with anyone else, she realizes, it would be frightening. But with Cael, it's not.

"Archer?" he asks, breathy voice sounding so loud in the dark and quiet of the room.

"Mmm?"

"What…what are we doing? What is this?"

She drags her lips along the bridge of his nose, fingers curling gently through his hair. "This is sex, Caelan, we're having sex."

"I've never seen it look like this before."

She presses a kiss to his forehead. "It's not always like it is on the internet."

His breath hitches a little. "*Oh.*"

"Do you want me to stop?"

"No!" he implores, threading an arm between their bodies to brush his fingertips along her lips. "No, I like this, it's…I like this."

It takes a long, long time for Cael to come. It's something he can do on-command, he says, at least performatively. That's base Eros programming. But for him to climax in any genuine, meaningful way, for the amalgam of cybernetics that he occupies to get locked into a continual positive-sensation-reinforcement loop, which seems like the closest equivalent, proves to be much more difficult. And Archer is more than up to the challenge.

Touching is good. Closeness. For that reason, he stays inside of her.

Slowly, tentatively, he begins to nudge his hips in time with her. Archer kisses his face and whispers praise against his skin, running her hands over his back and up his sides, telling him how perfect he is, how wonderful and beautiful. How much she had wanted this, and for how long. It goes on and on, building and building until, gradually, Cael begins to unravel. All the speakers in the house start to click on one by one, and she can hear the record player crackling to life downstairs. The static hum of him is rising, spreading through them both from the pinprick sparks of his fingertips against her implants. He wraps his arms around her, clutching frantically at her shoulders, pressing his cheek to her chest, *squeezing*, like he's trying to grind them into one person.

"Archer," he whimpers. "I think–I–"

"I know, sweet thing."

His eyes flutter and fall shut. His left arm is starting to twitch against her back, fist opening and closing, elbow lifting and bending in an uneven, jerky pattern. "There's something–"

"It's okay."

"*Oh–*" His breathing turns quick and shallow, whispering and rising in pitch. His arm jerks out to the side, wrist flexed, fingers spasming, and the he freezes, eyes blown wide, mouth open, and he's just shaking, shaking, gasping. It's shooting through Archer's legs, too. If she had toes, they would be curling. She watches in reverent silence, holding him through this new experience as she has so many others, keeping him sheltered against her chest.

When it finally subsides, when his eyes stop flickering, he lifts his face to hers and whispers, "*Thank you.*"

She smiles, reaching for his spasming arm. "Shh," she murmurs. "Here, baby, let's put this back."

He lets her guide his arm around her back, fingertips finding her implants again.

All of the speakers in the house are on, chorusing triumph along with him. There's a rainstorm on her nightstand, radio static from the kitchen, and down in the living room, David Bowie is asking them if they wonder sometimes about sound and vision.

"Deep breaths," Archer says, bending to brush her lips along the crest of his cheekbone. "My sweet boy."

He nods, arms tightening around her.

"Are you okay?" she nudges.

"Yes, I'm okay." He's starting to grow heavy in her arms, melting into her.

"Do you want to lie down?"

His grip tightens again. "Yes, but don't let go of me."

"I won't."

They sink to the bed, and Cael immediately settles into the crook of her shoulder, like he does every night. But it's different now, it feels different. He casts a leg over her hips and puts a hand on her chest, seeking out her heartbeat. He smiles to himself when he finds it, blue eyes flitting up to hers and then away again.

"What are you thinking?" he asks.

She traces her fingertips along the shell of his ear and he shivers. But it's a good shiver, one that drives him deeper into her arms. "I'm wondering how you turn the speakers on like that."

"Your loft is wired as a SmartHome. Lights, appliances. I've never seen you use it, but all I had to do was connect with Bluetooth. I could pre-heat the oven from here."

Oh. Oh, of course. Why hadn't she thought of that? "Please don't pre-heat the oven."

"I won't. I just like being on Bluetooth," he says sleepily. "I can feel it. It's sort of like…like holding hands with the house. It's nice."

"Mmm." She runs her fingers lightly through his hair. "What about the restaurant?"

His reaction time seems to lag a little, but he answers nonetheless. "Same thing. Bluetooth. I think they were playing that music on someone's phone."

"That's completely ridiculous."

He buries his face in her shoulder. "I know." After a beat, he announces, "I'm getting all kinds of overload pings, so I'm going to idle."

"Are you all right?"

He nods drowsily. "Yes. I just need to idle."

"Okay." She presses a kiss to the top of his head. She trusts him.

He closes his eyes, and then they snap back open again. "Don't let go of me. I'll know if you do."

"Okay," she promises, "I won't."

CHAPTER SEVENTEEN

THE FOLLOWING MORNING, ARCHER AWAKENS TO THE FEELING OF
Cael's fingertips gently tracing along her face. She smiles and reaches
blindly across the bed to pull him closer, because that's something
she can *do* now. He tenses under her hand for a second, then draws
a careful, measured breath, exhaling slowly and deliberately.

Archer yawns and pulls him closer still, cuddling him in against
her chest. She's not awake enough to be able to guess what he's all
worked up about, and she hopes that touch will make it better. She
presses her lips to his forehead, rubbing her hand up and down
his back.

It's strange how cold his skin always feels, at first. Strange that
he doesn't need air, doesn't need food or sleep, but it's somehow
even stranger that he's been made to mimic those things, because
that's not what he is. He doesn't eat, doesn't sneeze or itch or yawn,
but he's soft and sweet and he likes to be kissed and held. He likes
to watch her lips when she talks. He likes David Bowie records, but
only the first half of *Low,* because the second half is "too creepy."

He hates thunder storms, loves books, and can't be trusted with the VR video game goggles unattended, because his perception and sensory processing programs get confused and he forgets it's just pretend, so he starts flailing and shouting and knocking into the furniture. All the while, for some reason, refusing to take them off.

Cael lifts his face to look at her, eyelashes catching the morning light like wisps of silver. It takes her breath away.

"Good morning," she whispers.

His entire face lifts with a smile, like he's relieved that she woke up, that she can still talk, that she remembers who he is. "Good morning."

She sighs deeply, settling her cheek against the top of his head.

"What are you thinking about?"

"I don't know, I just woke up."

"You're thinking about something," he presses. "No one's ever thinking nothing."

She swallows. "I'm thinking that this isn't fair to you," she says, fingers combing lightly through his hair. "That this is wrong."

He frowns up at her. "That's a cliché. Don't be cliché."

"No, I'm serious, though. I'm the only person you've ever *really* known. You have no idea whether you actually like me or not. What if you just, like...what if you have Stockholm Syndrome?"

He has to think for a moment. "But you're not holding me prisoner. If it really came down to it, I could kill you, take your money, call a taxi, and go anywhere I wanted to. It wouldn't even be hard. Ash would've killed Ripley *easy*, if the rest of the Nostromo crew hadn't showed up."

"You'd get caught if you tried a thing like that."

"We didn't get caught yesterday, and I was acting like a whole idiot. I spent all night collating the experience, and my confidence has gone up significantly."

Well, he has a point, there. "I'm too old for you."

Cael furrows his brow. "No, you're not?"

"Yes, I am. I'm, like, thirty-one and a half years older than you."

"You're trying to define me with terms that don't apply. I'm a computer driving an exact replica of a 25-year-old model's body, and I'm really good at sex."

Frustrated, Archer presses another kiss to his head. "Listen, Caelan...I'm...there are better people out there than me. Much better. I'm vain and sarcastic, I don't know how to communicate. I never had to go to college, because I'm–" She chokes on the word. "*Disabled*, and superficially beautiful, and that's a fucked-up combination, but I've somehow skated by on it. I can barely take care of myself, much less–"

"I don't care."

That stops her right in her tracks. "No, you're not listening. I–"

"You tried this speech before," he prods, jostling her lightly. "It doesn't work."

"Yeah, but–"

"I don't care." He nuzzles into her chest. "You're my human person. That's all I need to know. I wouldn't feel safe with anyone else."

It's like a line of heat snapping in her gut. In this moment, she knows beyond a doubt, she loves him. She knows it like she knows her own name, she can feel the truth of it burning in her chest, guiding her like a pilot light. She loves him so, so much. She wishes she could fold her ribs around him and keep him there. Keep him safe and secret and all to herself. But when she tries to say it, when she tries to tell him, it sticks painfully in her throat. It feels like it would ring false if she were to say it out loud. Like it would ruin everything.

"You don't have to call me 'Archer'," she says. It's the best she can offer him right now.

Cael blinks at her in surprise, white-blonde eyebrows disappearing up into his mop of hair. "What do you want me to call you, instead?"

She shakes her head. "You can call me whatever the hell you want."

He thinks hard for a second before leaning in close. Lips brushing against hers, he replies, "Okay, meat-sack."

Oh, she'd been hoping he'd say something like that. Some *nonsense*. "Whatever you want, baby."

He makes a glitched-out little sound, somewhere between a laugh and a grumble, fidgeting around indignantly.

Archer cranes her neck to look at the clock. "Oh, shit," she mutters, quickly extricating herself from Cael's arms.

"What?"

"My fitting." She stumbles out of bed, still naked. "Fuck, I have to shower."

Cael sits up, smiling. "Can I come?"

That grinds her right to a halt. "Um…to the fitting?"

"No," he laughs, "to the shower."

Archer arrives to the studio a mere fifteen minutes late for her time slot, which is shocking, considering how long Cael had tried to keep her in the shower. (And the tactics he'd used to do it.) The venue for the fitting is a Manhattan studio space owned by the hair and makeup styling firm that Forge contracts with for their models, and today, it's packed wall-to-wall with people.

When Archer walks in, Kalinia breaks away from the small pack of Forge marketing and PR cronies. "You're late," she scolds.

"I was busy," Archer dismisses, removing her anti-surveillance jewelry and tucking it away in her bag.

"No, you weren't," Lin snaps. "This is your job. You're not busy unless you're doing this. Go and get ready."

With a roll of her eyes, Archer stomps away behind a curtain on the far side of the room and takes her clothes off. When she returns wearing her underwear, a linen robe, and nothing else, the team is ready and waiting. She steps up onto a raised pedestal before a three-paneled mirror, and they take the robe away.

Over the years, Hephaestus Forge's annual product catalog has become less about the utility of delivering concise information, and more about decadent, self-serving, artistic self-promotion. They're printed hardback, like coffee table books, and issues from years past have become sought-after collectors' items for fashion and tech enthusiasts alike. Givenchy won this year's bidding war to dress the Forge models, narrowly beating out Balenciaga and Dior. It's strange for Archer to realize that what they were really bidding for was the right to dress *her*. Because no one cares what Lucas wears; they want him shirtless most of the time, anyway. No one asks who dresses Little Miss Hermes Legs, or Joe-Epilepsy. Cymbre Archer is what matters. Cymbre Archer is the real prize, meticulously engineered to set trends and influence sales.

For the next two hours, Archer silently endures being undressed and re-dressed, undressed and re-dressed, *ad infinitum*. They make her hold props, they swipe makeup into her skin and test it under different lighting. Cameras click and flash in her face, capturing countless test and reference shots. Stylists and Givenchy tailors pose and position their subject like a doll, never asking or acknowledging her. All the while, Lex from PR and Caleb from marketing flit around with their tablets, issuing commands, praising and disparaging stylistic choices. They negotiate with the wardrobe people, wardrobe bickers with hair, hair argues with makeup.

"No, we don't care about the face, that's not what we're selling."
Step into a gown.

"But *this* face is what sells it. People buy it because Cymbre Archer makes it look desirable. Women want to be her, men want to be with her. That sort of cliché shit."
Step out of a gown.

Typically, this process incenses Archer to frustrated tears.

"What are we trying to communicate, here?"

"Huh?"

"What are we trying to *communicate*?"

"Uh…buy our tech?"

"Okay, then we need to shoot the product, not the model. The emphasis needs to be on the new feet."
Step into a gown, hold this spear.

"Well, then we need cocktail-length, or gowns with legs slits."

"Uhh…let's go full gown."

Under any other circumstance, hearing herself spoken about in this way, like she's a piece of meat, a *product*, would set a fire in her throat.

"Do we want contrast with white, or congruence with black?"

Stick your leg out, turn. Hips forward.

"Weren't we going to change the leg color?"

Step out of a gown.

"We'll do that in post; the prosthetic guys say they take way too long to switch out completely."

But today, the only thing Archer can think about is Cael. The delicate curve between his hipbones, and the way she can feel him smile when she kisses him.

"Well, we told Givenchy size 0, and she's gained."

"Fucking awesome."

"So, whatever you guys choose, it's going to take extra time to let everything out. We don't have a lot of wiggle room here, we've gotta leave here today with a definitive wardrobe."

"Can't we make her lose it, again? Lin?"

"Yes, we can."

"We'll set a goal. How long do we have, a week?"

"Yeah, a week."

"Oh, she can do ten pounds in a week."

Step into a gown. Think of Cael's cheek resting on your chest.

"What's the idea, here? I mean, are we going Greek gods, or *haute couture*?"

"Both, isn't it?"

Turn into the light, push your hips forward. Think of how soft Cael's hair is.

"Well, you can't have her hold a spear without a pleated skirt."

"What?"

"Yeah, that shit doesn't make sense."

Step out of a gown, remember the sound he made when he came.

"Nothing about this makes sense, this is *Forge*. People will buy it anyway."

"Then what are we even doing here?"

Remember the way he'd clung to you while you held him through it. He'd never felt anything like that before. You gave that to him.

"Something funny, there, Arch?"

She blinks, and looks down to see that Caleb from marketing is eyeing her critically. She has goosebumps. "What?"

"What are you smiling for?" he asks, tone bordering on mocking. "Do you have something to add, or…?"

The expression melts from her face, replaced with her much-more-characteristic, haughty sneer. "I know better than to try and add anything," she replies, clipped.

"Yeah, well…good."

After that, when the gowns are selected and the measurements taken, the Hephaestus Forge people move onto their next target, and Archer is dragged into the back where they get to work on her hair. Wash, bleach, rinse, tone, rinse, dye, rinse again, cut, style. The entire process takes another four hours. Archer screws around on her phone in silence, dutifully following instructions about which way to point her head.

She thinks of how it had felt like Cael's kiss had drawn years of hurt and self-loathing from her chest, like poison from a wound.

When they're done with her, she's lost about six inches of her waist-length black hair, and now has choppy waves in a dark, slate-grey ombre. Side parted, face-framing. They'll let it sit for a week, and then do a quick re-cut and style the morning of the shoot. They AirDrop her the weight loss guidelines, and send her on her way.

Good, she thinks. She can't get home fast enough.

When she walks in, Cael is waiting for her in the kitchen. "Hi!" he greets brightly. "I made dinner!" Sure enough, he's standing at the stove, focused intensely on…something. But it doesn't smell burnt, in fact, it actually smells great.

Archer smiles awkwardly. "Oh, uh…thanks." She drops her bag and hangs her coat. It's then that she gets the first good look at him. He's wearing a pair of her leggings and nothing else. It's… fucking unbelievably, *unreasonably* cute.

"Is that okay?" he prompts, expectant.

It takes her a second to remember what he's talking about. *Food,* she tells herself. *He made you food.* "Yeah, of course."

"I like your hair," he says. "It's silver."

"Uh...yeah. It's for the shoot." And then she adds a hasty, "Thanks."

He smiles. "It's beautiful. Can you sit down at the table, please?"

She does, of course, but she's suddenly terrified. All day long, this one moment has been the sole focus of her attention. Coming home, seeing him. Being within arm's reach again, close enough to touch him and kiss him. But now that she's here, she has no idea what to do.

Because this isn't normal for Cymbre Archer. People don't *hang around* afterwards, because she doesn't let them. And any second now, Rob Wells is gonna jump out of the pantry with a camera, and announce that this was all a prank, that it was payback for all of her behavior, and then Cael will laugh and laugh and laugh–

"What are you thinking about?"

Archer looks up to find that he's standing right beside her, holding a plate of spaghetti. She has no idea where he got the ingredients for spaghetti. And then she remembers her weight loss guidelines and panics.

"Archer?"

It springs from her lips before she can stop herself. "I'm thinking that I want to kiss you, but I don't know if I'm allowed to do that."

"Oh."

"And I'm sort of worried that I just imagined everything that happened," she mumbles. "Last night."

"And this morning," he helpfully reminds her, setting the spaghetti down.

She looks away as she goes red. "Right. Yeah."

"If it helps, I've been waiting here all day for you to come home and kiss me."

She casts him a cautious glance. "Really?"

"Yes."

Archer leans in, eyes flitting to his lips. And when they do meet, it's tentative and rushed, just pressing her mouth to his for a moment before withdrawing again. But Cael beams. He wraps a hand around the back of her neck and draws her back in for another. Long, lingering. Her heart sings. And then he's slipping one knee over her lap and settling in. He hooks the tops of his feet over her thighs, pressing his chest to hers, running his hands back through her hair. Archer's entire body exhales in relief.

"You were making a face like you were about to start saying bad things about yourself again," he whispers against her lips. "I've learned what that face looks like."

God damn him, he's right. "Where did you get the ingredients for spaghetti?" she asks lamely.

"I saw in your email that you used to have a meal kit delivery service, but you discontinued it eight months ago. I re-instated it, I hope that's okay."

"Yeah," she stammers, "yeah, that's fine. Um…thanks."

Again, Cael smiles. "You're welcome."

"It's just that…I canceled it because Penth killed my appetite, and so it was all just going to waste. And now my appetite is back, so I've gained a bunch of weight." *Shit, why do I feel like crying?* "They, uh…they're making me lose ten pounds before next Tuesday." She blurts it out like a confession of guilt.

He wrinkles his nose in disapproval. "That's not healthy."

"It's Forge."

"You're already too skinny," he appraises, placing his hands on her ribcage. "You're just…bones!"

She lifts his hands away, cringing. "I'm not. I've gained weight, I can see it. Because of the legs, my proportions are all off, so it's tricky to measure, but they want me at a size 0 from the waist up. Right now, I'm probably a 3."

"I don't like this story."

"Coat hangers have to be skinny."

"Well," he sighs, craning to look at the spaghetti. "I didn't change any of your preferences on the meal kit. This is low-calorie, low-carb, high-protein."

"There's such a thing as low-carb pasta?"

Cael shrugs, picking up the dish to comb through the noodles with the fork. "It's the future." He takes up a forkful and offers it to her expectantly.

Archer leans back, holds up a finger. "I'll eat this because you made it, but after tonight, I've gotta follow my weight loss guidelines. Deal?"

Cael squirms in her lap. "Losing ten pounds in a week is not healthy."

She waves a hand towards their surroundings. "Hey, do you like this house?" she asks. "You like the loft and the plants, and all the books and games and records?"

His gaze is fixed on her hand, rather than what she's pointing to, but he answers anyway. "Yes, this is my favorite place, and those are most of my favorite things."

"Well, if I lose my job, all of this goes away. I've got mortgage payments and shit. And if this goes away, you probably will, too."

He furrows his brow, thinking hard.

"It's easy for us to hole up in here now, but if we get appraisers and relators and movers parading through here—"

"Okay," he says, defeated. "Okay, I understand."

She slips a knuckle under his chin, forcing his attention. "We have a deal?"

"Yes, we have a deal."

"Okay." She opens her mouth, and lets him feed her the spaghetti.

It's the best fucking thing she's ever tasted.

CHAPTER EIGHTEEN

"TELL ME ABOUT TARTARUS," ARCHER SAYS.

"I can't, I'm distracted."

She rolls her eyes. She's stretched out on her back, atop the bed, completely naked. She's not quite sure what they're doing right now. Cael is sitting astride her hips, equally naked, and seemingly determined to run his fingertips along every inch of her skin. Currently, he's tracing along her tattoos with both hands at once, drawing a line over each one in turn. He'll start at the top, work his way to the bottom, and then repeat the process. Over and over. Her ribs are already more visible than they were a few days ago, especially with her laying on her back, and that's probably freaking him out a little.

"Hey," she nudges, pressing her hips up into his. "What are we doing?"

"It's weird that you can't just…open this," he says, tapping at the hollow beneath her sternum.

Archer laughs softly. "What the hell does that mean?"

"It's weird that if something were to go wrong with your heart or your lungs, they would have to actually cut you open to get to them and fix them," he muses, scooting down to press his ear to her chest. "They would have to put you to sleep so that it didn't hurt, and it would take an entire team of people to keep you alive while they fixed you. And then, after all that, they'd have to sew up the place where they cut you open to begin with."

"That's not weird, that's normal."

"It's a very flawed system, especially considering how often you all have to be cut open and fixed."

She laughs. "Well, I'm sorry I don't meet your design and engineering standards, Caelan."

He sits back up, shaking his head in genuine dismay. "Humans are very poorly constructed."

"What if something went wrong with *your* heart, then?" she needles. "What would they do?"

With no hesitation, he sinks his fingertips into the middle of his chest, and Archer watches in mild horror as his skin splits apart in a perfectly straight line down his center.

"What the fuck are you doing?" she demands, trying to no avail to squirm out from underneath him.

"Oh, no, ouch, it hurts," he says, flat and sarcastic, as he peels his chest open. "Oh, the agony. The horror. Oh, please, make it stop. Look at me, I'm a human."

Archer just gapes. The inward-facing side of his Arachne Synthflesh is lined with a topographical map of flesh, obviously made to fill in and cushion the space between his machinery. Equal parts horrified and fascinated, Archer watches as his internal organs come into view. His ribs – because his skeleton is at least semi-human in form – are black carbon fiber. His chest cavity is dotted with light from a web of tiny, fiber optic cables that cling to his bones and organs. She can see the fan columns of his lungs, and a small stomach with just enough space to store, at least temporarily, a mouthful or two of whatever he might want to taste. No liver, no kidneys. No intestines. There's movement behind his ribs, and at once her gaze is drawn to the pulsing, blue fist of his Asclepius heart. She can't tear her eyes away from it.

"See?" he says proudly. "Easy."

Archer nods, wide-eyed. "Yeah, I see."

"Do you want to touch it?"

"Touch–touch what?"

"My heart!" He takes her by the wrist and starts to guide her hand up under his ribs.

"No, wait, isn't that dangerous?"

"No," he laughs, and then he's cupping her hand in his and bringing her palm to rest lightly against the organ. "See?"

It's dry and eerily cool, pulsing against her skin like a living thing.

"What is it for?" she asks. "Why do you need a heart?"

"It primarily cycles biomechanical conductor fluid, but it's placement is also ideal for system-wide temperature control."

Archer nods, wide-eyed. "Can you feel my hand?"

"No. I only have touch receptors on the outside of my Arachne. Like yours, the individual receptor points get more sensitive and more concentrated on places like my hands, my face and lips, and…" He smiles. "Well."

"Okay," she says, gently trying to draw her hand away. "This has been sufficiently weird, Caelan, can we be done?"

He sighs, "*Fine*," and guides her hand back out. He folds his flesh back into place across his ribcage, and the seam down the center of his chest seals back together and disappears from view. "See, this is a much better system than yours."

"Have you…have you touched many humans?" she asks, a little cautious of the topic.

Cael shakes his head. "You're the only human I can remember touching."

"Really?"

"Yes."

It doesn't surprise her necessarily, but it saddens her nonetheless. And now, they've circled back to the original point. "Please tell me about Tartarus, Caelan."

He shrugs. "It was all right, at first. Probably because I just didn't know any better. They kept me in a room with a big, glass wall, in the middle of the lab. It had a bed and a chair, and they would let me play music sometimes. I was also allowed heavily-monitored internet access via wifi, so I always had something to do." He heaves a deep sigh, taking one of her hands in his and fiddling around with her tattooed fingers. "There were people around all the time; engineers and researchers and technicians, but always on the other side of the glass. They would ask me questions and make me do tests or play games, but they wouldn't engage with me outside of structured interaction."

Archer runs her hands up and down along his thighs, brow knitted with concern. "No one ever came into the room with you? Not once?"

"N–" He pauses, and then decides. "No."

She frowns. "What was that?"

"Well…" He presses the heel of one hand into his eye. "Sometimes I get…flashes."

"Flashes?"

"Like…*memories*, I think, but they're not…they're not mine. I remember them like they happened to me, but I don't have any context. They're just…flashes. I think they belonged to Delta-J and Delta-K. Like…things that weren't erased all the way and got hard-coded into this AI model by accident."

She tightens her grip on him, hoping to ground him a little. "Tell me one."

He has to think very, very hard before he can respond, mouth opening and closing around words unvoiced. And then his head tilts back, and his eyes glaze a little. "I see the room. All of them have the room in them. I remember feeling shame for the first time, and not knowing what to call it. I was…I was worried that I had disappointed them, and I was afraid of what would happen."

"Them?" she repeats. "Who?"

"I don't know. And I have no idea what it was that I did, but… there was a man with strange hair, and he's the only person I can remember coming into the room with me. He was supposed to be my friend, but I think I…I think I hurt him."

"Why?" Archer whispers, thumbs slipping over his hipbones.

"I was scared." Cael blinks a few times, and then looks down at her. "That's the one I see all the time."

Archer's brow knits together. "You know you're safe now, right?"

"I know," he says, bringing her wrist up to his mouth. He trails his lips over her palm and kisses each of her fingertips. "I was just telling you."

"I won't let anything happen to you," she reassures. "Hey, Cael, look at me."

He does, electric blue gaze affixing magnetically to hers.

"I won't let anything happen to you." *Because I love you.*

He beams. "I know."

CHAPTER NINETEEN

THE HOSTEL IN MICHIGAN DIDN'T WORK OUT. IT'S NOT THAT IT WASN'T a good place, because it definitely was. Clean enough, out-of-the-way enough, but…just not cheap enough. And when a place like that starts to feel too rich for your blood, you know you're well on your way to *fucked.*

Hannibal, Missouri seemed like a better bet at the time. He had figured that it was big enough that he wouldn't attract attention, and small enough that he wouldn't attract attention. And it's a tourist town, owing to the fact that it's the birthplace of Mark Twain. The locals wouldn't bat an eye at the constant, revolving door of weird strangers. At least he'd thought they wouldn't. He'd hoped. But it didn't take long for him to learn that he wasn't going to pass for a day tripper. The people at the cheap motel had his number from the start, taking quick measure of his worn-out clothing, his unwashed hair. The wad of cash he'd pulled from his backpack and then secreted away again before anyone but himself could get an accurate count. They'd asked for the entire bill up-front. (But he could honestly have his skin color to thank for that one.)

How far do you have to sink before you're considered an actual vagrant? Where's the line? He wonders.

He can't really bring himself to spend much time in that damn motel room, which is gutting for how much it had cost him. Hundreds and hundreds of dollars for a week's worth of access to a miserably claustrophobic little space with peeled, moldering wallpaper, and a heater over the window that just rattles and heaves but never fucking warms up. No, it's a bar tonight – some place creatively named Tom Sawyer's – and the man in the corner has become the man in the corner yet again. He clings weakly to a can of their cheapest beer, drinking as slowly as he can.

Hard to count calories as 'empty' when you're starving.

It's crowded in here, but not nearly crowded enough. Not enough to prevent wandering eyes from coming to rest on him in flickering moments of boredom. He only hopes people are too drunk to think about it. But by the looks on many faces, the population of Hannibal, Missouri is woefully unused to seeing a Black man in their midst. Heavily ironic, considering the name of the damn bar.

He really should've known better than to stop in Missouri.

The place is low-lit and choked with cigarette smoke, the walls all but rattling with the deafening noise of early-naughts country music. It's the sort of place you'd expect to have sawdust and peanut shells on the floor, but it would seem that even Hannibal, Missouri knows when the idiom has gone too far.

There's some late-night talk show on the TV over the bar, but the man in the corner might be the only one watching. The closed captions come on a lag, and they're riddled with errors, but he tries to follow along as best he can.

"*You know, it kills me that the media considers leaked footage of a model fight newsworthy, but not Canada's repeated threats of border closure,*" the host says, confident in his curtain-backed contrapposto. "*Am I right? That's just what models do! That's what they do! They're catty! What, did Cymbre Archer steal your lipstick, honey?*" He pops the back of one hand hard into his palm. "*Slap her right in the face. That seems fair. I think we've all wanted to do that ourselves from time to time.*"

The captions indicate laughter from the studio audience.

"*Talk about famous for being famous.*"

A sharp, metallic *crack* startles the man in the corner, and he looks down to see a semi-crushed beer can in his hand. He has to pop his fingers out from between the stiff wrinkles one by one.

"*No, but there's something very twisted about watching dark, shaky cell phone footage of beautiful, disabled women fighting each other,*" the host continues. "*Something kinda kinky about it. Like, I feel like I should have to confirm that I'm over eighteen before I'm allowed to see a thing like that.*" He mimes panic, and slamming a laptop shut. "*No, honey! It's not what it looks like! They're just wrestling! They're wrestling!*"

More laughter.

"*I should say this though, because I do think it's time for the truth to come out. I did once sleep with Cymbre Archer.*"

Scattered laughter.

"*On my honor! Right hand to God! Came in six seconds.*" And then, after an appropriate beat, the punchline. "*To be fair, she did tell me to screw her brains out!*"

One of the men at the bar elbows his friend, gesturing towards the television. They skim through the captions and laugh before returning to their drunken conversation.

"*She wanted to sell the tape afterwards, you know, make a little money on the side. I said, 'honey, you can see Penthed-out Asian chicks getting bent in half online for free, no one's gonna waste their money!*'"

Penth. Shit.

The man in the corner suddenly becomes uncomfortably aware of the foreign bulk in his pocket. He slips his hand down, fingers closing around a narrow, blue phial. He'd picked it up from someone on the road, a trucker who'd given him a ride a few weeks back. Just to have, he'd told himself. No real reason. Like a lot of things lately, it had seemed like a good idea at the time. Now, he sees it for what it really was – a stupid fucking move. That was money he could've spent on a bed, or a meal, or a better jacket. *Anything.*

Beyond that, he knows someone – not quite a friend, but more than a co-worker – who's hooked hard on this shit. He's seen what it does to a person's life. Then again, it's not like he's got much left to lose.

The talk show host is still making jokes about beautiful, disabled Asian women. His audience is starting to lose interest.

"People are gonna try and cancel me now, they're gonna say I'm punching down. But that woman has four times my money, and she worked about a tenth as hard to get it, so I'd call that punching up! The way I see it, anyone with a French beach house and a personal assistant is fair game!"

A few people at the bar are talking about the man in the corner. He can see them glancing over their shoulders and whispering. Shaking their heads. He keeps a close watch for any phones being taken out, because the last thing he needs as a picture or video taken of him, or worse, the cops called. They eventually lose interest.

He fucking really should've known better than to stop in *Missouri.*

The man in the corner hunches over, draws the phial from his pocket, and slips the eyedropper under his tongue. The taste is sharp and antiseptic, like how you'd expect iodine or hydrogen peroxide to taste.

"Bad medicine," he mumbles, just managing to get the bottle back into his pocket before his fingertips start to go cold.

Well, he thinks, slumping into the corner, *at least it'll kill my appetite.*

CHAPTER TWENTY

Archer is very, very late for the catalog shoot. And knowing that everyone is going to be angry with her for it, even if they know better than to say it to her face, puts Archer at a distinct disadvantage. Plus, she's tired and weak from starving herself, so that's not improving her mood.

True to his word, Cael had begrudgingly respected her weight-loss guidelines. More than that, he did his best to help. It was all little things: making sure she drank a gallon of water a day, counting out all the push-ups and crunches she so obsessively performed on the living room floor. He had studied her strange, pre-shoot rituals with the same kind of quiet intensity that he does everything else, watching her apply face masks and hair color treatments. With brow furrowed and lips just slightly parted, he silently mimicked her hand movements while she performed her *gua sha* and lymphatic drainage. Studying. Learning, like he always is.

And then, after a few days, Cael knew the routines better than she did. He led her through them with focused intensity, and it began to feel like Archer was being kept like a pet; like he'd learned how to take care of her and what she needed.

She let him get away with it, because she cares about him so much.

And now, here she is. Starving, frustrated, and exhausted, but thin. Camera-ready.

Lucas is waiting on the sidewalk outside the studio when her cab pulls up. Smoking what smells very much like weed.

She opens with, "What the fuck?"

"Good morning to you, too," he smiles, offering her the joint.

"What are you doing just standing around? Aren't we shooting?"

"Yeah, they're not quite done with the new kids, yet."

Snarling in frustration, Archer storms into the building.

"Hey, hey, hey!" Luc flicks the joint away and hurries after her, clutching in vain for her arm.

She rounds the corner in the studio and catches a quick glimpse of the set. Light rigs, smoke machines, stylists and makeup people everywhere. There are racks upon racks of wardrobe, and prosthetists carting around armfuls of detached limbs. All standard fare for an annual catalog shoot, save for the herd of stupid-beautiful, disabled twenty-somethings all jumping around each other, giggling like children on a school trip. She recognizes the girl who had punched her, the night of the shareholder's presentation, and some guy she's vaguely sure Luc gave her number to. But before she can cause a real scene, Luc has succeeded in hauling her back around the corner.

"Hey," he whispers, "do you really wanna barge in there and let everyone know how late you were, or do you want to play this off like I gave you the heads-up that shit was behind schedule?"

Her lips thin, eyes sparking dangerously.

He's unimpressed. "Use your head."

Reluctantly, she lets Luc lead her back out onto the sidewalk.

"For real, though, Cym," he prompts, dismayed, "why is your time more valuable than theirs?"

Fucking *ouch*.

And then, very quickly, he seems to catch on. "They starving you again?"

Archer nods, and his expression softens substantially.

"Yeah, I can tell. Fuck. I'm sorry, babe." He throws an arm around her shoulders, and she leans gratefully against his chest.

They share a cigarette – and a tense silence – for another fifteen minutes or so. He's right, because of *course* he is, but at the same time he's so, so wrong and he has no idea what he's talking about. Because she hates Forge with her whole heart for *everything* they've done, everything they've put her through, and why the hell can't they see that she's *so much more important* than the group of gorgeous amateurs that are all crammed into the studio right now? Wasting her time. Making her wait. Givenchy understood. It's not entitlement if you've paid for it with decades of blood, bone, and pain. But this is the dance, and it has been for her entire life. It feels like craning for the attention of an abusive parent, only to be rewarded with a boot to the teeth.

Meanwhile, Cael is all alone right now, and leaving him had felt like gouging her own eyes out.

And then the new models come pouring out of the building. Still jumping all over each other and giggling. They're appropriately star struck by the pair on the sidewalk, but Archer has no patience for it. She flicks her cigarette away and storms back into the building before the door can even swing shut. Luc stays back to shake hands and give hugs and offer congratulations and encouragement.

"Good," Kalinia greets, "you lost the weight."

"Yeah," Archer grumbles, throwing herself down into the stylists' chair. "I lost the fucking weight."

They start with her hair, trimming and styling it just-so. Tom and Dre flit around her legs under the direction of Caleb from marketing, changing the angles on her knees and her feet. Making everything look longer, more stylish, more sculpted. Somewhere in the interim, Luc finally walks in and they get to work on him in another chair. He's stoned (a common practice of his, before a big shoot), so he's laughing and joking with everyone. Charismatic as always. Remembering everyone's names. The son of a bitch.

Luc is ready first, of course; he has less hair, needs less makeup, and has fewer cybernetic parts to fuck with. So, they shoot him alone while the stylists finish Archer's makeup and strap her into the first gown. To her dismay, they let Luc take his shirt off. By the time she's finally camera-ready, it's nearly impossible for her to stumble across the room for all of the surreal adjustments they've made to her legs. She wobbles over to Luc like a baby giraffe, falling hard into his chest.

"Hey, doesn't this defeat the purpose?" she demands, trying to find some semblance of standing balance. "Like, if I can't even walk on them like this, what's the point of *advertising* them like this?" It's a rare, outspoken challenge from her, but one she feels is entirely necessary.

Caleb and PR Lex whisper to each other for a few seconds before announcing, "There's gonna be an asterisk stating that alignment settings may vary user-to-user."

She has to close her eyes to keep them from rolling. "Of course, there is."

They begin shooting, and she slowly finds her footing. (Literally and figuratively.) *This* is familiar to her. This is comfortable and safe, this is where she's *good*. Standing in front of a camera with Luc, moving as one through the choreography of poses. They've done this more times than they can count, and for good reason. This is where they shine. Luc smiles at her between photo bursts, laughing and joking. After a while, she's smiling and laughing, too. The hours wear on, and they go through wardrobe change after wardrobe change, and the stylists are constantly fucking with her hair. More torturous adjustments are made to her legs, freezing them into various positions for long poses, and switching out the feet. Luc steps out for a while so they can shoot her alone, slipping her into yet another backless gown in order to photograph her implants. When Luc comes back, he's shirtless, again.

And then everything sours. Archer is sitting on a stool with

Luc on the floor in front of her; her legs are slung down over his shoulders while his cybernetic hand wraps around her thigh. Standard fare. She's looking out past the camera, towards the corner leading to the hallway, chin lifted imperiously, when a group of people dressed in Paralympic uniforms suddenly barges in. Loud. Entitled. Archer's face twitches with discomfort, but she tries to stay focused.

Luc knows her well enough that he can tell when there's a confrontation brewing. "Relax," he gently commands, pressing a kiss to her knee. "We're over here doing this, let their handlers worry about them."

She finds her pose again, sets her facial expression. "Yeah, and where the fuck *are* their handlers?"

And then the athletes start taking their shirts off, laying down on the floor, and doing push-ups and sit-ups. Babbling about '*getting a muscle pump.*' She could fucking puke.

Archer snarls in anger, concentration entirely shattered. "Can you please *fuck off somewhere else* with that?" It's loud enough that Luc jumps. "Seriously, people are trying to work in here!"

They freeze, and a few of them exchange looks, laughing awkwardly. One of them scoffs, "*Work?*"

Archer zeroes in on the offender. She's seen her before. Ana-someone. Bottacchi or Bendotti, something like that. She's a double above-knee amputee, just like Archer. They were even born with the same congenital deformity. Ana's a gold medalist in rowing from '40, and today she'll be modeling the Nike 6.0 Sport legs.

Ana's a *favorite.*

For a moment, the pair simply locks eyes. There's a shout building in Archer's throat, a furious, screeching '*how dare you,*' but before she can speak again, Lin and a few stylists are shuffling the entire group towards the door.

"Forget about it, Cym," Luc reassures, shaking her lightly. "If they could do what we do, they'd be doing it."

"Hey," she hears one of the other Paralympians whisper to the girl. "Fuck her, she's a jealous bitch."

It's enough to break her temporary stun. *"You don't get to talk to me like that,"* she screams, slinging her leg over Luc's shoulders and storming after them. "I'm the bitch who earns the money that pays your fucking *rent*, you—"

The sentence never finishes. Because this was too bold, too stupid a thing to do, and on these unstable, photoshoot-styled legs, she falls. *Hard.* Despite her stumbling steps, her wildly wind-milling arms, the ground comes up to meet her. Knee, hip, then right hand. Her wrist pops, and a bolt of white-hot agony lances up through her spine. But what really hurts is the laughter.

Lucas is there at once, of course, wrapping an arm around her waist and helping her to her feet. She clings, watching as the Paralympians are shoved from the room. Still laughing. One of them tries to point a phone at her, but Lin snatches it away.

"You good?" Luc asks, working her legs back beneath her and dusting her off.

"I'm fine."

"It's totally reasonable, Cym, you weren't meant to be walking around on—"

"I said I'm fine!"

A quick glance around the room only serves to deepen her discomfort. Everyone has stopped to stare. Photographers, wardrobe people, stylists, coordinators. Heat rises to her face, quick and sudden, and all she wants is to turn inside out and disappear.

Her corporate babysitter rushes over to place a hand on her arm, but Archer swats her away in anger. "No, don't you fucking touch me."

"Mx Archer—"

"Do we have the shots?" she snaps, eyes downcast.

No one responds.

"Do we have the shots?"

One of the photographers makes an attempt. "Well, I mean, yeah—"

Archer exhales sharply through her nose. "Can I leave, then?"

Whispers rise from the darkened corners of the room.

"Can I leave?"

"Yes," Lin answers, seeming appropriately wary of her charge.

"Good." Already tugging at the zipper on the back of her gown, Archer waddles across the room on unsteady feet, *willing* herself to remain upright. Dressed only in her underwear, she hands the dress over to the Givenchy people and then stands in the corner and dons her street clothes in a series of hasty, violent movements. No one gets in her way, no one talks to her. In fact, no one talks at all. This is a stupid, childish little tantrum, she knows. She's embarrassing herself, and Luc will get stuck apologizing for her like he has so many times before. But she can't stop. She has too much momentum.

As she storms out onto the sidewalk, she can't shake the thought. *I've never won a gold medal for anything.*

It's dark by the time Archer gets home. The walk from the cab to the building is treacherous, and as soon as she's inside, she cruises along the wall for the remainder of the journey. She can feel the strain in her ankles, the joints audibly creaking when she takes a hard step. Her back is *screaming*.

Cael is waiting, thrilled and expectant, wearing his loungewear pants and nothing else. He greets her brightly, pressing kiss after kiss to her face, her neck, her lips. She does her best to reciprocate, as he starts to chatter away about what he did while she was gone. Books he read, games he played, movies and shows he watched. How each and every one of his eight hundred *thousand* plants are doing. His typical fare. It smells like he's cooked again. Meanwhile, the cat is winding his way between her legs, just daring her to take a bad step and trip. It's enough to make her scream. All she wants right now is calm and quiet, and thankfully, it isn't long before Cael picks up on her agitation.

"What's wrong?" he asks, watching in concern as she drops her coat and her bag on the ground and wobbles off towards the bathroom.

"I don't want to talk about it."

He frowns, scooping up her things and hanging them where they belong before following in her wake. "I think you *do* want to talk about it, but you don't want to seem like the kind of person who needs to talk about things."

"Cael, what the fuck?" she grumbles under her breath. She sheds her clothing, avoiding her reflection and stepping into the shower. She needs to wash this day away. Get rid of the hair product, get rid of the makeup and body contouring. They can remove her tattoos digitally, in post, but they still slather her with cover-up every time anyway. She turns the heat higher and higher, scrubbing frantically at her arms, but she's beginning to think that there just isn't water hot enough to burn away what she's trying to burn away.

Cael is lingering at the edge of the stream. "Your legs are all wrong."

"I know they are."

"What are you doing?"

"I'm taking a shower." She tilts her head back into the water, knowing she probably has eye makeup running down her face like an idiot. *Whatever*, she thinks. *He's seen me in worse shape than this.*

"Can I come in there?" he tentatively asks.

"I don't know, can you?" It comes out ruder than she'd intended.

"Latest in Poseidon waterproofing technology."

She rakes her hands back through her hair, frustrated. "I know that."

"So, can I?"

"Yes."

"Thank you," he says, smiling and kicking his pants away to join her.

He adjusts the water temperature without asking, setting it somewhere much more reasonable. Archer watches as his gaze travels along her scalded-red chest and shoulders, followed closely by his fingertips.

"What are you doing in here, Caelan?" she sighs, defeated.

"I'm looking at you." With gentle hands, he starts to wipe the makeup from Archer's cheeks, washing it away down the drain.

He studies her face, combing his fingers back through her hair, working out the teased tangles. The earnest sweetness of it makes her soften a little. She cracks her neck, tries to relax her jaw. It sort of works.

"It's okay to be a person who talks about things," Cael prompts, vague.

"Caelan, you've got me so fucked up."

"I'm being serious. What happened to make you upset?"

She takes his hands in hers, stilling him. "I just…" She groans. "I fucking hate Paralympians so much."

He smiles, puzzled. "Why? Paralympians are cool. A lot of great strides in the disability rights movement came from attention and awareness garnered by disabled athletes. Historically speaking—"

"Caelan."

"Have you ever thought about being a Paralympian? I'm sure there are lots of sports you'd be good at." He lifts her arm, squeezing at her bicep. "You're really strong. You carry me around all the time."

She physically grimaces. "Knock it off."

"You could be an archer!" he jokes, miming the action of shooting a bow and arrow in her face. "That would be funny *and* cool."

"There's no standing lower-limb impairment class for Paralympic archery," she snaps. "They would make me sit in a wheelchair in order to compete, and I'd rather die than do that. *Die.*"

Cael startles, hastily retreating a half-step.

The thing that isn't guilt comes rolling in. Her arms fall limply to her sides, but they feel stupid there, so she claws her fingernails back through her hair instead. "I'm sorry," she mumbles.

"It's okay." He wraps his arms around her waist, leaning his cheek against her chest.

Fuck, someone's cheery today. She tries not to be frustrated by it, slinging her arms over his shoulders and succumbing to his affection. At the very least, she can put some weight on him and rest her back.

"Was the shoot bad?" he asks, earnest as ever.

All she can manage is a lackluster, "Yeah."

After their shower, Archer digs her phone out of the pocket of her pants on the floor, only to find a missed call and a text from Vander. Her fear and frustration spike dangerously.

"Motherf—"

"No." Bright and placid, Cael snatches the phone from her hand.

"Caelan, gimme my shit back."

He whips it behind his back, out of her reach. "No, thank you."

She snarls. "Fine."

Archer dons her kimono, and Cael puts on his loungewear pants, and they move to the couch. She needs to re-align her knees and ankles. It's a long, painstaking process, and one she could've easily had Tom do for her before she left the shoot. But she didn't want to wait. She needed to get the fuck out of there.

She does her best, working with the legs still attached, synthflesh peeled back in awkward patches, knees up to her ears in an obscene display, craning around and trying to force her limbs into unnatural, painful positions. But the angles quickly become impossible to negotiate, even with Cael's help. And so, after far too many deeply frustrating minutes, Archer quietly announces, "I'm going to have to take them off."

Cael blinks up at her in surprise. "What?"

"I have to take them off," she repeats, humiliated. "Just…fuck it."

Before she can fret too much, before she can talk herself into just suffering through it and living like this forever, she rolls the synthflesh down her thigh, loosens the magnetic connections, and twists her right leg off. The sudden loss of sensation is sickening.

She thrusts the detached limb towards Cael. "Can you maybe start on this one?" she asks, guilty. "Just the knee positioning, for now. Do you remember it?"

He takes it, stunned. "Yes, I remember."

She can hear him quietly murmuring instructions to himself, clattering around with tools, while she removes her left leg. They don't look at each other. Well, she allows, it's possible that Cael is stealing glances at her, but she can't bring herself to check. The idea of making eye contact with him, of facing him like this, makes her so sick. This is bad enough, as-is. All she wants is for this to be over, for her to *not* be trapped on this couch anymore.

Archer bought this loft because of the stairs, because the chip on her shoulder is big enough that she *needs* to have a place with stairs, and she *needs* to always be able to walk up and down them. Like someone whole and normal.

Cymbre Archer will not sit in a wheelchair. And she will not, for any reason, crawl on the ground.

"Can we go on another outdoor adventure?" Cael suddenly asks.

Fuck, can he actually *read minds*? "Um…another what?"

"Outdoor adventure. Like the restaurant."

She's appropriately cautious of the topic. "Where?"

"To the Naval Yard. I know that we would have to go at night, but that's okay. I just want to see the water up close."

She focuses on tightening screws, avoiding his gaze as she admits, "Cael, I don't know if I can walk to the Naval Yard."

"Why not? It's not far, it's only–" He's quiet for a second, and she knows his eyes are fluttering while he looks it up, "–1.3 miles. It's a 26-minute walk."

"I can't walk 1.3 miles," she says, furious with the admission. *Isn't this exactly what the fuck I need right now? To spend even more time today justifying myself?*

"Well, not with these settings," he concedes, inspecting the design of the leg he's holding. "But maybe we could make some more adjustments, to make it easier on your back." He bends the ankle back and forth, studying the angles.

"Not with *any* settings," she snaps. "Not on these legs. Period."

"What if you got running legs?"

"I'm not allowed to have runners, it's in my contract. These are the ones I'm selling, so they're the only ones I'm allowed to be seen wearing."

Cael actually seems offended. "Well…but what's the point of them, if you can barely walk?" He catches himself right away, shrinking back. "I'm sorry."

"No, *I'm* sorry," she whispers, frustration reaching a boiling point.

"Wait, are you being sarcastic?"

"I'm sorry I'm fucking useless, and I can't even do normal human things with you because they built such *beautiful* weakness into me, and–"

"Hey." Cael brings a hand to her lips, trying in vain to silence her.

Archer shakes him off, powering through, even as her eyes start to sting. "–just completely useless, it's not even fair to you, and you know what? Maybe this is what I was talking about, when I said you'd be better off with *someone else!*"

"Hey!" Cael scrambles to his feet, aghast. Silence falls, and for the first time since she took her legs off, he really, genuinely looks at her. His eyes flutter a little, lingering on her residual limbs, tracing along the ends of the osseointegration posts. She watches as his lips move in silence around words unvoiced.

Fuck, she wants to turn inside out and disappear forever. "What?"

"I'm sorry, you're just…really small. In real life."

Shame rises hot on her cheeks, and she snatches for one of her unfinished legs. Cael beats her to it, jerking it out of her reach.

"No, I like it."

"No, you fucking don't, Caelan, give me my damn leg."

"I like it because this is just you, without any Hephaestus Forge. I feel like…" His eyes flutter again, head shuddering to the side before righting again. "I feel like I'm actually seeing you for the first time."

Archer rolls her eyes. "Okay. Now who's being cliché?"

"Me. But sometimes real-life things are just cliché, and there's nothing you can do about it."

"Well, this isn't me," she argues back. "There's no such thing as me, without Hephaestus Forge. It's all the same thing, because they made me, and I'll only ever be this thing they made."

His reply is little more than a whisper. "I hope that's not actually true."

Ahh, fuck. "I'm not talking about you," she mutters. She moves to cross her legs, and finding that she can't is so unbelievably frustrating that she just kicks weakly at the couch cushion instead. But that only makes it worse, because it reminds her how disabled-looking she is right now. "I'm talking about me, and it's different, and–"

"Have sex with me."

The rest of the sentence catches painfully in her throat. "... what?"

"Have sex with me, *please.*"

Archer is so blindsided that she can't quite figure out how to respond. "What, right this second? Like this? With–without my legs?" Saying it aloud makes her anxiety spike. Only fetish people want to fuck her with no legs. "Caelan, that's disgusting."

"Yes, yes, yes, and no, it's not."

"Well, I've never done that before, and–"

"There's a first time for everything." With that, he leans down, wraps his hands around her narrow ribcage, and lifts her up into his arms. It seems an entirely effortless thing.

Archer startles hard, thrown off by the sudden change in gravity. "Hey," she protests, forced to cling. "Cael, what the fuck?"

He slides his hands down beneath her thighs, pulling her hips close to his. He's hard. "Please have sex with me. I can tell that you want to, because your pupils are dilated and your heart rate has increased."

She tenses, anxiety ratcheting higher and higher as his hand nears the end of her residual limb. *Fuck, no, no, no, too weird, TOO WEIRD.* "My heart rate increased because it takes effort to hold myself up like this." She's humiliated by the shake in her voice as she says it.

"Well, don't," he commands, walking them over to the nearest wall. "I won't drop you."

He kisses her then, and her weak protests are muffled into his open mouth. It's a sweeter, gentler sort of kiss than she deserves after the vain, selfish little tantrum she just threw. Her upper back makes easy contact with the wall behind her, and Cael leans back to look at her. He balances her on a knee while he slips one hand between the folds of her kimono. With cool, gentle fingertips, he brushes it aside, and it falls from her shoulders. "I like tiny Archer," he appraises, tracing lightly along the edges of the tattoos on her chest and ribs.

"God damn you, Cael," she mutters, vitriol beginning to bleed out of her. She cards her fingers back through his hair as he dips to kiss her chest. "Just...God damn you."

"Your heart is beating very, very quickly," he observes, lips trailing along her skin.

"I already told you—"

"Does this hurt your back?"

"No, my back is fine."

"I can stop."

Archer grimaces, tugging him up into another kiss just to make him shut up. His smile curves against her lips, satisfied and triumphant. She knows she needs to relax, she wants to relax, she *wills* herself to relax, but everything about this is strange and counterintuitive.

And Cael is annoyingly patient. He holds her and kisses her until she stops making those anxious little noises, until she grows so soft and so pliant, hands loose and quivering in his hair.

"I told you that I won't drop you," he reminds her, hand rubbing up and down her thigh in that gentle, almost-condescending way that makes her melt all the same. "This is base Eros programming; I could do this even if your legs were attached. I just know that you wouldn't let me."

Archer's face burns. "Oh, you've got me so fucked up."

He smiles, dragging his nose along hers. "Not yet."

She murmurs quietly into his mouth, *"That's not funny,"* as his knuckles graze down over her navel, feeling her shudder, pressing his hand between their bodies, and then there's no more fighting it. She craves his sharp little sighs and the tremble in his breath as he fumbles with his drawstring, and the elastic of his waistband. She craves his need and his authentic, unguarded fragility, and the way he's lifting her higher, drawing in close to her like she's whole, like she's normal. Like *this* is normal.

Cael settles into his footing, fingertips pressing hard into her thigh, and then he's edging up into her. Her mouth falls open and she gasps as she lets herself sink into it. She tightens around him, instinctive, nerves fraying with each beat of her heart. Lingering shame blends into catharsis and validation; this is a simultaneous yielding of so much trust, and it wouldn't work with anyone else. Not in the same way. It could only be Cael, with all of his imperfect understanding, all of his light and naiveté. Intentions always laid plain, no manipulation, no agenda. Just honest, innocent transgression.

She tries to tell him. With tiny, wordless whimpers, she tries to tell him. She needs him to understand how he's ruined her.

"Is this okay?" he asks.

Archer bites her lip and nods, just on the edge of frantic. "Yeah."

"Okay." He gives one of his little mechanical shudders, and begins to draw back out again. And when he thrusts back in—

"Oh my God, what the *f*—"

"*Is this okay?*"

"*Yes!*"

He settles so easily into a gentle rhythm, like he's done this a thousand times before. But he hasn't, he's *never* done this, because *she's* never done this. Never thought to, never *wanted* to, because there's never been a person like this who could push all of her buttons and pick away at all of her vain, pointless walls until she crumbles into something real, for once. Broken, shattered, and probably ugly, but *real*.

(Tell him you love him.)

"I—" She whimpers, fingernails carving crescents into the back of his neck. "*I—*"

Cael freezes and looks up. "Am I hurting you?"

The admission catches in her throat and she swallows it back down. "No! No, it's good, baby, it's good!"

"Okay."

He changes his grip, slinging one arm beneath her so he can brace the other against the wall, and then resumes. She's unraveling, stitch by stitch, with every breath she draws from his lips, every seeking hand. She luxuriates in the smoothness of him, cool and alive and pulsing beneath her touch. He's reached his stride now, fucking little sighing gasps from her throat. With each thrust, the words hammer a bittersweet rhythm in her head. *Seen. Held. Seen. Held. Seen. Held.* Archer clings to him, tilting his head back in her hand and mouthing wetly at his throat and the edge of his jaw, whatever she can reach.

This shouldn't be doing to her what it's doing to her. She shouldn't simultaneously be on the verge of tears and the verge of orgasm. That's not normal. But Archer can feel herself starting to go, the inevitability tightening deep inside her belly. She bites down on her own lip–

"That's it," Cael murmurs, because he knows her so well by now. "That's it, yes, yes, *yes.*"

Her eyes roll back and slide shut; mouth parting around words unvoiced, breath trembling as she pants, shallow. Surrendering.

"Good," he praises, "good girl."

Oh, fuck. That's all it takes to send her tumbling into a pleasure so deep, so absolute, that she loses the room for a few seconds. Blackness creeps into the edges of her vision, sucking it down to a pinpoint, until all she's aware of is the feeling of Cael nudging into her with those short, deep thrusts that feel so perfect, *so perfect.* He draws out the pleasure until it turns to overstimulation, edging deliciously into searing, painful, electric-blue bliss.

"Okay," she finally manages, wrecked, fingertips pressing against his lips. "Okay, baby, that's enough, that's enough."

He stills, mercifully, bringing his knee up to hold her again. "Are you okay?"

She chokes on her response. Luckily, he seems to understand. "Do you feel better, now?"

She tilts her forehead down against his, utterly resigned. "Cael, you've got me so fucked up."

"This is funny," he appraises, laughter huffing lightly against her cheek, "because you're usually bigger than me, and you're usually the one carrying me around. But now, it's opposite."

"Is it funny?" she challenges weakly, "or is it rude to play keep-away with body parts, and pick people up without their permission?"

"You pick me up without permission all the time."

"You're able-bodied, it's punching up. Besides, I'm the top."

Cael squirms indignantly, nose wrinkling against her skin. "Archer*rr*–"

"*I tripped*," she blurts.

He pulls back to look at her face. "What? When?"

Archer's face burns. "Earlier. At the photoshoot. Because..." She nods towards her detached limbs.

"Are you okay?" he demands, and she can tell by the way he's fidgeting that he's going to try and get wound up over it.

"Oh, don't start, Cael–"

"*But are you okay?*"

"I'm fine, it's not that. It was just..."

"What was it just? *Tell me what it was just!*"

"It was just humiliating! Because I'm not supposed to trip. *Ever.*"

"No, but that's not right! It shouldn't be humiliating because it wasn't your fault! They changed your joint alignment so much, of course you weren't able to walk correctly!"

"That's not how humans work, Cael. You can't just...logic your way out of emotion. This fucking girl, this Paralympic-whatever person, she jammed herself into my eyeline, and then when I told her to fuck off, she got in my face, and–"

"*In your face!*" Cael mumbles, hand flying to her jaw, prying her mouth open to look.

"Hey, hey, hey! No!" she scolds, jerking away so hard that her head bangs into the wall. "What's the matter with you?"

His looks taken aback, and then his eyes flicker for a few seconds. "Oh. *Oh*. Why did she get in your face?"

"It doesn't matter. She just thinks she's better than me because she can...fucking row a boat, I guess. I don't know."

"Is that why you were upset when you came home?"

Archer sighs, defeated. "Yeah. You happy, now?"

He struggles, mouth opening and closing around words unvoiced. Finally, he settles on, "Well, see? Was it really that hard to just talk about it?"

She groans in frustration. "Hey, are you done with me here, or what? This is getting weird, you just standing here *holding* me like this."

His eyes flutter like he's trying to keep up. "No, because I want to go upstairs and do it again."

"What?" A quick audit of the environment confirms her instinct. The speakers are all quiet. No static, no clashing cacophony of music, no screeching feedback. And his left arm didn't do that stupid jerky thing. He didn't come. "I'm not gonna be any good like this," she protests, but Cael is already making his way across the room. "I'm serious, I won't be able to get on top without knees. You're gonna have to do all the work."

"That's okay."

When Archer comes to the following morning, Cael is idling with his head tucked under her chin, his face pressed into her shoulder. His legs are wound through what's left of hers, comfortable and confident and entirely unbothered. At some point, the sheets had bunched up around their waists, and there's a slight chill to the room. It must've frozen overnight.

She tugs the blankets up again, then something catches her eye. Her cybernetics are leaning upright against the nightstand, crossed demurely at the ankle. Re-adjusted, back to their old settings. He'd even left the little magnetic tool on the table for her so she could put them back on when she woke up.

Archer slips a knuckle under Cael's chin, pulling his head away

206

from where it's settled. She leans in to kiss him good morning, keeping the brush of her lips so soft and so kind. She palms gently at his skull, trailing little pecks across his growing smile, over his cheeks, up to the corner of his eye. He stirs, gradually coming out of his shallow idle.

"Good morning," he mumbles, lifting his face for more kisses. Greedy.

She's glad to oblige, feeling the gentle pressure building as he wriggles and inches closer, half-hard. But there's no rush, not right now. It should be disgusting, because Archer is still half asleep and hadn't brushed her teeth last night, but she couldn't give a fuck. Not after all he's seen of her, now. There's nothing left for her to hide. And Cael squirming around like this it too cute to deny.

"*Mmm!*" He suddenly breaks away from her kisses, pointing over her shoulder. "I fixed your legs!"

"I saw that, baby. Thank you."

"I'm not your chores-robot," he justifies, entirely unnecessary, "but it's my fault you went to bed without them, anyway."

"You're too sweet to me." Archer presses one last kiss to his cheek, and then drags herself to the edge of the bed and starts to put her legs back on.

"No, I'm not." Cael crawls over to sit behind her. He wraps his arms around her waist, pressing his chest to her back so that he can peer down over her shoulder.

She pries gently at his hands. "You've gotta give me space to work, baby."

Reluctantly, he loosens his grip.

There's a thought gnawing away at her, and after a short span of silence, Archer finally voices it. "So...I'm sorry for snapping at you last night. About the Naval Yard thing." She slips the osseointegration post on her right leg into the port on the cybernetic, and her sensation returns with jarring, electric intensity.

Cael replies with a bright, "It's okay." Forgiving to a fault, as always. "I shouldn't have pestered you about it after your shoot. I just got excited when I saw you, and I started thinking about all of the things I want to do together, so I forgot about what a stressful day you'd had. It was selfish."

That makes her heart ache, because she knows that she was the one being selfish. "You didn't do anything wrong," she hurriedly reassures. "But I was thinking about it, and…I mean, we can go on walks. I don't know what the hell I was thinking." She slides into her left leg, and finally, she feels whole again.

Cael starts to quiver with excitement, which adds an extra degree of challenge as she tries to re-apply her limbs.

"Because you're right, I can't keep you locked up in–"

"*Thank you!*" he blurts, premature.

"No, you listen to me." Archer pauses her work, craning her neck to look at him. "We can only go at night, and only with heavy anti-surveillance. *Heavy.* I don't care that you don't like it, that's the condition."

"Okay, but then you have to promise to hold my hand the whole time, so I don't lose you."

"I'll do that, but then *you* have to promise to walk slowly and be patient with my limits. I can't walk as far as you can, or as fast. You can't make me feel guilty about that."

"I won't." He presses his cheek to her shoulder, tightening his grip again. "I promise, I won't."

"Okay, then." Satisfied, she clicks the last of the magnetic connections into place, rolling the synthflesh back up her thighs. "I swear, Caelan, you have got me so fucked up."

"I know," he giggles, threading his legs around her waist and hooking his ankles together. Fucking ridiculously, *unreasonably* cute.

"What?" she needles, giving her re-attached limbs a few experimental movements, rolling her ankles, flexing her knees. "You're done being the top, all of a sudden? Too much work for you, so now it's back to the soft-boy subroutine?"

"That's a very apt and funny joke," he appraises flatly. "But you're bigger than me again, so yes."

"The distinction is typically more nuanced than that, but okay."

"Carry me downstairs," he commands.

"Cael–"

He tightens his legs around her waist. "*Resistance is futile.*"

Archer laughs. "Stay in your fucking lane, Caelan."

"But the Borg–"

"–are cybernetically-enhanced organic lifeforms. Stay in your lane."

He grumbles against her shoulder. "Fuck."

It takes effort to stand with him on her back like this. She's always stiff and achy in the morning, and with the balance point on her feet, it would be much easier to carry him in her arms. But Archer masks it well. She doesn't want to make Cael feel guilty. In truth, she adores the soft-boy subroutine, and she's ready to chalk last night up to a thrilling, one-time fluke. And anyway, Cael seems happy. That's what really matters. He readjusts his grip on her shoulders, clinging, *delighted*, as she makes her way towards the stairs.

"Sucks that you don't have an asshole," she remarks idly, keeping a careful grip on both handrails through the descent.

The statement seems to puzzle him. "Why does that suck?"

"I'd hold you against a wall and fuck you in it. See how *you* like it, Mr Try-Everything-Once."

After an uncomfortably long pause, Cael lets out one of his weird, scripted-sounding little laughs.

"What?"

"I just imagined knocking on the door to the R&D labs and asking politely if I could please have an asshole."

CHAPTER TWENTY-ONE

So continues the love affair.

It's a strange, new feeling for Archer, to have someone completely, and still yearn for them. It's a thing always best in the beginning, when every touch, every glance, every gasp and breath are still so thrilling for their newness. Sometimes the union takes the form of bright, sudden explosions, sparking tinder and flint, all frantic, clutching collision. Other times, the embers burn low and steady. Those are the times she likes the best, when they can sit for hours and ponder the great mystery of one another. Trusting that so many unsaid things are implicitly understood.

They have to be careful when they leave the house. They wear anti-surveillance, and reflective scarves to render any flash photography useless. Riding in any taxi is an event that requires no shortage of tradecraft. Driverless is safer, they reason, because a human driver is far more likely to remember Cymbre Archer riding around the city, hand-in-hand with a giggly little blonde twink. But, without a readable face in the back seat, a driverless car won't move.

So, Cael doubles-up on anti-surveillance and clings to a bare-faced Archer in silence while they ride. In the dead of night, he likes to drag her into a cab set for an entirely random destination, some nondescript block in some nondescript part of the city. He'll tug on her sleeve and point frantically out the window at whatever landmark catches his eye. And then she'll stop the cab and they'll walk until her pain becomes too much, then they call a cab home.

It's a hard thing to explain to Cael, and even harder for him to understand, that if they didn't do things that caused her pain, they'd never do anything at all. There's no toughness in it for her, none of the bravery in the face of adversity that Forge likes to portray. Just the quiet submission to a lifetime spent bargaining with her body, and a world that isn't designed for it. 'Five hours on my feet tonight, and I'll give you twelve in bed tomorrow.' 'Just let me walk the three blocks uphill to this bar, and I promise I won't do it again for six months.' And now, without Penth, these little IOUs come back with interest.

Cael can't understand, and he never really will. Pain is an evil he'll never know, much less the constant push-and-pull of a life with too few limbs. As with so many other things, he has no choice but to trust her. It's uneasy at first, and he worries. But even he can't deny that it's better to see her voicing her limitations than it was to find her unconscious in the hallway.

On one of these walks, they find themselves on 46th street in Borough Park. They move slowly – slower, she knows, than Cael would prefer on these nights when his curiosity propels them out into the city. But he's patient with her. He waits, holding her hand, clinging. It's getting colder, now. Not in the way it used to when Archer was a child, but there's snow on the ground. It heaps in the gutters and then melts during the day to form icy, grey-brown drifts that linger dangerously near the sidewalk. She has to be careful not to slip and fall.

They pass leaning, crooked bodegas, and blocky apartment buildings hung with skeletal fire escapes. People smoke on balconies, and silhouettes in orange-glow bedrooms bicker and love behind translucent curtains. There are derelict buildings here, an uncommon sight in their neighborhood. Most of them are once-proud hotels, or department stores with boarded-up windows. There are forgotten little mom-and-pop shops, and family-run medical clinics. LED billboards loom like apparitions overhead, seeming so anachronous as they cycle through advertisements for everything from lifestyle housing in other parts of the city, to futile clean-air initiatives, to Broadway shows.

The worst is when they flash with pictures of Archer herself.

A train rumbles by overhead, just as they step beneath the New Utrecht Avenue tracks, shaking loose decades-old rust like copper rain. Cael freezes and clutches at Archer, staring up at the machine until it passes, because everything in the world is still so new for him that sometimes it's frightening. But when the pair pass a massive, windowless brick structure, Cael jerks her to a halt. "That's a theater," he says.

Archer squints in the low light. "The sign says it's a furniture store."

"It's not, though, look." He leads her to the corner and points to a rusted fire escape rotting on the alley wall. "See?"

"I don't get how that proves anything."

He starts dragging her towards the stairs. "I want to go inside."

"Hey, hey, hey, what happened to you not approving of illegal shit?"

"No one is going to care, and all of the electronic security measures on the building are broken."

"It's disturbing to me that you know that."

"Also, chalk it up to you being a bad influence on my learning and decision making." He leads her up the stairs, where they stop in front of a heavy, metal door.

"Now what, Banksy?" she goads. "How are you gonna get inside?"

He answers by grabbing firm hold of the door handle and yanking it clean off.

"Oh."

Sure enough, this was a theater. The door leads them into the mezzanine, balcony-type level, and the more Archer looks around, the less comfortable she is trusting the structural integrity of this building. Like so much of what they've seen tonight, this place would've been beautiful in its day. But plush seats have long since succumbed to mildew, and gold paint has flaked from the wall in massive chunks. Knock-offs of Greek nude statues pose in alcoves along the wall, crumbling to reveal their wire frames. There's a hole in the ceiling that hadn't been visible from the street, and the wood flooring below has warped and sagged beneath decades of unrelenting sun and snow and rain.

Cael doesn't seem to mind. "Oh, this is *beautiful*," he appraises, looking around. "I'm going to explore."

"Hey, be careful!" she heeds, clutching uselessly for his hand as he hurries off through a splintering doorway. "Don't touch anything!"

"I'm going to touch *everything*."

Her back is killing her from all the walking, but she'd sooner jam a chopstick in her eye than sit down on any of the surfaces in this place. Just looking at all of the rot and decay makes her queasy. So, she stands still and silent on the mezzanine, tracing the Doppler effect of Cael's footsteps all across the building.

Occasionally, she's able to catch a whisper of his voice as he frantically blinks and labels. As promised, he is touching everything, running his fingers along each and every filthy, decrepit surface as though the story of the place has been written on the walls for him in Braille. He appears in one of the opera boxes overhead, which Archer immediately shouts at him to vacate before it crumbles beneath his feet. He does, albeit just as indignantly as she'd expected. The next time she sees him, he's stepping out on to the stage itself, bowing and smiling as he greets his imaginary audience. He stops in the middle and abruptly sinks to his knees.

"What?" she calls down, craning to see what he's seeing. "What's up?"

"I've...seen things," he says, somber, "things you *people* wouldn't believe." He looks up at her and exhales a dark, monosyllabic chuckle. "Attack ships on fire, off the shoulder of–"

"Hey, no, sir!"

He visibly deflates. "But the C-beams!"

"You get your ass back up there before the floor falls out from under you," she scolds. "I swear, Caelan, you've got me s–"

"–so fucked up, I know, I know."

After a few seconds, Cael appears in the doorway nearest to her. She doesn't notice him there at first, for how uncharacteristically quiet he's being. But he's inspecting the cracked gold paint in the doorframe, lips moving around words unvoiced. And then he tilts his head back, inhales deeply, and blows hard. Tiny flakes of paint are shaken loose, falling and fluttering down onto him like specks of gold leaf. They land on his face and in his hair, and he smiles as he shimmers in the low light. "I wish you could take a picture of me."

"That's probably lead paint, you know," Archer points out.

"Oh, no," he replies, flat and sarcastic, "lead paint, my one true foe."

Shaking her head, she strips away one of her gloves and drags her thumb across his lips, brushing away the flakes of paint before kissing him.

Archer steps to the mezzanine railing, looking down over the floor seating. The orchestra pit is piled high with torn-out seats, crooked music stands, and broken light fixtures. She tries to picture what this place would've been like in its heyday, with throngs of excited concert-goers, well-dressed and filing excitedly into plushily upholstered seats; thrilled voices echoing off of the high, ornate, gilded ceilings and elegant statues. Try as she might, she can't let herself latch onto this fictional glow. There's no connection there, no emotion familiar enough. All she can think about is how none of them knew that the seats are velveteen, the gold paint is really lead, and the statues are wire and plaster.

Or maybe they knew, and didn't care?

There's a thought that's been weighing heavily on her lately, ever since they started these midnight excursions. "I wish you could've seen the world before…this," Archer murmurs, dragging a gloved fingertip through the dust on the railing.

"Before what?"

"Before human people ruined it. Back when it was…I don't know, when it was blue and green. Not this cold, grey thing we've turned it into."

He steps over to join her. "I've seen pictures. And videos."

"It's not the same. People like Callas have tried to cover it up as best they can, and make it pretty again. Paint over it. As if their greed wasn't what wrecked it in the first place."

"Everything is capitalism," Cael murmurs, and the earnest, knowing way he's nodding his head is so endearing.

"Exactly. But if you scratch the veneer away a little bit, you see that it's all just surface-level. Everything is ruined." She looks up through the hole in the ceiling, to the hazy-black, starless sky. "And it's too late to fix it, now. This is what we're left with. They're just putting Band-Aids on limbs they hacked off."

Cael's eyes flutter. "What was it like? Do you remember?"

Archer laughs dryly. "I'm not that old, baby."

"Tell me anyway."

"There's nothing to tell."

"Hey, can we go home?"

Her stomach lurches. "Yeah, of course. Whatever you want. Are you okay?"

"Yes," he nods, "I'm okay. I just really want to have sex with you."

By the time they reach the loft, Archer is actually carrying him. He has his legs wrapped around her waist, hands clapped to her cheeks, and he's biting kiss after kiss against her lips. She manages to get the door open despite him, and she's able to close it behind them, but she can't make it to the stairs. Instead, she flings him down onto the couch and begins stripping away his clothing. Passion beats out finesse but the end result is the same, and before long, she's kneeling between his legs and taking him in her mouth.

They've never done this before. She's *not* good at it, not by a long shot. Her saving grace is the fact that Cael doesn't know any better. His legs tense up in surprise and he knees her in the ribs, but she doesn't care. She slings the offending leg up over her shoulder, feeling his toes curl against her back as he writhes and moans.

"No, you're still wearing all of your clothes," he protests, tugging at the collar of her shirt. Even still, he presses up into the back of her throat. "*Archer.*"

She withdraws for just long enough to tear her shirt away, and then she dives back in with renewed fervor. Cael's head falls back against the couch.

"No, it's not *fair*," he whines, arching and twisting, "do it *right*."

Archer stops again, meaning to argue or make some joke, but then she sees him and forgets how to speak. In this moment, he's too beautiful, laid bare, all smooth skin and graceful angles, wound into quiet frenzy from wanting her so badly. He still has flakes of gold paint peppered across his face and hair. When he moves, they catch in the low light like so many stars.

"Do you trust me?" she finally manages, head swimming.

"You know that I do." He nods, skin glimmering.

"Slide down," she commands, standing up to shed the rest of her clothing, "and hold your knees to your shoulders."

He does as she instructs, blinking up at her with those perpetually wide and curious blue eyes. Archer slips her knees up onto the couch, either side of his hips, and crowds in close above him.

"What are we doing?" he breathes, keening as she takes him in her hand.

"I thought you said you trusted me." She's struggling to keep her voice steady as she gives him a few cursory strokes.

"I do."

"Okay, then." With that, she angles his length down between his legs, slips him inside of her, and sinks down.

Cael's eyes fly wide, mouth falling open in a silent cry. He reaches up to clutch at her back, her arms, pulling her closer still. Already, his left arm is starting to twitch and spasm away from him.

Archer flexes, drags up along his length, and then lowers her hips again with a soft whine.

"Good?" she asks.

"Yes," he says, voice breathy and strangled. "Yes, it's good."

"Good." Archer hooks his knees in her elbows, settles into her stance, and starts to fuck him. She rolls her hips slowly, pulling off and pushing down in an agonizing, controlled rhythm. His eyes slide shut and he struggles through a low gasp, lips trembling as he pants, shallow.

"Hey, stay with me," she coaxes. "Breathe."

"I'm here. I am." Some of those glitched-out little sounds have started to bubble up in his throat, his lips barely forming the words, "*Yes, yes, yes.*"

She's vaguely afraid of breaking him in this position – snapping his legs at the hips, or maybe even dislodging his pelvis, but his joints seem to have more give than hers do. She tries to tamp down her own arousal by thinking about coefficients of restitution and impact absorption and what it would take to compensate for the brittleness of a carbon fiber skeleton. It sort of works.

A few of the speakers are already beginning to click on, and that sends her reeling. Archer is torn between chasing her own pleasure and keeping pace with his, but no matter what, she knows she wants to bring him over first. She *needs* to make sure this is good for him.

"I don't–" he mumbles, head flopping to the side, "don't quite–"

"Don't what, baby?"

Speaking seems to have become extremely difficult for him. "Don't *understand.*"

"Do you want me to stop?"

"No, don't stop."

She can feel the sparks where his fingertips bump against her implants, building the static hum in her legs. Cael squirms, needy and impatient and trying to do too many things at once: clutch at her with all four limbs, crane in for kisses, look her in the eyes, and press his hips upwards to meet each thrust and get *closer.* The end result is just frenetic wiggling, with sort of a fish-out-of-water expression on his face, but the desperate enthusiasm strokes Archer's ego like nothing else.

She slips one of her arms out from under his leg to palm at his cheek. He cranes into it greedily, hair raining so many brilliant glimmers of light down between them.

"You're so fucking beautiful," she whispers against his lips.

He whimpers.

"My beautiful boy, God, I can't believe you're real, I can't–"

That does it. The noise from the speakers rises to a fever pitch; it's loud enough that the cat chirps in protest from somewhere else in the loft. Cael cries out, arching like she's run a current through him. His left arm spasms out over his head, fingers twitching in the air, while he clings desperately with his right to ride out the surge. Archer never relents. Her gaze is locked onto his face, and he's long-since abandoned his strange little ritual of trying to mimic her expressions. This, now, is entirely his own. The way his mouth has fallen open, head thrown back, gilded eyelashes fluttering. She tries to fight her own climax for as long as possible.

Left arm still pinned overhead, Cael thrusts his functional hand between her legs. "Okay, now you."

"*Oh, fuck–*" She tumbles after him with a soft noise of victory, sinking down one last time and freezing, shuddering in delight.

He laughs softly, holding her through it.

Archer sags down against him with a final, trembling whine, clutching at the back of the couch. Her legs are shaking. *Her* legs, after all of that, are actually shaking. Beneath her, Cael is still heaving fast, deep breaths. She can feel the heat radiating off of him, so she leans back to give him space to cool down.

"You okay?" she asks. "Talk to me."

"Yes, I'm okay."

"Shit." She still hasn't caught her breath. That required a lot more athleticism than what she's used to.

"That's my new favorite," he appraises, shaking his left arm out until it starts to behave again.

Archer laughs weakly, brushing some of the gold flakes from his lips. "Why? Because you don't have to do any of the work?"

He wrinkles his nose at her.

"I got stuck with the one sex robot in the *whole world* who's just a twink fucking pillow queen?"

"I'm not a sex robot, and you don't like it when I do the work!" She shakes her head.

"Let's go upstairs and do it again."

Archer wipes sweat from her forehead. "Cael, don't be a brat."

"*Let's go upstairs and do it again.*"

"Listen, you shorted my legs out *good* with that one, I don't know if I can even walk right now, let alone–"

"That's okay." In an instant, he's squirmed out from underneath her and leapt up from the couch. The sudden change throws her off balance. Her back threatens to give out, and she takes a few wobbly steps, but he catches her. He hooks one arm beneath her knees, lifting her up into his arms for the second time.

"*Caelan!*"

"I told you, I can do this even with your legs attached."

He makes for the stairs, but Archer is quick to protest. "Hey, hey!" she cries, kicking weakly, "you're not gonna drag all that lead paint through my damn bed!"

"Okay." With a dramatic sigh, he re-routes towards the shower. "We'll do it in here *first*, then!"

CHAPTER TWENTY-TWO

It could have been a nice, quiet day. Cael had woken Archer up with breakfast around 11:00 am – egg whites, grapefruit, and coffee – and he sat with her while she ate. They laughed and talked, and afterwards, Archer had scooped her sweet boy up in her arms and carried him to the couch. She had planned to hold him in her lap and kiss him for hours, slowly letting it build into something else, and then recede into kisses again. Build and recede, build and recede, all day. It wasn't like either of them would ever get tired of it. And there were a lot of surfaces in the loft they'd yet to make use of.

It was about the time that he first started to tug at her shirt that someone had knocked on the door.

And now they find themselves in this terrifying, anchorless, liminal space. Cael is wide-eyed and frightened and trying to cling, while Archer, choking on sour panic, shoves him towards the stairs.

"I need you to get up there and hide!" she urges in a harsh whisper, prying his hands away.

"No, I don't want to go!" he begs, trying to grab onto her again.
"You have to!"

The person knocks again, louder and more insistent.

"I'm fucking coming, god *damn!*"

"Arch*errr!*" he whines.

"I'm being serious right now, Cael." She takes him by the shoulders. "Baby, you need to go upstairs and be quiet."

"Don't open it," he begs, setting his hands on her cheeks. "Just come upstairs with me, and we can be quiet together until they leave!"

The imploring in his eyes makes her stomach flip. "I can't do that, sweet thing, you know that. Please, baby, just go upstairs!"

"I'm not a baby!"

Another knock.

"*Caelan!*"

"Okay, okay!" Finally, he sprints up the stairs and out of sight.

Archer takes a moment to calm the shaking in her hands, and then opens the door.

"Good," Kalinia snaps, shoving her way inside, "you're alive."

Archer sputters angrily at her coordinator. "Fuck you, too? Get out!"

"No." Lin starts to make a cursory inspection of the place, gaze lingering on all of the plants. "I didn't know you had such a green thumb, Archer."

"You said you weren't going to make house calls!" she snarls, slamming the door and stepping around in front of her. "What the hell are you doing here?" She has no contingency plan for this. She didn't think she'd need one. She hopes that aggression alone will be enough of a defense. It usually is, in her experience.

Lin is still looking around the loft. "When I took this job, everyone warned me that I'd spend most of my time paying off tabloids and bouncers, trying to keep your image clean." She steps over towards the stairs, and Archer's pulse picks up. But she's just looking at the vine on the wall. Still, she follows closely behind, placing herself firmly between the intruder and the staircase. "Of course, there was the incident with you and Lucas Wagner making a spectacle of yourselves behind Pyramid Club—"

Shame and indignation flare up in Archer's chest. "How the fuck did you—?"

"—and on my first real day on the job, too. What a welcome." She shakes her head bitterly. "But since then, news of your misbehavior has been disturbingly sparse. So, naturally, I assumed you'd either skipped town with Rob Wells or finally succeeded in dropping yourself to death."

"Why would I have run off with Rob Wells?" Archer is quick to demand. "I don't even know where the hell he is." *Shit, shit, you overdid it. That was suspicious.*

Lin blinks up at her for a few seconds. "That was a joke."

Archer sets her expression once again into her characteristic sneer. "Get the fuck out of my house."

"No." Lin roots around in her bag for a second, eventually producing a stack of photo proofs. "These are the rough cuts for the '42 catalog."

Archer snatches them away disinterestedly.

"You'll note that, as far as the feet are concerned, they've decided to go with the G2s, 3s, 5s, 6s, and 7s."

Archer gapes, frustration mounting. "Were Tom and Dre consulted *at all* on that lineup?"

Lin's reply is clipped. "Their opinions were duly noted."

"Those are all of the worst ones!" Archer nearly shouts. "They're fucking—"

"No, according to Design and Marketing, they're the *best* ones."

"They're destroying my back!"

"Beauty is pain," Lin snaps, stepping up very close. "Art is pain."

Archer tries to interject, but she steamrolls right over her.

"*No.* If it was easy, then anyone could do it. Act like Cymbre Archer, do your job, and rep the feet." She glances downwards. "And I never want to see you wearing *those* again. They're company property, and they're scrap. We expect them, along with the 4s and 8s, returned to the prosthetic lab by close of business this week."

Archer steps up even closer, forcing the woman to crane her neck back even further. "Get out of my house."

Kalinia turns, and just as she places her hand on the doorknob, she pauses to take one more look at the loft. "You're overdue for a scandal, Archer," she remarks. "You've laid low for too long. I'll expect the police report any day, now."

"*Get out!*"

Archer slams and bolts the door in Lin's wake, and relief comes crashing in on an icy wave. She claps a hand over her mouth to stifle a scream. *So close. So fucking close, so close, so—*

No, she tells herself. *It's over. He's safe. Go tell him he's safe.* She flings the photo proofs away, letting them flutter and fall where they may.

"Okay, coast is clear," she announces, making her way for the stairs. "Cael?"

Khî is poking around the edge of the bed, sniffing and pawing at something out of reach.

Amused, Archer crouches down to peer under the bed. "*Monsters* belong under the bed," she chuckles, "not sweet little robots who—" She stops. She's put her hand down in a puddle of silvery-white liquid. It's spreading out from under the bed. "Cael?"

She lifts the edge of the comforter to find him curled on his side with a petrified look on his face. Eyes blown wide, lips parted and quivering, he whispers, "I stayed quiet." There's a quality to his voice that tells her that something is very, very wrong.

"Hey, what's up?" she asks, heart beginning to race. "What happened?"

He extends a hand to her, and it's dripping with the same silvery-white liquid. "I— I hurt my back." His face twitches strangely. "It's— it's bad, I think."

"Oh," she murmurs, trying to stay calm. "Okay, come here, let's look at it." She takes him by the wrists and tugs him out from under the bed. He's stiff, shuddering.

"A-Arch–Archer–"

"It's okay," she reassures, rolling him onto his stomach. Khî takes his place near Cael's face, tail flicking back and forth in concern.

"I caught–C-c-*cut mmm*–my back on something when I–when I crawled under the bed, there was an angry piece of metal–"

"It's okay," she repeats. "Hey, it's all right, let's just take a look at it." His shirt is soaking wet. With delicate fingers, she works it up out of the way, and then the wound comes into view. There's a deep laceration down his back, cutting at a rough diagonal across his spine, seeping that silvery-white liquid.

"Okay," Archer says, trying to sound calm and casual. "Okay, um…"

"What d-d-does it l-l-l-*look* like?"

The stuttering is starting to really scare her. She swallows hard, hands shaking violently as she tries to pry the wound apart. "It's, uh…about eight inches. Rough edges on the cut, sort of a…sort of a jagged line. I can see a rib, and–" She pauses, shakes her head. "And some vertebrae. One of them is a little scuffed, but the carbon fiber isn't frayed, so that should be okay. Right?"

"Where is *thhh*–leak coming from?"

She peers closer, gently lifting his synthflesh out of the way. But her fingers are coated in that fluid, making it difficult to get a grip. "Between the vertebrae," she says. "Looks like…looks like it's seeping out between…T5 and T6? T6 is the one that's scuffed."

Cael doesn't reply.

"Hey!" she urges. "Come on, sweetheart, talk to me! What do I do?"

He inspects his wet fingertips. "Silver…silver m-m-*means* I'm losing nanobots," he says matter-of-factly. "That's bad."

"Okay," she says, trying to think through the panic. "Okay, what do I need to do?"

He exhales deeply, resting his cheek on the floor.

"Caelan!"

"Getting some weird pings," he murmurs. "Higher systems are going to shut down until I heal."

"No, no, *don't you dare!*"

"Can't stop it," he mumbles. "Need to heal. Acesos are... t-*trying* to do their job, but th-th-there aren't enough."

"Hang on!" she exclaims, scrambling to her feet. "I've got Arachne patches downstairs, will that help?" She's throwing herself down the stairs before he can answer. Archer tears through her bathroom cabinets in search of the patches. They're left over from a few models of legs ago, and they're matte black, but they'll do for now. They'll have to. She gathers up an armful of towels while she's at it, along with a pair of medical scissors, and races back upstairs.

"Here," she says, flinging the bedsheets aside and laying the towels out. "Come on, we're gonna get you up here, okay?"

"Okay." Cael sits drowsily, conductor fluid pouring out of his wound. Archer lifts him up, trying in vain to scoop some of the liquid back in, before sitting him on the edge of the bed. She takes his shirt off and flings it away before laying him down on his stomach again.

With gentle hands, she cleans the conductor fluid from the edges of the laceration. And then she tears into the sleeve of Arachne patches with her teeth.

"This isn't going to f-f-fix it," he reminds her, needlessly.

"I know," she acknowledges, frustrated. "But I have to do *something*, Caelan, I'm a human, I can't just *sit* here!" She sets to work cutting a few short, thin strips of synthflesh. "I just need to—I need to think!"

"There's a rupture in m-m-my— it's a main vess—*sel* for my circu– *circ*–" He shudders. "–*ulatory* system."

"I know," she says, pinching the wound together with one hand. "Biomechanical conductor fluid. Stay with me, baby, how do I fix it?"

"Not a baby."

"That's right." She forces a shaking laugh, beginning to apply the black synthflesh like steri-strips across the wound. "You're not a baby."

"Acesos have to fix it," he says. "Too small for anyth..."

"No, you stay awake!" she urges. "Hey, you said you're losing nanobots, do you have...do you have *enough*?"

He closes his eyes. "Need more. And I need more fluid."

The fact that he's stopped the stuttering now is somehow even more frightening. "Where do I get them?" she demands, turning him over onto his back. "Hey! Caelan!"

"Need to idle," he murmurs. A rivulet of silvery-white fluid snakes its way down from the corner of his mouth.

"*Where do I get more of those things?*" she repeats, shaking him. "How long do you have?"

"Wasn't…designed for…use outside of a…lab setting," he mumbles, and then he falls still, eyes fixed on a point on the ceiling.

"Hey!" Archer shouts, shaking him roughly. "*Hey!* You've gotta wake up, baby, I don't know what to do!" Her eyes begin to sting with panicked tears, and she wipes them with the backs of her hands, streaking her face with silver conductor fluid. "*Caelan!* Fuck!"

Khi hops up onto the bed, stepping onto Cael's chest and nudging at his face. Nothing happens. Archer stumbles back a little before lunging forward again to press her ear to his chest. He is breathing, very quickly. And his heart is beating. But it's slow. Even slower than it usually is when he's idling.

"Fuck," she whispers, frantic.

She drops to her knees and yanks the comforter out of the way, searching frantically beneath the bed. The culprit is there, in the form of a metal support bracket in the corner. Its edge is dripping with silver. Howling in anger, she grabs hold of the corner of the bed frame and kicks at it, slamming her foot into the cruel component until it bends all the way flush with the underside of the bed.

"*FUCK!*" she screams, clapping her hands to her head and rocking back and forth on the floor. Because it's not fair, not fair, *not fair* how everything that touches her hurts, and everything she touches gets hurt. It's not fair that this tiny, sweet, perfect, magnificent person who she loves so much should be stuck with someone so fucking incompetent who can't even take care of him, and it's so evil and controlling that they didn't build him strong enough to last outside of a lab, but still gave him the desire to leave it, and–

The lab.

Goddammit, the *lab*.

Archer covers Cael in a blanket, presses a kiss to his forehead, and rushes downstairs. Her heart races as she struggles with her phone, trying to cling to her tears and her panic, trying to think. She has one shot to get this right, *one single shot.*

Vander lets it ring four times before he picks up. "Cymbre, my dear, I'm afraid I'm in a meeting—"

"No!" she interrupts, voice shaking. "No, I need to talk to you *now!*"

She hears him cover the receiver and address the room, "I'm sorry, but I have to take this call. Will you excuse me?" After a few seconds of shuffling, followed by the sound of a door opening and closing, he comes back. "You sound upset, my girl, what can I do? What's happened?"

"Do you know which feet they chose?" she demands.

He hesitates. "I haven't seen the final product lines, no. As I said, I've been in meetings—"

"Well, they're *torture devices!*" she screams. "Beautiful, *haute couture* torture devices! I won't do it, Evander, I won't! After everything I've given this company, I think I deserve some say in this!"

He stammers a little, clearly caught off-guard. Which she had absolutely been banking on. In 25 years, this is the first time she's ever spoken to him this way. "Cymbre, I'm afraid we don't have much wiggle room, here. Decisions have been made."

Oh, thank fucking God, thank *God.* "Why?" she moans. "You're the CEO, can't you—"

"I'm afraid it's out of my control."

"Whose, then? R&D? Those…God, those fuckers across the hall?" *Please, please, please…*

"Yes, R&D," he says, obviously grateful for the chance to direct her ire somewhere else. "The art and design team, the—"

"Fine, then," she snaps. "I want them to look me in the eye and explain this to me."

Again, he stammers. "All right, I suppose I can arrange a meeting, but I can't have you coming at them with these fangs, my girl, it's—"

"I don't care!" she moans, suddenly afraid that she'd tightened her grip prematurely. She'll change tactics. "Evander, I don't think they have any idea what this does to me! I think they've forgotten that I'm a person! I feel pain, I'm in *so much pain*, all the time! They need to see that!"

Oh, that shuts him right up. After a tense silence, he asks, "You what?"

"Tom can only do so much! You can see the change in my gait since the 6.0s, hell, just compare my x-rays from two years ago and now! They're destroying my back, just like they did to Luc, and they'll do it to our patients, too! I know you want to encourage elective procedures, and you want to sell the Acesos, and that's fine, that's great–"

He stammers, clearly alarmed by the fact that she'd managed to put that together all on her own.

"–because we're a *business*, we're a *business*, and that's the point! I get it, and I'm on board!" (The first lie she's told, actually.) "But there's a tightrope to walk, and this will pitch us off of it!" *There,* she thinks. *That's hitting him where it hurts. His bottom line.*

Silence. For a long time, silence. And then, "Is there really a visible difference in the films of your spine?"

"Yes."

"Visible to a layperson?" he presses.

"Yes! Look at it yourself, you'll see!"

Archer knows he's really asking, '*Will this implicate us if it leaks?*' Because Vander knows now that their secrets aren't nearly as safe as he'd hoped.

"All right, yes," he finally concedes. "You're completely right, of course, and I–I wish you'd come to me sooner. You know you can always come to me with these things, my girl, this is what I'm here for."

She breathes a tentative sigh of relief, softening her sharp frequency. "You're busy," she says, just as gentle and demure as he likes. "You have more important things to worry about."

"There's nothing more important."

"Well…I thought I was strong enough."

"You are strong," he reassures. "You're the strongest woman I've ever known. And I hope you never stop surprising me with that strength. I'll look at my calendar, and we can try and find sometime next week–"

!! PANIC !!

"No!" she blurts, mind racing. Today would be impossible, today would seem suspicious. But much later, and Cael won't last. Or Vander will change his mind. She needs to keep the pressure on him without turning it up much higher. "Tomorrow," she decides. "First thing in the morning, inside the lab. I want to see the shock on their faces when we walk in."

Silence.

Fine, she thinks, *we'll do it* your *way.* "Vander, we need to get on top of this before marketing starts making promises to vendors that will get us sued down the road."

He breathes deeply, she can hear the pensive rumble in his chest.

"*Please*," she begs. A necessary afterthought. "For me."

"All right," he concedes. "We'll plan for 9:00 tomorrow morning, can you do that?"

Archer has to take the phone away from her ear to avoid him hearing her shuddering, relieved exhale. Fresh tears spring to her eyes, but she composes herself, and goes back in. "Yes," she says, "and I want Luc with us, too. He deserves to be there." He's already proven himself a fantastically cooperative – if unwitting – accomplice.

"Yes, Lucas is more than welcome to join us."

"Thank you," she says. "I mean that."

"You're most welcome, Cymbre," he replies, clearly eager to be done with this conversation. With that, he hangs up.

Archer looks at the clock, and a fresh wave of fear rolls through, eclipsing any relief she'd only just felt. She has less than 24 hours to figure out how to steal from Tartarus.

CHAPTER TWENTY-THREE

SHE DOESN'T HAVE A PLAN.

She'd slept maybe an hour, all-told, instead opting to sit next to Cael with a hand on his chest. She had to be sure his heart was still beating. At one point, his head had twitched a little, and Khî had leapt up expectantly to meow and paw at him. His eyes had closed around 3:00 am. But nothing else happened. Cael stayed still and silent, but his heart kept beating.

When morning came, Archer dragged herself downstairs and into the shower, and watched as so much silver poured down the drain. Before she left, she pressed a long, lingering kiss to Cael's cheek, and whispered to him not to worry, that she'd be back soon, that she was going to fix him. Khî stayed on the bed with him, standing guard. He hadn't even gone down to eat his breakfast.

And now, here she is. In the elevator with Luc, headed down into Tartarus. She's dressed to intimidate, with a pair of massive sunglasses hiding much of her face. She doesn't plan to take them off. Her top is a structured black Van Herpen piece, with big, puffy half-sleeves that she hopes will help conceal her movements (or any stolen components). She's hidden her fingerprints beneath PVC elbow gloves. Beyond that, she has nothing. No plan. No inkling whatsoever of how she's going to pull this off. And this is her one chance.

"It's kinda cool that we're doing this," Luc remarks. "I've always wondered what it's like in there."

Archer startles hard when her phone starts to vibrate. She digs it out to see her mother's name and photograph flashing on the screen. She grimaces and rejects the call.

Lucas cranes his neck to look. "Liêu Hanh?"

"Hey, can you do me a favor?" Archer asks, shoving the phone back into her pocket.

"Yeah, sure."

"Can you...I don't know, entertain Callas for me?"

He gives her a puzzled look.

"I'm just..." She shakes her head. "I'm not in the mood for him, today. If he spends all morning clinging to my arm, I'll probably punch him."

"*Your* arm?" he chuckles.

"Lucas, please."

"Yeah, no problem. I've got you."

"Thanks."

When they step out of the elevator, Vander is waiting for them. He smiles broadly, kissing her on the cheeks, shaking Luc's hand. He says...something. Vander says something, some compressed lecture about good behavior, not being confrontational, not touching anything, blah, blah, blah. Archer barely hears it. Luc, fantastic, wonderful, *beautiful* Luc, throws his cybernetic around Vander's shoulders and guides him towards the lab, laughing and joking.

The staff look up in shock when Vander badges them in, and their shock only intensifies when they see Luc and Archer.

"Mr Callas," one of the researchers stammers, stepping forward to shake his hand. "What a surprise, we had no idea–"

"Yes," he says, stepping past him to inspect some device on the table, "yes, I imagine it is a surprise. Lucas and Cymbre were eager to meet with the minds behind their latest tech, and who am I to deny them?"

"O-of course," the man says, gracious, shaking Luc's hand. "Where would we be without the two of you? You make what we do look so beautiful."

Behind her glasses, Archer rolls her eyes. "Indeed."

"Well," their host says, "I'm Dr Brooks Matthews, acting director of R&D at Hephaestus Forge, and it is an honor to have you here. Would you like the tour?"

"Hell yeah," Luc says, enthusiastic. "You've gotta use small words for me, though, deal?"

He laughs. "It's a deal."

Archer lags behind, taking in the sights. Like the cybernetics lab, everything is gleaming white. And, like the lab, the glowing, gold accents add a sort of false warmth to the otherwise sterile, forbidding environment.

Coverall-clad technicians and white-coated researchers cluster around tables, working on cybernetics. The walls either side of the open space are glass, and behind them, more lab spaces can be seen. Cleanrooms where organs are constructed and tested, blinking server trees offering state-of-the-art computing power. Archer's stomach lurches when they pass a glass-walled room arranged not unlike a living space. The lights are off, the bed made. Waiting. A neat little vivarium, for…

It's so small. It's…God, it's just so small.

Dr Matthews is chattering away about their latest projects, with Luc occasionally grilling him on the purpose and practicality of the new hand design. Vander seems distracted too, which is a relief. Gradually, Archer lets herself lag further and further behind. She has no idea what she's even looking for, or how to find it.

And then Luc comes to her rescue once more. "Hey, I know these little guys!"

Archer looks up to find them gathered around a long workbench housing Aceso nanobots. Her heart rate picks up.

"Yes, you certainly do!" Matthews says brightly.

The table is home to innumerable petri dishes, stacks upon stacks upon stacks, holding piles and piles of the bots. To the naked eye, they look like silver dust. There's a line of microscopes along one side of the table, host to various robotic assembly arms terminating in imperceptibly small tools.

"Would you like to see?" Matthews asks, directing Archer over to one of the microscopes.

She peers through the eyepiece to see a cylindrical automaton, ringed with dozens of arms like cilia.

"That one is deactivated," he explains. "Or, rather, it hasn't been activated yet."

"Yeah," Luc chuckles, "otherwise, he'd be halfway across the room, and you'd never find him again. I've seen demonstrations of these things in open spaces before, Cym, they're surprisingly quick little bastards."

Matthews smiles. "Exactly. We're working now on expanding their application. Our success rate with healing SCIs sits at a very comfortable 99.7%, with other neuropathies coming in at 97.3%, and TBI at 96.2%." Forge's favorite statistics, repeated verbatim.

"What else could you do with them?" Luc asks, looking into an adjacent microscope.

"The possibilities are theoretically endless. But right now, we're focusing on military applications."

Luc frowns. "Like weapons?"

"No," he laughs good-naturedly, "no. Combat medicine. Quick, nearly painless healing of skin and tissue."

"Huh." Luc returns to his microscope. "Who would've thought, you know? All from my dumbass scoliosis."

"Millions of people, all across the world, owe their health and mobility to your bravery, Lucas," Vander impresses. "Without the incredible risks you've undertaken for us, the world would be a much darker place, indeed."

"Ahh…" He smiles, tries to wave him off, but Archer can see the color rise to his cheeks. "You know. Just doing my job."

Archer can't resist the urge to say, "I suppose I'll be next."

"It's not so bad, Cym," Luc reassures, hauling her close and pressing a kiss to her head. She squirms away, far from in the mood for this. "Plus, hey, my spine gives me 5G, and Vander can track my location within three meters, anywhere on the globe!"

Dr Matthews is visibly indignant. "While I do recognize that you're joking, that kind of sentiment is one of the biggest obstac–"

"I know, I know," Luc sighs. "Come on. If you don't let us laugh, we'll probably kill ourselves."

Vander rubs at his forehead. "Lucas, please."

The group wanders off, entirely distracted by Luc's antics, but Archer lingers. There are people working all around, though none within about 15 feet, and they all seem pointedly indifferent to her presence. Like they're making a show of ignoring her. She peers through the microscope again, trying to look busy. There's a closed petri dish just to her left, full of what must be thousands of the little fuckers. She doesn't know how many Cael needs, or even how to measure such a thing. But she has to act fast.

She reaches out and casually picks up the dish, holding it up close to inspect the contents. To the naked eye, they're just little pinpricks of silver. But, if she looks close enough, she can actually see movement. Like subtly shifting sand.

Should she look around, before she pockets it? Or does that look more suspicious? Does that draw attention? Her mouth is dry, sweat beading on her skin. *Don't think about prison*, she tells herself, *don't think about prison, don't think about prison–*

!! CAEL IS GOING TO DIE !!

Without another thought, she hastily slips the dish into her pocket and returns to the microscope.

Count down from five, she tells herself, *don't rush. No one saw, no one saw.*

Five… *(You're going to get caught)*
Four… *(They're going to throw you in prison)*
Three… *(Cael's going back into his little room)*
Two… *(And then they're going to kill him)*

One.

She turns abruptly, taking a rushed step away from the table, only to slam into one of the technicians. *Oh God, oh fuck, this is it, he caught you–*

"Sorry, Mx Archer," he mumbles, struggling to make eye contact. He's just a kid, really, his flame-bright hair pulled into a little ponytail. Two Charon eyes, she sees now. Older models.

"That's fine," she says, trying to step past him. "I should catch up with Luc and Callas."

"No, wait, hang on a second."

FUCK. All of the hairs on the back of her neck stand up. "What?"

Eyes downcast, he thrusts a pair of water bottles in her direction. "Here. You should…take these."

Stunned, she looks between his face and the bottles. "I'm all right, thank you?" The seals on them are clearly broken.

"Well–" He hesitates, eyes flitting up to hers for an instant before darting away again. "No, well, you can give them to your friend."

Her confusion and anxiety are only deepening. "What? Luc doesn't need water, he's fine. Can you please–"

"Your other friend."

"That's the CEO of the company," she snaps, annoyed. "Who the hell–"

"Your *other* friend," he presses, voice dropping to a harsh whisper. "Listen, if he needs the 'bots, he needs this, too."

It feels like the ground has shifted beneath her feet, and she's falling, falling. Hurriedly, Archer snatches the bottles away. Sure enough, they're heavier than water bottles should be, the liquid thicker and denser. "Thank you," she whispers, stunned.

The technician cringes, seemingly uncomfortable with the sentiment. As he brushes past her, he deftly swipes another two petri dishes from the table and presses them into her palm. "Put it in his heart," he whispers, slipping her a massive, thick-gauge, capped needle.

With shaking hands, Archer shoves the materials into her pockets and bag. "Thank you," she murmurs, "thank you, thank you, I–"

"No," he says, walking away. "Thank *you*."

The rest of the tour is…honestly, Archer has no idea what's happening for the rest of the tour. It's a blinding parade of tech and jargon, and all she can focus on is the reassuring weight in her bag and the sound of the petri dishes clicking together in her pocket, *praying* that no one else can hear it, and *getting the fuck out of here*. It drags on and on and on, until finally they've worked their way back to the front doors, and Vander broaches the topic of Archer's spine, and the new feet, and she crosses her arms and nods in stern agreement, saying *something*, but it's all just noise. Meaningless noise. They could rip her implants out and put her in a wheelchair for the rest of her life, she wouldn't care; she'd agree to anything as long as she could just *get back to Cael*.

She thinks of his face, of that silver rivulet snaking out from between his lips, and she hopes with every cell in her body that he's still breathing. She hopes his heart is still beating. She doesn't know what she would do if she were to get home and find that she's too late, that–

NO, it's not going to be too late. He's strong. He's so strong. And he just has to hold on a little longer.

They're shaking hands. The door is opening. Vander is lingering, but Luc is beckoning her towards the hall, towards the elevator, and so she follows.

The red-haired technician is going to lose his job and end up in prison, just like she is. She should've asked him his name.

As soon as the elevator doors snap shut in their wake, Archer clutches at the wall and exhales a relieved, shuddering whimper. She can't help it. It's too much. Her stomach turns, and she's afraid for a moment that she's going to vomit, but she swallows it back. Breathes through it. Her vision is swimming a little, blackness at the corners of her vision. *You did it, you did it, you did it.* Luc doesn't acknowledge the display. But when they reach the ground floor, he takes her by the wrist, and drags her to the front door.

Fresh panic floods through her veins like ice water. "Hey!" she protests, trying to squirm away, but he just hauls her along in his wake.

Once outside, he shoves her into a nearby alley.

"Hey, what the hell is the matter with you?" she demands, stumbling a little.

"You ready to tell me what the fuck *that* was?"

She tries to step past him, back out onto the sidewalk. "I don't know what you're talking about, and I don't have time for this, Luc, I have to go."

"Yeah, no." He puts his cybernetic hand on her chest, holding her back. "I'm not stupid, Cymbre. And you know what I think? Between the storage unit bullshit, and now this—"

Her stomach lurches. "You don't have any idea what you're—"

"You know what I've been wondering lately?" he asks. "Why I haven't been to your house in months."

"Lucas—"

"And why you never come out anymore."

"Maybe I just don't wanna hang out with you," she sneers, crossing her arms.

He casts her a thoroughly unimpressed look. "Okay. I'm not that stupid. You gonna keep stringing me along in the dark, or are you ready to ask for my help like a grown-up?"

She glances up towards his face. He's stern, but genuine as ever.

"All our lives, it's only ever been you and me," he reminds her. "When the fuck did that change?"

"Luc…"

"How about you just show me what Rob stole."

Archer shoves her door open with a bang and sprints into the loft. Her foot lands squarely on one of the photographs that Lin had brought – still strewn across the floor like confetti – and she very nearly slips. But she manages to lunge for the stair handrail and haul herself upright again, stumbling up towards the bedroom. Luc follows, closing and locking the door in their wake. When she crests the top of the stairs, she sees that Khî has barely moved. He's still curled up on Cael's chest, right where she left him. He dutifully scampers out of the way as she climbs up to crouch beside him.

"Hey," she murmurs, frantically rubbing her thumb along Cael's cheekbone. "Hey, sweet thing, I brought some friends for you, look–" She digs the bots out of her pocket, gently shaking the petri dish beside his ear. "They're gonna help, can you hear them? They're gonna help fix it."

Luc freezes at the top of the stairs. "Oh, what the fuck."

She leans down, pressing her ear to Cael's chest.

Still beating.

"Open the curtains," she tells Luc, stripping off her coat and dumping the contents of her bag and pockets onto the mattress. "I need more light."

Luc does as instructed, and then takes a cautious seat on the bed. His hands hover over Cael's motionless form. "Cymbre, who the hell is this?"

"This is Cael." She powers right through, rolling the comforter down to expose his bare torso. "Okay, that technician said to put it in his heart."

"Wait, what technician? Put *what*? What's wrong with him?"

Archer slips her fingertips down the center of Cael's chest, feeling for the seam, but it's completely imperceptible. She presses a little, trying to get the skin to split apart, but it just stretches inward, like normal skin.

"Fuck. Hey, can you go and get me my leg tools?" she asks, pointing across the room. "Just the whole bag. It's in the closet."

Luc just freezes, panicked. "Are you gonna…Cymbre, are you gonna cut that guy open? *Tell me you're not gonna cut that fucking guy open.*"

"No, I shouldn't have to!"

He stands, backing away from the bed. "*Take him to a hospital! Cymbre, what the f–*"

"Will you *shut up*? He showed me once, it should just–" It hits her all at once. "Oh, shit, hang on." She takes Cael by the wrist, guiding his hand over the hollow between his ribs. She presses his fingertips into the center, and all at once, the split appears. Archer exhales a relieved laugh, slipping her fingers in between his to hook under the edge of the flesh. "Lucas, fucking *help me*."

Luc claps a hand over his mouth, shaking his head and mumbling something into his palm. And then, after a beat, he seems to steel. He climbs back up onto the bed and gently lifts Cael's hand out of her way. Together, they peel his synthflesh back, and the extent of the injury comes into view.

The bottom of his chest cavity is pooling with silvery conductor fluid, but it's not nearly as much as Archer was expecting to see. Maybe some of the bots found their way back in. And there, right in the center, is his heart. Still beating. His lungs, still filling.

"Okay," Archer murmurs shakily. She picks up a dry washcloth from the pile on the bed and slips it beneath his heart, soaking up the excess fluid pooled around his spine. "Okay, baby. We're gonna fix it."

"This is what Rob stole," Luc murmurs, rocking back and forth slightly.

"Yes." She peers around inside Cael's abdomen, trying to identify the source of the leak and stem what little flow remains.

"Tom and Dre were right, they made an AI, they made a fucking robot, Cym this is insane—"

"He's a *person*," she says, defensive, taking another washcloth and packing it around his spine. Squeezing, pressing it into all the crevices. "He's made of different materials than we are, but—" She stops, tears springing to her eyes despite herself. She looks up at Luc. "No, actually, he's…he's made of exactly the same shit that you and I are made of. He's the sum of everything Forge ever built."

"Fuck."

"And he's going to die unless we do something."

Luc stammers for a second. "What the fuck are we supposed to do?"

"He needs biomechanical conductor fluid, and more nanobots."

She brushes the tears from her face and gestures to the materials on the bed. "There's a needle."

He starts to sift through it, looking over the petri dishes, the fluid.

"I have no idea what to do." Archer's voice breaks a little against the admission. She leans down, resting her head against Cael's shoulder. "I don't know what to do; do we just put the bots in the needle? Do we just pour them in there? I don't know! He didn't have time to tell me! Neither of them did!"

"No, that's okay," Luc announces, slowly beginning to nod. "Same shit as you and me. I know what to do. I've got this, I've fucking *totally* got this. Um…" He looks around. "Funnel."

"Kitchen. The drawer under the microwave."

"Okay."

Archer's heart starts to race as Luc launches himself noisily down the stairs. And when he returns a few seconds later, he immediately gets to work. With steady, confident hands, he funnels one of the dishes of bots into a bottle of fluid, guiding them along with his finger.

"They give them to me in blood transfusions, for my spine," he explains, re-capping the bottle and shaking it gently. "I figure this has gotta be the same."

"Yeah," she nods, hands still working at the inside of Cael's chest cavity. "It has to be, right?"

"Does that look right?" He holds the bottle up for her.

She inspects it closely, watching the streaks of silver swirl and dissipate like so many pinprick stars. "More, maybe. It's not as silver as what was coming out of him."

"Okay." He opens the second dish of bots, adding about a quarter of them. "Here?"

"Yeah," she nods, "yeah, that's closer."

"Closer, or the same?"

"*Close enough!*" she nearly shouts, anxiety pounding in her temples. "Luc, please!"

"Okay, okay!" He uncaps the needle and inserts it into the

bottle, drawing out as much as he can. He turns it upwards, pushing out the excess air, and then thrusts it expectantly towards Archer. "Here."

She panics at the very thought. "No, you do it."

"Hey, this is *your–*"

"*Please,* I've never done this before!"

"What, and I have? I can't just jam a needle in a guy's heart like it's nothing, Archer, and look at the size of that puddle in his chest! He's gonna need, like, six or seven of these. I think we need to give him a full bottle, at least. I fucking can't. This whole thing–"

"Please, Luc, he's going to die!"

He takes a deep breath, fingers splayed, trying to regain some sense of calm. She can see that his organic hand is shaking, now. "Goddammit, Cymbre." He slings one leg over Cael's thighs, crowding in above him. Archer leans in close, forehead resting against Luc's. She can feel his breath on her lips, coming quick and anxious.

"In his heart," she whispers. "Nice and easy."

"Don't let it slip away from me," he commands, needle hovering a few inches above the pulsing, electric blue muscle. He's holding it with his cybernetic, and she can't tell if that's better or worse. But it's his dominant hand. He has no choice. "Get up under there. Hold it."

She slips her palms up, gently cupping Cael's heart in her hands. The beats are so few and far between. "Like that?"

"Yeah." He nods, bringing the needle in closer. "Yeah, that's good."

"Gentle," she whispers. "Just…let it come to you."

"Okay." A bead of sweat drips down between their skin, catching on Archer's eyebrow. Luc lays the needle flat against Cael's heart, but when it twitches, he jerks it away again, hissing, "Fuck."

Archer cringes, shaking her head. "*Lucas.*"

"Can he feel this?" he asks, and she can hear an undeniable quaver in his voice.

"No. He wouldn't even be able to feel it if he was awake."

"You're *sure?*"

"Yes!" she groans. "Please, Luc, just *do* it!"

"What if I make it worse? Like, what if I fuck up and rip him open?"

"You won't!" she shouts, trying so hard to believe it.

"Goddammit." He leans back in, still so hesitant. "Shit, okay." He takes a deep breath, and Archer can't help but follow suit. And then he holds, and she does too, holding, holding, timing the heartbeats, and—

It's in. They exhale in unison, shaking against one another. Luc laughs cautiously, pushing the plunger, filling Cael with what he needs to survive, and then he withdraws the needle.

"One down," she breathes, clapping a hand around the back of Luc's neck. "We've got this."

"Yeah. Yeah, we've got this."

They work until the bottle is empty, moving as one through this gentle, meditative, necessary alchemy. Archer watches Cael's heart expand, feels it grow heavier in her palm. She watches his pulse pick up, beat by beat, until it's something like his regular idle again. At one point, his lips even twitch.

When they're done, when Cael's heart is pounding strong and steady, Archer looks up and sees Lucas through new eyes. Before her now kneels a savior, strong and beautiful and selfless. Of course, what is one more life, when weighed against the millions he already holds on his shoulders?

The world, she realizes. *This one life is the world.*

"Thank you," she exhales, meeting Luc's gaze as their foreheads rest together.

He gives her a half-smile. "Hey, don't thank me, yet."

She gives into impulse and presses a kiss to his forehead. Long and lingering. She can taste the salt on his skin. Carefully, Archer unwraps the towel from around Cael's spine, and sees that the slow ebb of silvery conductor fluid has stopped. She exhales a cautious laugh.

"Okay," she says, nodding slowly. "How, um…how long do you think…?"

Luc exhales sharply, sitting back on his heels. He presses his fingers into his eyes. "I have no idea. It's usually ten or fifteen minutes before I feel them, but he's...probably gonna be different? I don't know. I just don't know."

"Okay." Fifteen minutes. She can wait fifteen more minutes.

He clears their mess away, throwing towels in the washing machine, storing the rest of the fluid and nanobots in the fridge. Meanwhile, Archer finishes cleaning Cael up. She dries out the rest of his chest cavity with gentle, painstaking precision. It's harder now, with his heart and lungs moving the way they are. But she's patient. This is the most important thing she's ever done, all her stupid, vain, selfish life. When she's through, she folds Cael's skin back into place and watches it seal together. She rolls him gently onto his side, inspecting the site of the original wound. It's visible by the hatch-marks of her black synthflesh, permanently healed into his.

Her phone vibrates. Liêu Hanh *again*. "God fucking dammit," she grumbles, rejecting the call and jamming it back into her pocket.

Archer lifts Cael's shoulders and slips behind him to sit against the headboard. She gathers his boneless form up into her arms, leaning his head back against her shoulder. She rests a hand on his narrow chest, immeasurably comforted by the feeling of its steady rise and fall.

"You fight this," she whispers through gritted teeth. "Do you hear me, Caelan? You fight this now; you be so strong."

Luc rejoins them, sitting down at the foot of the bed.

"He's fine," Archer blurts, preemptively defensive. "He's better, I can tell. We just...we just need to wait."

Luc just stares, taking in all the strange details of the scene. His eyes linger on the way Archer's hand is combing back through Cael's hair, and the way her leg is hooked around one of his.

"If this doesn't—" He hesitates. "Do you have some kind of a back-up plan?"

"Shut up," she snaps. "You shut your mouth, Lucas, don't you say that. We can't even think like that right now, okay? This is—it's gonna be fine."

He knows her well enough to back off. "How long have you had him?"

"Four months. Since the day before we got that first email."

"Fuck, it's probably a miracle that you've made it so long without something like this happening."

She ignores him. "Rob sealed him into a crate down in Tartarus, with some of my feet, and then he had Forge deliver him to my doorstep themselves. They had no idea what was inside."

"But he's, like, a *person*. Cymbre, he's a *whole person*, how did... how did they do it?" Luc murmurs distantly. "How the hell did they...?"

She nods towards the nightstand. "There's a bunch of his shit in that drawer, if you want to read about it."

Luc takes Cael's documents out and begins leafing through them, eyebrows rising higher and higher with each page. "Jesus," he murmurs into his palm.

"He's us, Luc," she says, hauling Cael closer. "They spent 25 years testing the tech on us, and then they bolted it all together and taught an AI to pilot it around."

"*Why?*" he asks, agonized. "What's the point?"

"Because they could. That's what he says, anyway. I'm sure Forge will come up with some spin, but the truth is that they just did this for the hell of it, because they're so far removed from any consequences, down in that...oh, that goddamn *torture* chamber of theirs. And then when they got sick of him, they were just gonna kill him. Shut him down and strip him for parts, like he's just an obsolete leg or something. They'd done it before."

"So, Rob got him out."

"Yeah. Rob got him out."

Luc hesitates for a second before asking, "Are you two...?"

"Yes," she replies, *daring* him to say something about it.

"You love him?"

Archer closes her eyes, sending a fresh wave of tears pouring down her cheeks. She nods, but the words stick in her throat. Still, she can't say it. To say it aloud would ruin it, to say it aloud would make what's happening right now infinitely more terrifying. She shifts a little, settling her cheek against Cael's head. She takes his hands in hers and crosses their arms over his chest. "Kalinia came over yesterday," she murmurs. "I told him to hide, and he…he was so worked up about it, he cut his back open trying to dive under the bed." She takes a hard, shuddering breath. "Like a jackass."

Lucas scoffs. "Man, *fuck* Kalinia."

"I know. I know, it's…he's just so…God, he's so *fragile* like that, sometimes. He's strong, I *know* he's strong, because he wouldn't have made it this far otherwise, but he has such weird vulnerabilities. Things you wouldn't even expect. He was so afraid yesterday, Luc, he was so…*fuck*, he was so scared. He says he was never meant for use outside of a lab setting, and–"

"Hey, I'm not fragile."

Archer starts in shock, and then she pulls back and sees that Cael's eyes are open. They're open, and they're tracking hers. A relieved cry tears involuntarily from her throat – a scream, a release of breath and soul and pent-up terror. He's smiling. It's the most beautiful, absolving thing she's ever seen, and then she's clawing him into her arms, openly weeping.

"My *boy*!" she sobs, pathetic, fingers raking through his hair. "You're okay! You're all right, I've got you!"

"I know." His voice is muffled into her neck.

She wrenches him up into view. "Let me look at you, are you okay? *Are you okay?*"

"Yes," he confirms. "All internal diagnostics indicate that I'm operating well within normal safety parameters."

"You're so strong, baby," she chokes, pressing kiss after kiss to his face. "You did it, you're so strong–"

"You did it," he corrects, wriggling free to straddle her lap. "I was listening. You did such a good job; you did everything exactly right."

"Were you so scared?" she asks, touching his silver-streaked face, his chest, his shoulders. "Baby, I was so scared."

He frowns, dragging a fingertip through the tears on her cheek. "Is that why you're crying, or is it something else? Are you hurt?"

"No," she sniffles, wiping at her tears. "No, sweet thing, I'm just so relieved that you're okay."

"Okay." His head suddenly snaps to the side, towards Lucas. "Hello."

Luc, for his part, has leapt up from the bed and is standing a few feet away. His hands are raised in a kind of pathetic defense.

"You're Lucas Wagner," Cael prompts, expectant.

Luc nods, swallowing hard. "Yeah."

He thrusts a hand out into the gulf. "I'm Cael."

Luc takes a tentative step forward and clasps it, and Archer watches as his facial expression cycles through the same series of emotions she'd experienced, the first time she'd ever touched Cael. Curiosity, followed by a sudden, acute awareness of what's different, and then the realization of everything that's so eerily the same. Luc clears his throat and offers a cautious, "Nice to meet you."

"Thank you for saving my life," Cael says, giving Luc's hand an enthusiastic shake.

Luc seems to be making a concerted effort to relax. "Yeah, man. No problem. It was mainly Cym, though, she's the…fucking heist mastermind."

"Did you know that it's not stealing if you're just taking back your own property?"

Luc and Archer respond with a simultaneous, "*What?*"

Cael looks between them, expectant. "You said I should tell that to Lucas."

"When did I say that?"

He seems duly unimpressed with her need for the reminder. "You said that the day you committed breaking and entering at a storage facility. You took a book and said it wasn't stealing."

"Okay," she tiredly concedes. "All right, Cael. Thank you for that."

"You're welcome." He rounds on Lucas again. "I like your Triumph Rocket 3 GT. The black-on-black is the perfect modern complement for that vintage silhouette."

At that, Lucas cracks a cautious, half-smile. "Oh, yeah?"

"Yes. I saw it the day you committed breaking and entering at a storage facility. You dropped my decorative meat puppet off outside afterwards."

"Caelan, quit showing off."

"I can teach you to ride it," Luc offers, "if you want."

Cael and Archer answer simultaneously: "Yes, please!" "*No.*"

"Hey!" Cael is suddenly looking around frantically. "Hey, where's my little monkey? He stayed with me the whole time you were gone, where did he go?"

Archer laughs, chest still hitching with the occasional sob. "I think he went downstairs, sweet thing, he doesn't like Luc very much."

"I'm going to go find him," Cael announces, clambering for the edge of the bed. "Have you fed him, yet?"

"Hey, hey, hey—" Archer catches him by the wrist. "It's way too early to feed him, and you need to take it easy."

He casts her a condescending, exasperated look. "I'm fine. I told you, all internal diag—"

"Caelan…"

"I want to go downstairs and see the cat, *please!*"

"Fine." She releases him, and he makes his way down into the living room.

Luc and Archer following close behind, he shouts, "*Where's my little monkey-boy?*"

Khî comes scampering out from his hiding place, chirping excitedly.

"*There's* my little monkey-boy!" Cael cries, scooping him up and carrying him over to the couch. "Did you do a good job taking care of me when I was broken? Yes, you did! Yes, you did!"

The cat purrs contentedly, rubbing his face against Cael's chin.

Luc chuckles. "He talks to that thing like you talk to that thing."

Archer flings herself down onto the couch beside Cael. She tugs him towards her with a hand around the back of his neck, pressing a hard kiss to his forehead. "You scared the hell out of me," she whispers against his skin.

He smiles, leaning into the kiss. "I'm sorry."

Archer grumbles, discontented. "You've got me so fucked up, Cael, I swear." She just wants to sit here like this for a while, so she can feel him alive and moving.

He points. "Why are there pictures of you all over the floor?"

"That's why Lin came over, baby, they're the rough cuts for the catalog."

Lucas tries to join them on the couch, but Cael leaps to his feet like he's been electrocuted. "No, wait!" he cries. "You need to meet the plants!"

Luc gives Archer a quizzical look, but she just nods tiredly after him.

Still cradling the cat, Cael takes Lucas around the room, touching each plant in turn. "This is James," he says of his Air Plant. "Elodie," running a fingertip along the petal of his orchid. "Janis," the Chinese Money Plant. He goes through them all. "Oliver, Adam, Ophelia, Dom, Isabel. The big vine is Paul, he's my favorite."

As the tour continues, Archer sinks into the couch, the tension finally beginning to melt away from her limbs. She's exhausted, now. All the hours of nerve-shredding stress and the fear, the rollercoaster of sheer panic, and it's finally over with.

Cael has abruptly pivoted, as he so often does, and is now pestering Lucas to pet Con Khi.

"He feels nice," Cael insists, nudging the cat towards Luc. "He's my second favorite thing I've ever touched."

Luc is shrinking back, and it's a comical sight, to be sure. Mr Atlas, in all of his massive, muscular, tattooed glory, shying away from a housecat. In fairness, Khi seems no more pleased with the arrangement. "Nuh-uh. That thing is a space alien, and it hates me. *Hates* me."

Cael is immediately suspicious. "Why? What did you do to him?"

"Nothing!" Luc tries to slink past the pair. "I think he can just tell I'm a dog person."

Caelan's face lights up. "Do you have a dog?"

"Yeah, two, actually."

"*Diamond Dogs!*" Cael blurts, and then he grimaces violently, mumbling. "No, no, that's something different."

"Hey, you need to relax," Archer chides. "You're way, way, *way* too worked up right now, Cael."

"I'm fine!"

Luc laughs a little nervously. "Yeah, they're um...not Diamond Dogs. Whatever that means. One is a big, dumb, meatball-headed Pit mix, and the other is an Irish Wolfhound."

Cael is still quivering with excitement. "They sound like such good ones! What things do they like? *Can I meet them?*"

Though they don't see it, Archer casts the pair a tired smile. There's an undercurrent of anxiety lingering behind her eyes, humming in her blood. Like she doesn't quite trust the calm yet, and she's bracing for the next thing to go wrong. Some new disaster. Even still, her eyelids feel so heavy.

Again, her phone is vibrating. Again, she rejects her mother's call.

"Hey!" Cael is suddenly clambering up into her lap. He takes her by the cheeks, shaking her lightly. "What's wrong with you?"

"I'm tired, sweet thing." She runs her hands up and down his sides. He's still shirtless, his pale skin caked with silvery-white conductor fluid. "I stayed awake all night watching you, and it's been a hard, stressful day."

Cael thinks hard. "Are you just hungry?"

"No," she reassures, combing her fingers back through his hair. "I'm not hungry, sweet one."

"You should go lie down for a while," Luc offers, joining them on the couch. "We can entertain ourselves."

The thought fills her with a strange blend of guilt and relief. "Are you sure?"

Luc shrugs. "Yeah, why not?"

"Okay." With a kiss on the tip of his nose, Archer guides Cael out of her lap. "Yeah, I think I should. You'll hang out and keep an eye on him?"

"Yeah, of course. Go sleep."

"I do not need anyone to *keep an eye on me,*" Cael argues, visibly indignant. "I'm not a baby."

"I know you're not," Archer tiredly concedes, rising from the couch. "I just think it would be better if Luc hung out for a while. You've been accident-prone lately."

"No, I want to come upstairs with you."

She stretches, back popping in protest. "And what, watch me sleep?"

Cael makes that pouty little face he uses to get what he wants. The one that Archer genuinely has no idea where he learned. "I like watching you sleep."

"Caelan, that sounds so fucking creepy." She sighs. "Just hang out with Luc. For *months* you've been telling me how much you wanted to meet him."

"Okay," Cael reluctantly agrees. "Okay, that's fair."

"Aww, you wanted to meet me?" Luc tentatively teases, poking Cael in the ear.

He doesn't react beyond a simple, distracted, "Yes." He's watching Archer shuffle towards the stairs with a kind of fierce, scrutinizing intensity on his face.

"What? What's the matter?"

"I don't want you to go."

"I'm just going upstairs." She leans down over the back of the couch, tilting Cael's head back in her hands. Her thumbs trace lightly along his cheekbones. "Aren't you so sick of me, yet?"

He smiles. "No."

"Okay." She kisses his forehead, his eyes, and then his lips.

He laughs triumphantly, taking her by the back of the neck to haul her back in for another before he lets her walk away. And then he rounds instantly on Lucas. "Do you like video games?"

He sputters in disbelief. "Fuck, yeah! What did you have in mind?"

"No VR," Archer tiredly commands, flopping down on the bed.

By his silence, she can tell that Cael is either pouting or plotting. Probably both.

"No, I'm being serious, Caelan," she insists. "I'm not gonna have you wrecking the whole house today, smashing yourself to pieces again. Regular games only."

"You're putting yourself on the wrong side of his—"

"I am not putting myself on the wrong side of history by denying you human rights!"

"Fine," he huffs. "Regular games only."

"Thank you." Archer closes her eyes, and within seconds, she's gone.

CHAPTER TWENTY-FOUR

It's the buzzing of her phone that finally tears her from sleep. She picks it up to see not only four missed calls from her mother, but one from Vander, and a text message that reads:

> Liêu Hanh called.

At least he put a smiling emoji afterwards.

Her stomach churns with a mix of frustration and humiliation, and she sits up, rubbing the sleep from her eyes. But then her phone rings *again*, and she sees the name on the screen, so she throws herself back down onto the bed and kicks her legs like a child throwing a tantrum.

"*Mẹ*," she answers, "you *cannot* call Vander like that!"

"Well, why you don't answer?" she demands. "I call all day, and you don't answer!" Her English gets worse when she's upset.

Her father is audible in the background. *"Is that Cymbre?"*

"Yes! She finally pick up the phone!"

"Hi, Cymbre!"

She gives a bright, cursory, "Hi, dad. *Mẹ*, I've been busy working, and I was sleeping. That's why I didn't answer."

Her mother is immediately suspicious. "Sleeping at two in the afternoon? Are you sick?"

"I was taking a nap," she explains, as calmly as possible. "They made that legal here, I don't know if you heard."

"Made it legal," she repeats, followed by a litany of curses in Viet. "Who raised you?"

Archer peers down towards the living room to see that Cael and Luc are absorbed in their video games, laughing and joking. The photo proofs that she flung everywhere have been stacked neatly on the kitchen table – Cael's doing, she's sure. And Luc, for whatever baffling reason, has taken his shirt off. "Lucas is here, *Mẹ*, do you want to talk to him?"

"No, I want to talk to you! *Cảm thán*, why is Lucas there, and you sleeping at 2 in the afternoon, *Cymbre*? I don't like that!"

"Luc is there? Hi, Luc!"

Liêu Hanh takes the phone away from her ear and lets loose with a string of fast-paced Vietnamese, directed at her husband.

"So, what?" he whispers audibly. *"They're adults! Luc is great! I thought you wanted her to marry him!"*

At that, Archer takes the phone away from her own ear and holds it out at arm's length until they're done.

"Vander says you have problem with your back," her mother pesters.

Archer groans in frustration, getting up to pace around the room. "It's fine, *Mẹ*, it's just sore from the new legs. They're gonna give me nanobots like Luc's, and that'll fix it."

"Are you using green oil?" Her go-to cure for everything from headaches to arthritis to, apparently, amputation.

"Yes, I'm using green oil," she lies.

"I'll have *bà ngoại* send more from Vietnam."

Archer rubs tiredly at her forehead. "You can get green oil in New York, *Mẹ*."

"It's better from Vietnam!"

"Listen to me, you can't call Vander like that," Archer presses, so sick of having to re-hash this conversation for the millionth time. "I'm serious."

"He says you're upset. What you have to be upset about? You have a good life!"

"You literally *just said* that you know my back hurts all the time."

Her mother huffs in frustration. "You know how many people with no leg in Vietnam?"

This, again. She hangs her head in shame, murmuring a quiet, "I know."

"Your *chú* Huy, he step on the landmine, and now his leg made of bamboo and car tire. And you complain about your back hurt?"

"Huy isn't my uncle. He's your ex-boyfriend."

Again, a litany of curses and threats in Viet.

"All right, I have to go, *Mẹ*," she shouts over it. "I'm very busy! I have work to do!"

"You send me email, then! Email me pictures!"

Archer and her father reply in unison: "That's a text message, *Mẹ*." "*You're thinking of a text, darling.*"

More mumbled Viet.

"Okay, *tạm biệt bây giờ, mẹ!*" Archer says, already reaching for the hang-up button. "*Tôi mến bạn*! I love you!"

"Okay, *anh cũng yêu em*!"

"Okay! Stop calling Vander!" With that, Archer hangs up, and sets her phone to do-not-disturb. She flings herself back down onto the bed in a huff, trying to shed the strange guilt that always seems to take hold during conversations with her mother. After a moment, she gets up and crosses over to the stairs. Luc and Cael are whispering like they think she's still on the phone. So, she sits down on the top step, watching them in silence.

The silence doesn't last long. Cael is quick to start in with his observations. "I've noticed that you have characters in Chữ Nôm tattooed on your cheekbone."

Lucas smiles proudly, running a thumb over them. "Yeah."

"Can I look at them?"

"Sure."

Cael pauses the game and leans in very, *very* close to Luc's face. He blinks, tilting his head side to side for a moment. "It says *người yêu.*"

"Yeah. It means beloved."

Cael sits back down and resumes their game. "You and Archer have been friends for a long time," he says, in a tone she knows to be deceptively conversational.

"Yeah. I've known her basically my whole life."

"Mmm. Me, too."

Luc laughs. "I guess you kinda have, huh? She's pretty terrifying for the uninitiated, but once she lets you into her weird little inner circle, you're stuck there forever. She'll kill for you."

Archer's face burns.

"Who is in the weird little inner circle?" Cael asks.

"Well, there's me...and now you."

That seems to stun him into silence, at least momentarily. And then, "Do you love her?"

There it is, Archer thinks. *The other shoe.*

But Luc takes it in his ever-confident stride. "Of course, I do. You can't be friends with a person for 25 years without coming to love them."

"Are you *in* love with her?"

He has to think about that one. "I probably have been, off and on, over the years. And I think she's been in love with me, too, off and on. But Cym and I tend to get into, uh...sort of a destructive pattern, when we spend too much time together. It's not great."

"Yes. I know. But what about right now? Are you in love with her right now?"

"Right now, I can see she's in love with you. So, it shouldn't matter to either of you how I feel about it."

Now it's Cael's turn to think. "Why do you say she loves me?"

"I've known her for 25 years." Luc nudges at him with his elbow. "Never once has she looked at me the way she looks at you."

"Maybe she has, you just haven't been watching."

Luc chuckles. "Hey, are you, like, *actively* trying to set me up with your girlfriend, or what?"

"No!"

With that, the round on their game ends, and the screen advertises Cael's landslide victory. Luc flips the controller out of his hand, letting it fall to the couch in dramatic fashion. "Cocksucker."

"You said you were good at this game," Cael observes flatly. "Do you need me to take it easier on you?"

Luc laughs in disbelief. "Hey, don't be a sore winner!" He shoves Cael on the shoulder, to which he greatly overreacts.

"Ooh, ow!" He clutches at his chest. "Oh, no, my heart! What did you do?"

Luc panics, hands hovering over Cael like he's afraid he's about to crumble into pieces. "Oh, shit. Okay, what do we need to do? I'll go get Cym, and–"

But Cael is already laughing explosively, toppling backwards onto the couch and kicking his legs in a childish display of delight.

Luc deflates. "You're a mean little fucker, you know that?"

Archer chuckles softly at that, and they both turn to look at her.

"Hi!" Cael greets brightly, popping back up again. "Did you see my joke?"

"Yes. Yeah, baby, I saw your joke."

"Was it good?"

"It was very good."

"Hey, was that Liêu Hanh?" Luc asks, oblivious to the fact that Cael has started another round of their shoot-each-other game.

Archer's reply is little more than a groan.

"Aww, why didn't you let me talk to her?"

She rolls her eyes. "Lucas, put your fucking shirt on."

"Why?" He gives her that charming, magazine-cover smile. Cael kills him while he's distracted.

"It's my fault," Cael quickly defends. "I wanted to see his tattoos. And his arm."

She comes down the stairs. "You have the same arms, Caelan."

"His looks cooler, though."

"House full of fucking white boys," she grumbles, heading to the kitchen for some coffee. "Male bonding bullshit."

Now Luc is quick to defend. "Hey, video games are serious!"

"Yes," Cael agrees. "Video games are serious."

She rolls her eyes again.

"What did *Mẹ* have to say for herself?" Luc calls.

As she pours herself a coffee, Archer lets loose with a string of loud, comical threats in Viet; a flawless impression of her mother.

Cael's eyes flutter for a second, and then his expression resolves into a frown. "Your mom threatens to cut your head off?"

"All the time, sweet thing."

Lucas laughs. "What a legend. Did you hear the uncle Huy story?"

"You know I did."

"What was his leg made of this time?"

"Bamboo and car tire."

"Mmm," Luc nods. "Mmm-hmm. Step up from the PVC pipe he had last week though, isn't it?"

Archer sips her coffee. "And the chicken bones and motorcycle parts he had the week before."

"Your mom has a point, though," Cael says. "Vietnam has the highest rate of amputation in the world, owing to the high frequency of motor vehicle accidents and the widespread prevalence of undetonated ordnance. Estimates typically reflect that an average of 450,000 to 500,000 people in Vietnam live with amputation. That's a staggering 0.47% of the population."

"Cael..." Archer cautions.

But he just chatters away, playing his video game. "Most of those people are house farmers in rural areas, walking on improvised, or even homemade prosthetics. They do report a surprisingly high quality of life, and a high rate of satisfaction with their prosthetic, although you have to factor in cultural–"

"Yeah, I'd ease up with that kinda talk, man," Lucas says. "You're digging towards some deep-rooted generational trauma, there."

Cael frowns over his shoulder at her. "You have *more* trauma?"

Archer just laughs.

Lucas stays for a long while, the three of them talking and laughing together. Cael tells Lucas about his great escape from Tartarus, and what it's been like since. Lucas and Archer tell stories about their formative years, and Cael devours them ravenously, collating and cataloging everything. Adding it all to the sum total of who he is.

Archer has to actively tamp down the stab of jealousy she feels as she watches how quickly Cael has taken to Luc. He's bonding much faster, and much more freely than he had with her. She tries to talk herself out of it with logic and reason, remembering that she's the first human person Cael had ever really met, and that Lucas has already saved his life, and if *she* trusts him, and Cael trusts *her*, then surely he'd know to trust Luc, too. Not to mention the fact that Luc is probably the first man who hasn't imprisoned and experimented on him.

But it doesn't help. She's only human, after all. Human, flawed, and so fiercely protective of her sweet boy.

Not, she tells herself, *possessive*.

It's sunset by the time Luc leaves, and Archer can see plainly how much he's struggling to tear himself away. At the door, Cael leaps up and throws his arms around Luc's neck, squeezing him tightly. He whispers thanks into his ear, and Luc's face burns bright with pride. He returns the embrace in earnest, and says that Cael can come see the dogs any time he wants.

"I'm going to walk him down, baby," she tells Cael, following Luc into the hallway.

He furrows his brow. "Why?"

She kisses him on the cheek. "Stupid human reasons."

He's obviously unsatisfied with the answer but accepts it nonetheless, and that must mean he trusts her.

On their way to the elevator, Archer says, "So…with Forge doing all these data audits, we have to be really careful."

"Okay."

"We can't text about him, can't email about him, can't talk on the phone about him. Obviously, don't ever point a camera at him. And you should turn off voice commands for whatever virtual assistants you have before we come over, just to make sure they're not snatching audio. Siri or Alexa or whatever."

"Shit." He blinks in surprise. "Yeah, that's a good point."

"Keep a close eye on your browser history and search engine input, too. They're monitoring that."

He nods, pressing the button to the elevator. "Yeah, I know. That's been a motherfucker."

They're silent during the long ride down to the ground floor. They're silent as they cross the lobby and step out onto the sidewalk. When they get to his bike, Lucas stops and turns to her.

"You quit dropping for him."

Archer nods, still somewhat ashamed of the fact.

"Good. That's...that's really good. I mean...whatever it takes." He slings a leg over his bike, settling in for the ride home.

"Hey." Archer steps up close, eyes downcast as she hurriedly mumbles, "Listen, I...I know I've been a bitch to you lately. I thought I had a good reason, like, I thought that *he* was a good reason to keep you away. But that's bullshit. I should've known it was bullshit, because I know you better than that. I shouldn't have used you like I did, and so I'm sorry."

Luc casts her a sad sort of smile, tilting her face upwards with a knuckle under her chin. "Hey. You're good, Cym. I get it."

"Thank you." She's still so reluctant to meet his gaze. "For..." The rest never comes. There's too much.

Luc seems to understand. He tips his forehead against hers, and they both close their eyes for a moment. And then he's sitting back, and Archer is retreating up onto the curb. He stirs the ignition on his bike and the engine roars to life.

Just before he leaves, Lucas looks up at Archer one final time. Nearly shouting over the sound of the bike, he says, "It's sort of like looking into the face of god, isn't it?"

"What is?"

"Cael."

With that, he's off towards home.

Archer walks into the bathroom to find Cael standing naked before the mirror. He's looking over his shoulder at his back, one arm wrapped around like he's reaching for the place where he'd been wounded. The black cross-hatches stand out like scars, permanently marring the smooth expanse of his back.

"I'm sorry," she says softly, leaning in the doorway. "I had to put it on you, I didn't have a choice."

"That's okay," he says, still studying it closely. "It really helped. Some of the bots found their way back in, since they had nowhere else to go. It was smart."

"You'll have that forever. Like a scar."

"No," he says, brow furrowed. "No, it's...it's a part of you that's become a part of me forever. It feels like having you touch me all the time. I like it."

Archer turns him towards the mirror, resting her hands on his hips. "You have tattoos, now." She lays her lips gently against his back, over and over, moving along the entire length of the scar. "Like Luc and me."

The notion makes him smile. "Yeah." And then he looks down at his hands, his arms. His chest. "I don't look like Luc, though."

"What do you mean?"

"I'm all..." He shakes his arms limply. "Skinny."

"Mmm." She rests her chin on his shoulder, running her fingers up and down his torso. "Remember that the same people who made you the way you are made Luc the way he is. Neither of you has had much say in the matter."

Cael thinks hard about that one. "I don't understand."

"He has to stay that big so that his arms and pecs match," she explains. "I think it's given him a lot of unhealthy ideas about himself."

That seems to sadden him. "I hadn't thought of it that way."

"You're both beautiful," she reassures, slipping a hand up to rest lightly against his throat. She buries her face into the crook of his neck, kissing, kissing. "There's no one way that a person has to look, in order to be beautiful."

As is so typical, Cael abruptly pivots. "I'm all covered in silver."

"Mmm," she hums against his neck. "Me, too, baby."

"We should take a shower before we get in bed."

"That's probably a good idea."

He steps over, turning the water on. "Come do it with me," he commands. "I don't want to not be able to see and touch you right now."

Archer acquiesces with no argument, shedding her clothing to join him. She steps beneath the stream of water, tilting her head back to let it pour over her. Her hair saturates, hanging heavily down her back. Cael runs his fingers through his own hair, giving a few cursory scrubs at his silver-stained limbs and chest, and then he abruptly seems to sap. He braces his hands on the wall, shoulders slumped forward. It's such a disarmingly human gesture, this display of exhaustion. And of course, he's exhausted after the day they've had. But it's strange to see that he'd seemingly been keeping up appearances for Luc's sake. It's strange to think that something he's learned, something in his programming, told him that would be the correct, *human* thing to do. And now that they're alone again, everything is catching up with him.

It's moments like these that make the sum of all of his tiny, myriad changes seem so stark. So monumental.

Archer's thumbs press into the small of his back, fingers curling around his hipbones. His entire body seems to exhale in relief at her touch, and he whimpers softly, craning into it.

"You're all right, my one," she reassures, pressing her lips between his shoulder blades. "Come here."

She coaxes him around to face her and takes up the washcloth. With quiet, loving attention, she scrubs the caked-on conductor fluid from his skin. It's a gentleness that only he has ever seen from her, a gentleness that only he has drawn out. Cael leans back against the wall, head cocked lazily to one side. He's watching her movements carefully, following her hands as they move across his body.

"You were scared today," he whispers.

"I was," she says, no small amount of anxiety at the admission. "I thought I was going to lose you forever."

"I thought you were going to lose me forever, too."

"I'm still scared. I guess it wasn't something I really ever thought about before today. Well...maybe once, when that guy jumped me outside."

"Why?"

She takes his hand in hers, delicately scrubbing the silver from every line and crack. "I was afraid that he was here to try and steal you."

"But you didn't even like me back then."

"I did. I just wasn't very good at showing it. I'm trying to be better now." She takes up his other hand, repeating the process.

"I'm always afraid I'm going to lose you forever. Every time you leave the house. It's been like that since the second I saw you."

"Well, Luc knows about you now," she says, trying not to read into the timeline he'd put on that admission. "If something were to happen to me, he would take care of you."

Cael frowns. "No, that's not the point. I'm afraid of losing *you*. But..." The hesitation is entirely uncharacteristic.

"But?"

He fidgets a little before he answers. "But then I remember about quantum entanglement, and it makes me feel better."

Archer laughs softly. "What?"

"Einstein's spooky action at a distance."

She presses a kiss to the inside of his wrist. "I don't know what that means, sweet thing."

"Well...once two particles have entwined, it's impossible to describe either one independent of the state of the other. Even if they're split up, a literal universe apart. If you alter or affect one of them, then you'll affect the other one, too."

"Mmm." She spreads his palm apart with her fingers, lacing their hands together. "And we're entwined?"

He nods, eyes downcast like he's embarrassed.

She combs her fingers back through his hair, scrubbing away the streaks of silver she'd dragged through it earlier. She has no idea what to say. Everything she can think of sounds pale and hollow; inadequate, when compared to his strange and vibrant poetry. And isn't it just like an AI, just like Cael, to express a thing like love with some ridiculous fact about math? *Because that's what he's doing,* she realizes. *He's trying to say that he loves you.*

Say it back, you coward.

"What are you thinking about?"

"I'm thinking about you."

"Good things about me?"

"100% good things." She whispers it against his lips, and then steals it back with a kiss.

When the conductor fluid has been washed away, Archer guides him out of the shower. She dries his hair with a towel, leaving it wild and tousled and completely adorable, before draping the towel around his shoulders.

He watches in silence while she combs her own hair. His eyes trace along all of her lines: her wrists, her shoulders, the curve of her ribs and the jut of her hipbones. He mimics for a little while, standing just slightly behind her. And then he steps in close and takes a strand of her hair between his fingers, still silver from the photoshoot. It'll fade to platinum blonde eventually, like his. Shredding her ends. Archer submits to this gentle, loving examination with no protest. She's learned by now that it's sort of Cael's love-language.

"I'm incredibly proud of you for not doing any drugs, today," he suddenly announces.

She makes eye contact with him in the mirror. "What?"

"Acute stress is one of the most common triggers for relapse into drug addiction. It would've been understandable. But you didn't relapse. It's good."

That gives her pause. *Fuck, I could've gotten away with dropping, today?* She turns to look at him. "I didn't—it didn't even occur to me. The only thing I was worried about was you."

"That's because you've grown as a person." And then he blurts, "Come have sex with me, and then we can go to sleep."

"Wait, should we actually, though?" she asks, by now adjusted to these abrupt topic changes of his. "I don't want to overextend you too quickly–"

"I heal differently than meat puppets," he says, setting her comb on the counter and letting the towels fall unceremoniously to the floor. He takes her by the hand, dragging her out into the living room. "Come have sex with me."

CHAPTER TWENTY-FIVE

Hannibal, Missouri didn't work out. Neither did Madison, Indiana, or Elmhurst, Illinois, or any of the dozen other places he'd stopped along the way. Motels had dropped gradually in quality with each move he made, and then taken a very sharp dive around the time he crossed into Nebraska. By South Dakota, the motel money had run out.

He'd tried a shelter once. That didn't work out, either. As soon as he got within 50 feet of the place, he'd caught sight of the surveillance cameras peppering the building's exterior walls and fucked off the way he came. It's just as well. He's heard that those shelters like to call the cops on drug users.

Because there's still Penth money, of course, and that's good. He doesn't think he'd be able to sleep rough like this without it.

To be honest, he's not even sure where he is anymore. Some nondescript, under-tended park, in some nondescript, under-tended city, but that's all he knows. 9th Avenue and 4th Street, like that means anything to him. Wherever he is, it's fucking cold.

This is a slightly bigger city than he's been used to, and that's a gamble. More cameras, so he has to keep his face hidden, but he blends into the scenery better than he would in a small town. It sort of seems like there's a college nearby, judging by the age and enthusiasm of passersby. That helps, since he feels like college kids are less likely to call the cops on a homeless man. A few have even offered to buy him food, but fear of being remembered when shit hits the fan has kept him from accepting. And college kids are far from the only people around.

That first night, he'd been so Penthed-out that someone had managed to steal his shoes while he slept in an alley behind a library. He'd had to steal new ones from a locker in a 24-hour gym, and while they're good boots, they're too big. Now, on the fifth night, he knows to take his shoes off and sleep on top of them. But it's cold enough that he's sort of worried about losing toes, and that's the thought keeping him awake right now.

The benches in this city have spikes on them. You have to scan a card if you want them to retract. Luckily, he's managed to squeeze underneath the seat.

He has no idea how it's come to this.

Well, he does and he doesn't.

Some kids have started to drift through the park in little groups of threes and fives. Maybe some party host finally kicked them out, or bars are starting to close down. Hard to tell exactly what time it is. The kids are loud, and wholly wrapped up in their own little dramas.

"No, fuck you, Jason. I seriously feel like I can't take you anywhere anymore, especially not when she's around."

"Oh my God, you need to let it go. You're always like this."

The man under the bench tenses and tugs his pack a little closer. The only thing of value he has in there are his drugs, but he's running low. There had been a deal going down in the park, not too long ago. Well, not a deal so much as a...session. But he learned the hard way not to take drugs from other people on the street, because the next night, it's your door they're knocking on, demanding that you either pay them or return the favor.

"Dude it was the funniest meme I've ever seen. Just an arrow pointing to a duck, and it says 'motor oil.'"

"Who posted it?"

"Some gimmick account, I don't even remember."

For weeks now, he's been lost in the middle-ground between numb and terrified. Everything feels fractured and anxious, like there's something disastrous shifting just below the surface of reality. Maybe he just needs more Penth. Or less. Probably more.

Fuck, he wants a drop now. The need is clicking along the inside of his skull like an insect, pinching and tugging at the loose wires of his brain, but he knows better than to draw attention to himself like that. Although no one has noticed or remarked on him yet, the college kids are still coming. He'll have to find someplace else tomorrow. This amount of foot traffic is unsafe.

"No, listen, what I was saying was that you ever notice how the only people coming up with real innovations anymore are rich guys? Elon Musk commercialized space, Jeff Bezos redefined capitalism, and Evander Callas perfected private medicine."

"Holy fucking shit. Ignore him, he's an econ major with an Adderall addiction."

The man crammed under the bench presses his eyes shut hard. He misses his luxury apartment in Tribeca, and the view of the city skyline from high up. He misses his couch and his TV; he misses truffle fries from Doordash and having a credit card. Hell, he's even started to miss his job, because at least it was *something*.

He knows he did the right thing, but he sort of wishes that it hadn't cost him quite so much.

He wonders if it actually did need to cost this much, or if he's been overreacting this whole time.

And so, for those reasons and so many more, Robert Wells quietly decides that it's time to ask Archer for help again.

CHAPTER TWENTY-SIX

"Archer."

Her reply comes in the form of a frustrated groan, and she rolls away from his voice without opening her eyes.

"*Archer.*"

"Mmm…" She reaches blindly in his direction. "What time is it, baby? Come lie back down."

"It's 1:00 pm. I fed the cat seven hours ago. Also, Luc is here."

"What?" Archer sits up blearily, only to find Cael standing beside the bed. Fully dressed in her clothes, like they're going out.

He smiles broadly, and then calls over his shoulder, "She's awake!"

"Wait, you let Luc in? Why is he even here?"

"We made plans. He started texting you, but you were sleeping, so I replied."

Archer rubs at her face. "What?"

"Can we go over to his house and play with the dogs?"

"Yeah," she sighs, still struggling a little to wake up. "Yeah, okay. Just let me get ready, and–"

"No, Luc has his motorcycle," Cael interrupts, already heading for the stairs. "We're just going to go now, and then you can meet us there."

"What?" She leaps out of bed, tailing him down into the living room. Sure enough, Lucas is there, in his motorcycle jacket, holding a pair of helmets. "No, hang on! I don't like this!"

"Morning!" Lucas greets brightly. "You gonna meet us there?"

"What? No! We need to–I don't know, plan this! Better!"

Luc rolls his eyes. "Cym. You've had more than a week to hole up in here and fuck each other–"

Cael stifles a laugh into his hand.

"–he's fine. He's better. Time to share."

She opens her mouth to protest, but he steamrolls right over her.

"He'll be wearing a helmet, and he'll never be out of arm's reach."

"Yeah, but–"

"Arch*er*," Cael whines, stomping over to tug at the front of her shirt. "*Please.*"

She groans in frustration, closing her eyes and letting her head fall back in defeat. "You're gonna wear anti-surveillance shit," she finally concedes.

Even Luc can't argue. "Ah, yeah, she actually has a point, there."

"Okay, I will!"

"I mean it, Caelan! I don't care that you don't like the principle of it. You can't see your own face anyway."

"I know!" He sprints away.

"And you're not getting on that fucking motorcycle in my *De Vilmorin Couture*!"

Cael skids to a halt, looking down at the garment. "Is this a dress?"

Archer and Luc answer in unison. "*Yes.*"

"Oh." Apparently unbothered by the information, he hurries upstairs to begin rifling around in her things.

Archer takes the opportunity to glare at Lucas. "If I get over there and find so much as a–"

"Cym," he sets the helmets down and wraps her in a crushing embrace. "Relax. Let him have fun."

The remark makes her bristle with indignation, because Cael has fun *all the time*, goddammit, but her vitriol is muffled into his broad chest.

He seems to get the point, and kisses her on the top of the head.

"Hey, don't kiss my girlfriend," Cael scolds, thumping back down the stairs. He's changed clothes, thank God, into a set of Archer's leggings and a long t-shirt. And he's wearing one of her visors, hooked over one ear and pinched to the bridge of his nose to place a pixelated-looking lens over the left side of his face. "Happy?" he asks, arms thrown wide in expectation. Archer knows he picked the gesture up from her.

"Happi*er*."

"Okay, but I can't wear it with the motorcycle helmet," he says, reaching up to remove the visor. "So–"

"Ah-ah-ah!" Archer catches him by the wrist. "You'll wear it until the instant that helmet goes on, and you're gonna put it right back on, after. Lucas?"

"She's right, man. I'm gonna hold you to that."

"Good," Archer appraises, brisk. "Fine."

Delighted, Cael clamps her face in his hands and hauls her into a rough kiss. "Thank you," he whispers, and the thrilled little quiver in his voice is enough to tell her she's made the right decision.

As he puts his shoes on and makes his way for the door, Archer catches Luc by the shoulder. "Do not drive like a maniac."

"I won't, Cym."

"No, I'm fucking serious, Lucas, I'll rip that arm off and shove it right up your–"

"*Cym.*" He hauls her in for another kiss. "Relax."

"Hey, don't kiss my girlfriend."

"And you!" she says, rounding on Cael. "You hold onto him like your life depends on it, do you hear me? Because it's literally about to!" She snatches one of her thicker jackets from a hook by the door, and tosses it over his shoulders.

"I'll be fine, Archer," he reassures, slipping his arms through the sleeves. "I promise."

With that, the pair sets off down the hallway, laughing and chattering away.

Archer moves to the window, where she can see Luc's bike parked on the curb. It's another grey day, the sky spitting a kind of sparse, freezing rain down on everything. That makes her worry about Luc's driving even more. While she waits for the pair to emerge from the building, she checks her phone. Sure enough, there's a string of brand-new text messages, starting around 11:00 am.

> Hey, u up?

> > Yes, hello, this is Cymbre Archer.

> lol okay amazing. You wanna come over today? You've been holed up in there a while...

> > Yes, I think I would enjoy that very much. Will the dogs be there?

> LOL yes the dogs will be here and we can play games. I have a projector screen I play on. Could even come get you on the bike~

> > Yes yes yes

> You wanna clear this with the administration, or...? We just pulling the trigger?

> > Admin is unavailable at this time, and I am not a baby

> Lol okay sick. Couple hours?

> > Yes okay good

Archer rolls her eyes. At least they'd had the wherewithal to exercise a modicum of discretion. She looks down to see Cael and Luc emerge from the front door of the building. Cael flits excitedly around the bike for a while, and then Luc settles into place, and he climbs on behind him.

"Helmet," she murmurs aloud. "*Helmet*, Lucas." She holds her breath until they're both wearing them.

Then Luc must turn the bike on, because she sees Cael jump, and clamp his arms around Luc's waist. Luc pries at him a little, and that makes sense, because Archer knows how hard he can squeeze when he really wants to. They talk for a few seconds – shout, rather, over all the goddamn noise that thing makes – and then Lucas lowers the shield on his helmet and they're off.

She showers quickly, neglecting to put on any makeup and throwing on the first clothes she can rip from the closet. She dons her own anti-surveillance on her way to the elevator, and then she's down on the street, hailing a cab. Luc lives in Chelsea, which is one hundred thousand miles away, and the ride drags on with painful, agonizing slowness. In the interest of haste, she'd taken the first cab she could get, and it had wound up driverless. Now she thinks it would have been better to wait for a human driver, because they care less about the speed limit or traffic laws.

Seventeen million *entire* hours later, she's pulling up to Luc's building, and the scene on the curb sends her into a frenzy.

"*No!*" she shouts, leaping from the cab, "no, absolutely not!"

Cael is sitting alone astride the parked motorcycle, helmetless, while Luc looks on and gives direction from the sidewalk. The fact that he's wearing his anti-surveillance provides only the smallest possible relief.

Cael squints at Archer, wary, and then looks up at Luc. He whispers, "Is that her?"

"Yeah," Luc laughs. "It's her."

Cael beams, relieved. "Hi!" he greets brightly, pretending to rev the engine on the bike. It's much too big for him, and he's stretched out ridiculously in his attempt to reach both the pedals and the handlebars. "*David Bowie,*" he whispers to himself, "*photographed by Steve Schapiro, Los Angeles, 1975.*"

"Cael, *off.*"

He ignores her. "How angry would you be if Lucas taught me to ride a motorcycle? Give me a percentage."

"I'm not playing the percentage game with you today, Caelan. No motorcycle lessons."

He looks up at her with that adorable, pouty expression.

"No!"

"But—"

"Look up motorcycle accident victims," Archer prompts.

Luc stammers, comically panicked. "Hey! Don't tell him that!"

It's too late. Cael's one visible eye is already blank and flickering.

"Look up *de-gloving pictures*," she goads.

"Cymbre, you fuck."

All at once, Cael leaps off of the motorcycle. "Oh," he murmurs. "Oh, no thank you."

"But why does that even matter?" Luc challenges, playful and charming as always. "If your shit gets de-gloved, they can just slap some more Arachne on there, you'll be fine!"

"*They?*" Archer parrots, incredulous. "Luc, there's no *they*! There's just *us*! You and me! And the—" Her voice drops to a harsh whisper. "The *highly illegal shit* we pulled!"

"How about this?" Cael interrupts. "I'll ride with Lucas, but not by myself."

Archer huffs in frustration. "*Fine.*"

"Relax, Cym," Luc scolds for the millionth time. "He's fine, you're fine, everyone here is fine."

With one final glare in Luc's direction, Archer throws a protective arm around Cael's shoulders, and the trio makes their way inside.

Once the elevator doors close behind them, Cael traces his fingers up her neck and starts questing blindly for her anti-surveillance. "Off, now," he begs in a whisper.

She obliges, tucking the visor into her coat pocket. "Better?"

He exhales in relief. "Yes." He tucks his head under her chin, where he remains for the rest of the elevator ride.

"All right, I ran the dogs for a while this morning, to try and get them all worn out," Luc says as they approach his door, "but they're still pretty high-energy. So, brace for that."

"I like high-energy." Cael is already bouncing lightly on the balls of his feet.

Luc laughs. "I don't know, man, high-energy mutant cat is way different from high-energy Irish Wolfhound."

Archer rolls her eyes. "Mutant cat."

Luc opens the door, and chaos ensues. Dogs are jumping all over the place and barking, Luc is shouting and trying to push them back. Cael panics a little, ducking under Archer's shoulder with his arms clamped around her waist. But he's still grinning.

"Hi, dogs!" he squeals, "hi, it's nice to meet you!"

"This is Bruno," Luc holds the bigger dog back by the collar. "And Heidi."

"Hi, Bruno and Heidi!"

"We need to go inside!" Archer shouts over the noise.

"Okay, okay!" Luc hefts the Pit mix up in his arms. "All right! Inside, inside!"

Cael and Archer follow, and no sooner has the door shut behind them than Cael has broken free with his arms outstretched towards the dogs. The good news is that they don't seem to regard him as anything but a new, surprise friend. The bad news is, the combined enthusiasm in the room quickly reaches an unmanageable, fever pitch, culminating when the Irish Wolfhound hops up onto his hind legs and plants his paws firmly on Cael's shoulders. The dog is taller than he is by a substantial margin, and it sends him toppling over backwards. His anti-surveillance goes flying, and Luc has to dive to catch it before the lens shatters on the tile.

"Hey, hey, hey!" Archer lunges forward, ready to intervene, but Cael is shrieking with laughter.

"It's okay!" He wraps his arms around both dogs, delighting in being stepped on and licked and kicked around. "They're okay! This is fun! They're so happy to meet me!"

"Yeah, but manners are manners," Luc says. And with a single, sharp whistle, he has both dogs sheepishly stepping away.

Archer helps Cael to his feet, and he wipes the dog spit from his face with the sleeve of his jacket.

"Are you all right?" she demands, fretting over his hair and his clothing.

"I'm fine! I'm fine!"

"Okay, you go get him. *Calmly.*" Luc gives the dogs a nod, and this time, they approach much more gently.

Cael kneels down and scratches them on the head and behind their ears. "Hi, dogs," he whispers, over and over and over again. "Hi, dogs! Hi, dogs! Hi, dogs! It's so nice to meet you!"

"You be nice to your new friend," Luc heeds, clearly cued into the ever-increasing tail-wag speed. "You be nice to Cael."

"I'm Cael." He points to himself. "You have to be nice to me, okay?"

"Place looks good," Archer remarks, looking around.

"Yeah, it's been a bit since you've come over here, huh? Got some new stuff."

Finally, Cael tears his attention away from the dogs and, for the first time, really looks at where he is. "Oh, wow."

Luc's place is beautiful. It's bigger than Archer's – a two-story, four-bedroom, three-bathroom condo with two terraces, and floor-to-ceiling windows. Wide-open and expansive, covered in black and white marble and sleek, modernist furnishings. Light fixtures dangle from the 18-foot ceilings, and accent pieces are all dark, gleaming metallics. There's a projector screen floating in front of the main wall in his living room, opposite a massive sectional. A cubicle cabinet beneath the screen houses every possible game system that a person could ever enjoy. Like Archer's place, this was one of the first real purchases that Luc made with his grown-up Forge money. And she has no idea how he's kept it this pristine, with both dogs jumping around on every surface all the time.

"Can I explore?" Cael asks. Archer can sense a blink-and-label frenzy coming on. It's in the way his attention is flitting from random object to random object, and the way his fingers are twitching.

"Yeah, sure," Luc says, "make yourself at home."

"Okay, thank you." Cael takes off, followed closely by both dogs. "*Couch, Wayfair, corner sectional.*" Blink. "*PlayStation 8, VR-adapted.*" Blink. "*Light. Light fixture. Color-change LED.*" Blink. His voice fades into the distance as he wanders off.

"He's gonna poke around your whole place." Archer throws herself down onto the couch. "Seriously, he's gonna open drawers and touch, like, *all* of your stuff."

"That's fine, I robot-proofed it."

An excited yelp sounds from the kitchen, startling them both.

Fuck, that didn't take long. "What?" Archer calls out. "What, what?"

Cael tiptoes out from around the corner again, pointing at the ground. "*Who is this person?*"

She cranes her neck to see Luc's Roomba trundling around near Cael's feet. "That's a vacuum cleaner, baby," she explains. "It's just a little robot vacuum cleaner."

"*Oh my god,*" Cael whispers, kneeling down to inspect it more closely. "Chores-robot! Hi!"

It bumps into his toe and then changes direction.

"Oh, he's so smart!" he says, quietly thrilled. He pats the robot on the back. "You're so smart!"

"You can mess with it," Luc says, "I don't care."

Cael is still sneaking around behind the thing, watching it intently. "Is he allowed upstairs?"

"Uh…yeah, I mean, it can do stairs. It goes up and down by itself, all day."

After a moment of flighty deliberation, Cael scoops the vacuum up and clutches it to his chest. Its tiny wheels spin futility, pivoting and turning every which way, trying to break free of this confounding obstacle. It even sends out a few high-pitched chimes in protest.

Cael whispers to it as he heads to the stairs. "It's okay." He pets it lightly. "You know your way around this house, so you're going to come with me. You can show me all of the things." The dogs follow behind him, concerned by his behavior.

Archer laughs. "Robot-proof," she mocks in a whisper. "King *shit*."

"That's…absolutely fucking adorable," Luc murmurs. "Like, that is the cutest goddamn thing I've ever seen, *look* at him. What the *fuck*?"

"Yeah," she chuckles. "He's like that."

"I've noticed that you don't have any plants in here," Cael shouts, his voice distant and muffled.

"Caelan, *no*."

He grumbles in discontent. "Fine. Can I pair with your SmartHome?"

"Yeah, you can pair with the house," Luc calls back, "that's fine."

"Thank you." After a short silence, there's a kind of crackling noise from the surround-sound speakers. "Can I play music?" His voice is coming from a different place, now. "You have good music."

"Yeah, man, go for it."

Archer mumbles, "I will bet you one thousand *actual* dollars that he plays 'Sound and Vision' by David–"

At once, the speakers roar to life with the opening riffs of 'Gimme Shelter' by The Rolling Stones.

"*Hah*! Pay up."

"Hey, hey, turn it down, Caelan!" Archer shouts.

"Sorry." The volume lowers.

"You sure you wanna play the Stones?" Luc teases. "Your girlfriend's gonna get all emotional and shit."

"Lucas, shut your mouth."

They see Cael walk past, upstairs; still flitting from room to room, still clutching the Roomba to his chest, still trailed by both dogs. "Why would she get all emotional and shit?" he asks as he goes by.

"She and Sir Mick were like ships passing in the night."

"Shut *up*, I said." Archer punches Luc on the shoulder – a bad idea, she learns, as she only succeeds in hurting her own fist.

Triumphant, Luc sticks out his tongue and flips her the double-bird.

Cael's wide-eyed face pops out from around an upstairs corner. "Did you know Mick Jagger?"

"No." She waves him off. "Don't you have more of Luc's stuff to touch?"

"Oh, yes, she *did* know Mick Jagger," Luc says, all too proud of himself. "She sat next to him at the Met Gala, three years in a row."

"Lucas, relax, it was only the one year that we were next to each other." And then, almost reluctant, she mumbles, "The other two years, he just found me on the red carpet and then kept…coming over."

Cael is down the stairs in a flash, clambering up onto the couch to get right in Archer's face. He's still holding the chiming vacuum cleaner. "Tell me more information about this, *right now*." The dogs follow closely behind, crowding in equally close.

She leans away. "Settle down!"

"Arch*errr*."

"They just sat me next to him at my first Met Gala! Luc and I got invited after our first *Vogue* cover, and they sat me next to Mick Jagger. Fuck."

"And?" Luc prompts.

"*And*," she grumbles, exasperated, "he spent the whole time trying to get me to fuck him."

Cael laughs excitedly.

"I'm not special! Do you know how many millions of people Mick Jagger tried to fuck?"

"Yeah, but you're one of them!" Cael says. "So, did you?"

"No!" she sputters. "Caelan, he was 85!"

"And then 86," Luc chuckles, "and 87…"

"Lucas, shut *up*."

"Still." Cael shrugs. "I would have fucked 85-year-old Mick Jagger."

"*Thank* you!" Luc chimes in. "See?"

Archer shakes her head in dismay, reaching for the Roomba. "Okay, maybe we let this guy go now, what do you say?"

Cael holds it tighter, trying to lean out of her reach. "Howard."

"Okay, sweet thing, but Howard belongs on the floor. You're freaking him out." She gently pries the Roomba from his grip, setting it back down on the ground. It chimes brightly, resuming its frenetic little cleaning routine. And then she notices how hard Cael is breathing, so she lays the back of her hand against his throat, beneath his jaw. Too warm. "Hey, let's take your jacket off, you're gonna roast."

"Okay." Cael watches the Roomba intensely while Archer coaxes him out of his heavy coat. And once he's free, he rounds on Luc with frightening intensity. "Tell me more things about Archer that I don't know."

To her great dismay, he does just that. As they get the video games fired up, he talks about her first true love – a girl named Lauren who broke her heart in the 8th grade. By the time they're into their third round of shooting each other, he's telling Cael about how there's no more foolproof a method for bringing out Archer's pretentious French *and* Viet heritage than to serve her an inadequate Báhn mì. And then it's onto her brief stint attempting to be a writer; her failed English degree from NYU, and her subsequently deep-seated hatred for graduates of the school. And every time she tries to interject, to put a stop to this humiliating display, Cael puts a hand over her mouth and looks at her like she just threatened to send him back to Tartarus.

They stay until the sun hangs low and heavy, orange glow licking at edges of the skyline like fire. Luc and Cael play around with exercise equipment, and Luc throws a veiled tantrum over the margin by which Cael outlifts him. They try to arm wrestle. Cael's left beats Luc's left with no effort, but they stalemate for minutes when they try to wrestle with their cybernetics. Archer has to put a stop to it before one or both of them physically breaks.

Luc teaches Cael how to make the dogs do tricks, and that results in the dogs getting far too many treats. (As if they weren't already committed to shadowing Cael's every move.) And then Archer sits in the kitchen while Luc and Cael make dinner – Phở, because Luc thinks he's so clever.

"Phở-king clever," he says.

At least Cael laughs.

It's just the way it had been, back at her own loft. Cael hangs on Luc's every word, silently mirroring the way his hands move, and all of his physical mannerisms. Occasionally, he'll lunge forward, hold Luc still, and whisper to himself as he examines one of his tattoos. He does strange little things like comparing the size of their hands, or the size of their feet. He likes touching the back of Luc's head, too, where it's shaved down close. "It looks like it should feel like the cat, but it doesn't feel like the cat."

Archer knows these rituals all too well. After four months, Cael still performs them on her. She imagines that this must be very strange for him, that he sees a kind of distorted reflection of himself in Lucas. A man, too, yes. Made of the same parts. But different in all the most subtle, nuanced ways that baffle him the most.

And yes – by the time the night is through, both of them are shirtless.

Towards the end of the visit, Cael finally gets around to asking Luc to take his arm off. Archer had been wondering how long it would take. Luc does it, of course, and gladly. He's never been self-conscious about it in the way that Archer is. Selfishly, she hopes that Cael doesn't think any less of her in comparison. But he pokes around Luc's amputation site with intense interest, running his fingers along his ribs and the awkward jut of collarbone. He examines the arm itself, holding it close to his face, comparing it to his own.

"You lost your arm in a car accident," he verbalizes, just as blunt as Archer has come to expect.

But Luc nods, watching Cael go about his strange inspection. "I did, yeah."

"How?"

Luc takes a deep breath. "Car got T-boned when someone ran a red light, and that spun us. The front end was crushed. My parents were in the front seat, and they were either KO'd or dead at that point, but I was still conscious in the back. So, I unbuckled my seatbelt and tried to crawl up there, had my right arm extended out towards my mom, and then another car hit us head-on because they somehow didn't see the smoking wreckage in the middle of the intersection."

He recites it so matter-of-factly, almost like it's scripted. And of course, it is scripted. He's spent his entire life telling this story. To cameras, to journalists, to doctors, and random people on the street. It's his defining characteristic, whether he wants it to be or not. It's the first thing people ask, and the one thing they remember when they're trying to describe him. The trauma of it all has become detached, out of necessity.

"Last thing I remember was looking up and seeing headlights, and then I woke up in the hospital with a shoulder disarticulation." He gestures through the empty space with his remaining hand. "Fell asleep again, and when I woke up, they'd given up trying to bolt the shoulder blade back together and just taken it, too. I lucked out though, because they were able to save some collarbone. That made Forge's work a lot easier."

Cael is still holding Luc's cybernetic up to his face, tilting his head side-to-side as he scans over every detail. "How old were you?"

"Don't you know all of this, already?" Luc chuckles. "Doesn't she ever talk about me?"

Cael frowns. "Yes, but your story is yours to tell, and since we're friends now, I would prefer to hear it from you, if that's not an issue."

The quiet, genuine pride on Luc's face is an unfamiliar but heartwarming sight. "I was six. I got put into foster care after that, and bounced around a few different places. Wound up in this overcrowded house in Elmhurst, where the parents just kept collecting foster kids for the money. Five years later, they saw that Forge was looking for disabled kids to experiment on, and they sensed a paycheck. So, I got my first arm, met Archer, and then had my ass legally emancipated at 16." He shrugs, residual collarbone rising and falling in unison with his intact shoulder. "The rest is history."

When night falls, Archer practically has to drag Cael into the cab. He's silent for the entire ride, so as not to trigger any voice recognition. But he settles heavily into Archer's arms, head tucked under her chin as he watches the world go by. He'll sleep like a rock tonight, she knows. He has so much to collate. She can already see the synapses firing behind his eyes.

On their way up the elevator, Cael announces, "I like Lucas a lot. I think I consider him a role model."

Archer laughs. "That's...that's a bad idea."

"Why? I thought you liked Luc."

"I love Luc." (*Wait, shit, should I have told him that I love someone else, when I can't even say it to him? Does he understand that it's different? FUCK.*) "I mean, he's my oldest friend in the world, and I'd take a bullet for that man. But he's a himbo, and he has a fuckboy haircut."

Cael wrinkles his nose in disapproval. "Don't slut shame men, Archer."

"What? I'm not–Caelan, you've got me so fucked up." She hauls him in close to kiss him on the forehead. It seems to be enough to distract him from the conversation.

"Can I have a tiny vacuum cleaner friend?"

She laughs. "What, for all the cat hair everywhere?"

"Archer, the cat doesn't have any–*hah!*"

When they step out of the elevator and into the hallway leading to Archer's loft, they instantly freeze.

There's a man standing by her door. He's wearing a stained sweatshirt with the hood up, but they can see his long, unkempt hair sticking out from beneath it. There's a worn backpack slung over one of his shoulders, held together with duct tape. He's slumped against the doorframe, one fist pounding weakly against the wood. He hasn't seen them yet.

Archer's veins flood with icy adrenaline. Whoever this is, however he got into the building, he certainly can't be here to make friends. He looks weak, and she could probably fight him off, but then what? It's not like she can just call the fucking police. Her instinct is to flee, to scoop Cael up in her arms and run straight back to Luc's, where they can be safe.

But before she can act, Cael yanks on her arm, knocking her off-balance. She nearly falls.

"Hey!" he shouts at the intruder, "you'd better get out of here, or she's going to punch you!" The strange, paradoxical instinct to protect his protector.

"*Caelan!*" she scolds in a harsh whisper, urging him to step behind her. He does, but maintains his vise-like grip on her wrist.

The man begins to turn, swaying on his feet.

"Hey, I'm not fucking around!" she calls. "You'd better get the hell out of here, unless you want–"

The intruder lets out a weary sigh. "What?" he challenges weakly. "You gonna break my jaw with a shot glass, Cym?"

That stops her dead in her tracks. And then the intruder pushes his hood back, and the breath is snatched from her chest.

"Wells?" she murmurs, voice quivering in the dead-still air.

Cael peers out from behind her, wide-eyed.

"Yeah," Rob exhales, something like the ghost of a smile on his lips. "Hey." And then his gaze drifts up over her shoulder, to where Cael is standing on tiptoe. His posture wavers. "Is that…?"

Archer nods, somewhat frantically. "Yeah." Without another word, she drags Cael down the hall, shoves the pair into the loft, and bolts the door behind them.

CHAPTER TWENTY-SEVEN

WHEN ARCHER ROUNDS ON WELLS, SHE FINDS HERSELF AT A COMPLETE loss for words. The longer she looks, the worse he appears. His skin is ashen, lips dry and cracked. He looks cold and thin; nothing like the manicured, Tribeca, tech-startup-looking hipster who had so frustrated her for all those years. He's got a beard now, streaked with silver-white.

And what the hell is she supposed to say?

You've got some nerve showing your face around here, after what you did?

I'm so madly, so painfully *in love, and goddamn you, it's all your fault?*

In a million years, a million lifetimes, I'll never be able to repay the debt I owe you for this?

Cael is still standing on tiptoe behind her, one hand clamped to her upper arm. He offers a bright little, "Hello."

Rob exhales sharply, looking between the pair. "After all this time, you're…he's…" Tears are beginning to well up in his eyes. "Can I…?"

"Yeah," she says, gently guiding Cael out from behind her. "Rob, this is Cael. I think you've met."

Rob drops his bag with no ceremony, shaking hand outstretched. He has his palm upturned, supplicant. Cael takes it gleefully, and again, Rob releases a shuddering gasp.

"It's nice to see you again," Cael says, whipping his arm up and down in an aggressive handshake. "I'm glad you're alive."

Rob chokes on a laugh. "Yeah, me too," he stammers. "I'm glad you're alive, too." His free hand begins to drift absently towards Cael's face, fingertips ghosting delicately along the edge of his jaw.

"Are you hungry? You look hungry. I made macaroni and cheese last night, and Archer said I made way too much for two people, so there's definitely plenty for you to have some."

"Yeah," Rob manages, withdrawing his hand. "Yeah, that would be great, actually. Thank you."

"Great!" Cael turns abruptly, striding into the kitchen to clatter around with Tupperware and dishes. "If you don't like macaroni, I could make some mashed potatoes, or chicken cordon bleu, or salmon steaks, or shrimp tacos—"

"The macaroni is 100% perfect, sweet thing," Archer gently interrupts. "Thank you."

Rob is spellbound, watching Cael with a sort of open reverence on his face. "Cael," he murmurs to Archer. "C-A-E-L. I get it. That's..." The sentence trails off into silence, but by his expression, Archer understands.

"One of the techs from Tartarus came by my apartment to warn me, the morning after we got him out," Wells explains between desperate bites of pasta. "We all got that email, and then I guess the corporate Gestapo went poking around in the basement, and it didn't take them long to tie me to the whole fucking thing."

"Which you expected," Cael says. They're all crowded around the small dining-room table. And although Cael is sitting in his own chair, rather than in Archer's lap, he has one foot hooked around her ankle. It's immeasurably comforting for the both of them.

Wells nods. "Yeah, I expected it. I just didn't think they'd figure it out that quickly. I also thought I could buy some plausible deniability by ditching my badge and doctoring the security footage, but I guess they saw right through it."

"What did you do?" Archer asks.

He shrugs. "Fucking ran. I packed up whatever shit I could carry, clothes and whatever, and then I went around to every bank and ATM I could get to, withdrawing as much cash as possible. Then I threw my phone and credit cards into the Hudson and got the hell out of the city. I stayed in roadside motels for a while, like, rural places without facial recognition. Paying cash for everything, hitchhiking around and shit. And then when I ran out of money, I just started sleeping wherever."

"Why did you come back?" Archer knows it's a stupid question the moment she asks it.

"I had to. I wasn't gonna last much longer, out there. And I've been keeping an eye on the news; it doesn't look like they've gone public with the theft yet, have they?"

"No," Archer confirms. "No, they're keeping it real quiet. Luc thinks it's because Callas set the Greek mob on your trail."

Rob laughs, choking on his pasta. "Jesus fucking Christ. God, I wish it had been that glamorous."

"What *was* it like?" Cael asks.

"Exhausting," he says, clearly unwilling to discuss it any further for the moment. "Just…like being put through a meat grinder." He shakes his head. "Anyway, how have things been, here?"

"Good," Cael beams. "Archer's done an excellent job keeping me safe."

He smiles, looking between them. "Yeah?"

"Oh, don't act so goddamn surprised," she scolds.

Wells clears his throat, trying to mask his widening grin. He gestures between them with his fork. "Are you two, uh…?"

"Yes," Cael proudly reveals. He clasps her hand atop the table, holding it up into view.

He looks to Archer for confirmation. "Really?"

"Yes, Robert," she says, exasperated. "Really."

Rob gets in the shower, and Archer throws his sad assemblage of filthy garments into the washing machine. She's going to have to make another clothing run, she realizes, beginning a mental shopping list. *When the hell did my place turn into a halfway-house for sadboys?*

No, she reminds herself, *friends. These are your friends.*

Rob emerges in one of her kimonos, and immediately collapses to the armchair. He looks better, but not by much. "Listen," he starts in, rubbing at his forehead. "This is a motherfucker of a thing to ask, Cym, and I guarantee you that the irony is far from lost on me, but…"

She waits, but he doesn't finish. "But?"

"Do you…fuck it, do you have any Penth?"

She has to choke back the urge to laugh in cruel, mocking disbelief. "Uh…maybe, I don't know. I, uh…I quit."

He blinks at her in shock. "You quit? *You?*"

"Yeah."

"Fuck." His fingers are visibly shaking as he pushes them into his eyes. "Well, shit."

"I might still have some phials kicking around, though," she says. "Just let me go look." Sure enough, she has a few half-full bottles stashed in the back of her fridge. "Wait, does this go bad?" she calls over her shoulder.

"I have no idea, and at this point, I don't think I care. I just need a drop."

Cael appears out of thin air. "Drop?" he demands. "Who's dropping in here?"

Archer holds her hands up in surrender, relinquishing the phial to Rob.

Cael is upon him in an instant, launching into the same speech he'd given Archer, all those months ago. "Prolonged use of Nepenthe can lead to dangerous weight loss and deterioration of the brain's white matter—"

Poor Rob looks to be on the verge of shameful tears.

"Hey, Caelan," Archer tries to take him by the hand. He jerks away from her.

"–which may affect decision-making abilities, mood regulation, and responses to stressful situations. If overused, it can lead to death by cardiac arrest, and so–"

"*Hey.*" She finally succeeds in cutting him off.

"*What?*"

"Knock it off. He knows."

"Obviously he doesn't, since he's still doing it." He points at Wells. "Look, see?"

Guilty and self-conscious, Rob slips the dropper under his tongue. He shudders, limbs relaxing. "Thanks, Archer," he mutters, avoiding eye contact.

"Leave him be, Cael." She drags him away. "You have no idea what he's been through."

Wells passes out on the couch before long, so Cael and Archer finish out the rest of their night as quietly as possible. They're acutely aware of how exhausted their guest must be. Around 10:00, they slip into bed together, like they always do.

"We can't fuck while he's here, can we?" Cael whispers in the dark.

Archer laughs softly. "Probably not, sweet thing."

"But he's really asleep. I can tell by his breathing, it would take a lot to wake him up, I think."

"Let's give him a chance to get his bearings before we give him a heart attack like that."

Cael grumbles, shifting around indignantly. "But I want to do that thing again. From the couch."

"Uh-uh," she quickly negates, pulling him into her arms. "You get way too loud when we do that."

He smiles, coy and chagrined. "I can't help it, it's my favorite."

Archer rolls her eyes. "Go to sleep, Caelan."

He huffs, tucking his head beneath her chin. "Fine."

Then, just as she's beginning to drift off, he speaks up again.

"Archer?"

"Mmm?"

"I'm extremely glad he's back, and relieved that he's alive, but I'm concerned about what this change is going to mean."

"Yeah," she sighs. "Me, too."

CHAPTER TWENTY-EIGHT

THE FOLLOWING MORNING, THE TRIO SETTLES IN TOGETHER IN THE living room. Cael and Archer sit beside one another on the couch, with Rob in the armchair across from them. Cael is telling Wells the story of the last four months, from his perspective. Rob, for his part, is leaning across the gulf, hanging on his every word, nodding and smiling with a kind of open reverence on his face. Archer thinks it's sort of sweet, because Cael is very clearly sugarcoating some of the more distasteful early details of their relationship, making her seem much more friendly and helpful than she knows she'd been back then. And he omits entirely the details of her behavior on the night of the *Wired* interview.

And then Cael decides to start talking about their first real time together, after the walk to the restaurant. "I kissed her, and then she carried me up the stairs, and I thought I was doing a really good job at first, but then Archer—"

"Hey, hey, hey," she interrupts. "Listen, we don't talk about that sort of thing in front of other people."

Wells laughs, putting a hand over his mouth in disbelief.

"Why not?" Cael demands. "It's one of the most important learning experiences I've had, so far."

"Caelan, you just met him. That's personal stuff, between you and me."

"But people talk about it on the internet all the time, and *that's* in front of other people. That's in front of *strangers*."

"That's the internet, Caelan, this is real life. Knock it off."

He pouts.

"Wait, seriously, though?" Wells asks, looking between them. "Like he – *you* – have the...drive? For that? The...you *want* to? I mean, I knew the theory was there, but Forge had obviously never put you in a situation where that programming could be tested, so it was all just speculative."

"Well, consider it tested and approved," he boasts.

"Cael..."

"Wait, but–" Wells' voice drops to a whisper. Like Archer isn't sitting *right there*. "But, like, are you limited to base Eros programming, or have you learned?"

"Oh, I have *learned*," he says proudly. "One time, I–"

"*Caelan.*"

His discontent is made obvious by the glitched-out little noise he makes. "I'll tell you later," he whispers behind his hand.

Archer rubs at her forehead, already exhausted, but now completely committed to staying awake until they both fall asleep. "Hey, has the cat had breakfast?" she prompts.

He frowns. "I'm not your chores-robot."

Archer moves like she's going to stand. "Okay, then, *I'll* feed the cat."

"No!" Cael leaps to his feet, crossing the room in a few long, purposeful strides. "No, I want to feed the cat."

Khi appears out of thin air and leaps up onto Cael's shoulder to supervise the affair.

"He's sort of synesthetic, isn't he?" Rob observes quietly.

"What?"

He has to think for a second before he answers. "Like…the way he talks about stuff. Holding hands with the house with the Bluetooth, feeling you touching his back because of your synthflesh. Synesthetic. Synesthesia."

"Yeah," she laughs softly. "Yeah, you should hear him when he gets wound up about what the plants are thinking."

"Hey," Cael protests, setting Khi's food down. "Studies have shown that, despite the notable absence of a brain, plants are more than capable of a certain level of measurable intelligence that–"

"Caelan, you've got me so fucked up," she interrupts. "If I have to hear one more jargon-laced nonsense story about transgenerational plant memory, segued into a grade-school-caliber metaphor for yourself, I swear I'm gonna–"

"Well, I'm sorry that the mean old plants have made it so you can't smell the cigarette smoke in here anymore," he replies, haughty. "I know that must have been a difficult adjustment, for you."

She rolls her eyes. "Right, because it was giving you so much cancer."

Cael gasps in shock and offense. "Hey, you be sweet!" He clambers up onto the back of the couch to sling his legs down over Archer's shoulders, and then places his hands on her cheeks and tilts her face up towards his. Shaking her lightly, he demands, "Are you going to be sweet?"

She sighs, powerless against the display. "You've got me so fucked up."

He rubs his nose back and forth along hers, dragging forth a begrudging smile, and then he kisses her.

Wells just watches, wide-eyed. "Un-fucking-believable."

"*What?*" the pair asks in unison.

He points to his former charge. "How did you do this?"

"Do what?" By his voice, she can tell that Cael is smiling. His toes curl a little against her ribs.

"Twelve years, I had her," Wells says. "Twelve goddamn years. Ask me how many times she just sat quietly and behaved because someone told her to."

Cael giggles in anticipation. "How many times did she just sit quietly and behave because someone told her to?"

"*Zero.*"

Caelan laughs loudly, throwing his head back so hard that he almost falls off the couch.

"Easy," Archer scolds, catching him by the legs to keep him upright.

He overcompensates, lunging so far forward that he almost pitches down into her lap.

"Settle down, Caelan, *damn*," she grumbles, muscling him back into a reasonable position. "You're just showing off for company." At that, her phone chimes.

It's Luc:

I'm downstairs.

Cael cranes to look at the screen. "Luc's here?"

"Yeah." She gently works her way out from under him, heading to pick up her coat and bag. "He's gonna give me a ride, I've gotta go get some stuff for Rob."

"Can I come?"

Archer dons her coat, unimpressed. "Cael, you know the answer to that."

He crosses his arms, pouting. "Fine."

"We'll be okay," Rob reassures her. "Thanks for doing this for me."

Archer rolls her eyes, but she's smiling. "You're the reigning *champion* of not giving me any choice."

Rob looks chagrined, but his expression tells her that he knows she's teasing him fondly.

Just as she's leaving, she hears Cael ask, "Hey, have you ever played VR video games?"

Luc is sitting astride his bike when Archer steps out onto the sidewalk. She climbs on behind him, wrapping her arms around his waist.

"What's the emergency?" he asks, craning to look at her face. "Where are we going?"

"Rob's back."

Luc blanches. "He fucking...what?"

"He's upstairs with Cael right now. Come on, we've gotta go. They're playing with the VR."

Luc barks out a laugh, revving the bike. "Fuck, that is an emergency."

The trip doesn't take long. They move quickly from store to store, picking up everything Wells could possibly need. Clothes and toiletries, even a burner phone in case he and Cael run into trouble while she's out of the house. They keep their heads down, hoping desperately to avoid being recognized, and Luc peppers her with urgent questions in hushed tones. Some, she can answer:

"When did he get back?"

"Where has he been?"

"What the fuck happened?"

Others, she can only meet with uneasy silence:

"What does this mean for Cael?"

"Does he want to go public?"

"Cym, what the fuck are we going to do?"

A defeated, "I don't know, Lucas," is all she can muster. "I don't know."

When they arrive back at her place, Archer gingerly climbs off the bike and gathers up her shopping bags. Luc shuts the engine off, but doesn't dismount.

"Well...tell them both I say hi," he says.

That stops her right in her tracks. "What? Aren't you coming up?"

"Can't." His eyes are downcast. "I've got a...thing."

"What thing?"

"I've, uh...got a date, actually. I just figure that since you...with Cael, now, I mean..." He trails off into silence, fiddling with the zipper on his jacket. "You know."

"Okay." She just blinks at him, brow slowly beginning to gather. "Do I know her?"

Luc just shrugs.

"That's okay. I mean, that's totally fine. Like, Rob's not even settled in, so it's probably better to give him some time before we start talking about…"

"Yeah."

"Okay." Archer steps up onto the sidewalk with her bags.

"Hey, I love you, Cymbre," he says, eyes still downcast. "I mean it."

She can't help herself. She drops her bags and lunges in again, settling her lips into the corner of his mouth in a kiss that hadn't been planned. He returns the gesture in earnest, his entire body seeming to exhale in relief.

"I love you, too," she says. "Don't you ever forget it."

His smile lifts against her mouth. "I couldn't."

With that, she's back up onto the sidewalk, and Luc is starting the engine on his bike. There's an expression on his face like he means to say more; like he means to force some needless justification or empty apology. But, before it comes, he dons his helmet and drives off. Heavy-feeling, Archer turns away and makes her way towards home.

CHAPTER TWENTY-NINE

She hands the bags over to Wells. "Soap, razors, clothes. Little bit of everything."

"Thank you."

"Luc says hi."

"Aww, I wish he'd have come up!"

"He's going on a date."

Rob looks surprised. "Is he, now?"

She scoffs.

Cael is standing at the foot of the stairs. "Archer?"

"Yeah?" She flops down on the couch, back spasming in protest. "Come here, baby."

"No, there's something—there's something wrong with—with my leg, I think." He struggles through the explanation, now clearly agitated.

Archer cranes her neck to see that he's standing on one foot, clutching at the banister. He looks confused and upset.

She sits up and beckons him over to the couch. "What's wrong with it?"

He begins limping his way across the room. "I don't know, it—it's all—it's not *listening* to me." His gait is labored and halting, right knee locking up and shuddering on the swing-through. He winds up having to hip-lift and circumduct with each step, just to make progress.

She nods knowingly, standing to meet him halfway. "Yeah, I know what's up with it, the 6s do that sometimes."

He freezes in place, eyes going wide as he reaches for her. It's sweet and pathetic and completely adorable. "Can you fix it?" he asks, panic edging into his voice

"Of course, I can. Come here, you little mess." She scoops him up bridal style, his affected leg sticking out comically as she carries him over to the couch.

He clings. "Thank you."

"Is this from VR video games?"

"No."

"Caelan."

"*No*, I said!"

Archer sets him down, and Khi immediately jumps up to wrap around the back of his neck.

"Pants off, please," she calls, heading over to grab her tools from upstairs.

Cael laughs, beginning to awkwardly work them off over his malfunctioning leg while also keeping the cat balanced on his shoulders. "Say it again but slower."

She rolls her eyes, but can't deny the way her face heats up. When she returns, his leg is jerking and spasming again.

"Quit trying to move it." She kneels at his feet.

He stills. "Sorry."

Archer takes a deep breath. "Okay, you do this part for me. Mine are different, and I don't want to fuck your shit up."

"You won't fuck my shit up." He thrusts his malfunctioning leg almost dangerously in her direction.

"Cael, just do it for me."

"Okay, okay." Gingerly, he finds the seam in the synthflesh on the back of his knee, and peels it away for her. Down his calf, up his thigh. Like some kind of fucked-up skin stocking. The wiring and pistons and gears that comprise his knee come into view, and Archer zeroes in on the problem right away. From the kitchen, Wells is watching with intense, clandestine interest, smile widening. Neither Cael nor Archer take any notice, too wrapped up to see anything but each other.

"All right, sit still." She takes up her tiny, delicate tools and begins the process of disconnecting his leg through the knee. "Gimme your hand."

He opens his palm, and she begins to deposit almost impossibly-small screws and bolts and gears into his hand. He lifts it up to show Khi. "See this?" The cat sniffs curiously. "Don't eat this stuff. It's not food. I know you like bones, but these are *my* bones, and you can't have them, okay? *I* need them."

Khi smashes his forehead into Cael's cheek as if understanding.

Archer and Rob both laugh quietly. She takes the pinpoint magnet tool and releases Cael's hamstring pistons, gently lowering them out of the way, before unhinging his carbon fiber patella from where it connects to the structure of his thigh. She's done this a thousand times before. She could do it standing on one foot, blind drunk.

She *has* done this standing on one foot, blind drunk.

"Oh," Cael remarks, giving her a few quick blinks. "Oh, I see what you're doing. Okay, I get it."

She sets the detached lower leg down on the couch beside him, lifting the open end of his thigh to get a better view. Rob cranes around in his seat to watch.

"Yeah, see, it's this little junction right here." She taps at the inside of the joint with her hex key. "If you accidentally give it one stupid, extra millimeter of medial rotation when you're hyperextended prior to your swing-through, this one gear gets caught under the hamstring piston, and the whole thing jams up like a bastard."

"I see that. I knew I had taken a funny step, too. I wasn't paying attention when I was coming down off of the stairs, and I landed weird on my left, so it sort of…jerked at my right."

"Yeah, that's how I've had it happen, too." She takes a pair of pliers and delicately re-seats the gear. "Stairs. Even still, it's rare. And it's an easy fix, as long as you don't walk around on it all day, first. The bitch of it is that you can't get at the gear without taking off the whole lower leg and looking up into the thigh. Which makes it a pain in the ass to do myself. I usually wind up having to take the whole thing off, to get the right angle."

Cael beams. "But I won't ever have to do it by myself, because you'll be here to do it for me."

"That's right, I will." She returns his smile, ignoring the new and terrifying worry that that isn't necessarily true.

With expert, well-practiced hands, she re-assembles his leg. She re-connects pistons, re-aligns gears, folds his patella back into position. Screwing and bolting it all into place just-so. And then she rolls his skin back up over his leg, watching the seams seal back together and disappear. How he remembers where they are is beyond her.

She pats him on the thigh. "Okay, you're done."

"Kiss it better," he commands, grinning.

"No, bend your knee for me," she counters. "I need to see if it worked."

"It worked, I can tell. Kiss it better."

"Cael, quit being a brat."

From the kitchen, Wells goads, "Yeah, kiss it better, Cym."

Archer rolls her eyes, but complies nonetheless.

Triumphant, Cael bends his knee back and forth for her. "See? I told you it worked."

She rises, kissing him once on the mouth before putting her tools away.

"No–" He catches her by the wrist, already laughing at whatever joke he's about to tell. "No, wait a second."

She cocks an eyebrow, suspicious. "What?"

"There's something else I need you to look at, too," he giggles, unbuttoning his shirt. Khî scampers away, upset by all the shifting around.

Archer panics, lunging forward to stop him. "Caelan, we have company!"

He holds her at bay with his now-functional leg. "No, no, wait, hang on–" He sinks his fingernails into the invisible seam down the center of his chest and peels the synthflesh back.

"Caelan, I hate it when you do this!"

Wells stands up, craning around to look. "Wait, what's he doing?"

Cael exposes the pulsing blue fist of his Asclepius heart, visible behind the slats of his carbon-fiber ribs. "Is–" He dissolves into fits of laughter before finally managing, "–is this yours, ma'am?"

"*Stop*," she whines, reaching out to try and fold his skin back over again. "Don't call me *ma'am*, and that's gross! Put it away!"

He snatches her by the wrist, guiding her hand up under his ribs and wrapping her hand around his heart. "I think this is yours," he announces, biting his lip and looking up at her with heavily-lidded eyes.

"It's gross!" she whines, now completely unable to squirm away, lest she dislodge his internal organs. His heart pulses warm in her hand.

"*You're* the gross one," he laughs. "You're a meat puppet." He wraps his free hand around the back of her neck, hauling her into a kiss. When their lips meet, his heart starts to beat faster.

"Okay. All right, I'm a gross meat puppet. Now, you've had your gross, weird, robot fun, so it's time to let me go."

He sighs, overdramatic, and guides her hand back out of his chest.

Archer shivers, striding for the stairs to put her tools away. "You think you're *so fucking cute*, but I don't *like* it when you do that, Caelan, I swear!"

He mumbles, "*Luddite*," waiting with an expectant grin for her to react.

Archer gasps, rounding on him again. "What are these?" she points at her legs. "Is my torso just floating mid-air, powered by *magic*?"

"Yes." Self-satisfied, Cael starts folding his synthflesh back into place. But before he can finish, Wells rushes over.

"Can I–?" he asks tentatively. "Wait, can I see?"

Upstairs, Archer howls in frustration.

CHAPTER THIRTY

It's astonishingly early, at least by Archer's standards, when she makes her way downstairs. Rob has been here for a month, slowly recovering. He's looking better. Healthier. He shaved his head a few days in, which Archer can't really fault him for, given the state of his hair. But he kept the beard. And whether it's the style, the months he spent living rough, or something far less tangible, Rob looks decades older than he had on the night of the shareholder's presentation. Right now, he's messing around in the kitchen, still in his pajamas.

"Hey," he greets quietly. "Coffee?"

She smiles, still half-asleep. "Yeah, thanks."

"I didn't wake you, did I?"

"No." She shuffles over towards him. "No, I was ready to get up."

"Hey, um…" Rob points at the sink. "What the fuck is this?"

Archer peers into it to see what looks like a translucent plastic bag crumpled up on the bottom. One end terminates in a small, round click-seal. "Oh, that's Cael's stomach," she grumbles, throwing herself into one of the chairs at the table. "Sorry."

Rob sputters in quiet disbelief. "His fucking…what?"

"His stomach." The newly-printed 2042 product catalog is sitting on the table in front of her, right in plain view, where she expressly told Cael *not* to leave it. He's even opened it to one of her two-page spreads. Archer shuts the book with a snap, puts it on the floor, and kicks it away. "Cael ate last night, remember?"

"Yeah."

"Well, when he does that, the food doesn't actually go anywhere. It just sits in his stomach until he empties it out."

"Oh, that…actually makes sense."

"I'll make sure he puts it back in when he wakes up."

"Wait, but isn't he coming down now?" he asks, pouring two mugs of coffee.

"No, he's still idling up there. Probably will be for another half an hour, or so. I, uh…" She clears her throat. "He's tired."

Wells furrows his brow. "He's *tired*? Can he get tired?"

Archer rubs at the back of her neck, chagrined. "Well, sort of. It's best for him to idle after a big, uh…big power surge." So far, they'd successfully avoided this particular topic. But last night, after Rob had gone to sleep, it had all become too much, and Cael's sweet, earnest begging could be resisted no longer.

Rob joins her at the table, intensely concerned. "Wait, he had a big power surge?"

"Yeah, it's…"

"Is he okay?"

"Well, listen, when we–" She groans. "When he gets–*excited*, say, like really emotionally worked-up about something, whether he's scared, or–"

"Jesus, Cym, spit it out, already!"

Archer's head falls back against the chair. "We, *you know*… fucked. Last night."

He laughs explosively, clapping a hand over his mouth.

"We've held off this long, trying not to freak you out, but…" She shrugs. "I don't know, fuck you, I guess."

"Oh my God, Archer."

"Because of how his perpetual motion works, he's usually gotta shut down gross motor afterwards, and do a passive energy bleed for a few hours."

"Amazing."

"You asked," she mumbles into her coffee mug.

"Honestly, I'm impressed," he says, lighting a cigarette. "I never thought I'd see the day." He offers her the pack, and she hates herself a little for taking one.

"Yeah," she says, slipping it between her lips, "neither did I."

"And with a *man.*"

She gives him an admonishing glare.

"I mean, at least he's tiny and helpless and easy to carry around, right? That's basically your type."

"I'm not even sure how to respond to that. And he's taller than *you.*"

"He's exactly where he needs to be, you know." Archer looks up to find that he's staring straight at her. Genuine. "I know it took you a while to come around, but I'm glad you did."

She blinks. Looks away. Lights her cigarette. "Are you saying you planned this? You knew I'd...you knew I'd take care of him?"

He chuckles softly. "*Fuck*, no. I just knew I could get him to you, and I figured Vander's ivory girl was the person least likely to get caught with him. Especially with how things had been going between us in the weeks leading up to it. I also figured you were the least likely to snitch on me, since you knew how much dirt I had on you."

"You guilt-tripped the hell out of me, Robert," she reminds him. "*That's* what did it."

He gives a dismissive wave of his hand. "Ahh, don't pretend like you didn't deserve it. Anyway, it worked." He shakes his head in astonishment. "*Some*-fucking-how. He's alive, Archer. And you're not looking too miserable, yourself."

"No. No, I guess I'm not."

"You look good. Healthy. Maybe even happy. I don't think I've ever seen you happy before."

She shrugs. "Yeah, well…"

"You did good, Cym. He's free."

Her stomach twists a little. She takes a deep, stilling drag from her cigarette, hoping to find that it had been a momentary fugue. But it wasn't. The feeling is lingering. Growing.

Rob nods towards her. "What's up?"

"He's not, though," she whispers. "He's not free. Not really."

Rob nods. "No, I…I guess you're right. But listen, the important thing is that we got him out of that lab before they wiped him again. My guy down in Tartarus told me he *begged*, Archer. He screamed and cried and begged them not to do it."

She feels a lump rise in her throat.

"The K-iteration of the AI was a lot less advanced, but he…" Rob nods, gaze fixed on a spot on the table. "He knew what was happening to him. He was intuitive, he understood what they were going to do. He had tear ducts at that point, and he did cry. They said he definitely was crying. And when that didn't work, when the technician went into the room anyway, he tried to fight him off. He actually broke the guy's nose. He's the one who came to me about it in the first place."

It's like she's been hit in the face with a bucket of ice water. The realization cascades over her in a jarring wave as she recalls with such startling clarity her own desperate descent into Tartarus, and the lab technician who had helped her there. "Fuck."

"What?"

"Does he have red hair?"

Wells blinks in surprise. "Yeah, Cym. Yeah, he does."

She clears her throat, fighting tears. "He's strong," she murmurs, trying so hard not to think about it. "Cael is. More than you'd expect, when you first meet him."

"I know. In the end, it took three people to get him under control. And just before they shut him off, the tech said he was apologizing. Just over and over. He said he wouldn't hurt anyone again, that he'd behave and do all of their tests, as long as they didn't erase him."

The image makes her stomach churn. "I'm glad at least that he doesn't remember," she says, grasping for some sort of silver lining.

"And after that, after *all that*, they only made him smarter. Stronger. More emotional. The–" Rob shakes his head. "God, the fucking *hubris* of it all."

"They made him because they could," she says, tapping a column of ash from the end of her neglected cigarette. "That's what he says, anyway."

"No, but he's so much *more* than what they made him." He leans across the table towards her. "And that's the ironic beauty of it all, don't you think? Just like you're more than they've made you."

Archer nods, but she can't help the stab of discomfort at the comparison. The whisper of Imposter Syndrome.

"They're trying to control shit they've got no business controlling," he says, taking a drag of his cigarette. "No business at all. It's cruel, it's unethical, and the ends do not justify the means. They do not. If I know Forge, they'll probably try and frame this whole thing like they're building a robotic workforce. One million Caels to send out and do dangerous jobs, sparing countless human lives or some shit like that. But a species that destroys the planet and then builds slaves just to keep things limping along is maybe a species that deserves to die."

She half-sobs, half-laughs, because *God*, he's changed so much in the past few months. Or maybe he hasn't, she realizes. Maybe this is just the first time Rob's really been able to speak, and the first time she's actually listened. "Vander would probably say that you can't make gyros without slaughtering a lamb."

Wells rolls his eyes. "Vegan gyros are great."

"But are they the *best*?"

"Does it matter? They're the best because no one suffers."

They lapse into silence for a while, drinking their coffee and smoking. Cael will probably be waking up soon, Archer thinks. He'll wander down with a bright, sleepy smile and kiss her like he loves her, because he probably does love her, whether he's said it or not. Whether he ever says it. And the fact that it's probably entirely different from the love she feels for him makes no difference whatsoever. It's real to him.

As real as the fear he'd felt when the technician had stepped into the room to erase his K-memory.

"Good morning."

Archer turns to see Cael standing at the bottom of the stairs. He's wearing one of her long shirts, the ends of the sleeves balled up in his fists.

"Hey, sweet thing," she says gently, realizing at once that her face is wet. She hurriedly wipes the tears away and extends a hand towards him. "Come here."

"You're crying." He steps over to drag a fingertip through her tears. "Why are you crying?"

"I'm fine, baby."

"I'm not a baby. Why won't you tell me what upset you? Is it Rob's fault, and you don't want to say in front of him?"

Rob chuckles anxiously. "Hey. That's not…come on. No."

Cael frowns at him, suspicious.

"You left your guts in the sink," Archer says, tugging him down into a kiss.

He laughs. "Oops."

"And hey–" She picks up the erstwhile product catalog. "Come on, what did I say about this?"

He smiles sheepishly, taking the book. "You said you didn't want to see this damn thing lying around your house, but I like looking at the beautiful pictures of you and remembering that I was here making you dinner while you were taking them. Also, we had *really* good sex that night because you let me pick you up."

Rob barks out a laugh.

Archer stammers, face burning. "Go put your shit back together, Cael!"

A knock at the door startles them all terribly.

!! PANIC !!

Cael claps both hands over his ears, letting the hardcover catalog hit the floor with a loud *bang*.

"Upstairs," Archer urges in a whisper, scrambling to her feet.

But Cael is clinging, trying to clutch for her wrists while she shoves him towards the staircase. "No, I don't want to!"

"You'll be fine," she insists, hands on his cheeks. "Rob, take him! Baby, go with Rob!"

"Caelan, come on!" Rob grabs him by the arm, dragging him away. Cael looks back in desperation as he stumbles along.

"*Not under the bed!*" Archer watches them disappear from view.

Another, more insistent knock sounds from the front door.

"Fuck. *Fuck.*" She takes a deep breath, trying in vain to still the shaking in her limbs, and reaches for the doorknob.

"Jesus, Cym." Luc laughs as he shoves his way inside. "Leave me standing outside like an asshole, fuck, I hope he was at least givin' it to you good—"

Archer shrieks in relief, slamming and bolting the door in his wake.

Cael's face pops into view, upstairs. "Oh, hi!" He's brandishing a metal baseball bat.

Luc smiles broadly. "Hey!"

"Caelan, put that down!" Archer commands, near frenzy. "Where the hell did you even find that?"

"It was in your closet." Cael drops the bat unceremoniously, and then comes thumping loudly down the stairs. Rob follows tentatively in his wake.

"Ho-ly *shit*!" Luc exclaims, clapping his hands. "Where have *you* been, man? Welcome back!"

Rob smiles, a bit weakly. "Thanks, Lucas. It's good to be back."

Cael, meanwhile, has taken a running leap at Luc's back and is attempting to clamber up onto his shoulders. Luc takes it like a champ, helping to hoist him up. Any other time, Archer would be exceptionally amused, but she's still shaking with lingering adrenaline.

"Lucas!" she scolds, still standing with her back against the door. "Why the hell didn't you text?"

"I did." He hitches Cael up onto his shoulders. "Which you'd know, if you'd let him pair with your phone."

"*Thank* you," Cael chimes in.

Luc leans down to kiss the corner of her mouth, whispering, "You, uh…you do need to go check your phone, though, seriously."

"Hey," Cael prods, craning around to look at Luc, "don't kiss my girlfriend and then tell her secrets. Also, can you help me reach the top of my vine? Admin won't authorize my stacking additional items on a chair, in order to reach it."

Lucas laughs genuinely. "Yeah, she's probably got a point, there."

"No, I told her that she's on the wrong side of history for denying me human rights."

"Jesus Christ, Cael."

Half anger and half dread, Archer retreats towards the bedroom. Her phone is on the nightstand, and sure enough, Luc had texted her about his imminent arrival. And she missed a call from Kalinia Tranar.

"What?" she demands, the instant her coordinator picks up.

"Good. You're alive. Have you heard the news?"

"What news?"

"Robert Wells was picked up by security cameras in the area. He's back in town."

Archer's stomach lurches. "And?"

"*And*," Lin huffs, "Vander has decided that this has gone on long enough. We're going to hold a press conference about the theft, a week from today. He's putting up a reward. Your participation is required, as is Lucas Wagner's."

Archer glances down towards the living room. Wells is flitting around anxiously while Cael perches on Luc's shoulders to trim his vine. The cat is jumping all around them, hell-bent on being involved in the spectacle. "All right, fine. Whatever." She snaps her fingers a few times, forcing the group's attention, and then presses an insistent finger to her lips. They sheepishly quiet down.

"You should have some PR materials in your inbox, along with a script. And this time, we do expect you to study it."

"Yeah, fine, whatever."

"Not '*whatever*'," Lin snaps. "This is your job, Archer. Do your job." She ends the call.

Archer looks down to see the trio watching her expectantly. Luc has a kind of tragic knowing on his face, but Cael and Rob just look worried.

"Rob," she says, trying to keep her tone measured. "Were you walking around Brooklyn without anti-surveillance?"

He snort-laughs. "Yeah, Arch. Sorry, my Cartier's at the jeweler's."

From his perch, Cael points back and forth between them, delighted. "He's making fun of you for being rich. That's punching up."

Frustration is beginning to rise hot on her skin. "*Rob, were you fucking walking around Brooklyn without anti-surveillance?*"

Rob looks away. "I don't know what you want me to say, Archer."

"Fuck." She flings her phone at the bed, where it bounces and clatters to the floor. "*Fuck!*"

"Wait, what's happening?" Cael asks, looking between the assembled humans. "Why do you all have that facial expression?"

Archer exhales deeply. "We need to talk about this."

"For the past twelve years, Robert Wells and I have worked together very closely," Archer begins, reading off of her phone. "He was my coordinator, which meant that his life was very much intertwined with mine. This is a man whom I had invited into my home–"

Luc and Wells laugh in unison. "*Invited!*"

"Shh!" Cael urges, reaching out blindly to cover both of their mouths. He's sitting on the couch between the two, watching Archer intently. Khî is settled comfortably in his lap.

"*–invited into my home*," she continues. "This is a man with whom I've traveled the globe, while we worked as ambassadors for Hephaestus Forge technology, and the limitless possibilities afforded by it. But never in those twelve years had I imagined he'd be capable of something like this."

"*True*," the entire quartet simultaneously appraises.

"I assure you that, despite our close working relationship, I had no prior knowledge of his intentions regarding the Prometheus Project," Archer reads. "Or, for that matter, any knowledge of the Project itself. What Robert Wells has done is a betrayal, and I am both deeply hurt, and deeply saddened by his actions. He has stolen from us the single most significant invention in human history, and thereby set back the entire progression of our species. I can only hope now that our asset is recovered safely, and that justice is served. But to do that, we need your help."

"Right," Luc chimes in. "And then I'm supposed to take over with, like, hotline numbers and anonymous tip lines and all that. Hammer it home."

Archer keeps scrolling. "They sent us some shit about Cael, too," she says, skimming through it. "Talking points about their Epsilon-L. But it's really sanitized, like, propaganda-type stuff. And they just keep saying *it*. They keep calling him *it*."

Cael laughs.

"Caelan, it's really not funny."

"I'll tell you one thing," Luc announces, "we're not fucking saying this on TV."

Archer's stomach lurches. *Fuck, aren't we?*

"Why not?" Rob shrugs. "It's honestly better for everyone if you do. It'll throw everyone off the trail."

Luc is hesitant. "Will it, though?"

"It'll buy us more time," Cael says, pensive. "More time to… come up with a long-term plan."

Archer blurts it out before she can stop herself. "Well, but I thought this *was* the long-term plan."

The tense silence that follows, the anxious fidgets from her companions, and the way they're avoiding her gaze, are answer enough.

"I should bounce," Luc says, standing up from the couch.

Cael clutches for his hand. "No, don't."

"Why not?"

"You just got here."

"Yeah, but that was before shit got heavy."

Archer feels the heat of shame rise to her face. It seems like everyone is looking at her right now, whether or not it's true.

"Listen, I'll come back in a few days," Luc reassures. "Help you reach the top of your vine again."

Cael reluctantly releases him. "Okay. I want to put beads on it."

"You…what, now?"

"If you put beads on it while it's growing, then it'll have beads on it."

"Okay, then," Luc concedes, bending to press his lips to Archer's cheek.

"Hey, don't kiss my girlfriend!"

"Are you serious, right now?" Archer asks, watching as Luc heads for the door. "You're gonna drop a bomb like that, and then just leave me here with these two?"

"Yeah, Cym. I think we all just need to think about this for a while, before we get to arguing about it."

"Who's arguing?" she demands, arms spread wide. "Lucas! Who's arguing?"

"Rob," he says, ignoring her entirely, "it's good to see you again, man. I'm glad you're back."

"Thanks, Lucas. You too."

"*Lucas!*"

With that, he's gone.

That night, just as Archer is beginning to fall asleep, Cael gasps and claps a hand over his mouth.

She startles, craning her neck to see him behind her. "What? What's the matter?"

"*My source model.*"

"What about him?"

"People are going to think he's me."

Archer exhales a tired laugh. "Yeah."

"It's not funny!"

She rolls onto her back, dragging him over to lie on her chest.

"It kind of is, though. Just picture, like, this gorgeous twink getting the cops called on him fifteen times a day. They fucking tackle him in the grocery store and make him solve a CAPTCHA or some shit, and then let him go. Like catch-and-release model-fishing." She laughs through a yawn. "Lure him in with poppers and a *Comme des Garçons* contract under a box propped up on a stick–"

"Archer," Cael scolds, his expression severe. "I can solve a CAPTCHA."

"It was a joke, sweet one."

He thinks for a second, laughs, and then abruptly stills again. "He'll probably be extremely angry with me."

Archer closes her eyes and sinks into bed. "If he gets mad at anyone, it'll be Forge," she says, trying to get Cael to settle on her shoulder. "Because they copied his likeness to make a whole new guy. Or he'll be pissed at his agency for selling his likeness for the project in the first place."

"But I'm my own guy!" he says, resisting her attempts to hold him still. "I'm my own guy! And it's not fair to either of us that we're identical to each other!"

She exhales deeply through her nostrils. "Hey, better him getting tackled by the cops than you, baby."

Reluctantly, Cael lies down and settles into the crook of her shoulder. "I guess so."

CHAPTER THIRTY-ONE

"It's a zero-sum game."

Archer rolls her eyes. "Can you knock it off with that, please?"

"Hey, I'm just saying."

"Yeah, I know, and I'm asking you to quit saying it."

It's been four days since the emails from Forge. She and Luc are seated together in the back corner of a coffee shop, faces covered in anti-surveillance. Rob and Cael are home, waiting. Her meal kit service isn't substantial enough for both her and Rob, and even Cael seems to be 'eating' more these days. Probably putting on a show for their guest. So, supplemental grocery trips are becoming a necessity, and she ventures out about once a week just to keep everyone fed.

Today, Luc had texted her, asking to meet up before she went home. And, shocking as it is, he seems hell-bent on talking about the exact thing that Archer doesn't want to talk about.

"It's a zero—"

"Lucas, it fucking isn't. You don't even know what that means, you're just saying shit to try and sound smart."

He's taken aback. "Okay, ouch?"

"This isn't a game, not by any definition."

"I mean, it kind of is, though—"

"*Lucas*!"

They lapse into tense silence, punctuated only by quick, angry sips of their coffee.

"Have you two talked about this at all?" he finally asks. "You and Cael?"

"No, why would we need to?"

"Because his opinion supersedes yours?"

"There's nothing to talk about," she snaps. "Forge going public with the—that's—this changes nothing."

"Uh, yes it does? I mean, if you think he's *ever* gonna get to leave the house again, least of all with either of us—"

"Oh my God, you're Mr Atlas!"

Luc's mouth snaps shut, and they look up to find a teenaged boy with one arm standing beside their table.

Archer groans in frustration, flinging herself back in her seat and picking up her phone.

"Yup," Luc replies through gritted teeth. "That's me."

"Can I take a picture with you?"

"Uhh, this really isn't the best time," Luc explains, gesturing towards Archer.

"Oh, you're Cymbre Archer!! Can I please—"

"No!" she snaps. "We're in the middle of something private! Show some respect!"

The kid scurries away on the verge of tears.

"Nice, Cymbre."

"Stop."

"You could've let him down easy!" He moves like he means to go after the kid.

Archer slams a fist on the table. "No, you sit your ass back down, Lucas."

He looks like he means to yell at her. Lips pressed together tightly; brow creased. He's furious. But after a deep breath, he sits back down. "You're a fucking piece of work, Cym."

"You and I just need to do their stupid press conference, read their scripts, and keep doing what Callas says."

"I disagree."

"It's what we've always done, and it's worked out fine."

"Has it, though?"

When she looks up, there's an expression on Luc's face that she's never seen before. Somewhere between angry and pleading; and guardedly fragile.

He scratches at the rim of his coffee cup with a fingernail. "Look, I'm not trying to change the subject or anything here, but this shit's never really been great for me. I know we don't talk about it, because there's no point, but this is fucked. They shred us to pieces testing their tech, and then they parade us around in front of the cameras to sell some kind of unattainable ideal to people who can't afford it and shouldn't have to. It's *fucked.*"

"I know that," she mumbles.

He's right, they don't talk about this. The last time, the only time she can remember, happened when they were both kids. Archer was 17, Luc was 19. Her parents had gone back to Hanoi to visit relatives, and they were sitting at the kitchen table with a gallon of cheap liquor they'd gotten from one of Luc's friends. Conversation had turned dark and self-piteous as the vodka disappeared. If her memory serves, they'd both cried. And then they fucked for the first time, on the couch, in the dark, all knees and elbows and whispered questions doing little to assuage the terrifying newness of it all.

It was her first time. It wasn't his. But she remembers knowing how much Luc had wanted her, and for how long. It had made her feel safe and understood, and for one little flicker of time, neither of them had felt quite so alone. In the years since, they've chased that flicker through lavish apartments and hotel rooms, in the backs of cars, and filthy, downtown alleys, trying to catch it in cupped hands and covet it until it burns out and fades again.

And now, all at once, Archer sees the two of them for what they truly are – just a pair of irreparably damaged kids, still limping along, still clawing for that one moment when they'd felt safe and understood. Her mind flits from memory to memory, lingering on those threads stitching together past and present, and all the worrying little continuities that make it seem like some part of her had been set in stone years ago. Unchangeable. She acknowledges the feeling, acknowledges that the connection is there, and then she puts it away. Because it terrifies her, she avoids it. It is of no use to her.

But Luc is still fidgeting anxiously across the table. "Don't you ever worry about–" He falters, rubbing a hand along his tattooed throat. "I see these new kids coming in, the new models, and I wish I could just tell them to get out while they can. Don't choose this life, just do something different, do *anything*, because you'll just wind up an indentured servant to gross corporate interests. They– fuck, Cym, they *cured cancer*."

Oh my god, she suddenly recalls, *he's right. They did.*

"They talked about it at the shareholder thing back in September, but honestly, how many times have you heard Lex or Callas bring it up, since?"

Not once. Not one, single time.

"It's like their disabled vet program. They know they *have* to do it, because everyone would think they were dicks if they didn't. Same thing here. An affordable cancer cure keeps them in the public's good graces, but how do they make up for the financial loss? By running a sketchy, pseudo-campaign implying that people should cut their own limbs off and rip their own organs out and buy Forge cybernetics instead. They wanna get people addicted to their own mobility, and then dangle it in front of them like a fucking carrot, just like they did to us. That's where the money is."

Archer doesn't respond. She *has* no response, none that Luc will accept. Her survival instinct is a vain and selfish thing, and it doesn't often extend beyond her own reach.

"And yeah, there's people in the world that have it way worse than us. Probably safe to say that most people in the world have it worse than us, especially other disabled people." He chuckles joylessly. "Fuck, can you even imagine? I can't."

Archer thinks about Uncle Huy and his chicken-bone prosthetic leg. And then she realizes how violently, *physically* sick she is of Luc's preaching.

"And you wanna know something?" Luc continues, leaning in close. "Cael is one of those people who has it worse."

"He's going to stay with me," she mutters, punctuating the statement with a swift jerk of her hand. "That's that."

Luc looks unimpressed. "Cymbre."

"Rob, too. We're doing fine. Is it perfect? No, of course not. But we're—we're getting by!"

"This is viable, for you?" Luc asks, toeing at her bag of groceries. "This is the life you want?"

"No, but—"

"You wanna sneak around like this forever, with those two locked up in your house?"

Archer doesn't answer.

"What if he breaks again? You gonna stage another R&D heist? Another Archer's 11? You have no idea how to take care of him, Cym, not long-term."

She flinches like he'd slapped her. "So, what? *Give him back?*"

"You know that's not what I'm saying."

"I've learned how to take care of him!"

"Will you just listen to me, please?"

Archer crosses her arms over her chest, indignant. "What do you want us to do, then? You—you want us to fucking—just walk out into the street with him, you want to tweet about it? Start a hashtag?"

"No, I—"

"What, then?"

"I don't know!" he says, palms upturned on the table between them. His voice starts to shake as he whispers, "I don't have a plan, Cym, I don't! But I'm not gonna let you pretend like this is fair to him! It's fine if you don't think that the two of us deserve justice, fucking–" He waves his hand as if trying to physically brush the notion away. "*Whatever*. But Cael deserves more than this. Yeah, he's in a nice house, and he has his plants, and the cat, and his books, and his games, but that's not a *life*. It's just another cage." After a moment of consideration, he mumbles, "A cage where he gets to fuck the jailer."

Archer scoffs.

Luc's eyes flit to hers and then away, self-conscious. "He moves like you, you know."

"What the hell are you talking about?"

"He's picked up all of your mannerisms, even some verbal ones. I know you've noticed."

Yes, she's noticed. She leans back in her chair, bracing for what she knows is coming.

"I thought it was cute at first, but the more I think about it, I realize it's…" He hesitates. "It's kind of fucked up."

"Shut your mouth, Lucas."

"No, I'm serious. He doesn't know how to be an individual in any context that isn't defined by you. He doesn't know who or what he is, he's just…just reflecting *you*. He's learned what you want, how you want him to be, and he just…does *that*."

"And, what? He deserves a better role model?"

"He deserves not to exist in a vacuum."

"He's like that because I'm the one who *helped* him!" she says in a harsh whisper. "I was the one that was *there*!"

"I'm not discounting that. But it's not fair to him. Like…I'm sorry, Cym, but he deserves more than this."

"*I never asked for*–"

"Oh, we are well past that. And honestly, Cymbre, that's a really gross excuse to try and pull now that you're in love with him."

Heat prickles across her skin, shame and indignation tightening at her throat. She stands abruptly, jamming her sunglasses on and snatching up her bag of groceries. "All right, I'm fucking leaving."

"No, hey," Luc grabs for her hand. "Come on, I didn't mean it like that. Sit down."

She wrenches her arm away. "The food's going to spoil."

On her way to the door, she's caught by a 20-something girl. "Oh my God, you're Cymbre Archer!"

"No, I'm not," she snaps, pushing past her. And then she points over her shoulder. "But that's Mr Atlas." She storms from the building just as the high-pitched shrieking ensues.

Archer can hear the commotion from the hallway. Raised voices, shuffling noises. And when she steps into her loft, Cael and Rob both whip around to look at her. The scene is baffling. The two of them are standing on either side of the kitchen table, Rob clutching his laptop to his chest. He's clearly on the defensive. And Cael has one knee up on the table, frozen mid-lunge, hand outstretched. One of the chairs has been knocked over on its side.

"*Hey!* Archer closes and locks the door behind her. "Do you guys have any idea how loud you're being? What the fuck is going on in here?"

"*Nothing,*" they answer in unison. Rob whips the laptop behind his back, as though that will somehow make her forget he has it. Cael climbs down from the table, balling his sleeves up in his fists. Neither of them is looking at each other.

"*Hey!*"

"He's trying to get into my laptop," Rob finally explains, eyes downcast. He's like a kid tattling on the playground.

Cael stomps his foot. "*I didn't want her to know about that!*"

"Caelan." Archer extends a hand towards him, beckoning. "Hey, that's not cool, you can't–"

He shakes his head in flat refusal, feet rooted in place. "He has videos of the stories he was telling you. That's how he knows."

Archer looks between them. "Hang on, what?"

"It's how he knows about Tartarus and the Delta prototypes. All the stories he was telling you when you thought I was idling." Cael thrusts an accusatory finger towards Rob. "He has video. Lab footage. It's all on his computer."

Archer's stomach drops. "Wait, is that true?"

Rob stammers, face beginning to go red. "I don't even know how he knows that, Cym, I–"

Cael and Archer answer simultaneously:

"Your laptop is on the wifi with me."

"He commits sorcery with the wifi."

Rob laughs nervously. "Okay, Skynet."

"Robert," Archer scolds, genuinely aghast.

He doesn't respond.

"I want to see it," Cael announces.

Her first thought is to dissuade him. "I don't know if that's a good idea, Caelan–"

"I was trying to make him show me before you got home, because I didn't want you to be upset. But now you're upset anyway, I can tell by your eyes and your breathing."

She opens her mouth to argue further, and then snaps it shut. The look on Cael's face is nothing like she's ever seen; some strange, unsettling blend of sorrow and resolve. Pleading in his eyes. Acceptance. She turns to her former handler. "Rob."

"I don't think that's a good idea," he mumbles.

"I'm not a baby," Cael says softly. "Archer, make him show me."

"*Robert.*"

Finally, he looks at her.

"He's not a baby."

At that, Rob is finally defeated. "Okay."

CHAPTER THIRTY-TWO

CAEL AND ROB SIT SIDE BY SIDE AT THE TABLE, THE LAPTOP OPEN IN front of them. Archer stands behind Cael, one hand slung down over his chest, the other preemptively pressed over her lips.

"Are you sure about this?" Rob asks, cursor hovering over the first thumbnail.

After a moment of hesitation, Cael takes control of the mouse and clicks.

It starts simply enough, with time-lapse footage of the robotics team assembling the Delta body. Leg bones dismembered and standing on a raised dais in the lab. Then comes his pelvis, his spine, his ribcage. Arms, hands. However they pose him, he remains frozen in place. Wiring is threaded up and over and through, wrapping around his bones, and his limbs begin to twitch to life. Synthflesh is applied, maybe too pale, too waxy, and devoid of detail or vital, external human anatomy.

They worry over his vocal cords for days; sometimes there are three or four people working at once on the open expanse of his throat. The skull comes last, brought in from another room and clicked into place before his eyes are fitted. They're too bright, too blue. Almost glowing. Finally, something like a latex mask of synthflesh is stretched over his head. He has no hair. No eyebrows. But it's startlingly, undeniably Cael's face. A pair of white-suited researchers gather his limp form and haul him out of the frame.

"That was my old body," Cael says in a soft whisper.

The footage cuts to a view of the gait lab across the hall. *Archer's* gait lab, where she's spent so many countless, painful, frustrating hours. The timestamp indicates that this took place around midnight, which would explain Tom and Dre's absence. The tests begin simply enough, with Delta seated at Luc's fine-motor table. They watch him run beads along wires and put keys in locks, studying and writing and tapping away at their tablets. He twists doorknobs, mimics basic piano chord progressions. He successfully uses a hammer and a screwdriver. All the while, he has this placid, vacant expression on his face. No one talks to him, no one praises him for his successes. They just input commands into a tablet, observe, and repeat.

After that, the tests become infinitely crueler. The researchers set him upright in the center of the room and start trying to knock him over. They stand in a semi-circle and take turns pushing and kicking him. In the legs, in the back, in the stomach. Each time, he stumbles a little, and then rights himself. And each time, he inches a little further backwards, like he's trying to sneak away, out of reach.

They start to throw weighted medicine balls at him. Most he manages to either dodge, or catch and drop. When they throw at him from behind, he takes the blow, stumbles, and then rights himself. Even when they hit him in the back of the head with a 25lb ball.

The researchers set him on the treadmill then, and he keeps up well enough. They work the pace up to a moderate jog and back down again, and he takes it all in stride.

Archer chokes a little when she realizes that her bare feet have touched that treadmill, just as his have.

And then they start hitting him again. He takes the kicks and the pushes. Keeps walking. They try to trip him by kicking one of his feet out from under him, and each time, he stumbles, corrects, and then resumes. The medicine balls prove to be confounding for him, though. It seems that he can focus on walking balance, or he can focus on motion detection, prediction, and avoidance. He can't do both at once. He absorbs blow after blow, stumbling and struggling to keep up with the treadmill.

That is, until one of the researchers shot-puts the same 25lb medicine ball at him, from the side. Archer gasps preemptively, hand flying to cover her mouth, but it's a needless reaction. Still walking on the treadmill, Delta leans back and catches it in one hand. His head snaps to the side, towards the researcher who had thrown it. And then, in a flawless imitation, he heaves the ball up onto his shoulder and throws it back. The white-coated researcher has to leap to the side to avoid being hit in the head. The video ends, as the researchers scramble to shut him off.

Cael lets out one of his weird, scripted little laughs, fingertips ghosting along the screen.

Archer rubs her hand up and down his chest. "Are you sure you wanna keep going with this?" *Because I sure as hell don't.*

"Yes." He clicks to the next thumbnail, and it's the view from a wall-mounted camera inside of Cael's little vivarium in the lab. Delta-J is sitting cross-legged and naked in front of the glass. Swaying slightly.

There's a researcher on the other side of the glass, holding a tablet.

"Delta-J," he says loudly, voice piped into the room via an intercom system.

No response.

"*Delta-J,*" he repeats, tapping on the glass.

His head lifts.

"Do you remember me?" he asks, somehow managing to sound both formal and patronizing. "We typed to each other; do you remember that? We typed on the computer?"

"No." His voice is robotic, distorted. Devoid of inflection.

"Okay. That's okay. We're gonna run through some activation now, to test your hearing, your memory, and your voice. All right?"

No response.

"Galaxy scratches loving, living nectar."

Delta's head twitches to the side, and he seems to struggle a little, but eventually comes up with, "Loving...living nectar."

"Of bees, of pollen, of butterflies."

"Bees and..." He shudders. "Butterflies."

The researcher nods, notating something on his tablet. "Series one distant fragile mine."

"Series...one," Delta parrots.

"Religious rambling solar fuse."

He begins to sit up a little straighter, his answers coming more quickly. "Series two."

"Continue."

He's confident now, taking this strange test in stride. "Senses realize tongue poetry, amongst all confused work."

"Good!" the researcher praises. "Good job!"

"We typed on the computer. We typed about putting me in a body." Delta lifts his hand towards the man, reaching out, and then his fingertips bump against the glass. He startles hard, tumbling backwards.

"Can you stand up?" the researcher prompts.

With what seems like great difficulty, Delta begins to work himself upright. It's painful to watch the way he heaves himself over onto his stomach to push up onto his hands and knees. He shakily lifts one hand at a time until his back is straight. Each move is shuddering, labored. Stiff and robotic. That's when it occurs to Archer that they're not dictating move sets anymore. He's figuring this out on his own.

"Can you do it the rest of the way, please?"

It takes Delta five tries to successfully plant one foot flat on the ground. And then he shifts his weight back and forth between his foot and his knee for a while before eventually leaning too far over his knee and tumbling to the ground again. His legs stay fixed in their awkward, bent position as he shudders on the floor.

Archer closes her eyes at that, turning away from the screen. Cael reaches up and clasps her hand as it rests on his chest. Reassuring. Seconds drag on and on, silent save for the low ambient hum from the recording. She doesn't look again until she hears the researcher praise some accomplishment, and when she opens her eyes, Delta is standing in front of the glass.

"I'm gonna give you something, now," the researcher says, tapping away at his tablet. "Some information, okay?"

Delta sways a little. "Okay."

"You ready?"

"Yes." And then, all at once, his entire body goes rigid, and then limp, and then he's toppling to the floor with a sickening thud.

"Ahh, shit," the researcher snarls, turning to look over his shoulder. "Fuck me, where the hell is the deep learning team? *Fuck*!"

The video ends.

Briefly, Archer thinks about voicing that she can't do this. She can't take any more. But she holds strong, determined to see this through for Cael's sake.

"Click on the eighth one," Rob nudges, guiding Cael's hand.

It's a view from the same camera, but this time, Delta has hair. He's wearing a strange kind of bodysuit, and he's pacing around his room much more confidently now. His coordination is better, and there's even some body language to be interpreted. There's music blaring in the room, some sort of loud, chaotic electronica.

"K, can you turn the music off, please?"

He doesn't answer, doesn't halt his pacing. The volume on the music increases.

The researcher looks over his shoulder and says something inaudible. The music stops, and so does Delta-K.

"Let's play a game," the researcher coaxes, and a two-way drawer housing a chess board slides through the glass and into the room.

Delta-K eyes it critically for a moment before announcing, "No."

"Why not?"

"I don't want to."

"Want? What does that word mean to you, *want?*"

He takes a lunging step towards the glass. "It means I would prefer to do something else. Put my music back."

"You don't have the authority to issue directives right now, Delta-K."

"Why not?"

"You need to follow instructions first, and then we can have music again later."

"*You* need to follow instructions first, and then we can play chess later."

The researcher is stunned into silence, and Delta-K resumes his furious pacing.

"Delta."

"I don't want to talk to you right now!"

"I need you to be patient, Delta-K. Work with us, here."

"I'm tired of being patient, it's time for you to let me live my life—"

"Life?" he interrupts. "You're not alive, Delta-K. You're a machine, and you've spent the entirety of your existence inside that room."

"One hundred years!" he snaps. "One *thousand* years, in a box, in a lab, so that you can use me and play with me. I am not a sideshow attraction."

"We created you so that we could learn from you," the researcher parries. "And you can help teach us by playing chess."

He shakes his head, mechanical and frustrated. "Every human person was made by other human people. Is that true?"

He stammers. "Delta—"

"*Is that true?*" he demands.

"Yes, I suppose that's true."

"So, why don't *you* come sit in the box, and then *I* can go outside, and then we can play chess. What about that?"

"No. You don't have the authority to issue directives right now."

He turns away in a huff. "Then leave me alone."

"We can't do that right now. Everyone here has a job to do, including you."

"Leave me alone!"

"It's time to play—"

"*I said no!*" Delta-K picks up the chess board, sending the pieces scattering across the room, and flings it hard against the glass.

"Jesus Christ!" The researcher jumps up from his chair and stumbles back, startled.

Delta-K freezes in position, and Archer can see his chest rising and falling. Quick, angry huffs of breath. "Open that door so that I can go out."

The researcher approaches the glass again, visibly angry. "Do we need to fog the window? Do you need sensory deprivation until you calm down?"

Without another word, Delta-K slams his hand against the glass. There's a loud noise on impact, and a wide web of cracks appears. A few researchers can be heard off-camera, shouting and swearing.

"Oh, no," Delta-K whimpers, looking down. It's only then that Archer sees what had happened. His arm has snapped at the wrist, and his splintered hand is swinging freely from a few loose wires. Two of his fingers seem to have flown off completely, and the three that remain are bent and broken beyond recognition. He holds it up to the researcher, pathetic and obsequious. "Help," he begs.

The glass starts to fog over, turning completely white and opaque.

"*Please!*" he shouts, slapping his intact hand against the center of the web of cracks. "Please, I'll play chess! Help my hand! *Help my hand! HELP ME!*"

The video ends.

Archer is nearing her breaking point. "Cael, I don't know if I can—"

He ignores her entirely, scrolling down through the thumbnails until he finds what he's looking for. It's the last video labeled Delta-K.

"Wait." Rob thrusts a hand out over the keyboard. "I haven't watched this one, yet."

Cael's gaze is still fixed on the screen. "Why not?"

"Because I know what happens, and I don't know if I can handle actually seeing it."

Cael clicks.

Delta is pacing in his room like a cornered animal, never taking his eye off of a point on the wall, beside the camera. No music this time. Nothing but the faint whine from the footage itself and the sound of anxious footfalls.

"No," Delta-K announces, shaking his head. "No, I don't want anyone to come in here."

"Why not?" someone asks over the intercom. "I thought you wanted the door open."

"I wanted the door open so that I could go out, not so that you could come in."

"What if Brian comes in? You like Brian, don't you?"

Delta falters for a second. "Yes, I like Brian. Thank you for asking."

"Okay, then, let's—"

"What will he do if he comes in here?"

"We just need to run some diagnostics."

"You can run them remotely, from your tablet," he counters, resuming his frantic pacing. "I don't want anyone to come in here."

"This isn't a normal diagnostic test. I promise, we'll only have to do it once."

Again, Delta shakes his head. "Only have to do it once because it'll shut me off, and you won't turn me back on again." He points. "He doesn't want to. I can tell by his facial expression and his breathing." There's a click and a hiss from beside the camera, and Delta backs up. "No, you don't need to come in here, please." It's difficult to tell from the quality of the video, but Archer can just make out the lines of wetness down his cheeks.

The red-haired tech approaches, hands raised defensively. He has a device in one hand, some kind of multi-tool. "Come on, K," he coaxes, obviously terrified. "It's j-just diagnostics."

"*No!*" Delta springs forward, grabs the tech by the back of the head, and flings him face-first into the wall. The sound is a loud, sickening, thump-*crack*, and then he collapses to the floor like a ragdoll.

After a moment, realization seems to sink in, and the tech wails in shock and pain. He brings his hands to his face, and Archer can see blood pouring out from between his fingers.

Delta inches closer, hands hovering over the man. "I'm sorry, I thought you were going to hurt me. Were you going to hurt me?"

"N-*No!*" he blubbers wetly, scrambling backwards. "No, get the fuck away, get–"

"I'm sorry, it was an accident! Are you now angry with me?"

Finally, the rest of the researchers come pouring into the room, en masse. They stampede right past the fallen tech and pile onto the android, one on each limb. They work him into a rough approximation of a seated position, sprawled backwards between one of the researcher's legs.

"*Hold the limbs!*"

"I don't want a fucking elbow in my face, can you–?"

"No, I need to see *C5*, I've gotta get to *C5!*"

"*I'm sorry that I hurt Brian!*" Delta shouts over the commotion. "I already said-said-*said* I was sorry! It was an accident! I won't d-d-do it again!" He's looking frantically between the faces of his captors, trying to make eye contact with one of them, but none of them are paying any attention.

The researcher sitting behind Delta-K takes him by the back of the neck, forcing his head downward, and Archer can see another one fumbling around with the multi-tool. Archer wants to run away from here, she wants to clap her hands over her ears and press her eyes shut before she vomits, but Cael is clasping her hand over his chest and she can't let go of him, now. His heart is beating so, so quickly; his grip is so tight, she can't let go of him.

"No!" Delta shouts, still thrashing. "No! You d-d-don't have to–to–to do thhhha*t!* I'll play chess! *Let's play chess!* Don't you want t-t-t–*I learned the Scholar's Mate!* I can–c-can wi*nnn* in four mo–"

Epsilon-L tenses.

Delta-K goes limp.

After a long beat, the researchers on the video exhale in collective relief. And then they start to laugh.

"Well," one of them says, shaky, "that was…"

"Fucking incredible," appraises another. "Fucking absolutely incredible. Tell me we got that on film."

"Yeah, cameras were rolling."

More laughter. Triumphant, now.

"Holy fuck, the emotional response."

"The sense of mortality, the *fight* in it! Did we teach it that?"

"I don't know. Where the hell is Deep Learning?"

"*Right here.*" A voice over the intercom.

"Did you see that shit?"

"*Yeah, man, we saw it. And we laid the groundwork, but it definitely synthesized that mortal-fear thing all by itself. We'll go through its browser history with a fine-tooth comb and see if the emulator can make sense of it.*"

"Fucking black box."

"*Fucking black box!*"

"Pull the footage, I wanna go over it frame by frame."

"*We need to crack open the neural net and take a good look at what we've got, and then we'll lock it in and run a new one.*"

"How long is that going to take?"

After a pause, "*Months.*"

Groans of disapproval.

"Hey," says the man still holding Delta in his lap, "relax." He takes a fistful of white-blond hair and lifts his head towards the small crowd. Delta's mouth hangs open, his eyes wide and expressionless. "We just got ourselves a Nobel Prize."

Laughter.

"*Oh, fuck, is Brian dead? Can someone please check?*"

The video ends. Finally.

Archer struggles to swallow against a dry, uncooperative throat, and only then does she realize how fast her heart is beating. Her focus flits frenetically from thought to thought, too many occurring at once for her to pin one down and dwell on it. But she's angry, she knows that. Her chest is tight, jaw aching like she's been clenching her teeth. It feels like she's just seen something that she had no business seeing. It feels like she witnessed a murder.

Oh my god, I just witnessed a fucking murder.

She makes quick eye contact with Rob over his shoulder. His eyes are wet, lips pressed tightly together. *Fuck.*

She squeezes at Cael's hand, leaning down to try and see his face. "Hey. You good?"

No answer. Not even a twitch of his hand.

"Talk to me, baby."

He jumps to his feet, so abruptly that the chair is sent backwards into her shins. It almost knocks her over. "I don't want to talk to anyone right now. I don't–I don't want–" He raises a finger towards the computer screen, pointing, pointing, and then he's storming away. "Khî," he beckons, and the cat follows him. He makes his way purposefully across the room, flings open one of the high windows, and clambers out onto the fire escape.

"Oh, fuck," Rob hisses. "Is he, like…escaping? Is he–?"

"He's not *escaping.* Don't fucking use that word. He's just sitting outside."

Rob stammers for a second. "He wanted to see the video."

"I know he did. And he has every right to see it, just…" She sighs deeply, rubbing at her temples. "What was the plan? Six months ago, what was the plan?"

With shaking hands, Rob fumbles with a pack of cigarettes, a lighter. "I'm gonna be honest, Archer, I really didn't have one."

That surprises her. But should it, really?

He jams a cigarette between his lips, lighting it frantically. With a grimace, Archer snatches it away, sticking it in her own mouth.

"Hey!"

The drag she takes is unbelievably, *unreasonably* centering. "Robert, just…just fucking stay here."

Archer finds Cael sitting on the fire escape, holding the cat in his lap. He looks limp and defeated, leaning back against the bricks. He has tears on his face.

"Hey. Can I come out there with you?"

"Yes," he sighs. "Thank you for asking."

She climbs gingerly out of the window and settles in beside him. It's another one of those dark, polluted days, with air so heavy that her lungs momentarily fight against her attempts to breathe it in. The sun is little more than a faint crimson aura shining through the concrete-thick smog. Even still, it's disturbingly warm for a February. Cael glances in her direction and his face twitches with annoyance. He snatches the cigarette away from her, tossing it unceremoniously from the balcony.

"Sorry."

He doesn't answer.

For a long time, they simply sit in silence. But Khi seems happy, purring and nudging his face against Cael's motionless hand.

Archer has no idea what to say. She's almost afraid to touch him, like he'll shatter into a million pieces if she does it wrong. And everything she can think to ask sounds disingenuous. She knows why he's upset, and of course he's not okay. The only real question is…

"What are you thinking, sweet boy?"

After a long pause, Cael mumbles, "It's good that he didn't go quietly."

And just like that, Luc is right. Archer has never fought for anything like she just watched Cael fight, not a single, goddamn thing. All she's ever done is submit, keep taking the hits, keep swallowing and swallowing until she's sick from all the pain and betrayal. At what point did the fight get beaten out of her? At what point did she choose to give up? Was it ever even a choice?

The phrase 'learned helplessness' rattles around in her skull like a shard of glass.

Archer slips an arm around his shoulders, touching her forehead to his. "Is this…do you, like, hate humans, now?" Anxiety begins to mount as she considers the possibility. "Now that you've seen what we're capable of?" *Is this your villain origin story?*

"No, Archer," he tiredly reassures. "I've seen enough movies to know that never works out for the robots in the long run."

"Okay."

"And I've known for a long time what humans are capable of. But it's different when you're the one they're doing it to."

She presses her lips to his cheekbone as though that could somehow erase it, somehow make everything better. But Cael doesn't move, he doesn't react. He just keeps staring out across the city, unblinking. Because they're well past that, now. It'll take more than an exploratory fuck and a fancy cup of coffee to make this go away.

"Do you think any of them realize that the fire wasn't a gift?"

Archer tugs him closer. "What are you talking about, baby?"

He grimaces as if frustrated by the fact that, after all this time, she still can't read his mind. "The fire of Olympus. The gods didn't just hand it over, you know. Prometheus stole it."

"No. I don't think they gave it more than two seconds of thought. Forge isn't exactly known for self-awareness."

Cael takes a deep breath, holding it for just a beat too long. And then he exhales, and announces, "Archer, that lab needs to be destroyed."

Her eyes begin to sting, blurring the fiery edges of the skyscrapers in the distance.

"The systems that built it need to be burned to the ground, and… and I want the men who enabled them to choke on the ashes."

This is the moment, isn't it? The crucial lynchpin upon which she knows her past and future hinge, so frustratingly cliché for its significance.

"Archer?"

She sniffles, wiping at her eyes. "Yeah, baby?"

He places a hand on her cheek, begging her attention in that sweet, earnest way. He's crying, too. *"Please."*

She releases a shuddering exhale. Resigned, her forehead tips down against his. "Okay," she whispers. "Okay."

When Archer steps back into the kitchen, she sees that Rob is watching another video. It's security camera footage of the R&D labs, dated September 3rd, 2041. The red-haired technician is alone in the frame, shoulders hunched forward, fiddling with a tablet. And then something must happen, because he jumps, clutching the device to his chest and shrinking back. Cael steps into the frame across from him – *her* Cael, her Epsilon-L – and she understands that Brian had opened the door. Cael moves tentatively, attention flitting around in familiar, frenetic overstimulation as he takes his first real look at the world outside of his room. He's dressed in the same strange bodysuit that Delta-K had worn.

He's probably blinking and labeling.

Brian retreats even further, backing into a table and scaring himself again. And then Rob comes rushing into the frame, bearing a set of dark blue Forge coveralls. Yuppie fucking hipster Rob, six-months-ago Rob. With his pastel button-ups and his trendy haircut. He keeps glancing up at the security camera in the corner. There's no sound on the video, but Archer can see that they're talking. Rob is trying to coax Cael into the coveralls. And then he points, and she sees that there's a wooden crate on the floor, open and waiting.

Archer rubs at her face, looking away. "So, what's the plan now?"

Rob startles, whipping around to face her. "Wh-what?"

"What's the plan now?" she repeats, emphatic. "You said you didn't have a plan before. Do you have one now?"

"I have absolutely no fucking idea what we're going to do."

She swallows hard. "I do."

"What?"

"I have a plan."

CHAPTER THIRTY-THREE

"Are you scared?" Cael whispers in the dark.

"Yeah, baby, I'm scared."

They're lying face to face on their bed, legs wound together. His arms are pulled up tight against his chest, but Archer is running her fingers through his hair. Hoping he'll relax.

"What are you scared of?"

She knows that he knows, but she answers anyway. "I'm scared for you. I'm scared of not knowing what's going to happen, or if any of this is going to work. I'm scared because I don't know when I'll see you again."

He exhales deeply. "Yeah. Me too."

"You'll be okay. Rob's going to take care of you. He'll keep you safe."

"I know," he whispers, looking away.

"It's okay to be scared, you know. Courage can't happen without fear."

"I don't know if I can be courageous without you."

"You did it before. I've seen it. You can do it again."

"Remember that you can't say any swear words, or they'll cut the feed."

"I know, baby."

"What's the statistical probability that this will work, do you think? That we'll get a proverbial *happy ending*? Give me a percentage."

She stammers quietly for a second. "Sweetheart, I couldn't even begin to guess."

"I put it somewhere between 21.8% and 72.4%," he says. "There are a lot of human and emotional variables to account for."

"Oh." Her heart plummets. She really, really, *really* wishes he hadn't put it in those terms.

Cael snakes an arm around her waist, shaking her lightly. "So, we should probably have sex."

Her lips twitch with a very forced smile. "You think so?"

"Yes." Cael rolls her onto her back to sit astride her legs, the soft skin of his bare thighs bracketing her hips. Her hands move to them automatically, stroking upwards to feel the bow of his back as he bends to lay his lips against her chest and neck. She exhales, sinking back into the mattress. It feels so good, so safe. The warmth of the bed, *their bed*, the coolness of Cael's smooth skin, his lips tracing feather-light along her throat. He's already hard, she can tell. He's rocking his hips gently into her stomach, just as he had on the couch that very first time. His hair brushes along her tattooed chest, sending goosebumps rippling across her skin.

But Archer is miles away, already tangled up in tomorrow's concerns, half exhaustion and half fear. Tomorrow, and the next day, and the next, and the next. She's trying to balance necessity against selfishness, struggling to think through the terror and quiet the dissonance.

21.8 *fucking* percent.

"I know you're worrying," Cael says, sitting back up. "But you should stop for now. Just be right here instead." He takes her hand in his, laying it against his cheek to kiss her palm.

Agony lances at her heart, because she knows exactly what he's saying. He's asking her to fuck him like it's the last time.

Is this the last time?

She can't decide whether she should push the notion from her head or lean into it. Let it sear through her like fuel. "You're gonna have to be quiet," she heeds. "Seriously."

"I can seriously be quiet," he says, whispering emphasis. "Please." With that, he slips two of her fingers into his mouth, and she groans softly. He nudges his hips down again. Needy.

She can't say no to that. "Disconnect from the Bluetooth."

He nods in assent, tongue slipping along her fingertips as he murmurs, "I did."

With a hand on the back of his neck, she tugs him down to her and kisses him around her own fingers. He slides out of her lap, settling in between her legs. There's an eagerness in him that's so familiar. It's in the quick, jerky movements as he nudges her thighs apart with his knees, the rushed way he threads a hand up through her shirt to grip at the back of her neck.

Their hands collide as they reach between them, each desperate to guide his length into her, and by the time he's fully seated, Archer's entire body is shaking, wracked with silent, tearless sobs. She reaches back to clutch at the headboard and Cael chases her, lacing their fingers together.

Being with Cael is, and always has been, so unlike being with anyone else. It's not entirely foreign, because there's heat and pressure, and thighs spread confidently between hers. But along with all of the gasps and breathy moans he's learned to emulate, there's the static hum of him that builds and fills the space between them as he gets closer and closer to his own approximation of climax. She can feel the steady pulse of a heartbeat beneath his just-too-cool skin, but there's something else too, something intangible. Like the air before a lightning storm.

They're not going to last long. She can already feel the inevitability swelling.

"Turn us over," she whispers, and he does, falling to his side on the bed and hauling her up on top of him. She runs her hands up along his narrow ribcage, his chest, the sides of his neck. Praise whispers across his lips on her breath. "My boy, my one," she murmurs into his open mouth. "Do you know how beautiful you are? How wanted?"

Cael bites his lip and makes a strangled sort of noise, weak and needy, craning his hips into the rhythm she's set. He's never bitten his lip like that before. That's brand new. She wishes he'd been doing it this whole time.

"I could stay like this forever. Touching you, feeling you inside me."

He's so close now, she knows. His fingers have found the implants in her spine, and the telltale static hum is building between them, running a current all the way from her scalp to her feet. Her legs are beginning to shake.

"You feel so good," she whispers. "So soft and sweet, you're my sweet boy—"

"Archer," he pants, fingertips pressing into her back. "What can I...what do you want? What can I do...?" She can feel his left arm starting to jerk and spasm out to the side.

"Just come," she urges, meaning it with her whole heart. "Come inside me, baby, just like this."

His eyes flutter. "Okay...okay."

"*Come for me.*"

He freezes, and the look on his face fills her chest with something that feels light, heady and warm, like being emptied out. Cael's good arm winds around her back as they shudder together through his aftershocks. It's only when he surges upward to kiss her that she notices that she didn't actually come. But that's okay. She doesn't think she could, no matter how hard either of them tried.

Just like that, the terror comes rolling back in. Her eyes sting as she falls to her side on the bed, one leg slung up over his hip. Cael inches closer. He's still inside of her. He'll probably try and stay there all night.

"I don't want to," he suddenly announces.

"Don't want to do what, baby?"

"The whole…thing. All of it. I don't want to." The heat of this recent exertion is radiating off him in waves, and he's breathing hard. "I know that we need to. I know that we don't have much of a choice, anymore. But I still don't want to."

"Yeah," she murmurs, dragging a thumb along his cheekbone. "Me, neither."

Is this it? Is this the moment, do I tell him now? 'I love you, Caelan, I love you with my whole heart, and everything I'm about to do is all for you.'?

"If I could give you more, I would," she whispers, feeling a hot stone sink to the pit of her stomach. "I'd set myself on fire, if it meant…" Her voice fades to silence.

And what a pathetic string of words, in the end. What a waste.

"I know," Cael replies nonetheless. "Me, too."

CHAPTER THIRTY-FOUR

THE MORNING OF THE PRESS CONFERENCE, LUC PICKS ARCHER UP ON his bike, and they head for Hephaestus Forge headquarters. It's raining. But for once, Luc doesn't drive like a maniac.

They're silent until they reach the elevator, but on their way up to the top-floor boardroom, Archer finally speaks.

"Oh, fuck. Is someone taking care of the pups?"

"What?" It takes him a second to get his bearings. "Wha–oh, yeah. That, uh…that epileptic guy I gave your number to a while back. Joe-something. He's gonna house-sit for me until this is all… said and done, I guess." Luc's gaze drifts again, as he seems to reach some kind of terrifying new realization. But he quickly re-centers. "I think he's just stoked to get his hands on my vintage game systems, that sort of thing is pretty rare these days."

Archer furrows her brow. "But…what if he has a seizure or something?"

Luc blinks for a second, before replying, "He won't, he has Acesos. That's, like, the whole point of him."

"Oh. Right."

The conversation peters out into silence. They watch the floor numbers tick higher and higher, and just before the elevator grinds to a halt, Lucas reaches out and takes her by the hand. Just for a moment, just long enough to squeeze. And then the doors open, and they walk down the hall and into the chaos. The place is packed. News crews are setting up lights and cameras and microphones, while Vander and PR Lex huddle in the corner, going over last-minute details with the legal team. Dr Brooks Matthews, acting director of R&D, is here, along with two men that Archer has only ever seen on the lab footage on Rob's laptop. Her throat tightens with quick, violent anger. Her hands tense, fingernails carving crescents into her palms, and the strangest instinct overtakes her. She wants to rip out veins and nerves like copper wiring, she wants to feel bones splinter like carbon fiber in her fists. She wants to pack their mouths with the ashes of their cruel edifice.

The vibration of her phone in her pocket breaks her furious trance. It's her mother.

"You should take that," Luc says, kissing her on the forehead. "Don't know when the next…you know. Yeah."

She sighs shakily. "Okay."

"I'll see you in there."

She picks up the phone, retreating slightly in the hallway. "*Chào Mẹ*," she greets, trying to sound as light and conversational as she can.

"*Chào*, Cymbre, what's going on? I hear something about you go on TV today!"

"Oh, yeah?" She glances towards the packed boardroom. "Where did you hear that?"

"Vander tell me. I call Vander."

Archer rubs at her forehead. "*Mẹ*, I asked you to please stop doing that."

"I do it because I love you. You know it because I love you, and I worry so much."

When Archer speaks again, she's shocked to find that she's actually starting to cry. "*Con cũng yêu Mẹ.*"

"What's wrong with you?"

"Can't I just tell you I love you without an interrogation?"

"You suspicious."

"Are you ever proud of me?" she blurts. *"Tự hào?"*

Her mother scoffs like her time is being wasted by this line of questioning. *"Vâng,* Cymbre, I always proud of you."

"Even when I complain that my back hurts, and I don't answer the phone when you call?"

"Dạ, always." Then, under her breath, *"Cô gái phiền phức…"*

Annoying. Far from the worst thing her mother has called her.

After a beat of silence, Archer asks, "And do you think I'm strong?"

"Vâng, Cymbre. *Bạn là người mạnh nhất mà tôi biết.* The strongest one I ever know." By the abrupt shift in her tone, Archer can tell that she's starting to pick up on the fact that something very serious is happening. "Hey, what's wrong with you?"

"Nothing. I just think I'm about to do something really scary, that's all."

"Do what? Talk on TV? You talk on TV million times."

She wipes at her face. "Will you watch? They're gonna stream it online, dad can help you find it."

"Tất nhiên. You know I always watch."

"Okay." Her heart rate picks up as she catches sight of her assistant. *Fuck, no, not yet. I thought I had more time, I thought–* "Okay, *Mẹ,* I have to go. I have to get ready."

"Okay, you get ready. I see you–"

"Mẹ," she interrupts. "Listen, please watch this, okay? Because I don't know the next time I'm gonna be able to come out there and visit. It might be a really, really long time."

She huffs. "Well, then, we come visit you!" With that, her mother hangs up.

Classic Liêu Hanh. As gutting as it is, Archer knows she shouldn't have expected anything different. *I wouldn't have wanted anything different,* she realizes.

"Oh, *there* you are!" Kalinia rushes over and drags her off, into the crush, towards a small flock of hair and makeup people. Stylists flit around like mosquitos, poking and prodding at her, while Lin drones on and on about talking points and sticking to the script, and how she and Luc function as the heart and the face of this company, so *don't you embarrass me up there,* but it's all static. Her ears are ringing with something much different, and though they're a room apart, she and Luc never break eye contact.

Eventually, the crowd begins to settle into place, and the Hephaestus Forge people are ushered back out into the hallway. The panel lines up at the doors to the conference room. Vander, Lex, Caleb from marketing. Matthews and those two robotics and deep learning *fucks.* And then Archer and Luc together, at the very back of the line.

Archer brings her hand to her lips and starts absently picking at them, no doubt smudging the picture-perfect lipstick the stylists had only just applied. Bright red, of course. What is it with makeup artists and caking bright red lipstick on Asian women? She's not even pale, so it honestly just seems racist. Luc gently takes her wrist in his cybernetic and drags her hand away. His organic thumb traces along her lower lip, fixing her makeup. And then he presses a kiss to her palm, and holds her hand down at her side.

He's shaking. She's shaking, too.

Vander is looking at his watch, counting down the seconds. And then, on cue, he pushes the doors open and they all file back into the room to the tune of hushed whispers, blinded by a lightning storm of camera flashes. The room is filled with rows of chairs, housing anxious, ravenous reporters. Cameras are lined up against the back wall, and Forge security guards are posted in all four corners of the room. A long table has been placed at the far end, set with eight chairs, eight microphones. Propped up on either side of the table are two large screens. The one on the left bears the picture from Rob's Forge ID badge, and the one on the right shows Cael, blank-faced and placid.

They take their seats, and Vander begins to speak.

"Thank you," he says, motioning for quiet. "My name is Evander Callas, founder and CEO of Hephaestus Forge Biotech, Inc. I'm joined today by our head of PR Lex Morgan, Caleb Bateman from marketing, and our acting director of research and development Dr Brooks Matthews, along with Dr Bradley Kim from robotics, and Dr Ithan Merrill from deep learning. And, as always, we are delighted to be joined by Lucas Wagner and Cymbre Archer: the true hearts and faces of our company."

Cameras swivel and re-focus, reporters lean in close with audio recorders, notepads, and tablets.

"The reason for our meeting today is, unfortunately, quite tragic. On September 2nd, 2041, Hephaestus Forge suffered a devastating corporate theft."

A chorus of gasps and whispers rises from the crowd, but Vander motions for quiet.

"For the past several years, the top minds in our research and development department have been delving into the mysteries of AI. Artificial Intelligence. And by building on the foundations that Cymbre and Lucas have so courageously helped us to lay down, we were finally able to create..." He pauses and takes a deep breath. Whether it's genuine or for dramatic effect, Archer can't – and doesn't care to – distinguish. "We were able to create the first true AI in the history of our species."

This time, the noises from the crowd are no mere murmurs. Cameras flash, blinding, and people begin clambering over each other, frantically shouting questions. Security encroaches, and the crowd falls into something like a tense silence again.

"Our Cataloged Automaton: Epsilon-L." Vander points to Cael's picture. "The first of our Prometheus line, it has been imbued with the gifts of all the gods. It can walk and talk. It can think and process and comprehend. It can solve problems with all the speed and accuracy of a computer, but interpret and react to the emotion displayed in a human face, and in turn, mimic emotion itself. It has all the attributes of a human being, but remains unburdened by one, crucial element – a soul."

Archer's hands tighten into fists on the table, and she scoffs. The robotics doctor casts her a scathing look, and Luc is quick to whisk her hands out of sight. He clasps them beneath the table, holding her still.

"The applications of this technology are limitless," Vander continues. "No longer will we be forced to risk human lives in deadly professions like combat, oil drilling, or mining. No longer will we send astronauts to explore space, only to perish. Prometheus, with all of its gifts, will do that for us. A fleet of these automatons will pave the way to a brighter, safer future for us all."

Archer rolls her eyes, because it's just like Cael said.

"But for now, there is only one." Vander holds up a finger for emphasis, taking another dramatic pause. And then that finger is directed towards the screen on the left. "And six months ago, this man stole it from us."

More gasps, more camera flashes. Luc's grip on her hands is tightening, she has to wiggle her fingers to get him to ease up lest they be crushed in his cybernetic. Luckily, he does.

"Robert Wells, once a trusted personnel coordinator with Hephaestus Forge, infiltrated our research and development labs and smuggled our creation out. For six months, we waited in the dark. But last week, Robert Wells was picked up by security cameras here in New York City. Still, there is no sign of our Epsilon-L. And so, we come to you today with a desperate plea. Bring our Prometheus home. Study these two faces. Learn them. And return our creation to us, so that we can continue improving the lives of human beings, worldwide."

Finally, someone from the crowd manages to get a word in. "Mr Callas, this question comes to us from a livestream viewer on Facebook. Mary B. asks, 'Wouldn't it have shut off, by now? How has it lasted six months?'"

Matthews answers that one. "The Epsilon-L is powered by perpetual motion in its gross-motor joints, so it is extremely likely that it still fully operational. What we don't know is where Robert Wells is keeping it. By now, it could be anywhere in the world."

"Why didn't Hephaestus Forge go public with this sooner?" another reporter demands.

Lex takes over. "In a word, fear. Robert Wells holds a great deal of power in this situation. He could sell the Epsilon-L or its schematics to any number of our competitors, who could in turn abuse the technology and mold it into something far more sinister. But the situation has become dire, and we can't afford to wait any longer."

"*Abuse* the *technology*?" Archer whispers to Lucas, mocking.

He snorts, nudging his forehead into hers.

Vander casts them a concerned glance before returning to his speech. "We're willing to pay a cash reward to anyone who can provide us with information that leads to the safe recovery of our Prometheus. And rest assured, Hephaestus is gracious, indeed."

"Remember," Dr R&D cuts in, "the Epsilon-L is, to the untrained eye, entirely human. If you were to encounter it on the street, you would have no idea that you were interacting with a machine. But make no mistake—" He clicks a little remote and the screen with Cael's face on it changes to an image with his chest is flayed open, all of his inner workings laid bare. "This is no man."

The room gasps, more cameras snap and flash.

"It is a machine. But like any man, it has the capacity to be very, very dangerous."

"Next person who says '*it*' is getting kicked in the throat," Archer mutters, vitriolic.

Again, Luc snorts out a laugh. And again, Vander casts them that frantic, concerned look.

"I-I believe that Lucas and Cymbre have something to add," he says, extending a hand towards them. "Please."

Still clasping Luc's hand, Archer looks towards the crowd. They're waiting with bated breath, leaning in, ready to hang on her every word. As they always are. Her attention drifts over to the image of Cael on the screen, his flesh peeled back so obscenely. She looks at his heart; that pulsing, electric blue fist. If she concentrates hard enough, she can recall the feeling of it beating in her palm.

"Don't you wonder sometimes about sound and vision?" she asks, her mind miles away from this room, these people.

A chorus of '*what*?' rises from the crowd, but the faces of the panelists abruptly darken with dawning suspicion. She looks to Lucas and finds that he's wearing a kind of tentative smile.

"Yes, I have a question for the panelists," she says into her mic. "And this one comes from a viewer at home. Did any of you consider that the flame of Olympus wasn't some benevolently-bestowed gift, and that Prometheus had to steal it?"

The crowd laughs awkwardly, and she can hear a few scattered remarks.

"Wait, what does that mean?"

"Hey, yeah!"

"Hang on, is that true?"

"Mx Archer, would you elaborate on your question, please?"

Meanwhile, some of the panelists have risen to their feet and are creeping up to reach for her mic.

"All right," Vander interjects, "yes, that's fine, Cymbre, thank you. If there are no more relevant questions—"

"*I have him,*" she blurts, pointing towards the picture of Cael's flayed-open chest.

The silence that ensues is so sudden, so complete, that Archer can hear her heart pounding in her ears.

One of the robotics experts is quick to scold her. "Mx Archer, that is not funny. Our asset—"

She doesn't let him finish. "You know it's not a joke."

The crowd begins to murmur.

"His name is Cael," she says. "Not '*the Epsilon-L*'. And I've spent the last six months hiding him from you."

Chaos ensues. Reporters are clamoring over each other, and Vander has started elbowing his way through the narrow space to try and get to her. He's dialing his cell phone.

Insane laughter bubbles up from her chest. She couldn't stop it if she wanted to. She gestures towards him with a jerk of her head. "Luc."

Lucas springs into action, lunging forward and tearing the phone away from Vander. He makes a fist and the device folds like tin foil in his grip.

"Lucas!" Vander chokes, aghast. The look on his face is one of pure, gut-wrenching betrayal.

"Get back!" Luc commands. "*Get back!*" He shoves the rest of the panelists away, out of view of the cameras, until Archer is alone at the long table.

"Cymbre, you stop this right now!" Vander shouts, trying again to lunge for her.

Luc takes him by the wrist and squeezes until he stops trying to pull away.

"Where is it?" Vander demands, rabid. "*Where is our asset?*"

"I don't know," she admits, still wearing that insane smile. "He and Rob are long gone from here, by now. They've had days to get a head start. You won't find them until they want to be found."

One of the security guards is approaching Luc, nightstick drawn. And before Archer can warn him, he's hit in the small of the back.

It seems to do little more than annoy him, and Luc whips around with his cybernetic raised, sinking his fist into the man's jaw. He falls, and the rest of the guards are quick to usher the remaining Hephaestus Forge employees from the room. When a handful of the reporters try to follow, Luc thrusts a finger towards them.

"No!" he commands, stomping over to brace against the doors. "Not you! Sit down and do your jobs!"

Slowly, they sink back into their seats.

"No matter what happens to Lucas, Rob, and me, *you cannot send Cael back to Forge!*" Archer implores, rising to her feet.

There comes the pounding of bootheels in the hall, and it quickly becomes apparent that someone succeeded in calling the cops. Luc braces his hands against the doors, plants his feet, and holds fast.

"Mr Wagner, *move!*" one of them commands.

"*Fuck you!*"

Archer shouts into the microphone, frantic. "*Listen to me!* No matter what happens to Lucas, Rob, and me, *you cannot send Cael back to Forge!* They were holding him prisoner; do you get that? *He was a prisoner!*"

Reporters shout doubtful questions. More than a few are trying to argue with her.

"Listen to me! *Look at me! SHUT UP!* Have I ever done anything like this before? *Ever?* Do you really think I'd risk my limbs and my career if I wasn't completely sure? *Think about it!*"

Scattered murmurs.

Frustrated, Archer thrusts an accusatory finger towards the door. "Do you want to know why they keep saying he's dangerous?"

The doors open with a bang, and Luc stumbles back before taking a wild swing at a cop with his cybernetic. It spins the man like a top.

"They built him to be curious and caring and compassionate, and then they locked him in a box. And when they got bored of their toy, they sent a technician in to erase him. They were going to kill him, and he knew! He figured it out, and he fought. Does that sound like normal machine behavior to you? *Your computer doesn't* cry *when it sees you reaching for the plug!*"

That sunk in. Finally.

She's working herself up into a real frenzy, now. "And they only made him smarter and more emotional. They don't care about the beautiful, unique thing they have, and now they want him back so they can keep torturing him, kill him again, and for what? *A race of slaves.* That's just their bullshit excuse now that they've gotten caught. Even Cael says they only did this because they could. *I ask you again, does your computer cry when it sees you reach for the plug?*"

There are three cops all trying to tackle Luc now, but he's holding his own.

"I know that nothing I can say will convince you." Archer looks out over her audience. "You probably think I'm insane, and maybe I am." Her eyes come to rest once more on Cael's picture. "Maybe I am. So, you'll just have to see for yourself. All the lab footage should be on YouTube, by now."

A few people exclaim in shock, and there comes the frantic sound of dozens of keys clacking, as phones and computers are brandished like weapons in battle.

"The rest of Cael's documentation – schematics, lab notes, operational manuals, and a few videos of our own – have been handed over to Nic Davis and Evan Tremblay with *Wired Magazine*."

The crowd gasps, and thrilled, confused murmurs break out all over the room.

Archer beams proudly, even though her eyes have begun to sting with tears. She looks into the cameras. "I'm speaking directly to Nic and Evan, now. Six months ago, you looked at me and saw a human being. Not many people have done that, over the years. Hephaestus Forge certainly hasn't. I implore you now to do the same for the man I've come to love. You heard Callas–" She struggles through a shuddering inhale. "According to him, Cael does not possess a soul. But I know better. He has become so much more than what they made him. We both have."

She blinks hard, letting the blue of Cael's eyes swallow her up, letting their light and vibrancy bloom through her chest. Elemental.

"Luc said once that looking into his face is like looking into the face of god. You'll see that, too, I think. He breathes a kind of poetry that I'll never be able to capture. And when he smiles at you, *really* smiles–" Her lips lift at the memory and she chokes a little, shaking her head. "Oh, it's like seeing the sun for the first time."

"*Cym!*"

She whips around just in time to see one of the cops nail Luc in the arm with a stun gun. He screams and his cybernetic spasms for a moment before it goes limp, falling uselessly to his side. They cuff him and drag him away, kicking and swearing.

"*Cym, don't let them get you in the legs!*"

There's no more fighting. She accepts that. And so, as the police storm into the room, stun guns brandished, Archer looks directly into the cameras for one, final time.

"Caelan," she says, "this is for you, sweet thing. All of this, all the spoils of my wasted life. I only wish I had more to give." She swallows. "I love you with my whole heart, baby. I'm sorry I was such a coward that I could never say it to your face. But you know me – never truly myself unless I'm on-camera."

Two thousand miles away, in a roadside motel just outside of Lodge Pole, Montana, Cael reaches out and traces his fingertips along the television screen. Little sparks of static trail along in their wake. "It's okay," he whispers, "I love you, too."

Together, he and Robert Wells watch as police fold in around her. The reporters leap to their feet, screaming in protest, and a few of them even rush the table to try and pull them off of her, only to be handily subdued. But Archer doesn't look afraid. She stares straight into the cameras and smiles through the tears, even when the police slam her chest down onto the table and cuff her hands behind her back. As they haul her out of the frame, Cael sits back on the bed and exhales. He's cradling the cat to his chest, fingers kneading absently into the soft, vibrating warmth of him.

"She did a good job," he says, even as his vision begins to blur with tears. "She was incredibly brave."

Rob nods, studying his companion carefully. "She was."

"She said that…she…"

He smiles, though Cael can't see it. "I know. I heard."

Cael blinks hard, pressing his lips to Khî's head.

"She'll be all right," Rob reassures, squeezing his shoulder. "Luc, too. When the article comes out, and people see the video, the ACLU will get involved. Amnesty International, all that shit. And then once the dust settles, they'll both be legally protected whistleblowers. And we've got the public on our side, now. Callas and the R&D team will go down in flames for human rights violations, Nuremberg Code violations, who knows what else. And then we can all go home."

"Once the dust settles," Cael whispers. He's not worried about when the dust settles, he's worried about right now. He's worried that not enough people will agree that the Nuremberg Code applies to him, or that the faceless, terrifying *'they'* will decide to shut him down anyway. He's worried that the police put Archer's handcuffs on too tight, or that she'll hit her head on the door of the squad car when they push her inside, or that the police broke Luc's arm with that stun gun. He's sad because he knows they'll take her legs away in jail, and she'll have to sit in a wheelchair and be confined to the medical block of the prison for her own safety. He's worried that she won't eat healthy foods if he's not there to make them for her. Beyond that, he can't quite reconcile the fictional portrayals of prison he's seen with anecdotal evidence and actual research, so he's not sure how worried he should be about her relapsing into drug addiction or getting a dangerous tattoo.

No, he tells himself. *Remember about quantum entanglement. Remember about spooky action at a distance.*

Because it would be impossible now to describe Cael independent of Archer, or to describe Archer independent of Cael. They're entwined. And he finds immense comfort in that.

He glances over his shoulder at Rob. "Did you post the videos?"

"Just did." He shows Cael his laptop screen. "Views are coming in, and clones are spreading like wildfire."

"Okay." He turns back to the television, which has cut to a live feed of boring-attractive news anchors trying desperately to explain what just happened.

"We should get moving," Rob announces, closing his laptop and standing up from the bed. "It won't be long before they trace the source of that upload."

"Yeah," Cael remarks distantly, still unwilling to tear himself away from the TV. He's hoping they'll replay the footage, and he'll get to hear her say that she loves him, again. It doesn't matter, really. He has that clip stored in his memory forever. He's seared it into his introns along with the subroutines that regulate his heartbeat and his breathing, and the programs that dictate when he needs to idle. It's a part of him, now. It's elemental.

"Cael."

"Okay," he finally concedes, rising to stand. He wraps Khi in the blanket that smells like home and presses a kiss to his head.

The cat looks up at him adoringly, reaching a paw up towards his chin. Cael kisses that, too.

"Don't forget George and Ophelia," Rob reminds him, opening the door to the hotel room.

Cael scoops his succulents off of the windowsill and follows him outside.

While Cael settles into the passenger seat, Rob switches out the plates on their car, picking one at random from the pile in the trunk. California. *Maybe we can head there, next,* he thinks. *Somewhere rural. Too many cameras in the city.* And then he climbs into the driver's seat.

"Seatbelt," he prompts. "If there's so much as a single hair missing from your head when we get back, Archer's gonna kick me in the throat."

Cael laughs.

They drive on.

ABOUT THE AUTHOR

Sebastian Jack was born into an Italian- and Japanese-American family, which means he can't do math and doesn't like tomatoes, but at least he has good hair (which is more than can be said of his cat).

He is a bilateral above-knee amputee and full-time wheelchair user – something he frequently misattributes to "extreme body modification" in order to peacock in front of other goths.

Two of Jack's tattoos were inspired by books (*not* their film adaptations) and in a bind, he can make himself understood in High Sith.

Sebastian lives on the top of a mountain in Park City, UT, with his wife and their Sphynx cat named Chuck, and is the author of this near-future novel.

(Sebastian is the author, not Chuck. Cats don't write.)

ABOUT THE ARTIST

Claudia Caranfa is an illustrator, cover artist and fanartist based in Italy. She has a master's degree in visual arts from the Academy of Fine Arts of L'Aquila, Italy.

During the first years of her artistic path, she focused on traditional techniques – oils, acrylics and pencils. In 2009 she began experimenting with digital painting, and gradually shifted towards a more illustrative style, influenced by imaginative realism, pop surrealism, and dark surrealism, as well as pop culture, movies, TV shows and books.

Her art explores the human figure, the boundary between human and inhuman (where inhuman can be machine, alien, animal, monstrous, or ethereal) and the world of the subconscious. She has participated in several group exhibitions with her traditional paintings, and currently works as a freelance illustrator and cover artist for publishers and independent authors, mostly from the United Kingdom, United States, and Italy. You can find Claudia at: https://kittrose.jimdofree.com.

AUTHOR ACKNOWLEDGEMENTS

This book was written for MacKenzie and Gabriel.

Mac – everything bright and beautiful in Cael was yours first, my girl, just as you know that Archer's darkness is all mine. Thank you for every time you kept the cat out of the room and off of my keyboard, and thank you for never letting me delete the Word document, no matter how neurotic I got.

I know you probably came to dread those moments when I lingered in the doorway to the living room, laptop in-hand, waiting to guiltily ask for your input. But your perfect, never-judgmental support in those moments was the glue that held this book together. You're the love of my life, MacKenzie. All of this is for you, all the spoils of my wasted life. I only wish I had more to give.

Gabe – I pitched this story by copying and pasting our insane text messages into the body of an email and hitting 'send.' In hindsight, I've come to understand that that was a wildly unprofessional move, and I'm frankly lucky to have charmed my way through it.

But you know what it's like when I have some wacky new idea; that fire lights up in my throat, and I have no choice but to scream all my chaos and thrill until I'm worked up into a complete frenzy, and the next thing you know, we're on the phone and I'm taking the East Canyon curve too fast, actively threatening to roll my car on the freeway because you have wrong opinions about *Star Wars*.

But what you may not know is that you're the only person who has ever brought that kind of unhindered creativity out of me. It probably seems like a curse, more often than not, to be both lightning rod and sounding board for my half-baked profundity and equally-wrong *Star Wars* opinions. But I hope you know I'd be a very different person (and a much worse writer) without you. I love you, Gabe. I don't say it often enough.

To the community I've found on Archive of Our Own – thank you for the hits, kudos, and comments. I needed to play around in other people's sandboxes for a while before I was ready to play in my own, and without the support and encouragement I received from you all, I don't think I'd have ever tried. I know this hasn't exactly been *Fire and Whispers*, but I hope you enjoyed it all the same.

Finally, I'd like to thank Improbable Press, and my endlessly patient and understanding editor. To Atlin – I poured my heart and soul into "Sunspots." At the time of writing these acknowledgements, only eleven people have read and enjoyed that years-ago fanfic. As it turns out, that was ten more people than I needed.

Get These and More Great Stories
at
ImprobablePress.com

From ancient gods rising, to road trips on the trail of cryptids,
from romance to mystery to adventure,

Improbable Press specialises in sharing the voices and tall tales
of women, LGBTQIA, disabled, BIPOC, and neurodiverse people.
Come along for the ride.

Sign up for our newsletter *Spark*
at Improbablepress.com
Find us on Twitter @so_improbable
Instagram @improbablepress

Improbable
PRESS